Praise for *Fated* by Alyson Noël

"Alyson Noël paints a magical New Mexican landscape."
—*New Mexico Style*

"Noël does a terrific job of slowly unspooling secrets and motivations with writing that is both charismatic and spunky."
—*Los Angeles Times*

"A rush of romance will sweep you away in this hauntingly mystical read. I'm already as addicted to Daire and Dace as I was to Ever and Damen. Next book, please!"
—*Justine* magazine

"With fantastic characters and an amazing plot, *Fated* will suck you in and leave you breathless. Noël is a master with words. . . . With passion and thrills around each corner, this book is a must read."
—*RT Book Reviews* (Top Pick)

"Atmospheric and enjoyable . . . Noël's many fans will be eager to find out what happens next."
—*Publishers Weekly*

"Readers will feel the pull of Daire's quest just as forcefully as Daire herself does, and will count the days until the release of *Echo*."
—*Shelf Awareness, Maximum Shelf*

"A fast and enjoyable read . . . with some very unique plot twists and balance among the romance, conflict, and family relationships."
—*Deseret News*

"Two boys, one light and one dark, factor heavily into the intriguing, twisting story line, which is sure to draw Noël's numerous fans."
—*Booklist*

how [she] can create a world filled with fast-paced, heartbreaking plots along with awesome characters and such a magical world."

—*Cover Analysis*

"I loved this book. All the characters were beautifully developed, including some of the minor characters. . . . I, for one, had high expectations of this book because of *Evermore,* and *Fated* definitely met those standards."

—*Flamingnet*

"The world-building in *Fated* is fantastic. . . . The plot is amazing, and the rich Native American history, along with the supernatural elements of the book, just made it even better. . . . *Fated* is a story of *pure* magic—breathtaking and wonderful, *all at once.*"

—*Kindle and Me*

"*Fated* was absolutely original in its own way! From the vivid descriptions to the spiritual world the author, Alyson Noël, has cleverly created, I was so intrigued and stunned by this book that I can't wait to see where Noël takes this series to, because she sure as hell has a winner right here!"

—*Tales of the Inner Book Fanatic*

"This novel is something different than anything I've encountered. *Fated* has a rich mythology, full of spirit animals, spirit journeys, fate, soul-seeking, and, of course, good and evil."

—*Thirteen Days Later*

also by alyson noël

In memory of my *Abuela*

fated

alyson noël

st. martin's griffin ⬚ new york

FATED. Copyright © 2012 by Alyson Noël, LLC. All rights reserved. Printed in the United States of America. For information, address St. Martin's Press, 175 Fifth Avenue, New York, N.Y. 10010.

www.stmartins.com

Design by Anna Gorovoy

Library of Congress Cataloging-in-Publication Data

Noël, Alyson.
    Fated / Alyson Noël. — 1st St. Martin's Griffin trade paperback ed.
        p. cm. — (Soul Seekers)
    ISBN 978-0-312-66485-5 (hardcover)
    ISBN 978-1-4668-0254-4 (e-book)
    ISBN 978-0-312-57565-6 (trade paperback)
    1. Supernatural—Fiction.   2. Love—Fiction.   I. Title.
    PZ7.N6718Fat 2012
    [Fic]—dc23
                                    2012032021

10 9 8 7 6 5 4

acknowledgments

A big sparkly thanks goes to the following people who either know-ingly, or unknowingly, contributed to the creation of this book:

Alicia Gates, for guiding me on a wondrous journey to the Lower-world.

Daniel and Emily in Taos, for their willingness to share their sto-ries and give me a glimpse into their lives.

Javin in Santa Fe, who took time out from a busy schedule to talk about life on the reservation.

The kind and generous staff at the amazing Inn of the Five Graces—if I could live there, I would!

Mary Castillo, for the friendship, the laughs, and the book on *Curanderas*.

Marlene Perez, Debby Garfinkle, and Stacia Deutsch—gifted writ-ers and good friends, our "coffee talks" mean more than you know!

The awesome people of St. Martin's Press, including, but certainly not limited to Matthew Shear, Rose Hilliard, AnneMarie Tallberg, Rachel Ekstrom, Elsie Lyons, and everyone else who helps turn my manuscripts into books.

My wonderful agent, Bill Contardi, and my wonderful foreign rights agent, Marianne Merola—you guys rock!

My husband, Sandy, for pretty much everything.

My family—you know who you are and you're awesome!

And, last but not least, my readers—thank you for allowing me to live this wonderful dream!

Animal Spirit Guides

Raven

Raven represents mystery, magick, and a change in consciousness. Raven teaches us how to take the unformed and give it form. By helping us to confront our shortcomings, Raven reminds us that we have the power to transform anything we have the courage to face. A natural shapeshifter, the spirit of the Raven allows us to disguise ourselves as necessary in any situation, even to the point of being invisible to others. Raven helps us to work the magick of spiritual laws to manifest that which we need and bring forth light from darkness.

Coyote

Coyote represents humor, wiliness, and reversal of fortune. Coyote teaches us how to strike balance between wisdom and folly. As a cunning adversary, Coyote reminds us to understand circumstances fully before developing a plan to achieve our goals, but as a survivor, Coyote will take extreme measures to insure the well-being of its lineage. A resourceful trickster, the spirit of the Coyote shows us how to adapt to and find fun in virtually any circumstance. While Coyote's use of magick doesn't always work as intended, it always serves a purpose.

Horse

Horse represents freedom, power, and enlightenment. Horse teaches us the benefits of patience and kindness, and that positive relationships are cooperative ones. Possessing great stamina and speed, Horse encourages us to awaken our power to endure and reach our full potential. A strong and powerful animal, the spirit of the Horse reminds us of our inner strength and gives us the courage to move forward and head in new directions. Horse calls on us to carry the burdens of life with dignity, while remaining solidly grounded in our spiritual quest.

Wolf

Wolf represents protection, loyalty, and spirit. Wolf teaches us to balance our needs with that of community, while informing us of the importance of ritual to establish order and harmony and that true freedom requires discipline. An intelligent animal with keen senses, Wolf encourages us to go out of our way to avoid trouble and fight only when necessary. A great teacher, the spirit of the Wolf urges us to listen to our internal thoughts to find the deepest levels of self and intuition. Wolf guards us as it pushes us to take control of our lives, find a new path, and honor the forces of spirituality.

Eagle

Eagle represents illumination, healing, and creation. Eagle teaches us that while free to choose our own path, we must respect the freedom of others to do the same. With its ability to soar and survey all directions, Eagle reminds us to see life from a higher perspective. As a symbol of great power, the spirit of the Eagle means taking on responsibility greater than oneself and using the gift of clarity to help others through dark times. Having wings and strong legs, Eagle transcends worlds, encouraging us to soar to spiritual heights while remaining well grounded in reality and to fulfill our full potential as a creative force.

We don't receive wisdom; we must discover it for ourselves after a journey that no one can take for us or spare us.   —Marcel Proust

then

First came the crows.

An entire murder of them.

Circling the graveyard in strict formation, their dark beady eyes watching, relentlessly watching, their sleek black bodies buffeted by the wind. Oblivious to the dry sweltering heat, the oxygen choked air—the result of the raging wildfires that scorched the sky crimson and rained hot squares of ash onto the mourners below.

For those attuned to such things, it was a sign that could not be missed. And Paloma Santos, sure that her son's sudden death was no accident, saw the crows for what they truly were: not just an omen but a herald of sorts—signaling that the next in line had arrived—was in fact, right there in that cemetery.

Her suspicions confirmed the instant she slid a comforting arm around her son's grief-stricken girlfriend and sensed the life form growing within.

The last of the Santoses.

A granddaughter whose fate had long been foretold.

But if the crows were aware, then there were others who might know as well. Those who'd like nothing more than to destroy the unborn child—ensure she never get the chance to lay claim to her birthright.

With her granddaughter's safety in mind, Paloma abandoned the burial long before the first handful of earth spilled onto the casket. Vowing to stay silent, out of sight, until the child's sixteenth year when she'd find herself in need of the counsel only Paloma could offer.

Sixteen years in which to prepare.

Sixteen years in which to restore her own dwindling powers—keep the legacy burning—until it was time to pass down.

She hoped she would last—her son's death bore a price far beyond grief.

If she failed to survive, failed to reach her granddaughter in time, the child's life would end tragically, prematurely, just like her father's. It was a risk she could not afford.

There was no one to follow.

Too much at stake.

The unborn child held the fate of the world in her hands.

now

one

There are moments in life when everything pauses.

The earth hesitates, the atmosphere stills, and time shrinks and folds onto itself until it collapses into a big tired heap.

As I push through the small wooden door of the *riad* where Jennika and I have camped out the past several weeks, trading the hush of the rose-and-honeysuckle-scented courtyard for the chaos of the serpentine maze of medina—it happens again.

But instead of mimicking the stillness like I usually do, I decide to go with it and try something fun. Easing my way along connecting salmon-colored walls, I pass a small, thin man caught in midstride, press my fingers against the soft white cotton of his *gandora*, and gently spin him around until he's facing the opposite way. Then after ducking beneath a mangy black cat that, caught in midleap, appears to be flying, I stop at the corner where I take a moment to rearrange a display of shiny brass lanterns an old man is selling, before moving on to the very next stall where I slip a pair of bright blue *babouches* onto my feet, decide that I like them, and leave my old leather sandals along with a fistful of crumpled-up dirhams as payment.

My eyes burning with the effort of keeping them open,

knowing the instant I blink, the *gandora*-clad man will be one step farther from his destination, the cat will land on its mark, and two vendors will gaze at their wares in total confusion—the scene will return to one of perpetual chaos.

Though when I spot the glowing people hovering on the periphery, studying me in the careful way that they do, I'm quick to squinch my eyes shut and block them from view. Hoping that this time, just like all the others, they'll fade away too. Return to wherever it is that they go when they're not watching me.

I used to think everyone experienced moments like that, until I confided in Jennika who shot me a skeptical look and blamed it on jet lag.

Jennika blames everything on jet lag. Insists time stops for no one—that it's our job to keep up with its frantic forward march. But even back then I knew better—I've spent my entire life cross-ing time zones, and what I'd experienced had nothing to do with a whacked-out body clock.

Still, I was careful not to mention it again. I just waited quietly, patiently, hoping the moment would soon return.

And it did.

Over the past few years they've been slowly increasing, until lately, ever since we arrived in Morocco, I've been averaging three a week.

A guy my age passes, his shoulder purposely slamming into mine, his dark eyes leering in a way that reminds me to arrange my blue silk scarf so that it covers my hair. I round a corner, eager to arrive well before Vane, so I can catch the *Djemâa el Fna* at dusk. Banging into the square, where I'm confronted by a long line of open-air grills bearing goats and pigeons and other un-identifiable meats, their skinned and glazed carcasses rotating on spits, shooting savory clouds of spice-laden smoke into the air . . . the hypnotic lull of the snake charmer's tune emanating from cross-legged old men perched on thick woven mats, playing their *pungis* as glassy-eyed cobras rise up before them . . . all of it unfolding to the spellbinding pulse of *gnaoua* drums that continuously thrum in the background—the soundtrack for the nightly resurrection of a bewitching square returning to life.

I take a deep breath, savoring the heady blend of exotic oils and jasmine, as I cast a final glance around, knowing this is one of the last times I'll see it this way. The film will wrap soon, and Jennika and I will be off to whatever movie, on whatever location requires her services as an award-winning makeup artist. Who knows if we'll ever return?

Picking my way toward the first food cart, the one beside the snake charmer where Vane waits, I steal a handful of much-needed seconds to crush that annoying ping of weakness that grabs at my gut every time that I see him—every time I take in his tousled sandy blond hair, deep blue eyes, and softly curving lips.

Sucker! I think, shaking my head, adding: *Fool!*

It's not like I don't know any better. It's not like I don't know the rules.

The key is to not get involved—to never allow myself to care. To just focus on having some fun, and never look back when it's time to move on.

Vane's pretty face, just like all the other pretty faces before him, belongs to his legions of fans. Not one of those faces has ever belonged to me—and they never, ever will.

Having grown up on movie sets since I was old enough for Jennika to sling me into a backpack, I've played my role as the kid of a crew member countless times: Stay quiet, stay out of the way, lend a hand when asked, and never confuse movie set relationships for the real thing.

The fact that I've been dealing with celebrities my entire life leaves me not so easily impressed, which is probably the number one reason they're always so quick to like me. I mean, while I'm okay to look at—tall-ish, skinny-ish, with long dark hair, fair-ish skin, and bright green eyes that people like to comment on, I'm pretty much your standard issue girl. Though I never fall to pieces when I meet someone famous. I never get all red-cheeked and gushy and insecure. And the thing is, they're so unused to that, they usually end up pursuing me.

My first kiss was on a beach in Rio de Janeiro with a boy who'd just won an MTV award for "Best Kiss" (clearly none of those voters had actually kissed him). My second was on the Pont Neuf in Paris with a boy who'd just made the cover of *Vanity Fair.* And other than their being richer, more famous, and more stalked by paparazzi—our lives really aren't all that different.

Most of them are transients—passing through their own lives, just like I'm passing through mine. Moving from place to place, friendship to friendship, relationship to relationship—it's the only life that I know.

It's hard to form a lasting connection when your permanent address is an eight-inch mailbox in the UPS store.

Still, as I inch my way closer, I can't help the way my breath hitches, the way my insides thrum and swirl. And when he turns, flashing me that slow, languorous smile that's about to make him world famous, his eyes meeting mine when he says, "Hey, Daire— Happy Sweet Sixteen," I can't help but think of the millions of girls who would do just about anything to stand in my pointy blue *babouches.*

I return the smile, flick a little wave of my hand, then bury it in the side pocket of the olive-green army jacket I always wear. Pretending not to notice the way his gaze roams over me, straying from my waist-length brown hair peeking out from my scarf, to the tie-dyed tank top that clings under my jacket, to the skinny dark denim jeans, all the way down to the brand-new slippers I wear on my feet.

"Nice." He places his foot beside mine, providing me with a view of the his-and-hers version of the very same shoe. Laughing when he adds, "Maybe we can start a trend when we head back to the States. What do you think?"

We.

There is no *we.*

I know it. He knows it. And it bugs me that he tries to pretend otherwise.

The cameras stopped rolling hours ago, and yet here he is, still playing a role. Acting as though our brief, on-location hookup means something more.

Acting like *we* won't really end long before our passports are stamped RETURN.

And that's all it takes for those annoyingly soft girly feelings to vanish as quickly as a flame in the rain. Allowing the Daire I know, the Daire I've honed myself to be, to stand in her place.

"Doubtful." I smirk, kicking his shoe with mine. A little harder than necessary, but then again, he deserves it for thinking I'm lame enough to fall for his act. "So, what do you say—food? I'm dying for one of those beef brochettes, maybe even a sausage one too. Oh—and some fries would be good!"

I make for the food stalls, but Vane has another idea. His hand reaches for mine, fingers entwining until they're laced nice and tight. "In a minute," he says, pulling me so close my hip bumps against his. "I thought we might do something special—in honor of your birthday and all. What do you think about matching tattoos?"

I gape. Surely he's joking.

"Yeah, you know, *mehndi.* Nothing permanent. Still, I thought it could be kinda cool." He arcs his left brow in his trademark Vane Wick way, and I have to fight not to frown in return.

Nothing permanent. That's my theme song—my mission statement, if you will. Still, *mehndi'*s not quite the same as a press-on. It has its own life span. One that will linger long after Vane's studio-financed, private jet lifts him high into the sky and right out of my life.

Though I don't mention any of that, instead I just say, "You know the director will kill you if you show up on set tomorrow covered in henna."

Vane shrugs. Shrugs in a way I've seen too many times, on too many young actors before him. He's in full-on star-power mode. Thinks he's indispensable. That he's the only seventeen-year-old guy with a hint of talent, golden skin, wavy blond hair, and piercing blue eyes that can light up a screen and make the girls (and most of their moms) swoon. It's a dangerous way to see yourself—especially when you make your living in Hollywood. It's the kind of thinking that leads straight to multiple rehab stints, trashy reality TV shows, desperate ghostwritten memoirs, and low-budget movies that go straight to DVD.

Still, when he tugs on my arm, it's not like I protest. I follow him to the old, black-clad woman parked on a woven beige mat with a pile of henna bags stacked in her lap.

Vane negotiates the price as I settle before her and offer my hands. Watching as she snips the corner from one of the bags and squeezes a series of squiggly lines over my flesh, not even thinking to consult me on what type of design I might want. But then, it's not like I had one in mind. I just lean against Vane who's kneeling beside me and let her do her thing.

"You must let the color to set for as long as it is possible. The darker the stain, the more that he loves you," she says, her English halting, broken, but the message is clear. Emphasized by the meaningful look she shoots Vane and me.

"Oh, we're not—" I start to say, *We're not in love!* But Vane's quick to stop me.

Slipping an arm around my shoulder, he presses his lips to my cheek, bestowing on the old woman the kind of smile that encourages her to smile back in a startling display of grayed and missing teeth. His actions stunning me stupid, leaving me to sit slack faced and dumb—with heated cheeks, muddied hands, and a rising young breakout star draped over my back.

Having never been in love, I admit that I'm definitely no expert on the subject. I have no idea what it feels like.

Though I'm pretty sure it doesn't feel like this.

I'm pretty dang positive Vane's just cast himself in yet another starring role—playing the part of my dashing young love interest, if only to appease this strange, Moroccan woman we'll never see again.

Still, Vane is an actor, and an audience is an audience—no matter how small.

Once my hands are covered in elaborate vines and scrolls, the old woman reminds me to allow the stain to take hold while she gets to work on Vane's feet. But the moment her attention turns, I use the edge of my nail to scrape away little bits. Unable to keep from smiling when I see the paste fall in a loose powdery spray that blends with the dirt.

It's silly, I know, but I can't risk there being even the slightest sliver of truth to her words. The movie will wrap soon, Vane and I will go separate ways, and falling in love is an option I just can't afford.

With our hands and feet fully tended, we make our way along the sidewalk grills, devouring five beef and sausage brochettes, a pile of fries, and two Fantas between us, before drifting through the square's nightly circus that includes snake charmers, acrobats, jugglers, fortune-tellers, healers, monkey trainers, and musicians. There's even a woman who's set up shop removing black rotted teeth from old men, which the two of us watch in horrified fascination.

Arms slung around each other's waists, hips rubbing together on every other step, Vane's breath tickles the curve of my ear when he slips a mini bottle of vodka from his pocket and offers me first swig.

I shake my head. Push it away. In any other place I might be game, but Marrakesh is different, and mysterious, and a little bit scary even. Not to mention I have no idea what the local laws are, though I'm guessing they're strict, and the last thing I need is to end up in a Moroccan jail for underage drinking.

It's the last thing he needs too, but it's not like he listens. Vane just smiles, unscrews the cap, and takes a few swallows before he tucks the bottle back into his pocket and pulls me into a dark abandoned alleyway.

I stumble. Squint. Grasp at the wall as I fight to find my way. Steadied by the warmth of his hands at my waist, and the reassuring phrase that flits through my head—the one Jennika used to wean me from my night-light back when I was a kid:

You gotta adjust to the dark so the light can find you.

He pushes the scarf from my head, leaving it to fall around my neck, as his face veers so close all I can really make out are deep blue eyes, and the most perfectly parting lips that are quick to claim mine.

I merge into the kiss, tasting the lingering traces of vodka still coating his tongue, as my hands explore the muscled expanse of his chest, the taut curve of his shoulders, the clean edge of his jaw. My fingers twisting into his silky mane of hair, as his slip under my jacket—under my tank top—seeking, discovering—bunching the fabric higher and higher as he works his way up.

Our bodies melding, conforming into a tangle of grinding hips—a crush of lips. The kiss becoming so heated, so urgent, my breath grows ragged, too fast, as my body ignites like a freshly struck match.

So delirious with the feel of him—the warmth of him—the promise of him—I surrender to the nudge of his fingers working inside my bra—circling, pulling, as my own fingers move south. Wandering over a well-defined abdomen, then lower still, down to his waistband. Ready to venture to places I've yet to explore, when he breaks away, his voice no more than a whisper when he says, "C'mon, I know a place." The words thick, eyes bleary, as we fight to catch our breath, fight to keep from pressing forward and claiming the kiss once again. "Seriously. I can't believe I didn't think of it before—it's gonna be epic—follow me!" He finds my hand, pulls me out of the dark and back into the bright, lively square.

At first I go willingly, prepared to follow him anywhere. Though it's not long before I'm seduced by the sound of that incessant pulsing rhythm—the trance-inducing lure of the *gnaoua* drum.

"Daire—c'mon, it's *this* way. What gives?" He frowns, brows slanted in confusion when I drop his hand and keep going, not bothering to check if he follows—no longer caring about anything other than locating the source of that beat.

I squeeze through the tightly packed crowd until I'm standing before it—my head filled with the hypnotic rhythm of that red leather drum, my eyes swimming with the flash of crimson silk, gold coins, and a carefully veiled face revealing nothing more than a pair of intense, dark, kohl-rimmed eyes.

"It's a dude—a trannie!" Vane shoves in beside me, mesmerized by the sight of the caftan-clad male with his hands thrust high, golden cymbals clinking, body wildly writhing.

But that's all that Vane sees.

He doesn't see what I see.

Doesn't see the way everything stops.

Doesn't see the way the atmosphere changes—growing shimmery, hazy, like peering through carnival glass.

Doesn't see the way the glowing ones appear—hovering along the perimeter.

Doesn't see the way they beckon to me—beg me to join them.

Only I can see that.

Even after repeatedly blinking, trying to return the scene to normal, it's no use. Not only are they still there, but now they've brought friends.

Crows.

Thousands and thousands of crows that fill up the square.

They land on the drummer, the transvestite belly dancer—soaring and swooping and settling wherever they please—turning the once-vibrant square into a field of dark beady eyes that relentlessly watch me.

The glowing people creep forward—arms outstretched, fingers grasping—stomping the crows to a mess of black, bloodied bits.

And there's nothing I can do to stop their progression—nothing I can do to convince time to march forward again.

So I do the only thing that I can—I run.

Bolting through the crowd, pushing, screaming, shoving, shouting for everyone to get out of my way. Vaguely aware of Vane calling after me—his fingers grasping, pulling me close to his chest, urging me to stop, to turn, to not be afraid.

My body sags in relief as I lift my face to meet his. Wondering how I'll ever explain my sudden bout of craziness now that everything's returned to normal again, only to gaze past his shoulder and find the crows replaced with something much worse—thousands of bloodied, severed heads hanging on spikes that fill up the square.

Their gruesome mouths yawning into a terrible chorus that calls out my name—urging me to listen—to heed their warning—before it's too late.

One voice in particular rising above all the rest, its grisly battered face bearing an eerie resemblance to one in a crumpled old photo I know all too well.

two

The light zooms toward me, bright and unexpected—prompting me to squint, to cover my face with my hands, only to find that I can't raise my arms—and when I struggle to sit, I fall back again.

What the—?

My limbs lie useless, stretched out to either side, and after lifting my head, trying to get a grip on my predicament, that's when I discover that someone's restrained me by tying me up.

"She awakens!" a female voice shouts, bearing an accent so thick I can't tell if her tone is one of fear or relief. "Miss Jennika—please, to come quickly! It is your daughter, Daire. She is up!"

Jennika! So my mom's in on this?

I roll my head to the side, taking in blue color-washed walls, terra-cotta tiled floors, and the ornately painted octagonal table that serves as a convenient drop spot for my banged-up tin of Rosebud Salve, my silver iPod and earbuds, and the water-warped paperback I've been lugging around. Watching as an old woman wearing the traditional long, black, hooded *djellaba* rushes from the room that's served as my home for over a month, returning with a frantic Jennika who drops down beside me, and brings her cool palm to my brow. Her familiar green eyes, nearly exact replicas of mine, appearing lost, set adrift, among her shock of bleached platinum hair and pale worried face.

"Oh, Daire! Daire—you okay? I've been so worried about you! Are you in pain? Are you thirsty? Is there anything I can get you—anything I can do? Just tell me, and it's yours!" She veers closer, peers at me anxiously, as her hands fret at the pillows just under my head.

My lips are so cracked, throat so sore, tongue so parched, when I open my mouth to speak, direct the words at her, it comes out sounding garbled and senseless even to me.

"Take your time," Jennika coos, patting my shoulder and indulging me with an encouraging look. "You've been through a lot. There's no need to rush it. I'm not going anywhere. We'll stay for as long as it takes for you to feel better."

I swallow hard. Try my best to drum up some saliva to speed things along, but my supply is so depleted, my second attempt isn't much better.

"Untie me," I croak, yanking hard against my restraints, hoping the action will convey what words can't.

But if Jennika understood, and I'm pretty sure that she did, she chooses to ignore it and reaches for a bottle of water instead.

"Here, drink this." She shoves a long red straw into the bottle and wedges it deep between my lips. "You've been asleep for so long—you must be dehydrated by now."

Despite my mounting frustration, despite wanting to turn away, deny myself the drink until she unties me, I can't help but guzzle it greedily. My mouth locked around the straw, my cheeks sucked in as far as they'll go, overcome with relief when the cool, welcome liquid washes over my tongue and soothes my dry, scratchy throat.

The moment the bottle's drained, I nudge it away, my gaze narrowed on hers when I say, "Jennika, what the hell are you doing to me? Seriously!" My arms and legs flop crazily as I try in vain to break free.

Watching in frustration when she turns, abandons me for the other side of the room where she takes her sweet time consulting with the old Moroccan woman, murmuring something I can't quite make out, then listening intently when the woman shakes her head and murmurs something back.

Finally returning to me, she takes great care to avoid my gaze when she says, "I'm sorry, Daire. I really, truly am, but I'm not allowed to do that." She runs a nervous hand over the front of her black tank top—correction, *my* black tank top—and I don't remember telling her she could wear it. "I've been given strict orders not to untie you, no matter how much you plead."

"What?" I shake my head—sure I misunderstood. "By *who*? Who instructed you to bind me like this? Her?" I nod toward the old woman. With her plain black robes and matching headscarf that covers all of her hair and most of her face, she looks just like every other woman I've ever passed in the souk. She hardly looks official enough to lay down the law. "Seriously, Jennika, since when do you follow orders outside of work? Is this some kind of joke? 'Cause if so, I'm telling you right now, it's not funny—not funny at all!"

Jennika frowns, fidgets with the silver etched ring she wears on her thumb—the one I gave her last Mother's Day on location in Peru. "Do you have any idea how you got here?" she asks, the mattress shifting when she perches beside me. "Do you remember anything?" Her long, silk skirt swishing as she crosses her legs and her gaze pleads with mine.

I close my eyes and sigh, pretending to lose all my fight as I force my body to settle into the cocoon of pillows she's placed all around me. I have no idea what she's talking about—no idea what's going on—how I ended up being held prisoner in my own hotel room, by my own mom. All I know is that I want it to stop. I want her to untie me. I want my freedom back. And I want it now.

"I have to use the bathroom." I pop one eye open and sneak a quick peek, confident she'd never deny me such a simple courtesy.

"You think you can untie me for that? Or would you prefer I go right here in this bed?" I open the other eye, shoot her a challenging look, only to watch her bite down on her lip, take a quick glance at the woman standing guard in the corner, then shake her head firmly, refusing to oblige me.

"I'm sorry, but I can't do that. You can either hold it or use the bedpan," she says, and I can hardly believe my own ears. "I'm not allowed to untie you until the doctor returns. But not to worry—it shouldn't be much longer." She nods toward the cruel-eyed sentinel in the corner. "Fatima called him just after you woke. He's on his way."

"Doctor? What the—?" I try to sit up, it's a reflex, I can't help it—but just like the last time, I slam back again.

So frustrated, so completely over this insane situation I find myself in, I'm gearing up to do something drastic, scream—cry—demand she untie me or else—when the memory ignites, and fragmented pieces spark in my mind.

Images of Vane—the square—the transvestite belly dancer—the incessant throb of the *gnaoua* drums . . . all of it coming in pulsating flashes—a dizzying flicker of snapshots that pop in and out of my head.

"Untie me," I say, voice full of venom. "Untie me *right now,* or so help me, Jennika, I'll—"

She bends toward me, the pink stripe in her hair falling onto my cheek as she presses a finger over my lips. Her gaze a warning, her voice betraying the full extent of her fear when she says, "You can't afford to say things like that." Her eyes dart toward Fatima as her tone drops to a whisper. "That's exactly the kind of thing that landed you here. They're convinced you're a danger to yourself and others. They tried to admit you to the hospital, but I wouldn't let 'em. Though if you insist on talking like that, I won't have a choice. Please, Daire, if you want to get out of this place, you're gonna have to learn how to contain yourself."

Me? A danger? A menace to society? I scoff, roll my eyes, sure

I'm caught in some kind of nightmare—one that feels freakishly real.

"O—*kay* . . ." I drag the word out as my eyes meet hers. "And exactly what did I do to deserve such a verdict?"

But before she can reply, the rest of the memory flares. More flickering images of glowing people, thousands of crows, and a square crowded with severed, talking heads hanging on spikes . . .

One in particular . . .

And then Vane.

Something happened with Vane.

He grabbed me. Tried to convince me that all was okay. But he couldn't see what I saw. Couldn't begin to comprehend what I knew to be true. Insisted on calming me, subduing me—leaving me with no choice but to do whatever it took to break free, get as far from the scene as I possibly could . . .

"You really made a mess of things." Jennika's voice catches as she stifles a sob. "You scratched up Vane's face and arms pretty good. They had to delay the rest of the shoot until he's fully healed since there's no way to hide the wounds with makeup—and believe me, I tried. Not to mention the harm you did to yourself." She trails a gentle finger down the length of my arm until she reaches a spot where I can no longer feel it. And that's when I realize I'm bandaged. From my elbows down, both of my arms are covered in gauze—the tips of my exposed fingers bearing only the faintest trace of my *mehndi* tattoo.

Just as I thought—he loves me not.

I sink my head back onto the pillow, not wanting to see any more than I already have.

"Daire, you completely freaked," she continues in typical Jennika fashion—her expression is sad, but she doesn't mince words. "You had a meltdown, a total breakdown—a rift with reality, according to the doctor who treated you. It took a whole group of locals to intervene and pull you off Vane, and once they did, you went after them too. Luckily, no one's pressing charges, and Vane's publicist is working overtime trying to bury the incident and keep it out of the press. But you know how these things go in the age of the Internet." Her shoulders lift, as her eyes tug down at the sides. "I'm afraid at this point damage control is the best we can hope for." She lowers her voice until I can just barely hear, speaking to me like a fellow conspirator. "Vane claims there were no drugs or drinking involved, but, Daire, you know you can tell me the truth. You know our deal. You come clean with whatever you did, and I promise you won't be in trouble." She leans close. So close I can see the whites of her eyes are now shot with spidery lines of red—evidence of a recent cry-ing jag. "Were you two partying? I mean, it was your birthday and all. Maybe you just wanted to celebrate in a really big way?"

Her voice lifts at the end, propelled by a sudden surge of hope. She's looking for a fast and easy explanation—something solid to pin the blame on. An episode of teenage debauchery gone too far would be preferable to the horrible, hard to swallow truth: That after I attacked Vane, a host of innocent bystanders, and myself, I babbled like a crazy person, going on and on about crows, severed talking heads hanging on spikes, and a tribe of scary glowing people intent on capturing me for purposes un-known. Continuing to fight, kick, and scream until I was finally subdued, carried away, tied to this bed, and injected with some-thing that burned and stung its way through my veins before it sunk me into a deep, dreamless sleep.

The memory now fully resurfaced. I remember it all.

My eyes slew toward Jennika's, seeing the fear displayed on her face, begging me to give her what she wants, confess to some-thing I didn't—wouldn't—do.

But I won't. Can't. She and I have a deal. She'll trust me until I give her a reason not to, and so far I haven't broken that trust. Vane's the one who drank; I refused to touch it. And as far as drugs go, I've been offered plenty over the years, but I've always said no.

What I saw was no fantasy. I was totally sober. I wasn't hallucinating. I need at least one other person to believe that—and if I can't convince my own mom, then who?

I shake my head, voice small and tired when I say, "I wasn't partying." I shoot her a meaningful look, desperate to convince her of the truth. "I didn't renege on our deal."

She nods, presses her lips together until they turn white at the edges. And despite patting my arm in a way that's meant to be comforting, I can tell she's disappointed. She'd rather I'd broken our pact than deal with a truth she can't comprehend.

The silence looming between us so heavy and fraught I'm just about to break it, desperate to find a way to convince her that the crazy things I saw really did exist—that they weren't the imaginings of a freaked-out mind—when there's a knock at the door, a muffled exchange of voices, and a thick-figured man looms in the archway that leads to my room, with the ever-present Fatima lurking behind.

My gaze glides the length of him, starting with his highly shined shoes, freshly pressed suit, starched white shirt, and boring blue tie. Noting the way his eyes fail to shine, the way his lips practically disappear into his skin, and how his tightly controlled curls seem to repel the bright light shining just overhead.

"Daire, nice to see you're awake." He turns to Fatima, motioning for her to grab the chair by the desk and drag it over to my bedside where he drops a heavy black leather bag to the floor and takes up residence. Nudging Jennika out of the way, he lifts a stethoscope from his neck, secures it in place, and tries to lower my sheet so he can get down to business and eavesdrop on the inside of my chest.

But before he can get very far, I squirm and buck and do what I can to push him away, glaring as I say, "Aren't you at least going to introduce yourself first? I mean, it's only polite, don't you think?"

He leans back, his dark eyes meeting mine as an insincere flash of stretching lips and widening cheeks stand in for a smile.

"My apologies," he says. "You are most right. I have forgotten my manners. I am Dr. Ziati. I have been attending to you since the night of the . . . incident."

"The *incident*? Is that what you call it?" My voice bears a sneer that matches the one on my face.

"Is there another name you'd prefer?" He crosses his legs, runs a manicured hand along the sharp crease in his pants, settling in as though he'd like nothing better than to sit around and debate this.

Jennika shakes her head in warning, urging me to let it go, to not push my luck. And while I choose to give her that, she can't stop me from saying, "How come your English is so good?"

I eye him suspiciously, noting the way his sudden laugh causes the skin around his eyes to crinkle and fan, while his teeth flash straight and white in a way not often seen in these parts. A clue that leaves me not the least bit surprised when he says, "I studied medicine in the States—at the University of Pennsylvania, to be exact. Though the truth is, I was born right here in Marrakesh. So after several years of residency abroad, I returned home. I do hope this meets with your approval?" He nods, waits for my reply, but I just shrug and look away. "Is there anything else you'd like to know before I check all your vital signs?" He waves his stethoscope at me.

Interpreting my sigh as consent, he lowers the sheet, causing me to cringe under the press of cold metal that works its way along the edge of my tank top as he orders me to take several deep breaths. And after looking into my eyes with a harsh lighted instrument, staring into my mouth and depressing my tongue with a smooth wooden stick as I'm told to say, *Awwww*, he places two fingers to the side of my neck, just under my jaw, where he locates my pulse as his gaze tracks the second hand on his expensive gold watch.

"Excellent," he says, nodding when he adds, "I trust you slept well?" He tucks the stethoscope into the bag and busies himself with inspecting my bandages, turning my arms this way and that without bothering to untie them, which really burns me up.

"You want to know if I slept well?" I lift my head and frown. "Untie me. Untie me right now, and I'll fill you in on whatever you want to know."

The disingenuous smile that seemed glued to his face just a moment ago quickly fades, as Jennika rushes to my side and rubs her hand over my shoulder in a failed attempt to subdue me.

"You can't keep me like this! I have rights and you know it!" I shout, but my words fall on deaf ears.

Dr. Ziati just looks at me and says, "Young lady, do you have any idea what brought you here in the first place?"

Yeah—glowing people, decapitated heads, and crows—thousands and thousands of them. And because of it, I had no choice but to maul a major up-and-coming movie star so that I could break free. What of it?

But of course I don't say that; it's a truth no one wants to believe, much less hear.

"Do you remember the things that you did—the things that you said?"

I shrug in reply. There's no use going on. One look at his smug expression tells me he'll never be on my side, wouldn't so much as consider it.

"You exhibited all of the symptoms of one who is under the influence of drugs—a hallucinogen of some sort. I've witnessed this type of behavior before—always with tourists." His tone smacks of the same disdain that glints in his eyes. "Only in your case, it has just been confirmed that the blood sample we took came back clean. Which leads me to my next question—have you experienced this sort of delusion before?"

I glance between him and Jennika—her face stricken with worry, his creased with morbid curiosity—then I roll my head 'til I'm facing the other way, preferring a view of the elaborate blue-tiled bathroom to either of them. There's no point in defending myself to those who refuse to be swayed.

"You spoke of glowing people chasing you, large black crows taunting you, along with thousands of severed bloodied heads that filled up the square and beckoned to you."

A gasp fills the room, prompting me to turn just in time to see Fatima clutching the small golden *hamsa* charm that hangs from her neck, her head bowed in hushed, fervent prayer, until a sharp word from the doctor warns her to stop.

"I'm afraid these can easily be classified as delusions of a rather paranoid nature." He returns to me. "And while I have no idea what might have provoked the episode as there were no drugs or alcohol involved, I will say that it's not uncommon for a genetic, chemical imbalance to begin showing signs of itself during the latter part of adolescence." His words now directed at Jennika when he adds, "It is my understanding that Daire has just reached her sixteenth birthday?"

Jennika nods, lifts a hand to her mouth and chews on a purple-painted nail.

"Well, excuse me for asking, but is there any history of mental illness in your family?"

I slide my gaze toward Jennika, seeing the way her face tightens. Her eyes brimming with barely checked tears as she stammers, "What? No! No. Or at least not—not that I'm aware of . . . nothing that I can think of . . . at least not offhand anyway . . ."

Her gaze grows distant as she shakes her head—two sure signs that she's lying—holding on to some pertinent piece of info she refuses to share. A suspicion so horrible she's unwilling to admit it to herself, much less the doctor, which only makes me even more curious. I have no idea who she could possibly suspect.

Jennika's an only child who's been on her own for a really long time. Didn't even realize she was pregnant with me until after my dad had passed on. And though it took a while for her parents to adjust to the idea of their seventeen-year-old daughter giving birth when she should've been sitting for her SATs, they came around eventually. Helping her get her diploma, looking after me

while she went on to get her cosmetology license at night school—
she'd just scored her first job as an on-set makeup artist when they
perished in a small plane crash on their way to a much-anticipated
weekend in Napa Valley.

After selling the house and just about everything in it that didn't
fit into a duffle bag, Jennika and I hit the road, moving from set to
set, staying either in short-term rentals or with random friends
between gigs. She enrolled me in Internet school as soon as I was
eligible—ensuring that we never slow down, never commit to anything we might miss when we lose it.

"Life is impermanent," she likes to say. Claiming the majority
of the people spend the majority of their lives trying to dodge all
signs of change only to find that they can't. As far as she's concerned, we may as well embrace it—may as well seek the change
before the change can seek us.

I'm the only lasting attachment she allows herself to have. For
as long as I can remember, our family's consisted of her and me
and a slew of random people that stream in and out of our lives.

Somewhere out there is a grandmother I've never met—my
dad's mom. But Jennika refuses to talk about her. From what little
I've managed to glean, my grandma disappeared right after she
lost her only son. Pretty much just fell off the face of the earth, as
Jennika tells it, and since she had no way to reach her, my grandma
doesn't even know I exist.

All of which brings me right back to . . . nothing. I have no idea
who in the family might have gone psycho. Might've caused me,
through some faulty genetic link, to go psycho too. Jennika is the
only family I know. And while she certainly has her fair share of
crazy, it's normal crazy, not clinical crazy.

Like any parent, her only goal has always been to protect me, but
from the distraught look on her face, I see that she's beginning to
doubt that she can.

Dr. Ziati glances between us, his voice calm, face placid, looking as though he's spent a lifetime dispensing exactly this kind of

life-changing news. "I'm afraid your daughter is in serious need of help. Left untreated, this sort of thing will only get worse. And while we've managed to stabilize her for now, it won't last. It is imperative that you return to the States as soon as you can. And when you do, you must get her to see a mental health care provider, preferably a psychiatrist, without delay. They've made great advances in psychiatric drugs in the past several years. Many people with imbalances such as Daire's go on to live normal, healthy lives. With the right kind of treatment, regular counseling, and provided she stays on course with her prescribed medication, I see no reason why she can't move forward in a productive and positive way."

Jennika nods, her eyes so watery, face so weary, I can tell she's *this* close to crumbling.

Then before either of us can form any sort of reply, the doctor reaches into his bag, retrieves a needle, flicks it on the side, squirts a spray of whatever into the air, and stabs me in the crook of my arm. Causing my body to sag, my tongue to grow heavy and flat, and my eyelids to droop until I can no longer lift them.

Dr. Ziati's instructions to Jennika are the last thing I hear: "This should hold long enough for you to pack up your stuff and make preparations to leave. When she wakes, give her one of these tablets every four hours to help you get through the flight. After that, you need to get her the kind of help she so desperately needs. If not, I'm afraid the delusions will only get worse."

three

It happened again on the flight.

About a quarter of the way across the Atlantic, poor exhausted Jennika collapsed into a heap that saw her sleeping well past the alarm she'd set on her watch.

Well past the four-hour allotment between Dr. Ziati's prescribed doses.

Awakened by an angry flight attendant who was quick to fill her in on my breakdown. Telling her it took five crew members and three passengers to contain me—to stop me from shrieking, and raging, and trying to bolt through the mid-exit door—before they were able to shove me into a seat and restrain my arms and legs with the same kind of Ziploc ties normally used on trash bags.

And while I can't recall any of it, I'm told that because of my actions, the pilots were consulted, calls were made, and we were almost diverted to Greenland.

What I do remember is being met by a team of very angry, very official-looking authorities who whisked us off to a window-less room, where I slumped on a table in a drug-fueled stupor, as a tearful Jennika fought to explain. The whole thing ending with my flying privileges being revoked for the next several years, along with a hefty fine they told us to be grateful for. Supposedly, it could've been worse.

A psychotic break—that's what they're calling it. That's what a battery of tests and in-depth interviews have seen me reduced to.

Another sad story in a succession of many—another teenaged girl held hostage to her own paranoid delusions.

These things happen.

It's nobody's fault.

But all it takes is one look at Jennika to know she blames herself.

We sit in silence as she starts the borrowed car, cranking the ignition once—twice—until the newly restored sky-blue Karmann Ghia is sparked back to life.

I stare out the window, watching the ugly gray cinder block hospital shrink smaller and smaller as we trade the black asphalt parking lot for black asphalt streets that lead us to Harlan's—Jennika's on-again, but mostly off-again, photographer boyfriend, who was kind enough to lend us the use of his car and his place while he shoots an editorial piece somewhere in Thailand.

"What did you say to them?" Jennika's eyes dart between the road and me as she punches all the presets on the old FM radio. Finally settling on Janis Joplin singing "Me and Bobby McGee"—a song I know well because Jennika always sang it when I was a baby, even though it stems from a time well before hers.

I shrug in reply. Force myself to concentrate on the horizon, hoping it will somehow work to stabilize me, ground me. This latest dose of pills is making my head so light and airy I fear I might flit through the window, drift with the clouds and never return.

Jennika brakes at a light, turns in her seat until she's fully facing me. "Seriously, Daire." She uses her *determined* voice, the one that tells me she will not rest until I acknowledge her. "What on earth did you tell them back there?"

I slump down in my seat, shielding my gaze from hers. "Nothing." I sigh, tucking my chin to my chest and allowing my hair to fall in a long, thick drape over my face. "Trust me, I barely said anything. I mean, what's the point of defending myself when everyone's already made up their minds—convinced themselves of the worst?"

I peek at her through the strands, seeing how she mashes her lips together and grips the wheel so tight the blood retreats from her knuckles and turns them the color of bones. Two very good signs she's debating whether or not to believe me, which is all I need to return to window gazing. Taking in a stucco slab of a mini-mall featuring a dry cleaner, a nail salon, a tattoo parlor, and a liquor store running a weekend special on beer.

"Well, you must've told them something," she huffs, her voice competing with Janis's until the song fades into "White Rabbit" and she lowers the volume. "Because now they want to *institutionalize* you." She glares, pronouncing the word as though it's fresh, breaking news—as though I wasn't sitting right there alongside her when the doctor first mentioned it.

I swallow hard. Gnaw the inside of my cheek. Aware of the way her breath hitches, how she swipes the back of her hand under each eye in an effort to steady herself.

"Do you get the significance of this?" Her voice rises to the point of hysteria. "*None* of the meds are working! And I don't know what to do for you. I don't know how to help you—how to reach you—and I'm no longer sure that I can. But if you continue to insist that—" She pauses, sighs. "If you continue to insist that these delusions are real, then I'll have no choice but to—"

"They're *not* delusions!" I swivel in my seat until I'm fully facing her, staring hard into a pair of green eyes that look remarkably like mine, except hers are lined with glittery purple eyeliner, while mine are shadowed with drug-induced dark blue half-moons that spread to my cheeks. "The glowing people are *real*. The crows are real too. It's not my fault I'm the only one who can see them!"

Jennika's face crumples. Scrunches in a way that tells me I've failed to make my case. "Well, that's the thing—according to the doctors, that's what everyone in your condition claims."

"Everyone *in my condition*?" I roll my eyes, shake my head, swivel back in my seat 'til I'm facing the window again. Counting an import furniture store, a vegan café, and a psychic with a blinking neon eye in the window among the local offerings.

"You know what I mean," she says.

And something about her tone—a tone that perfectly mimics every smug doctor who's ever had the pleasure of reviewing my case—causes me to lose it. To let out every pent-up thought I've held back until now. "No, Jennika, I don't know what you mean. I really, truly *don't*. And while I get how hard this must be for you—trust me, it's not like it's some kind of picnic for me! When your doctor friends aren't drugging me into a stupor, I'm being terrorized by images that are all too real despite the fact that no one else sees them. And even though you refuse to believe, I'm here to tell you that *time really does stop*! There are moments when everything just comes to one big crashing halt. And, for the record, I am not suffering from some sudden bout of adolescence-induced crazies, this has been happening for a while now. Ever since I mentioned it that time we were on location in New Zealand when you refused to believe me, just like you refuse to believe me now. But just because I stopped mentioning it doesn't mean it stopped happening. I mean, have you ever stopped to consider that maybe, just maybe, you're wrong? That there just might be more to this world than you and the oh-so-smart-white-coat-crew want to believe? You're all so eager to draw scientifically based, logical conclusions—to reduce me to some convenient, textbook diagnosis—but you *can't*. It's just not that easy. And I wish—" I pause, curl my hands into fists that lay useless in my lap as I fight to catch my breath. "I wish that just this once you would listen to me instead of them! I wish that just this once you would trust what I tell you!"

My voice ends on a high, frantic note that seems strangely out of place in this quiet Venice Beach neighborhood. And when Jennika noses the car into the drive, she's barely come to a stop before I've already opened the door and made a mad dash for the house.

"I'm exhausted," I tell her, using the key Harlan gave me to let myself in. "The meds are starting to kick in and . . ."

I've barely made it past the threshold before my knees fold and buckle beneath me, as Jennika rushes up from behind, anchors her fingers under my arms, and half-drags, half-carries me to the sofa bed where she eases me down onto the soft yellow sheets, props a pillow under my head, and carefully tucks the blanket around me as I drift into a deep pool of nothing.

I wake to the sound of Jennika's phone—her Lady Gaga ringtone making it as far as the second verse before she rushes out of the kitchen and snatches it up from the recycled-glass table.

Careful to keep her voice muffled and low on the first *hello,* she checks on me, sees I'm awake, and repeats herself in her normal tone, chasing it with, "Yes, this is Jennika." Which is soon followed by an incredulous, *"Who?"*

She squints in confusion, drops onto the nearest chair. Her free hand reaching for the Diet Coke she left on the side table, bringing it to her lips, then abandoning it to the table again before she can even take a first sip. And though I strain to hear the voice on the other side, all I can determine is that it sounds like a female.

Maybe.

I can't be too sure.

"I'm sorry, but—" She shakes her head, her voice growing edgy, fingers plucking at the long silver necklace she favors this week. "I don't get it. If you truly are who you claim to be, then why now? Where've you been all these years? It's not like I haven't tried to reach you, you know? But you were nowhere to be found. It's like you fell off the face of the earth!"

When she catches me staring, she's quick to abandon her spot and head for the kitchen, shooting me a backward glance that warns me to not even think about following.

I lay still, pretending to comply. But really I'm just waiting to hear the familiar sounds of Jennika settling—the screech of a chair sliding away from the breakfast table—before I creep toward the doorway and press my body hard against the wall in an effort to listen without being seen.

Trying to remember when she'd used that phrase before. So many people have come and gone from our lives—Jennika has made sure of that—but there's only one she's described in that way, as having dropped off the face of the earth.

There's only one other person who's proved to be even more elusive than Jennika and me: my dad's mom. My long-lost grandmother, who, according to Jennika, didn't even make it through her son's funeral.

Paloma Santos is her name, and it's only a moment before Jennika confirms it.

"Fine. Let's just say that you are Paloma. You still haven't answered my question, which is—why *now*? Why nearly seventeen years later? What could possibly be the point of all this? Do you have any idea how much you've missed?"

And while I have no idea how Paloma might've answered, since from where I stand the call is pretty one-sided, I do know that whatever she said was enough to silence Jennika. Other than a sudden hitch in her breath, it's a while before she speaks up again.

"How—how did you know?" she asks, her voice growing thready, thin. The words soon followed by: "Well no, I'm afraid you *can't* speak to her. It's—it's not a very good time."

I press closer, daring to peek around the door frame. Spying a glimpse of Jennika now slumped over the breakfast table, one hand propping up her head, while the other clutches the phone to her ear. Her words coming quickly, hard to follow, when she says,

"She's a smart and beautiful girl. She's a lot like her father. She's got my green eyes and fair complexion, but the rest is all him. I'm sorry you missed it, Paloma, I really, truly am. But now is not a good time. We're going through a bit of a rough patch. There's been an . . . incident. And while I—*what?*" Her spine straightens as she grips the phone tighter. "How could you possibly know about that?"

She turns toward the doorway, more as a precaution than having any real sense of my presence. But I'm quick to slip out of sight, biding my time until she pipes up again and I venture a peek.

She rocks the chair back on two legs, absently rolling the hem of her vintage Blondie concert tee between her forefinger and thumb. Jaw clenching as she nods, listens, nods again. Carrying on like that until I'm practically bursting with curiosity, wondering what the heck my long-lost grandmother might be confiding.

"Yes, I remember," Jennika finally says, setting the chair right again and staring blankly at the table's intricate zebra wood grain. "He loved you deeply. Respected you immensely. But he wanted to live his own life, his own way. He wanted a life outside of New Mexico. And now, after failing with him, you think you can get a second chance with Daire? Surely you're joking—"

While the words sound strong, Jennika doesn't. And I can't recall one single time in all of our lives when I've seen her looking so lost and defeated.

"She's been treated. Sedated. The first doctor in Morocco kept her heavily medicated, but it didn't last. Nothing does. They just keep playing with the doses, trying to find something that clicks. They're treating her like a guinea pig, and now they tell me they're running out of choices. Claim they're going to have to—" Her voice breaks as she covers her face with her hands. Taking a moment to steady herself before she straightens her spine and says, "They want to institutionalize her. Keep her under lock and key and heavy surveillance. And to be honest, I'm at my wit's end. I don't know what to do. I've taken some time off work, but soon enough I'll have to return. I have bills to pay, a living to make, and it's not like I can drag her along like I used to. She can't fly, and even if she could, it's not like I can keep her constantly drugged and restrained. And now you call. The last person I ever expected to hear from. Just out of the blue. How's that for coincidence?" She laughs, but it's not a real one, it's more like a longing for one.

Her shoulders slump as she returns to heavy listening mode, her silence broken by occasional comments like "Herbs? Seriously? You think that'll work?"

Followed by, "Paloma, with all due respect, you haven't seen what I've seen—you have no idea what she's capable of!"

And then, "So those are my choices? Really? Sixteen years of parenting and that's what I'm left with? And excuse me for asking, but how can you be so sure? I hate to say it, but Django was just seventeen when you lost him!"

When she goes quiet again, I'm just about to bust in—just about to let her know I've heard every word—or at least Jennika's part—and I'm not the least bit happy about it. They're deciding my future without my consent. Not stopping to think that I might want a vote.

My arm outstretched, about to grab hold of her shoulder, really let her have it, when she turns, her smeary, red-rimmed eyes meeting mine, not the least bit surprised to find me lurking behind.

The phone dangling between long skinny fingers with bitten-down nails, her smile defeated, voice gone hoarse with unspent tears, as she says, "Daire, it's your grandmother. She really needs to speak with you."

four

"Close your window so I can crank up the heat—it's cold out there."

I glance over my shoulder long enough to shoot Jennika a scathing look, but I've been shooting her so many of them over the last few days it washes right over her. She's grown as immune to my scowls as she has to my protests.

I bring my knees to my chest, allowing my heels to hang off the edge of the seat as my index finger prods the small square switch next to my armrest.

Pushing, then letting it go.

Pushing until it's almost there—then lifting my finger and watching it pause.

The window rising and halting in annoyingly short little spurts, but she ignores that as well. Preferring to divert her attention to more pleasant things like driving within the lines and fiddling with the rental car's radio—correctly assuming her refusal to acknowledge my game will bore me into obeying.

I force the window all the way up and shift toward the door until I can no longer see her. My shoulders hunched, arms hugging my knees, trying to make myself smaller, more distant, pretending that I'm not really here.

I wish I wasn't here.

My forehead pressed flush to the window, I blow a small patch of foggy circles onto the glass as I say, "I can't believe you're doing this to me."

It's about the hundredth time that I've said it. The hundredth time I've shot her a disparaging look to go with it. But to her credit, she just looks at me sideways and says, "Trust me, I can't believe I am either. But since neither of us could come up with a better solution, this is the solution that stuck."

"You realize you're abandoning me?" I gnash my teeth together, fight to get a grip on my temper—the fear I can't shake no matter how many times we rehash it. "You do get that, right?" I twist in my seat, stare hard at her profile, but she just keeps her hands on the ten and two position, and her eyes on the long stretch of road that meanders ahead. "You're putting me in the care of some crazy old man, so I can go live with some crazy old lady you've only met once. *Once!* And even then it was only for like ten seconds at my dad's funeral. I mean, what kind of woman bails on her own son's funeral?" I glare, challenging her to explain but only allowing a few seconds to pass before I'm at it again. "And yet, here you are, speeding across state lines so you can dump me off and be rid of me once and for all. Nice job, Jennika. Seriously. Way to parent." My hands clench so hard my nails bite into my palms, leaving deep red crescent marks that take a while to fade.

That's it, I tell myself. *Do not say another word. It's a waste of your time. Her mind is made up.*

But I can't commit. I'm far too wound up and it'll only get worse. Despite the fact that it doesn't really matter what I say or do at this point—doesn't make the slightest bit of difference either way. Nice—mean—calm—freaked—the result is the same. Ever since Paloma called, I've tried them all, and the verdict hasn't changed.

"It's not like I was flooded with options." Jennika looks at me,

her gaze narrowed in a way I know all too well. "I could either
send you to stay with your grandmother, or lock you away in
some mental institution for an undetermined amount of time,
where those doctors you hate so much promise to keep you in a
permanently drugged state until they can come up with a better
plan. And yeah, maybe you're right, maybe I barely know Paloma,
but as I've already told you, your father loved her dearly, never
once said a bad word about her, and at least for the moment anyway, I'm afraid his endorsement will have to suffice. If it turns
out she can't help, then we'll go to plan B. But, in the meantime,
we all agreed this was the best way to proceed. Besides, Paloma
promised to let me know right away whether or not she can help
you."

    "And you trust her?" My lip curls to a sneer. "You trust some
woman you don't even know? You trust her to tell you the truth,
to not drug me—or—or do something worse? And what about
the guy she's sent to meet us? You're just going to hand me over to
some creepy old man you've never even met? What if he's a pervert or a serial killer—or *both*?"

    The accusation hangs heavy between us, a barrier that cannot
be breached—or at least that's what I think until she says, "I trust
you." And when she looks at me, my throat goes so lumpy I can't
speak. "I trust that what you see and experience is all too real for
you, even if I can't see or understand it myself. But, Daire, we've
been given a chance, an opportunity to help you in a nonclinical,
all-natural kind of way, and I feel we have to at least give it a go.
It kills me to sit back and watch you suffer like this. As your
mother, I should be able to help you, spare you the pain you're going
through, and yet everything I've done so far, every choice I've
made, only seems to make you feel even worse than before. So
yeah, I think we have to at least give Paloma a chance—see what
she can do. You may not know her, but she is your grandmother.
And just so you know, I would never just drop you off and hand
you over to some creepy, old, serial killer, pervert as you claim.

He happens to be Paloma's close and trusted friend. He's also a well-respected, much-sought-after veterinarian. I did Google him, you know."

"Oh, so you *Googled* him? Oh, well, that changes everything then, doesn't it? What could I possibly worry about now that I know you've conducted such a thorough Internet search?" I roll my eyes, shake my head, and gaze out the window again, adding, "As for my dad—if Grandma's so great, then why'd he leave home at sixteen? Hunh? Do you have an excuse for that too?" I frown. Slide a finger under my bandage where I pick at the thick trail of scabs on my arm, waiting to see how she'll wiggle out of that one.

"For your information, Django wasn't running from *her*—he was running from what he considered to be a stifling life in a very small town."

"*A stifling life in a very small town?*" I repeat the words back to her, my voice loaded with sarcasm. "Charming, Jennika, seriously charming." I huff under my breath, push my hair off my face. "Do you even listen to the things you say? You actually sound happy about condemning me to live in the same stifling Siberia my dad couldn't wait to escape."

"So you'd prefer the institution? Is that what you're saying?" She looks right at me, her green eyes narrowed on mine, but I refuse to respond. "Besides," she continues, pushing her pink strip of hair off her forehead and tucking it behind her multipierced ear. "According to you, Paloma's already helped. According to you, you've been feeling much better since we got you off the drugs and onto the herbs, and you certainly seem to be doing better from what I can see."

"Whatever," I grumble, unwilling to tell her the truth, that the effect is temporary at best. As much as I don't want to go to Paloma's, I want to go to the mental institution even less. "But did you ever stop to think that there might be a third choice—one that you never considered? Now that I'm doing so much better, I don't see why I can't just continue with the herbs and follow you to Chile."

"No," Jennika says, though her tone lacks the venom the word implies. "It's not even an option. The fact that you're doing better only leads me to think that Paloma just might be able to help you kick this for good. Besides, it's not like I won't check in. I'll call every day—I'll write to you too! And before you know it, I'll be headed your way. As soon as we wrap, I'll catch the first plane out, I swear."

She lifts her hand from the wheel, extends her pinky toward me, her silver ring catching the light, winking at me, as she waits for me to curl my pinky around hers. But I don't. Instead, I just say, "So it's settled then. There's no room for debate. I'm going to live with some crazy old witch doctor who counts a creepy, old, perverted, serial killer, veterinarian among her friends. Awesome." I nod, gracing her with a smile that's anything but genuine. "If I live through it, I'll be sure to include it in my memoirs. And if not, you can include it in yours."

Jennika shakes her head in a way that tells me I've pushed all her limits. "She's not a witch doctor and you know it." Her nose twitches with the effort of keeping her voice steady—the movement causing the tiny diamond that flanks her right nostril to shimmer and blink. "She's a very respected healer, and honestly, Daire, I get that you're upset. I get that you feel abandoned and choose to express your fears by acting out. And while I'm very sorry for all that you're going through, for all that's happened to bring us to this point—I can't help but wonder if you ever, just for one single moment, stopped to consider how this whole scenario might play for *me*?" She pauses, gives me a chance to reply, but since we both know I haven't considered this, she's quick to move on. "If you think this is easy—if you think I feel good about this—if you think I don't second-guess this decision every chance that I get, think again. You're all that I've got. You're the only thing I truly care about. If something happened to you—" Her breath hitches as her eyes go so bleary I can tell she's picturing her version of a life without me and she doesn't like what she sees. "Well, let's just say that I'd never forgive myself. And yet, there's no doubt this thing is bigger than me, bigger than both of us. Leaving me with only two choices, neither of which thrill me. Though I think you'll agree that going to stay with your grandmother is by far the lesser evil."

I shake my head in response. I roll my eyes too. But the fight's seeping out of me and that's all I can bring myself to do.

The conversation fading as quickly as the ribbon of highway that streams under our wheels. Leaving me to stare out my window, unwilling to look back at where I've been, too frightened to look forward into the big vast unknown.

I just close my eyes tightly and strive to hang onto whatever remains of my sanity. Not wanting Jennika to know that Paloma was right—the herbs only hold for a while, and after that time stops marching and the glowing people appear once again.

Unwilling to admit that as much as I don't want to go—as much as I dread the moment when Jennika will leave me in the care of my grandmother's friend who will drive me to New Mexico while Jennika heads for the Phoenix airport where she'll trade in the rental car for an airplane bound for Chile—I can't help but hang onto the small seed of hope that Paloma's really not some crazy, sorcerer, witch doctor. That she'll be able to save me—spare me a future of sterile-faced, white-coated men with their long, sharp needles and fast-draw prescription pads. So far, she's the only one who hasn't accused me of going stark-raving mad.

"Wake me when we get there," I mumble, settling in as though I might sleep, when really, I'm just doing what I can to shut out the glowing ones, who are already popping up along the side of the road. Their piercing eyes following—watching—wanting me to know that, like it or not, they're not going away until I do what they ask.

five

We meet in the clearing.

It always begins in the clearing.

And though I've no idea how I get there, there's no other place I'd rather be.

I lift my face toward the trees, watching the leaves glimmer and dance in the wake of a soft trailing breeze, as a large, purple-eyed raven stares down from above—our gaze meeting, holding, until the boy appears just behind me.

His mere presence causing my breath to catch, my cheeks to heat—and when I turn and gaze upon the dark and startling beauty of him, that's all it takes for my heart to skip several beats, for my knees to fold and grow weak.

"Daire," he says.

Or does he merely think it? I didn't see his lips move so there's no way to be sure. All I know is that the sound of his voice causes the smile that widens my cheeks as my eyes graze the length of him. Pausing on icy-blue irises banded by a nimbus of gold, reflecting my image thousands of times—the stream of glossy black hair that flows down his back—the silky smooth skin—the long and lean limbs—the hands that hang open *and loose by his sides, giving no indication of the pleasure I know them to give.*

Those same hands curling around mine as he leads me out of the clearing, and down toward the bubbling hot spring where he gestures for me to wade in. My dress growing damp, transparent, clinging like skin—I head for the far side and eagerly await him.

Anticipating the feel of his lips upon mine, the burn of his fingers traveling over my flesh. His teeth nip at my neck, my collarbone, and then lower still, as he unbuttons my dress, slides it down past my shoulders, and gazes upon me in wonder . . .

"Hey." Jennika's blue glitter-painted nails scratch at my shoulder, refusing to stop until she's sure I'm awake. "Daire, wake up, we're almost there."

I unfurl my legs and straighten my spine, using the back of my seat as a guide to haul myself up. Taking a moment to get my bearings, blink the fog from my eyes, and reestablish my place—making the transition from the dream state to the waking state, despite the way the images cling.

It's a dream I've had before—one that I actually look forward to—and I'm relieved to know the meds haven't banished it for good. I stretch my arms overhead, lay my palms flush against the roof of the car—holding fast to the image of the boy's smooth brown skin, glossy black hair, and the lure of those icy-blue eyes.

I have no idea what his name is, despite the fact that he knows mine. Still, I like to think of him as my dream boyfriend. He's been visiting me for the last six months, give or take, which pretty much makes him my most enduring relationship to date.

Jennika parks outside the restaurant, glances between her watch and me, and says, "This is the place. Looks like we're early."

I shake my head, causing my dream boy's image to disinte-grate, much like the pictures on the portable Etch A Sketch I lugged around as a kid. Trying my best to appear stoic, brave, despite the way my stomach dips, my heart skips, and my hands go all hot and clammy and shaky.

"But it looks like he's earlier." She nods toward some tall, dark, solidly built stranger climbing out of an old pickup truck, its faded blue paint glinting dully in the afternoon sun.

"How do you know it's him?" I squint, straining to get a better look as he crosses the parking lot and pushes through the smudgy glass door. Trying to glean a little something about his character—his measure of trustworthiness, whether or not he really is some creepy, serial killer, pervert like I fear—from a glimpse of his dark Wrangler jeans, black cowboy boots, starched white cotton shirt, and the shiny black ponytail that falls just shy of his shoulders.

"He fits the description," Jennika says, and when I look at her and see the way she's looking at him, I know she's as nervous as I am. "So, what do you say, shall we head inside and make sure?" She grasps my hand in hers, squeezes tightly, if not briefly, then props her door open, slides from her seat, and motions for me to follow suit.

I shove my hands deep into my pockets and walk in behind her. My feet dragging across worn beige tiles, my head tilted in a way that encourages my hair to fall forward, obscuring my face. Determined to get a better look at him than he can of me, carefully noting all the small details I missed at first glimpse: his turquoise-tipped bolo tie that falls halfway down the front of his carefully pressed and starched shirt, his high cheekbones, broad nose, and startling dark eyes that are filled with such kindness my shoulders sink in relief.

You're in good hands.

The thought swirls through me, though I'm quick to discard it. I can't trust the things that I hear any more than I can trust the things that I see. Besides, it can't be that easy; he needs to earn my respect.

We head toward the back, toward the very last booth where

he sits. Watching him rise when he sees us, moving in a way that's surprisingly agile for someone his age. And as much as I'm prepared to hate him, as much as I'm determined to find some big glaring flaw that'll change Jennika's mind and cast a final vote against him, the smile that greets us is one of the most genuine I've seen in a very long time.

He reaches forward, offers his hand, and introduces himself as Chayton—Chay for short—and I'm pleased to find his grip both firm and sincere. He doesn't give me some wimpy handshake just because I'm a girl.

I slide onto the opposite bench, moving toward the wall as Jennika slides in beside me. And when Chay folds his hands on the table, leaning forward as he speaks, I can't help but like him even more for not talking about sports or the weather or some other dumb thing that ignores the disturbing reality of what brought us all here.

He gets straight to the point when he looks at me and says, "I won't pretend to imagine how you feel right now. Only you know that. And whatever feelings you're experiencing, whatever thoughts you may have, I have no doubt they're justified. What I can say is that the drive to Albuquerque runs around seven hours. And then it's another three from there to Enchantment where your grandmother lives. You and I have a long trip ahead, but we can spend it however you chose. We can talk if you want, and if you don't, that's fine too. If you get hungry, we'll stop. If you need to get out and stretch your legs for a bit, we'll stop for that too. If you just want to speed on through, aside from filling up on gas when we need it, we can manage that as well. I have no expectations. I ask nothing from you. Whatever it takes to make your trip comfortable, you tell me, and I'll do my best to see that it's done. Any questions? Anything you'd like me to know about you?"

I pause, unsure how to respond. The speech I'd prepared—the one where I make clear that I'm not one to be messed with—is no longer appropriate. So I shake my head and stare at my menu instead. Studying laminated pictures of hamburgers, sandwiches, salads, and pies as though a pop quiz will follow. And still, when the waitress comes for our order, I ask to go last, needing more time to choose something I probably won't eat.

Jennika orders a coffee with cream, says her stomach's too nervous—she'll grab something at the airport or eat on the plane—while Chay forgoes all thoughts of nutrition and asks for a slice of pecan pie with a scoop of vanilla ice cream on the side—an act that scores him another point in my favor. And though I'm tempted to do the same, I ask for a cheeseburger, fries, and a Coke. Telling myself that if nothing else, it'll provide a distraction, give me something to toy with if the conversation becomes as unbearable as I expect.

"So, how's Paloma?" Jennika asks, the moment the waitress moves on.

"Good." Chay nods, splaying his hands on the paper place setting before him in a way that showcases his intricate silver ring that, from what I can tell, bears the head of an eagle, with deep golden stones standing in for the eyes.

"What's she up to these days? Still growing herbs, I know, but what else? Is she still in the same place? What does she do for a living? Does she get by purely with the healing? You know I haven't seen her in years. Not since Django's funeral, and even then she left early—strange, don't you think?"

I cast a nervous glance at Chay, wondering how he'll respond to Jennika's machine-gun approach. How she shoots a whole spray of questions at a person, then sits back and waits to see which ones, if any, get answered.

But Chay is calm, if not methodical, and he addresses each one as best he can. Saying, "She keeps the same small adobe she's always had. And it's true that her garden grows so plentiful she is able to support herself with the money that comes from the healings and herbs. Seventeen years is a long time to go without a word, but I suppose all different people mourn in all different ways."

Jennika squirms. Chews her bottom lip. Furiously drumming up a whole new set of questions, I can tell just by looking, but stopped short when Chay looks at me and says, "How are *you* doing? I hear the herbs have provided relief?"

When his eyes meet mine, I have no doubt he'll know if I lie. A fact that causes me to admit, "They help for a while, but as soon as they wear off, the visions start up again."

Jennika gasps. Her face a mask of shock, hurt, and an undeniable anger at what she surely views as my betrayal. Holding her words long enough for the waitress to place our dishes before us, then launching into a full tirade the moment she's gone. "You told me you felt better! You said you weren't seeing those things anymore! Did you lie to me? I can't believe this, Daire. I truly can't believe this!"

I take a deep breath and pluck a fry from the pile, dangling it for a moment, watching it wag back and forth, before I plop it into my mouth, chase it with another, and mumble, "I didn't lie. I really do feel better." I duck my head low and take a sip of my Coke. Using the opportunity to sneak a quick peek at Chay, curious to see how he's reacting to this, but he busies himself with his pie, wisely steering clear of Jennika's and my awkward mother/ daughter dispute. "It works for a while, and it doesn't make me feel all lazy and foggy and weird like the drugs do. Still, the second it wears off, the visions return. But I didn't see the point in mentioning it, since it's not like it would change anything. You'd just end up worrying even more than you already do."

I shrug, try for a bite of my hamburger, but I don't have it in me, so I return it to my plate, while Jennika frowns into her coffee. And though it may look tense and awful on the surface, the truth is, I'm grateful for the silence.

That's how we eat—Jennika alternately frowning and sipping, me toying with my pile of fries, as Chay scrapes his spoon hard against his plate, making sure to get every last trace.

After dabbing the paper napkin over his lips, he leans back

against the shiny red banquette, and says, "The food absorbs the energy it's prepared with, as well as the energy it's met with. Bad energy, bad meal." He nods at my uneaten burger, but his eyes flash in kindness.

Then, without another word, he plucks a small pile of bills from his wallet, covers the tab with what looks to be a sizable tip, and ushers us all outside where my entire life changes in the amount of time it takes to transfer a single black duffle bag from a generic rental car to an ancient pickup truck with New Mexico plates.

Just that one simple act, and it's done. Leaving Jennika to come at me, her face distorted by grief, her shaky arms enveloping me. The two of us clinging in a soggy, incoherent heap of whispered promises and apologies—until I force myself to be the first to withdraw.

Force myself to be strong.

To smile like I mean it, and to not look back no matter how much I long to.

Climbing into Chay's truck, its engine already idling, getting myself settled beside him as he pulls out of the lot and onto the road, heading toward the place that offers my only real hope.

six

Since Chay gave me permission not to talk, I spend most of the trip napping, reading, and occasionally window gazing. It's only when we cross state lines into New Mexico that I crack open the red leather journal Jennika gave me, figuring I may as well jot down my impressions while my expectations are few.

You can only see a place objectively once. And even then, every other place you've ever visited manages to come into play. Once you've settled, spent a little time, and gotten to know a few people—forget it. From that point on, your opinions will be tainted by all kinds of bias, based purely on the negative and/or positive charge of your experiences.

It's only at first sight, when the mind's a blank slate, that you get the purest look.

So I fold the flap back, and write:

Tumbleweeds.

Watching as an entire family of brush traipses across the highway as Chay expertly maneuvers around them without losing speed.

The word soon chased with:

Blue skies
BIG, dark blue skies
Even the sun looks bigger than normal—like a huge, blazing
fireball, falling out of the sky and plummeting toward earth!
The transition from day to night making the horizon appear
infinite—endless!

Then just below that, I add:

I don't remember ever seeing a sky quite so <u>vast</u>.

Underlining *vast,* so when I go over it later, I'll know that I meant it.

My pencil clocking the page, keeping time with the thoughts in my head as I continue to window gaze—seeing what was at first a dry, barren landscape consisting of grays, and browns, and dull faded green shrubs suddenly give way to a rich palette of red earth, swaying yellow grasses, and towering, rugged, flat-topped mesas rising from deeply rutted canyons.

"Wow," I whisper, but what I'm really thinking is: *Small. Tiny. Woefully insignificant*—and I'm referring to me.

This place is too big. Too immense. Too *vast.* Appearing almost *cosmic* in the way it seems to meander for eternity.

Even though I'd decided to give it a chance, I've no doubt in my mind this place will dwarf me.

The sudden realization causing a deep pang of longing for my old life—a physical ache that only the bustling pace of a movie set with its well-defined borders, and small-town environment where everyone has a name, a title, and a purpose, can remedy.

"Welcome to the Land of Enchantment." Chay smiles.

"Are we here? Is this where she lives?" I squint into the distance, unable to see any houses, just miles and miles of uninterrupted land that seems to sprawl with no end. The sight of it making me wish he'd just stop, turn the car around, and take me back to where I came from.

Chay laughs, the sound pleasant and deep. "New Mexico is known as the Land of Enchantment. The town of Enchantment, where your grandmother lives, is still a ways away. There's a gas station on the other side of this pass. I figure we'll fill up and take a few moments to stretch our legs before we move on. Sound okay?"

I nod. Slip my pencil back into my notebook. Too agitated to write, too agitated to do much of anything other than gaze out the window, anticipating the moment when the landscape will be completely blotted out by the absence of sun.

Chay pulls into the station and stops at the first vacant pump, and the moment I exit the truck, I'm amazed at how good it feels to finally stand and walk around for a bit after so many hours of being pent up.

I throw my head back, stretch my mouth into a yawn, and take a long deep drag of New Mexico air. Surprised to find it even drier here than it was in Los Angeles, Phoenix too—must be the altitude. Stretching from side to side before bending down toward the earth—my fingertips brush across pebbly grains of asphalt, forcing myself well past the pain of my cramped and sore muscles now screaming in protest.

"Why don't you go inside and grab us some Cokes." Chay reaches for his wallet, but I'm quick to wave it away, already crossing the lot to the Circle K to check out the offerings.

The moment I push through the door, my stomach emits a loud, embarrassing rumble. And when I take in the array of pre-packaged, processed foods on display, I can't help but regret having left my uneaten cheeseburger and fries back in Phoenix.

I drift along the aisles, piling my arms high with supersized bags full of candy, doughnuts, and chips, along with two quart-sized bottles of Coke—one for me, one for Chay. And after adding a roll of mints to the stack, I dump it all on the counter, exchange a pleasant, if not generic greeting with the cashier, and busy myself with tabloid gazing while she busies herself with ringing me up.

Jennika hates when I do this—always quick to remind me that the majority of stories they print are either completely fabricated or carefully orchestrated by the subjects themselves. Still, it's a guilty pleasure I cannot resist. The fun lies in determining which is crap and which isn't.

Besides, it's the only way I have to keep up with old friends. Some people have yearbooks and Facebook—I have the gossip rags.

As always, I start with the cheapest, most outrageous one of all. The one that boasts an enduring fascination of alleged space alien abductions and sightings of Elvis's ghost. Smiling for the first time in hours when I see this week's cover does not disappoint— claiming that a very famous, Oscar-winning actress is being haunted by the specter of a long-dead director hell-bent on revenge for the abysmal remake she's producing.

Passing over the one that accuses every peasant top–wearing starlet of hiding a baby bump, I reach for the most respectable rag in the bunch—the one whose glossy covers are not-so-secretly coveted by most if not all of the up-and-coming stars.

This week's cover boasting a seemingly candid photo of—

"That'll be twenty-one sixteen," the cashier says, but her voice is just noise in my head.

I barely tune in. Barely make out the words. The counter, my pile of junk food, the clerk—it all just fades into the background, until there's nothing left but the cover of this magazine and myself.

It requires both hands to steady it—that's how shaky they've become. My cheeks heating, my breath trapped in my chest— unable to lift my gaze from those piercing blue eyes, golden skin, tousled mop of blond hair, lazy half-smile, and the bandaged arm he raises in greeting.

And it *is* a greeting. Of that I've no doubt.

Despite his trying to act as though it's a gesture of protest—as though it's some failed attempt to fend off the camera's intrusive telephoto lens—I know better.

Vane's never met a photo vulture he didn't secretly adore.

He's new at the game—still craves the attention. His entire life spent vying for this kind of coverage, and now, thanks to me, he's clinched it.

"Hello? Anyone home? Your total is twenty-one sixteen," the cashier barks, adding, "with the magazine, it's another three fifty."

I don't respond. I just grip the rag in my trembling hands, the dampness from my fingers causing the paper to grow crumbly, soggy, causing the ink to seep into my skin. Unable to peel my eyes from the bold-faced headline that screams:

Collision on the Vane Wick Expressway!

That's what they call him—the Vane Wick Expressway. Nicknamed after the most miserable, most traffic-choked highway that leads to that filthy den of chaos otherwise known as Kennedy Airport.

Having hailed from Podunk, Vane loves his oh-so-clever moniker. Loves every single part of his fame.

In the picture, his face is a mess of raw jagged scratches and dull purple bruises, while his left brow—the one he likes to quirk—appears to be slashed right in half. But damn if it doesn't leave him looking even hotter. Making him appear vulnerable but tough—like a guy who's seen some stuff, and then some.

Thanks to me, he's gone from *insanely cute* to *completely irresistible*—though I doubt I'll get so much as a thank-you note.

And speaking of me—I'm featured too.

Represented in the form of a small blurry photo set in the bottom right corner.

A photo I recognize as being lifted straight from Vane's cell phone.

A photo he insisted on taking, even though I tried to discourage him. Seeing no point in documenting what I knew to be a brief and fleeting hookup. And so, because I wasn't what you'd call a willing participant, when he raised his phone to shoot, I scowled in return.

He laughed when he saw it, even promised to delete it, and I guess it never occurred to me to check.

And I certainly never thought he'd use it against me—that it would end up providing fodder for my own, unfortunate nickname: "Fan from hell."

As in:

Fan from hell goes berserk on Vane Wick!

And just below that:

Nice guy Vane decides not to sue, says: "It's the price of fame—I can only hope she gets the kind of help she so clearly needs." Full story on page 34!

I don't turn to page 34.

I don't need to see any more than I already have.

And while I never thought Vane was a particularly nice guy like they claim, I did think he was nice enough—but I guess I was wrong.

It also looks like his publicist wasn't trying quite so hard to bury the story like Jennika claimed. She probably waited for the bruises to bloom before she hid in the bushes and took the photo herself.

It's not like I don't know the drill. Hollywood thrives on this stuff—it's the grease in their wheels. And now, because of my freak-out, Vane's own personal star meter shines even brighter.

"Listen—you want that or not? I don't got all day!" The cashier glares, even though from what I can see, the exact opposite is true. I'm the only one in here, and before I appeared, she was reading a book.

I'm tempted to drop the magazine on the rack. Wipe the image clean from my mind and act as though I never saw it in the first place. But there's no going back. No way to un-see what's now seared on my brain.

I waver. Wanting nothing more than to be rid of the thing, yet all too aware that it was my sweaty hands that caused the cover to run until it's all smeary and drippy.

"Add it," I say, hating to have to pay for it but unwilling to leave her with damaged goods.

I dig through my wallet, fingers trembling as I hand over a crumpled wad of cash and reject the change she tries to give back. Running smack into Chay as I push through the door, my eyes so unfocused, everything appears before me in big, wavering splotches.

Chay steadies me, placing a hand on each arm when he says, "Everything okay? Do you need to take your herbs?" He looks at me in a way that can only be described as tempered alarm.

I shake my head. Slip out of his grip. Unwilling to confide the truth—unwilling to tell him that the vision that haunts me is not just confined to my head—that it's out there for the whole world to see. Probably already gone viral—smeared across the Internet— awaiting its own extended segment on some cheesy gossip show on network TV.

My fingernails slash at the cover, shredding it to tiny, unrecognizable bits. Then after dumping the mess in the trash, I find my way to Chay's truck where he waits with a look of grave concern on his face.

"I'm fine," I tell him, handing over one of the Cokes and settling in for the ride. "Just eager to get there, that's all," I add, realizing it's true the moment the words are out.

seven

When Chay first mentioned that Paloma lived in a small adobe home, I guess it was one of those details I chose not to focus on. But after traveling the paved highway for over an hour of seriously bumpy dirt roads that offer little to no light other than that supplied by the moon, my eyes start to burn from all the squinting I've been doing in an effort to guess which adobe is hers.

They're everywhere.

I mean, there are other types of homes too, and plenty of trailer homes as well, but this particular area features mostly adobes, making pueblo style the overriding look of the place.

New York City has high-rises and brownstones; the Pacific Northwest has clapboard façades; Southern California has, well, a little bit of everything, but Mediterranean seems to reign supreme. And from what I can see, this part of New Mexico boasts a proliferation of rectangular homes with flat roofs and smooth rounded walls that look like baked earth.

Which means every time we approach a new one I can't help but think: *Is this it? Is this the house where Paloma lives?*

Only to sigh in defeat when Chay drives right past it and then past the one after that.

So by the time he stops before a tall blue gate surrounded by smooth, curving walls, I'm so jacked up on junk food and nerves, I'm too nauseated to react in any meaningful way.

"This is it," Chay says, his smile as good-natured now as it was at the start of this journey. Appearing as though the last ten hours of chauffeuring a sullen teen was not only a pleasure but also a breeze.

He heaves my bag from the small space in back where it's wedged behind the seats, slings it over his shoulder, and motions for me to follow. Reminding himself to oil the gate after it greets him with a loud squeal of protest, he ushers me through and steps in behind me.

The moment I'm past the threshold, I freeze. My feet planted on the stone and gravel pathway that leads to the door, unwilling to go any farther—unwilling to be the first to approach it.

I have no idea what Paloma looks like—what she'll be like.

I have no idea what to expect.

I should've asked more questions.

I should've used the last ten hours to grill Chay until he broke—until he confided every dark and dirty secret Paloma is hiding.

Instead, I chose to eat. And read. And dream about some phantom boy with smooth brown skin, icy-blue eyes, and long glossy black hair—a boy I've never even met in real life.

Lot of good it did me.

Before I can ask Chay to return to the truck and haul me right back to Phoenix so I can steal a second shot at doing it right—the front door swings open, revealing a small, dark figure surrounded by a halo of light.

"*Nieta!*" she coos, her voice surprisingly throaty and deep. But as hard as I stare, I can't make out anything more than a black silhouette—the light shining behind her in a way that causes a yellowy glow to shimmer around her.

She steps onto the stoop, stands directly underneath the porch lamp, which allows for a much cleaner look. Lifting a delicate hand to her chest where it flutters briefly over her heart before reaching for me. Her eyes brimming, cheeks pink with happiness, she repeats, "*Nieta*—my granddaughter. You are here!"

I squirm. Feeling oversized and awkward beside her diminutive form—aware of her hand moving toward me but unsure what to do. It seems oddly formal to shake it, and yet I'm not quite ready to go the hugging route either. Genetically speaking she may be my grandmother, but at this moment she's no more than a small, attractive stranger with flashing dark eyes, a generous smile, a nose that reminds me of mine, and long, lustrous black hair with occasional streaks of silver that shine like Christmas tree tinsel.

I mumble a greeting, chasing the words with a quick wave of my hand before I bury it in my jacket pocket again. Feeling bad about such a cold gesture, but under the circumstances, it's the best I can offer.

Though if Paloma's offended, she manages to hide it. Smiling warmly, she ushers me inside as she says, "Come now, child. Come inside. Come out of the cold. It is late. You've had a long journey. I will show you to your room, get you settled in for the night, and tomorrow we will get to know each other better. But for now, it is rest you need most."

I step inside, aware of Chay slipping around me and disappearing down the hall with my bag, as I pause on a colorful woven rug just shy of the entry and try to take it all in. The thick soft-edged walls, the heavy exposed door frames, the sturdy wooden beams that dissect the ceiling, the corner fireplace formed in the shape of a beehive, stuffed with vertically stacked logs that fill the space with the warm scent of mesquite.

"Your mother was right," Paloma says, moving into the kitchen. Her light cotton dress swishing behind her, her bare feet skimming the floor in a way that prompts me to blink, stare, then blink again—making sure that she's not really floating, despite how it looks. "Other than the eyes, you look just like your father, my Django." Her own eyes moisten, as I fidget before her. The only picture I've ever seen of my father comes from one of those black-and-white strips you get from a photo booth.

There were three pictures in total: one of Django alone (smiling), one of Jennika alone (eyes crossed/tongue sticking out), and another of them crammed in together with a teenaged Jennika desperately trying to channel Courtney Love's mid-nineties look with her bleached-blond hair, dark red lipstick, and extremely short baby-doll dress—her body draped across Django's lap while he made a big show of kissing her neck as she threw her head back and laughed.

Needless to say, the third pic was my favorite.

They both looked so young and in love—so untroubled and free.

And while I definitely appreciated that part of it, it was the message that really stirred me.

It was a message of warning.

A cautionary tale at its best.

All the visual proof I would ever need that life could change in an instant.

A reminder of how just like *that*—your whole world can get flipped upside down and there's nothing you can do about it.

Three months after that photo was taken, Django was dead, Jennika was pregnant, and nothing ever felt free or untroubled again.

At first I asked for the whole strip, but Jennika just laughed and said no. So then I asked for the one of the kiss—it was the one I really wanted anyway—but she shook her head, grabbed a pair of cuticle scissors, and snipped off the one at the top and gave it to me.

So while Django moved into my wallet, Jennika hid the other two. Having no idea that every time she booked a new job, I'd spend the first day scoping out her hiding place so I could stare at the kissing photo while she was in meetings.

Paloma fiddles with a pot on the stove, alternately stirring its contents with a large wooden spoon, and lifting that spoon to her nose and inhaling deeply. Finally deeming it ready, she pours the contents into a large, handmade mug and makes her way back to me.

"Drink this while it's warm," she says, the mug held in offering. "It'll help you sleep. Help you keep calm."

As much as I hate to admit it, I'm reluctant to take it, unwilling to risk it. Even though Paloma seems completely nice and non-threatening, and not at all like the scary witch doctor I feared—being here, in the house where my dad lived for sixteen years before he ran off to California where he met first my mom, then his death—well, it's all beginning to feel a little weird.

Still, Paloma is patient—holding the cup in a way that leaves no doubt she'll stand there for hours if that's what it takes. And since the night can't get any more strange and awkward than it already is, I heave a deep sigh and consent. Wrapping my fingers around the smooth ceramic handle, instantly drawn to the wonderful, enticing scent the strange brew emits.

The next thing I know, I've already drained it. Watching Paloma place the mug on a nearby table as she says, "It should start to take effect very soon, so we best get you to your room."

Her touch light and warm as she steers me by the elbow, leading me down a short hallway past one closed door and then another, before ushering me through an arched doorway where I collapse on the bed.

Her nimble fingers tucking the blankets around me as she says, "In the morning, we will talk about everything, but for now, sweet *nieta,* sleep."

eight

I'm in the forest.

A cool, windless, lushly green forest consisting of moss-dappled earth and towering trees bearing a canopy of branches so long and entwined only the faintest trace of sun filters in. The light glinting on the leaves in a way that makes them seem animated, alive—as though swaying in harmony to the raven's sweet song.

My feet move quickly, nimbly, gliding along an unmarked trail with the raven riding high on my shoulder. His alert purple eyes sweeping the area as a vague awareness tugs at my memory, reminding me that I've no reason to fear, the raven will lead me, he is my guide. I am meant to be here.

We scale boulders, wade through swiftly moving streams. The water rising higher and higher until it swells past my ankles and soaks through my dress. Wetting and snarling my hair all the way to the tips of my ears, until my fingers grasp for the rock at the far bank, curl around its hard jutting edge, and I heave myself up and sprawl across the top with the raven perched just beside me. The two of us warmed by a bold beam of light that wicks the moisture from my dress, my hair, and my skin— returning it to the sky where it promises to find me again in the form of dew, snow, or rain. Though it's not long before the raven's curved bill *pecks at my shoulder—signaling that it's time to get up, start moving again.*

Our journey continuing across densely forested terrain, and ending the moment the raven's clawed feet squeeze my shoulders so tightly they nearly puncture my flesh. His wings fluttering, spreading, lifting him high into flight—and though I turn my gaze skyward, do my best to track him—it's only a blink until he's vanished from sight.

His mission complete, I've no further need of him. Having reached my intended destination in the form of this beautiful grass-covered clearing I'm in.

I run an anxious hand over my dress—hoping I look presentable, pretty, for the friend who awaits me. Sensing his presence well before I can see him, I shutter my eyes, inhale his deep earthy sent—savoring the rush of adrenaline that kick-starts my heart into a flurry of spasms—stretching the moment for as long as I can, before he calls to me, begs me to face him.

The sound of my name on his lips causing a smile to widen my cheeks as I admire him, absorb him, in the way he does me. My eyes grazing over this beautiful, nameless boy with smooth brown skin, and glossy black hair that sweeps over his face. His torso lean and bare—his shoulders wide and capable—while the hands that dangle by his sides merely hint at the promise of the pleasure I know them to give.

He reaches for me, entwines my fingers with his, leading me away from the clearing, to the other side of the forest where a beautiful, bubbling hot spring awaits. Its clear thermal waters eliciting a fine misty heat that swirls and dances and skims along the surface.

I'm the first to step in, the water claiming my dress until it clings just like skin. I wade toward the far bank, where I eagerly await the sweet burn of his fingers exploring my flesh. My need like a fever raging within—relieved only by the feel of his hands cupping my face, his lips meeting mine—merging and melding—tasting and teasing—the kiss so bewitching it causes a spark of images to blaze through my mind.

Visions of a flower budding, blooming, falling from its stem, only to rise up and bud once again—fading into one of a crowd of dazzling souls that shine brighter than day, butting against souls turned so dark they blend with the night. The souls becoming one with the elements, showing the sky's constant recycle of snow, dew, and rain—the wind's two faces of harm and respite—fire's equal ability to heat or destroy—and the earth's stoic patience as it struggles to absorb all we demand . . .

The images repeating until the message is clear:

I am the hydrogen in the very water I float in.

I am the oxygen in the air that I breathe.

I am the small bubble of heat in this mineral spring.

I am the blood that courses through the boy who kisses me—as sure as I'm the beat in the raven's wings that led me to him.

I am an integral part of everything—and everything is an integral part of me.

A truth that was never made clearer—revealed in one soulful kiss.

His fingers move swiftly, deftly. Trailing along the front of my dress, pushing the fabric down past my shoulders, down past my waist, where he ducks his head low and his lips find my flesh. His progress halted by the press of my palms pushing hard to his cheeks, needing to see him, really see him, in the way he sees me.

My thumbs smooth the sharp rise of his cheekbones. My fingers play at his damp tangle of hair. Pushing it back from his temples, back behind his ears, revealing a pair of icy-blue eyes banded by deep flecks of gold that mirror my image thousands of times.

Kaleidoscope eyes.

I gasp, unable to tear my gaze from his, unwilling to look anywhere else—possibly ever again.

"It is time," he says, his stare deepening until it's burning on mine.

I'm quick to agree and nod in reply. Sensing the truth behind the words though I've no idea what they mean.

"There is no going back. You are meant to be here."

Going back?

Why would I ever want to go back?

I was born to find him—of that I am sure.

I move past my thoughts, press closer to him. Hooking my legs around the back of his knees, bringing him to me, eager to claim his kiss once again.

My lips swelling, pressing, only to be met by cold empty space.

My friend is no longer before me—someone else has taken his place.

Someone who bears the same strong, lean body—the same sculpted face—but while the hair is glossy and black like my friend's—this hair is clipped short, kept close to the head. And while the eyes share the same color, flecked by the same bands of gold, the similarity ends there.

These eyes are cold.

Cruel.

And instead of reflecting, they absorb like the void I sense them to be.

"I'll take it from here." He gives my friend a hard shove.

"You'll do no such thing." My friend quickly recovers. His body tense, muscles coiling—prepared to defend me.

The boy snickers, moves to push past him but doesn't get very far before he's blocked once again. His words edged with a sneer when he says, "Not to worry, brother—it's the soul that I want, the heart is all yours."

My friend stands before him, a solid wall of protection. "There is no heart without the soul. I'm afraid you'll get neither."

The boy's gaze grows darker, deeper, more determined and cruel, discarding the threat with the words: "Then I guess I'll take yours."

It's a moment before it sinks in.

A moment before it begins to make sense.

A moment lost.

Wasted.

The threat realized so quickly I'm left wide-eyed and gaping when the boy—the one with the cold, empty eyes—becomes something else.

Something unrecognizable.

Otherworldly.

Something monstrous, demonic—born of dark fetid seed and other wicked foul things.

His mouth turned jagged, bloodied, and obscene—bearing sharp, fanged teeth that sink into my friend—flaying his flesh. Rendering his chest to a crushed, pulpy mess that stains the water a terrible red.

He rears his head back, emits a horrible growl. His eyes glowing the same crimson that drips from his chin as a hideous snake flares from his lips, inhabiting the space where his tongue used to be.

I reach for my friend, grasping, fumbling, in a frenzy to save him.

I can't lose him.

Can't let this happen.

Not when it's taken sixteen years to find him.

Though the word has yet to be spoken, there's no denying it is Love that we share.

Love that brought us both here.

We are bound.

Fated.

Some things you just know without question.

I lunge. Kick. Fight. Scream. Though my efforts are in vain—I'm no match for the snake.

It swerves around me. Plunges straight into the now-gaping cavity of my friend's battered chest.

Returning with a sacred, shimmering sphere it suckles gingerly, gently, before consuming it whole—snuffing the life it beheld like a flame.

The demon grins—a hideous sight forever sealed in my brain. Then he winks out of existence—leaving me alone with my friend—my one true love—my destined one—now an empty sack of lifeless flesh lying limp in my arms.

nine

I wake with a scream. Lying facedown, my mouth mashed into a pillow in a way that muffles the sound. Still, I can't help but worry that Paloma might've heard, might decide to come check on me and make sure I'm okay.

I kick the tangle of blankets and sheets from my legs and push them to the foot of my bed. Hauling myself up against the short wooden headboard, I cock my ear toward the hall, alert to any sign of my grandmother, convinced it's just a matter of time before she bursts into the room bearing some strange herbal brew she'll force me to drink. But all I make out is the comforting noise of kitchen sounds seeping under the door.

Water running, butter sizzling, along with the soft sucking sigh of a refrigerator door opening and the firm no-nonsense thump when it closes again. The everyday domestic soundtrack most people take for granted—that I only know from watching TV and movies.

For the past sixteen years, Jennika and I have been on the road, which means that most of my meals have come from airplanes, restaurants, foreign cafés with questionable health codes, and, when I'm lucky, the huge catered spreads they serve on the set.

The only time I've come even remotely close to experiencing anything resembling "normal" domesticity was when we found ourselves staying at Harlan's on my twelfth birthday and Jennika tried to surprise us by making French toast. Only she got distracted while waiting for the edges to brown, and the next thing we knew the toast was smoking, the fire alarm screaming, and after the drama was handled, Harlan squeezed us all into his car and treated us to brunch at some vegan place near Malibu Beach.

But Paloma's nothing like Jennika. From what I can see, she's a living picture of Old World, Latina hospitality. Though as much as my rumbling stomach urges me to get out of bed and go join her, the rest of me is determined to hold off—to delay the moment just a little bit longer.

I push a clump of damp, sweaty hair from my face and waste no time exchanging the clothes that I slept in for the soft cotton robe Paloma draped over a chair. The horror of the nightmare so fresh in my mind that for the first time ever I fervently hope I never dream about that boy again.

I curl my toes into the soft sheepskin that hugs the floor by my bed, and put myself through a quick series of stretches. Working to release the crick in my neck that always comes from sleeping in the face-plant position, before moving about my new room, exploring it in a way I didn't get to do last night, since whatever Paloma gave me knocked me out good and fast.

There's an old wooden desk and matching chair by the window with my father's initials carved into the grain in the upper-right corner. The D S so hard-edged and angular it looks almost Greek. And though I try to picture him sitting there—talking on the phone, doing homework, even plotting his eventual escape to L.A.—it's no use. It's impossible to make the transition from a smiling black-and-white photo to a real flesh-and-blood person—Paloma's only child who felt so suffocated right here in this town, right here in this house, he couldn't wait to get away.

Even when I spot his framed photo on the dresser, it's still hard to place. Though despite his neat appearance, the photo definitely hints at his unhappiness.

His shirt is clean and pressed, his dark hair freshly trimmed, and while his smile is pleasant enough, if you look closely, you can see more than a hint of restlessness in his gaze. And I can't help but wonder if Paloma was aware of it too—or if she's just like every other parent, allowing her eyes to skip past all the things that are too unpleasant to see.

"He was sixteen in that photo." Paloma pokes her head around the now-opened door, her voice so unexpected I can't help but jump in response. "Same age as you," she adds, but all I can do is stare, one hand clutched to my chest, aware of my heart pumping madly against it, the other returning the photo, feeling oddly guilty for studying it.

"I heard you get up." She moves toward me, lifts the photo from my fingers and holds it in hers.

I don't say a word. I'm not sure what to say. I'm pretty sure my muffled scream hadn't carried all the way to the kitchen—so does that mean she was camped outside my door, waiting for just the right moment to barge in?

"Oh, I suppose I didn't so much hear you, as sense you." She smiles, glancing between the photo and me. "He left not long after this picture was taken. He called on occasion, sent a few post-cards, but once he was gone, I never saw him again."

She replaces the photo, taking great care to set it precisely where I'd found it, before moving toward the window where she pushes the soft cotton curtains aside, allowing a single slant of pale light to stream in.

Her gaze following mine when she says, "It's a dream catcher."

I reach toward the delicate weaving hanging just over the sill. Its round, webbed center woven with yarn and beads, with a delib-erate hole left smack in its center—while soft buckskin fringe and an array of light feathers dangle from the ends.

"Do you know the story of the dream catcher?" she asks, her

flashing dark eyes reminding me of the color of earth after a night of hard rain.

I shake my head and scratch my arm even though it doesn't really itch—a nervous habit that's been with me for years. My own horrible dream lurking just under the surface, leaving me to wonder if I should maybe confide in her—an impulsive idea I'm quick to dismiss.

"Like people, each one is different—and yet, they share common traits. This particular dream catcher is Navajo in origin, made by a friend. It is said that dreams come from someplace outside ourselves—and so the dream catcher is hung over the bed or the window, acting as a web that catches the good dreams that ease us through the day, while allowing the bad dreams to pass through the hole you see in the center, so that it can be burned up by the rays of the sun. And those feathers at the bottom—" She motions toward the feathers I've been flicking with my fingers without even realizing it. "They're meant to symbolize the breath of all living things."

She turns to me, her gaze lightly probing as though she's waiting for me to reveal something big. And though I'm tempted to tell her that her dream catcher doesn't work—that while it's a nice little piece of hand-crafted art, as far as functionality goes, it's a total fail, doesn't work worth a crap at keeping the bad dreams away—her eyes are too kind, too hopeful, so I swallow the words and follow her into the kitchen for breakfast instead.

"You know there's a rock jutting out of the wall, right?" I drain my juice and carry the glass to the sink where Paloma stands, elbow deep in suds, since there's no sign of a dishwasher from what I can see. Not meaning for the words to sound as abrupt and rude as they did, though I do find it strange that we just got through an entire brunch (little did I realize, but I'd slept well past breakfast, and even past lunch as it were), including a huge, heaping plate of delicious blue-corn pancakes topped with warm maple syrup, a side of assorted organic berries plucked straight from her garden, fresh squeezed juice, and a nice warm mug of piñon coffee so aromatic I can still smell traces of it clinging to the room—with absolutely no mention of the boulder 'til I just now brought it up.

Paloma's lips curve, granting a small smile as she says, "We should not disturb nature. We should never demand it conform to our ways. Rather we must learn to live in harmony with it, for it offers many gifts."

Oh boy.

I've heard that sort of talk before. Usually coming from some crazy-eyed starlet who just returned from a life-changing yoga session. The newfound enlightenment lasting a few weeks at most—until the next fitness craze hit and the starlet moved on.

But Paloma's no starlet. Though I've no doubt she could've been—back in the day. If my math is correct, she's got to be somewhere in her early fifties, though she's still really pretty in a no-fuss, organic sort of way, with her long, dark braid that trails to her waist, clear brown eyes, tiny frame, thin cotton shift dress that reminds me an awful lot of the one I wore in my dream, and bare feet.

I trace my fingers over the rock, amazed by the way it just butts right into the room, solid and insistent, demanding everything else find a way to exist around it.

The house looks different this morning, and not just because of the rock I failed to notice before. Last night the house seemed so warm and glowy with the fireplace blazing and the assortment of table lamps lit. But now it seems simple, almost plain. Bearing a handful of Navajo rugs, simple wood furniture, jam jars crammed with small clusters of yellow and purple wildflowers, and these odd little nooks that punctuate the walls, each of them filled with hand-rendered carvings of various saints.

Still, as monastic as it is, it offers an undeniable sense of comfort I can't quite place. Though that might have something to do with its size. It's small, cozy, impossible to get lost in. Consisting of this big open space that hosts the kitchen and den, two bedrooms—one for me, one for Paloma (and I'm guessing two bathrooms as well, since I don't remember her using mine)—and another room at the far end that's clearly a recent addition. The short brick ramp that leads up to it ending in an arched doorway that frames an entire wall of shelves filled with bunches of drying herbs, jars filled with weird-looking liquids, and all kinds of other miscellaneous *stuff*, for lack of a better word.

"What's that?" I motion toward the strange room.

"That's where I work with my clients; think of it as my office, if you will." Paloma pulls the stopper from the sink, allowing the water to gurgle down the drain as she dries her hands on a blue embroidered towel. "But not to worry, I've cleared the day to spend with you, so that we can talk and get to know each other better, without interruption."

I glance between the room and her, saying, "Well, maybe we should start in there. After all, I'm the crazy one who was sent here to be cured."

She gives me a look I can't read—is it compassion, sadness, regret? It's impossible to tell.

"You are *not* crazy." She leans against a counter crafted from colorful Spanish tiles, her head cocked in study. "And I'm afraid there is nothing I can do to *cure* you, as you say."

My eyes bug, as her words repeat in my head. My reply just shy of hysteria, when I say, "Then why am I here? Why'd I travel all this way if you can't help me? What's the point of all this? Why'd you take me away from Jennika?"

"You've misread my words." She pushes away from the kitchen and motions for me to join her in the den where she stokes the vertically stacked logs in the fireplace, causing them to spark and spit, before she moves to the couch and lowers herself onto the cushions. "I didn't say I can't *help* you, I said I can't *cure* you. There is nothing to be cured, Daire."

I glare. Fidget. Pull hard on my robe, yanking it so tight it practically wraps twice around me. Perching on the arm of a chair, having no idea what she's getting at. It all sounds suspicious, like some kind of doublespeak.

I'm *this* close to calling Jennika. Demand she fly here right now and come get me, when Paloma says, "It happened to your father as well. The onset is always around the sixteenth year."

I heave a deep sigh. Shake my head. "So I *am* psycho. Great. And, according to you, I got it from my dad!" My teeth grind, as I twist my sash so hard I hear the fabric give way.

This is great.

Just great.

I travel all this way only to receive the same diagnosis I got in Morocco and L.A.

"No." Paloma's voice is as stern as her face. "You are *not* crazy. It may feel like crazy—even look like crazy—but it's anything but. What you're experiencing is the onset of your biological inheritance—the family legacy that's been passed down through each generation, always to the firstborn."

Wha—?

I shake my head, peer at her again. Her mouth is still moving, desperate to explain, but it's too much to take in—too weird to comprehend. My head so muddled with the sound of her voice, her nonsensical words—the best I can manage is, "So why keep having kids if you all know this? Seriously—you have no idea what it's like. Why would Django take the risk? Why wouldn't he use protection or warn Jennika at the very least?"

"Because Django was as young and idealistic and stubborn as any other sixteen-year-old. He refused to believe. Refused to acknowledge my warnings. He thought that by running away, he could outrun the visions, outrun what I told him. But as you've already seen, there is no escape. The visions found you all the way on the other side of the world, and if you try to run, they will find you again. I'm told the symptoms appeared in full force in

Marrakesh. Though I'm sure you experienced signs long before that."

My stomach twists. My lungs shrivel and shrink. Forcing me to fight for each shallow breath as my eyes cast about wildly, urging me to flee.

"I couldn't reach Django. I failed to reach my one and only son—failed to convince him of his duty. His responsibility. His destiny. But, Daire, I will not fail with you. I know exactly what you're going through. Sure, the visions are different for each of us, but the message stays true. You need to heed the call before it's too late. " Her short, unvarnished nails pluck at the hem of her dress. "And while I'm sorry for your current state of suffering and confusion, I can promise you that it won't always be this way. With the right guidance, the right diet, and the right training, you will surpass all of that and realize your destiny, your birthright, the role you were born for."

I blink. Stare. Blink again. Aware of myself saying, "*What?*" as I shake my head and shoot her a baleful look. "Do you have any idea how crazy this sounds?"

"I do indeed." She nods. "My own reaction was quite similar, I assure you. But you must work past your prejudice—you must look beyond the ideas you've been conditioned to believe. There is too much at stake. This town holds secrets you cannot begin to imagine. It is full of coyotes, and Coyote is a trickster you must learn to outsmart." Her gaze levels on mine, letting me know she means business. She will not mince words. "If you fail to learn, if you fail to accept what you were born to do, I'm afraid I can't save you—no one can. If you continue to fight your calling, it's just a matter of time before your fate will become that of your father's. And, Daire, sweet *nieta,* I can't let that happen. I won't lose you, and I won't let them win. Until you've made peace with what you must do, until you fully understand what's ahead of you, what's being asked of you, the only safe place for you is right here in this house. My property is protected—you have nothing to fear as long as you're here. It'll be weeks until you've learned enough to leave."

I balk, my expression incredulous—her words ridiculous. No way is she holding me prisoner. No way will I listen to another crazy word.

And before she can stop me, I bolt from the room and race down the hall—her voice chasing behind me until it's blocked by the slam of my door.

ten

I dress in a hurry. Swapping my wrinkled white robe for a freshly laundered black tank top, slipping on the same dark denim jeans I arrived in, the black flats too. Then after reaching for my olive-green army jacket, and scraping my hair into a haphazard ponytail, I zip my bag shut, swing it over my shoulder, and call Jennika.

Again.

Only to have her phone go straight into voice mail just like it did the first time I called.

Flying is out of the question. I've been banned from all commercial aircraft.

Driving is out too. I may be sixteen, but I don't have a permit, much less my license. Up until now, I had no real need of it.

All I know for sure is that I can no longer stay here. It's not even an option. I'll take a bus—walk if I have to. I'll do whatever it takes to get the hell out of this horrible place.

I glance at my father's portrait—taking Django's restless, troubled gaze as a warning to bust free before it's too late.

No wonder he fled—Paloma's a freak.

She knocks, whispers through the wood, calling me *nieta* as she twists the handle and tries to come in. Her efforts rebuffed by the old wooden chair I've wedged under the knob, barring her from entering 'til well after I'm gone.

I press my ear to the door frame, listening for the reassuring sound of her retreating step—a temporary surrender I'm determined to exploit by making a run for the window, propping it open, heaving myself up to the ledge, and dropping my bag onto the stone courtyard below where it lands with a thump. My gaze fixed on the big blue gate and the adobe wall that surrounds the place, noticing for the first time the strange wooden fence constructed from juniper branches that sits just inside it, and just inside that is a thick border of something grainy and white—as though someone went a little crazy with the saltshaker.

A layer of salt, within a wooden fence, within a thick adobe wall—*is this what Paloma meant when she claimed the house was protected?*

I shake my head and swing a leg over, scrunching and contorting until I've freed my other leg and eased my way out. The tickle of the dream catcher's feathers brushing softly against my scalp serving as yet another reminder of why I need to flee—this is the house where crazy lives. If I stay any longer, I'll never see normal again.

I crouch next to my bag, grab hold of the strap, and dash across the courtyard as fast as I can. The gravel crunching under my soles so loud it reverberates through my head—the gate shrieking in protest, causing me to curse under my breath, until I'm free of it—free of her. Sprinting down the dirt road, following the same route I came from. My feet pounding so hard, small clouds of dust stir in my wake.

I run for a while. Run for much longer than I'm used to. The strap on my bag cutting a deep wedge into my shoulder, as my cheeks flame, my eyes sear, but still I continue. Refusing to stop until the small cramp in my side explodes into a pain so white-hot and stabbing, I lose my balance and land in a big crumpled heap. My duffle bag strewn to my side, my arms wrapped tightly around me, I tuck my chin to my chest and fight to grab hold, to steady my breath. Coaxing the pain to go away, convincing it to subside so I can get moving again.

I inch my way off the road, crawl deep into the shoulder where a narrow, dirt gully runs alongside it. Taking great care to pace myself, go slower than I'd like—making sure to stay crouched, out of sight, hoping to make it harder for Paloma to spot me, should she decide to go searching.

A small army of dried-out shrubs on their way to becoming tumbleweeds prick at my jeans as I pass one anonymous adobe house after another. Each of them in a similar state of disrepair, with crumbling chimneys and patched-up windows—featuring an assortment of rusted-out cars, freely roaming chickens, grazing cattle, and sagging, overloaded clotheslines meant to stand in for landscaping.

This has got to be the most poorly named town I've ever visited. There is absolutely no sign of anything even remotely *enchanting* about it. It's one of the worst cases of false advertising I've seen.

I've traveled a lot. Done considerable time in my share of dead-end dumps. Or at least that's what I thought until I came here.

I mean, where do people shop for clothing and food?

Where do the teens all hang out—the ones who haven't already hopped the first bus out of this godforsaken place?

And, more important, where do I catch that very same bus—how soon 'til it leaves?

I reach for my phone, trying for Jennika again, but just like before it goes straight to voice mail. And after leaving yet another angry message, followed by an even worse text, I consider calling Harlan but nix it just as fast. I have no idea how he and Jennika left things, have no idea if he's even back from Thailand. Besides, one look at my watch tells me there's only a short time standing between sundown and me, and I really need to locate the town by then; if not, I'm in for a long, spooky night.

I follow the gully to its end and find myself back on a succession of dirt roads once again. One ends, another begins, and after a while it's just one big blur of depressing, desolate streets that seem to lead nowhere in particular.

I've just decided to approach the next house I see, march right up to the door and ask for assistance, when I turn a corner and miraculously stumble upon some semblance of a town—or at least the closest thing I expect to find in these parts.

The street is wide, sprawling the length of three stop signs until it fades into nothing again. And not wanting to waste any more time than I already have, I head into the very first storefront I see, the sign overhead reading: GIFFORD'S GIFT SHOP * NOTARY * & MAIL STOP, with a smaller sign beside it advertising freshly brewed coffee.

I push inside, causing the bell on the door to clink so hard the patrons halt their conversations long enough to turn and stare—eyes widening at the sight of my snarled hair, reddened cheeks, and filthy jeans.

Great. Just in time for rush hour.

I sigh. Heave my bag high on my shoulder, straighten my clothes, and take my place at the end of the line. The rise of voices resuming around me as I snag a postcard from a nearby rack, which features the word *Enchantment!* scrawled in pink across the top, with a picture of this miserable street just below—and I can't think of a better depiction to show just how dismal this place really is.

Using the pen that's chained just beside it, I scribble the address for Jennika and my box at the UPS store, then write:

Dear Jennika—
Thanks for sending me to this dump and then refusing to take
my calls.
I don't feel at all abandoned by you.
Nope, not one bit.

Your kind consideration is very much appreciated.
Your loving daughter,
Daire
xoxo

Even though I know I'll be well out of here before the card has
a chance to reach her, the small burst of sarcasm makes me feel
better.

The line moves quicker than expected, and it's not long before I'm inching my way toward the counter. Warning myself
not to look at the magazine rack, no matter how tempting, but I
can't seem to obey. My gaze keeps getting pulled to the one featuring Vane and me on the cover. All too aware of that annoying
pang in my gut the moment I see him—only this time it's more a
pang of anger than weakness, and I consider that progress.

I lower my sunglasses and tuck my chin to my chest, hoping no
one will make the connection between me and the glowering girl
on the tabloid's glossy cover, though it's probably not necessary
since from what I can tell, they've made the transition from gawking at me to ignoring me, which I truly appreciate.

"Help you?" the man asks, as I edge my way to the front and lean
against the gray Formica counter. His snug jeans, Western-style
shirt, and big silver belt buckle make him look like some old, retired
ranch hand. Though his clipped East Coast accent hints at a whole
other life before he found himself here.

I perch my bag on my hip and slide the card toward him. Digging for my wallet as I say, "Just the postcard, some postage, and
hopefully some directions as well."

He hums under his breath and affixes a stamp to the back.
Shamelessly pausing a moment to read what I wrote, before his
eyes meet mine and he says, "Planning a jailbreak, are you?"

I quirk a brow, wonder why he chose to phrase it that way.

But he just shrugs and hooks his thumb toward the door.
"You'll find the bus stop at the end of the block. Bus to Albuquer-

que leaves every two hours." He consults his watch. "Unfortunately for you, one just left, which means you're stuck with the likes of us for just a little bit longer." He laughs in a way that causes his eyes to disappear into a riot of wrinkles, and though I'm sure he means well, I'm in no mood to join in.

I just pay for my stuff and shoot for the door. Squinting into the fading sun, searching for a good place to hide so Paloma can't find me before I've had a chance to run.

eleven

I make my way down the street, passing a bakery displaying elabo-rately frosted birthday cakes, a used bookstore featuring a random assortment of dog-eared paperbacks, and a small clothing boutique with sad sagging hangers bearing the kind of sparkly clothes I would never think to consider. Pausing before the corner liquor store, waiting for traffic to clear so I can see what lies just beyond, I sense the strange weight of someone looking at me, and turn to find a guy about my age leaning against a brick wall.

"Got a light?" His voice is low and deep as he waves an unlit cigarette at me.

I shake my head. Fingers picking at the ends of my ponytail as my eyes greedily roam the length of him. Taking in brown leather boots, faded jeans, a light gray V-neck sweater, damp black hair that's combed away from his face, a square chin, a strong brow, eyes that remain hidden behind a pair of dark glasses, and widely curving lips that smile flirtatiously.

"You sure?" He cocks his head, allows his smile to grow wider. Revealing a perfect set of flashing white teeth that stand in sharp contrast to his gorgeous brown skin.

It's the move of a charmer—a guy who knows he's good-looking. A guy used to getting his way.

I shake my head again, try to force my gaze away, but it's no use. My instincts warn me to leave, while my curiosity insists that I stay.

"That's too bad," he says, mouth quirking at the sides. His smile growing wider when he holds the cigarette before him and it turns into a shiny black snake that slithers up his arm and into his mouth invading the space where his tongue ought to be.

I freeze. Waiting for time to stop, for the crows to appear. Convinced it's another hallucination, when he laughs—the sound loud, booming, lingering in the background as he says, "Guess I'm on my own, then." He reaches into his pocket, retrieves a silver and turquoise lighter, and brings it to his lips where a cigarette waits in place of the snake—his thumb striking the ribbed metal wheel, sparking the blaze that flames in his face.

He inhales deeply, the two of us staring through dark lenses it's too late to wear. And before he can exhale, before he can blow a string of smoke rings my way, I'm gone. Crossing the street, my breath quickening, heart racing, punching in Jennika's number the instant my foot leaves the curb, leaving a stream of messages and texts so ugly they make the postcard read like a love letter in comparison.

I'm acting ridiculous. I seriously need to get a grip on myself. What I saw wasn't real. Still, I'm left unsettled in a way I can't shake.

With only a few feet of asphalt standing between the bus stop and me, I can't help but consider it. But it's too open, too exposed, consisting of no more than a splintered wooden bench and a shabby plastic shelter that looks ready to collapse under the next burst of rain. Not to mention it's probably the first place Paloma would look. She may be crazy, but she's not stupid, of that I am sure.

Needing to find a place to hide out, maybe even grab a quick bite to eat, I drop my phone in my bag, just about to set off again, when I notice the way the battery flashes in warning, as a glaring neon sign switches on right before me.

THE RABBIT HOLE.

And just beside the glowing red words is a glowing jagged green arrow pointing toward a steep flight of steps.

A basement bar.

The perfect place to hide until my bus comes to take me away. The last place Paloma or Chay would ever think to look.

Taking it as the first good omen I've had in weeks, I tackle the stairs and rush through the door, entering a place so dark and dim it takes a moment for my eyes to adjust.

"ID." An overly muscled, no-neck bouncer eyeballs me carefully.

"Oh, I'm not drinking, I just want to grab a soda, and maybe a bite." I force a quick smile, but it's wasted on him. He sees himself as a badass, a tough guy, someone who's immune to small pleasantries.

"ID," he repeats, chasing it with, "no ID, no enter."

I nod, slide my duffle down to my elbow, and dig through a tangle of clothes until I fish out my passport and hand it right over. My breath bubbles in my cheeks as he studies it, mutters something I can't quite make out, then motions for my right hand where he presses a stamp to the back before dismissing me with an impatient look.

Once inside, I take a good look around. My gaze darting along red vinyl banquettes, dark wooden tables, wall-to-wall carpet of indeterminate color, and a long mahogany bar crowded with patrons—the majority bearing the tired glazed look of people who've been teetering on their bar stools too long.

Searching for an empty seat, preferably one in a dark, undisturbed corner where only the waitress can find me, it's not long before I spy an older couple vacating just the kind of small booth

I need, and I'm quick to claim it well before their dirty plates can be cleared.

I pluck a menu from its holder, taking great care to maneuver around its sticky edges as I study the array of salty bar snacks on offer—all of them chosen to whet the thirst and make you drink more.

"Somethin'?"

I look up, startled. I hadn't heard her approach.

"Would. You. Like. Somethin'?" The waitress smirks, makes a point to over-enunciate every word. Tapping her pen against her hip in a way that tells me she's so used to getting crap for tips, she sees no point in trying anymore.

"Um, yeah," I say, knowing if I ask for more time she'll never pass by again. "I guess I'll just have the buffalo wings—oh, and um, a Sprite too. Thanks," I add, committing the cardinal sin of sliding the menu toward her, and watching as she huffs, shakes her head, and punches it back into the holder where it came from.

"Anything else?" she asks, and despite her surly, beaten-down tone and defeated, hardened slant of a mouth, I'm guessing she's only a handful of years older than me.

I'm also guessing she might've once been the town beauty queen. There are traces that linger by way of her long acrylic nails, freshly filled from what I can tell—carefully tended dark roots bleached a light, yellow blond—and black lace push-up bra that heaves her breasts so high and round they threaten to spill out the top of her tight white tank top, causing the name tag that reads: MARLIZI to teeter like a seesaw—but for whatever reason, it still wasn't enough to buy her escape.

"I need to charge my phone," I tell her. "Is there a vacant outlet I can use?"

She jabs a thumb over her shoulder, her modest bump of a bicep jumping in a way that begs me to notice the intricate snake tattoo that winds its way from her wrist all the way up to her shoulder and unseen points just beyond. "Talk to the bartender,"

she barks, turning to tap an overworked busboy on the back, or-
dering him to clear my table *ASAP,* before she heads into the
kitchen, her hip leading the way through a set of swinging doors
that appear to swallow her whole.

I head for the bar, making sure to keep an eye on my stuff as I
flag down the bartender, which is easier said than done. But before I can speak, he's already eyeballing my hand, the one with
the stamp, and directing me back to my seat.

His back turned toward me when I say, "Hey! Excuse me—I'm
not trying to order a drink—I just want to charge my phone. Do
you think you could help me with that? I'm pretty sure you must
have an available outlet somewhere."

He stops, heavily lidded dark eyes gazing down the long strip
of bar, studying me in a way that causes everyone else to lower
their drinks and study me too. Making me wonder if I should just
grab my bag and retreat. Get myself to that bus stop and take my
chances on getting spotted by Paloma or Chay or whoever else
she has working for her.

I don't like being stared at, especially like this. It reminds me
too much of the way the glowing people watch me. The crows
too. Reminds me of that awful night in Marrakesh, when the
Djemâa el Fna turned into a sea of dark flashing eyes and bloody,
severed heads hanging from spikes.

I take a deep breath and rid my mind of the image. Glancing
over my shoulder to check on my stuff as the bartender says, "Got
a charger?"

I nod, unable to tear myself from his gaze once I've returned it.

"So . . ." He flattens his palm, looks at me like I'm the dumbest
thing he ever saw.

And even though I'm reluctant to hand it over, it's not like I
have other options. Still, I can't help the way my stomach lurches
when he closes his tattooed fingers around the phone and leaves
without a word. Disappearing down a long corridor as I return to
my seat, where I slurp my Sprite and pick at my basket of buffalo

wings, all the while keeping tabs on my watch, willing the hands to move faster, never having wanted to leave a place so badly as this.

A crowd of people push past the bouncer—four guys trying to look tough in their baggy jeans, beer-brand tees, and camouflage hats—while their dates try to look hot with their puffy hair, tee-tering stilettos, cleavage-baring tops, and jeans slung so low their assortment of tramp stamps and belly rings are neatly displayed. Their eyes narrowing when they catch me staring, then forgetting me just as quickly once the song changes from an old Red Hot Chili Peppers tune to a classic Santana song that gets the girls dancing.

Their hands circle each other's waists, as they swarm and grind in a way that practically begs their boyfriends to notice. And it's all I can do to grab hold of the table, my fingers curling around the edges, squishing a stale piece of petrified gum someone saw fit to leave there—as my head swirls with the beat of that in-cessant drumming. The sound so persistent it turns the chorus into a meaningless flurry of words that fade into nothing.

It's happening.

I'm getting pulled under. Lost in the noise.

The atmosphere turning first hazy, then shimmery, and it's not long before everything stops, and time screeches to a big slamming halt.

The waitress now frozen with a tray of plates balanced on her palm—as the busboy pours a solid arc of water that never reaches the bottom. The dancing girls caught in mid-wiggle—lips puck-ered, eyes slitted—their boyfriends' tattooed arms caught reach-ing for freshly poured beers.

No matter how many times I blink, the scene refuses to change, refuses to march forward again. The beat so insistent, so rhythmic, it causes something inside me—something ancient and deep—to tremble and stir and rise to the surface.

I squeeze my eyes shut. Fight for control of myself. Aware of the crows swooping down all around me, landing on my shoulders, the table, pecking hard at my fingers—as the glowing ones nudge up against me, urge me to listen, to heed their warning.

I reach for my bag, fumbling for whatever remains of the herbs Paloma gave me. They'll make me sleepy, there's no getting around it—still, sleepy is better than this—anything is.

Dumping it into my soda, I give it a quick swirl with my straw, then chug it so swiftly it spills out the corner of my mouth, flows down my neck, and lands in small sticky globs on my chest. Then I lean back in my seat, wrap my arms tightly around me, and wait for the vision to end, for time to pick itself up and march forward again.

My eyes still shut when the waitress comes by and says, "That it?"

I lift my head, meeting a pair of eyes caked with eyeliner so thick I'm not sure if Jennika would cringe or cheer. Nodding when she repeats the question, too shaken to say anything more, all of my energy spent hoping the herbs will hold long enough to get me to Albuquerque. If not, who knows where I'll end up?

"Better get moving then, don't want to miss your bus now, do you?"

I narrow my gaze, searching her face once again. Noting a pair of overplucked brows that leave her looking more surprised than she's probably capable of. "How do you know I'm catching the bus?" I ask, pretty sure I hadn't mentioned it.

But she just smirks and plops the check down before me, voice trailing over her shoulder when she says, "If you're smart, you'll get out while you can. Don't be a lifer like I am."

I stare at her retreating back, calling, "I gave my phone to the bartender, do you know where he took it?"

She cocks her head toward the long corridor and disappears into the kitchen. So I toss some bills on the table, grab my bag, and head in the direction she sent me.

The place is big—much bigger than it appears at first sight. A huge, cavernous, underground space with numerous corridors that lead off in all different directions, reminding me of an old bunker from a movie set Jennika worked on back when I was a kid.

Since I have no idea where I'm going, I just follow the noise. Figuring at the very least it'll lead me to someone who might be able to help, and finding myself even further surprised when I enter a really large, crowded room with a stage, and a band, with a whole swarm of teens dancing before them.

Teens.

People my age.

Who would've thought?

They're even dressed like teens—though I can't imagine where they shop. The only boutique I saw didn't sell anything even remotely trendy and cute.

Maybe there's more to this town than I thought? Though it's not like I'll stick around to find out.

I head toward the bar, hoping this bartender will be nicer than the last, and after screaming to be heard above the noise, I head in the direction she sent me, attracting all kinds of unwanted attention as I push my way across the dance floor.

Two dark-haired girls snicker and glare as I make my way past, muttering a word I can't understand. But with only twenty minutes standing between me and my permanent emancipation from this gawd-awful place, I choose to ignore it—can't afford a delay. Can't afford the slightest mistake.

I rap hard on the door. Once. Twice. Desperate to get some traction, I raise my arm again, ready to bang even harder this time, when the door springs opens, and an older man catches my flailing wrist in his fist as he says, "Yes?" His eyes dance, his teeth flash, and on the surface at least, he appears to be the friendliest person I've met so far, but something about him makes me step back—makes me wrench my hand from his grip.

He stares, blinks, waits for me to speak up, and knowing I need to get this over with quick, I force the words from my lips. "I'm here for my phone."

He gives me a quick once-over, and while it's pleasant enough, I can't help but notice the chills that run down my arms, prickling my skin in a way that's disturbing. Then he swings the door wider, motions for me to step in. Calling to a guy staring at a wall of security screens documenting everything happening inside and out of this place, saying, "Son, the girl needs her phone."

I glance around the office, taking in desks, phones, computers, printers, chairs—all the usual stuff, nothing ominous about it, and yet, something about it leaves me on edge.

The boy reaches toward the wall and yanks hard on the plug, his glossy black hair gleaming under the fluorescent light in a way I can't miss. And when he turns, my phone and charger in hand, I can't move. Can't speak. Can't do anything but stare hard at his eyes.

Cold. Cruel. Icy-blue eyes banded by brilliant flecks of gold that fail to reflect.

Eyes I've dreamed about.

"This yours?" His voice is light, flirtatious, overly confident— a voice that belongs to a guy used to charming girls speechless.

A voice that recently asked for a light just outside the liquor store.

My hands tremble, my heart hammers, as I reach toward him, reach for the phone, only to find he has other plans.

His fingers curl around mine, catching my hand in his—as his strange blue eyes deepen in a way that challenges me to resist.

Though his touch is cool and smooth and undeniably inviting, something about it makes me jerk back, causing my phone to crash to the ground, and it's all I can do to tear my gaze away long enough to kneel down and retrieve it.

"I hope you'll stick around long enough to check out the band." His voice floats over my head. "They came all the way from Albu- querque. They're only here for tonight. Be a shame to miss it."

I swallow hard, settling my bag high on my shoulder, as I

struggle to settle myself, needing to play it cool for now, then bolt when I can.

"'Fraid I'll have to miss it," I say, striving for nonchalant, but my voice betrays me with the way it trembles and pitches. "Gotta bus to catch, so . . . if you don't mind." I wriggle my fingers, motioning for him to step out of my way. But he remains right where he is, blocking my exit with a grin on his face.

He cocks his head, allowing a clump of hair to fall across his eyes as his gaze sweeps over me and his tongue flicks across his front teeth. "Now you're just being mean," he says, smile broadening as he rakes a hand through his bangs. "Least you could do is stay a while. Give us a chance to get to know each other better. I had no idea Paloma was hiding such a pretty granddaughter— did you?" He turns to his father, their eyes meeting in a private joke that escapes me.

I start to speak. Start to ask how he knows about Paloma and me. But before I can get there, he says, "Trust me, Enchantment is even smaller than it looks. Hard to keep a secret in a town where everyone knows everyone."

His eyes meet mine, but instead of that odd, nonreflective blue they once were—they're now crimson. And when his lip quirks to the side, they part just enough to allow the snake to slip out and dart straight for my chest.

I gasp. Shove him aside and make for the door. Fingers straining for the handle, just inches away, when the walls begin to melt, the roof begins to sink, and the space shrinks so small it swallows the door and bars my escape.

The room crushing, pressing, forcing me to the floor, forcing me to my knees—depleting it of oxygen, making it impossible to breathe—to see—to do much of anything other than scream.

I scream until my head swells with the sound of it.

Scream until my eyes fill with bright swirling circles.

Scream until I realize I haven't screamed at all—the sound stayed inside me, never found its way out.

A cool, firm hand clamps hard on my shoulder, as the boy peers at me and says, "Hey—hey there, you okay?"

I stare at him sideways, seeing him for what he truly is—no longer a demon but rather a beautiful, overconfident boy wearing a false mask of concern.

"Can I get you some water? Do you need to sit down?" His eyes crease with amusement as the room settles around me, returning to normal again.

He reaches toward me, offers a hand, but I'm quick to jump up, slip out of his grip. Noting the way his dad watches, his face placid, unreadable, while the boy hovers beside me, pretending to care.

"Get away from me," I mumble, my voice weak, whimpering—my body a trembling mess of nerves. Assuring myself that what I saw was real, even though it's ridiculous, even though they do their best to pretend not to have noticed.

"Hey now." He reaches toward me again. "That's no way to—"

"I said, *don't touch me!*" I grab hold of my bag—bolt for the door.

The boy calling after me as I shove through crowds of people my age, people I might've befriended had Paloma succeeded in keeping me here.

Knocking into girls and bouncing off boys, until one in particular catches me, steadies me. His fingers circling my arm as he peers down and says, "You okay?"

I struggle against him, fight to break free. Though it's not long before I'm overcome by a cool wash of calm chased by a comforting warmth that folds like a blanket around me. My movements slowed, my thoughts becoming so hazy and loose, I abandon my flight. Robbed of all recollection of why I wanted to leave when I'd do anything to always feel so secure—so safe—so loved and at peace.

So at home in his arms.

I melt against his chest—lift my gaze to meet his. Gasping when I stare into a pair of icy-blue eyes banded by brilliant flecks of gold that shine like kaleidoscopes, reflecting my image thousands of times.

The boy from my dream.

The one who died in my arms.

Brothers.

As the boy claimed they were:

"Not to worry, brother—it's the soul that I want, the heart is all yours."

But I know it can't be. My mind is deceitful. I can longer trust the things that it shows me.

I break free, jolted by the sudden loss of warmth—the crushing chill that surrounds me the instant I sever his touch.

"I'm sorry—I just . . . I thought you needed—" He peers at me, gaze fraught with worry, head cocked in a way that causes his long, glossy black hair to spill down his side.

But before he can finish, I'm gone. Racing across the room, I blow past the exit and make my way up a steep flight of stairs—convincing myself the boys aren't real, or at least not in the way that I think.

The hallucinations and dreams are merging as one. I just need to get out of here—just need to—

I'm about halfway down the alley when I allow myself to stop beneath the only street lamp that's lit, where I sag against the wall and fight to catch my breath. My body bent forward, fingers clutching hard at my knees, as slick waves of hot, clammy sweat course under my clothes—thoroughly wetting me.

I yank on my ponytail, pry it away from the place where it clings fast to my neck, and when I return my hand to my knee, my gaze is caught by the stamp I'd failed to notice 'til now:

A red ink coyote with glaring red eyes.

This town holds secrets you can't even begin to imagine. It is full of coyotes, and Coyote is a trickster you must learn to outsmart.

The memory of Paloma's words causing me to push away from the wall, fumble blindly toward the street, as the glowing

ones surge toward me, their numbers increasing until they surround me.

Having overpowered the herbs, they jump out of windows,
leap from shadowed doorways—as the crows swoop down to my
ankles and peck at my feet—squawking in outrage as I stumble
right over them, turning them to clumps of bloodied feathers that
cling to my shoes.

Only a few yards of asphalt lying between the bus stop and
me—one double lane road and I'm free.

Free of the Rabbit Hole, this alleyway, this horrible town, the
glowing people, the crows, and the boys with the unearthly blue
eyes.

I can make it.

I can do it.

I have to.

I've no choice.

Never mind that my vision is narrowing, turning everything
to bright shining spots that shimmer before me.

Never mind that my legs are wobbly, knees no longer willing
to carry me.

I bang into the street, arms outstretched, struggling to see
through the glare. My lips moving in a silent plea:

Help me—please—just a few more steps and I'm there!

The sound of tires squealing, voices shouting, now crowding
my head. Leaving me blinded, swaying, darting around the shadows
dancing before me. My vision filling with bright wavering circles
of light as a sudden thrust of hot metal sends me flying, flailing,
soaring high into the sky with arms spread wide, raven-like—
until gravity hits and the asphalt roars up to catch me in a bed of
razor-sharp rocks that slice through my clothes and embed in my
flesh—jamming my nose with the stench of burnt rubber, charred
skin.

An image of the old black-and-white photo bearing my dad's
smiling face the last thing I see.

His dark eyes narrowed in judgment—disappointed with me.

I didn't listen to his warning.

I was too focused on the gruesome state of his head back in that Moroccan square to listen to the words he tried to tell me.

And now, because of my failing, I am like him.

Only worse.

I failed to escape.

Failed to find a way out.

And now, because of it, I will die in this town.

the
spirit
road

twelve

Paloma leans over the grave site; murmuring in her native Spanish, she clears the film of dirt with her fingers before placing the flowers just so. A handful of blooms plucked straight from her garden—bright blossoms of violet and gold that continue to flourish despite the onset of fall.

Her gaze solemn, mouth set, knees pushing into a patch of dried grass, as her long dark braid slips over her shoulder and sweeps the length of the simple, rectangular marker, before she grabs the braid, tames it, turning to me when I ask, "So, is this where he rests?" Regretting the way my words came out much louder than planned.

She shakes her head, eyes fixed on mine, surprising me when she says, "No."

I cock my head, peer at the grave marker again, ensuring the mistake isn't mine.

"This is where he was *laid* to rest. This is where we *buried* his body. But make no mistake, Daire, he no longer remains in this place."

I do my best not to balk, but I'm pretty sure I did anyway. You'd think I'd be used to Paloma's plainspoken ways, but really, it's just so odd to hear a parent speak about her dead child's body in such a frank and clinical way.

"Don't make the mistake of confusing this place with your father." Her eyes narrow, urging me to listen. "This is *not* where he lives. If you want to come here to visit, have a place to speak with him, commune with him—if you find that it helps, then by all means, go ahead. It's perfectly understandable, and I would never move to stop you. But never forget that your father is every-where. His soul's been released, unbound from this earth, left to become one with the wind that blows through your hair, the dirt that shifts under your feet. He's the rain in the storm cloud that hovers over those mountains beyond." She extends a slim, elegant arm, gesturing toward the beautiful Sangre de Cristo Mountain range—a wide sweep of navy and gray with a cap of white snow at the top. "He's the bloom in every flower. He is one with the en-ergy of the earth. He is everywhere you look. Which means you can speak to him here, just as easily as you can speak to him any-where. And if you go very quiet and listen with care, you just might hear his reply."

I swallow hard, still caught on the part about my dad being one with the wind, and the dirt, and the rain. Her words remind-ing me of the dream I had the first night I arrived. The one where I realized that I was an integral part of everything—and not long after that, my true love was dead.

I lean hard on my crutches, my gaze sweeping the length of the graveyard, still unused to the quiet humbleness of this place. In Los Angeles, the cemeteries are carefully planned, heeding strict zoning laws and consisting of wide, grassy, well tended knolls with the occasional pond near which to pause and reflect. They go by glossy Hollywood names like Forest Lawn Memorial Park—encouraging the illusion that your loved one isn't really gone, but rather they've been recruited for some elite, afterlife golf tournament.

But this place is nothing like that—it's raw and accessible, with no fancy, euphemistic name, no shiny marble mausoleums. It's not pretending to be anything other than what it is—a place for common folks to bury their loved ones. Set right off the side of the highway, pretty much in the middle of nowhere—it seems random, unplanned, crowded with handmade crosses and markers that, at first look, all seem to clash.

But as shabby as it seemed at first glance, now I see that the graves are often visited and well kept. Marked with generous handfuls of flowers—some plastic, some real—set alongside freshly filled balloons grounded by rocks and left to sway in the wind. All of it making for so much color, so much comfort and love, I can't help but feel oddly peaceful here. And it's not long before I realize I'm in no hurry to leave.

"How did he die?" I ask, using my more or less unscathed leg to rub against the one with the cast. The plaster makes it itch, and I can't wait to be rid of it. "Jennika would never tell me," I add, when I see the way Paloma hesitates, averts her gaze.

"Why do you call her Jennika?" she asks, her voice soft, eyes returning to mine.

And though it would be just as easy to answer, *"Because it's her name,"* I don't. There's no need for sarcasm. I know what she meant.

"She was barely seventeen when she had me—I raised her as much as she raised me. Also, I grew up surrounded by adults, which didn't make for a whole lot of baby talk. Everyone called her Jennika, so one day when I really needed her attention, I called her that too. Of course I didn't pronounce it correctly, but she got the drift. It was the first word I ever spoke, and it stuck."

Paloma nods, a small smile sneaking onto her face.

"And now, your turn—what really happened to Django? Was it an accident like mine?" I gaze down at my bruised and battered self, which, thanks to Paloma's careful ministrations and advanced healing knowledge, not to mention Chay's having arrived on the scene mere seconds after the impact (just as I'd thought, Paloma had sent him to look for me), I was spared a grave in this place. Actually, I was spared a lot more than that. It was just two weeks ago, and I'm already up and about.

"It was an accident," she says, her tone becoming earnest when she adds, "but it was nothing like yours."

I squint. Nod. Wishing she'd hurry up and get to it. I'm dying to know the rest of the story. But I'm also beginning to realize that Paloma works on her own schedule. She is not one to be rushed.

She rises to her feet, brushes the dirt from her knees, and faces the mountains as though speaking to them and not me. "It happened in California—on a Los Angeles freeway. He was riding his motorcycle, on his way to pick up your mother, when the truck in front of him stopped short and the load of lead pipes it was carrying broke free of their restraints and plowed into him. He was thrown from his bike. Died instantly. Decapitation was listed as the *official* cause."

She turns, her face bearing the expression of someone who's told the story too many times. Someone who's grown used to such grisly facts. Someone unlike me. Which is probably why my insides start to curl as my throat fills with bile.

Decapitation was the official cause.

The words swirl in my head, causing me to toss my crutches to the ground and crumple beside them. My arms wrapped tightly around my waist, as I duck my chin to my chest and fight to steady myself.

It's only a moment's delay before Paloma's beside me. Her hands smoothing over my hair in a way that sends a wave of calm coursing through me, her breath cooing in my ear when she says, "*Nieta,* what is it? Please tell me."

Two weeks ago I never would've obliged her.

Two weeks ago I fled from her, convinced she was far more enemy than ally.

But a lot's happened since then.

I'm starting to accept that I'm living in a world most people couldn't even begin to imagine.

That old saying—*ignorance is bliss*—finally makes sense.

The ignorant are definitely the lucky ones here.

Though unfortunately for me, I'm no longer part of that group. I've split from their ranks.

Now that I've seen what I've seen, know what I know, I can no longer turn my back on the truth, no matter how much I'd like to.

According to Paloma, I have to find a way to embrace it—otherwise, I won't just be sitting at my father's grave, I'll be lying right there beside him, six feet under.

"In Morocco . . . in the square, the *Djemâa el Fna* . . ." My stomach churns, my head screams, warning me not to say it, afraid of having it confirmed, but I force myself to push past it. It's time I finally tell her. "I saw him." I lift my gaze to meet hers, needing to see how she reacts to my words, but Paloma just nods in her usual calm, sage way, encouraging me to continue. "The square was filled with horrible, bloody heads hanging from spikes—and the one front and center, the one that called out my name—well, I recognized it from the old black-and-white photo I keep in my wallet. It was Django. I knew it the second I saw him."

My voice cracks, my eyes start to sting, and Paloma wastes no time in comforting me. Her slim, cool fingers brushing over my forehead, over my cheeks, murmuring a stream of words I can't understand, as I fight to gain control of myself.

"Jennika mentioned it," she says, switching back to English, her voice steady, matter of fact. "She relayed the stories you told her. After we spoke, I did a little research and discovered that the area you mention—the name translates to *meeting place at the end of the world,* and in its earlier history, it was used as a place for the public to view the severed heads of criminals that hung on stakes around the square."

I pull away. Gaze hard into her eyes. Torn between the relief of confirming I'm not crazy—that what I saw was real—and wondering how that could possibly be considered a good thing in this particular case.

"I've no doubt what you saw was as real as the glowing people and the crows you've already told me about. Your father had similar visions. I did as well. They're terrifying, I know. And as you've already discovered, you cannot outrun them. They'll go to great lengths to get your attention—they've no choice; there is too much at stake. They can't afford to lose one, and luckily it's not often they do. It puts great stress upon the one who is meant to pass down the gift, and leaves everything in a perilous state."

I'm not entirely sure what that means. She's always so cryptic, and while she's willing to answer some of my questions, for the most part she usually just shakes her head and says, *"In time, nieta. In time."*

Still, it's not like that stops me from trying. "You said the *official* cause of death was decapitation—but what was it really? Was it the crows? Did they cause the accident—or maybe something like them?" I peer into her eyes, desperate to understand.

"It was neither the crows, the glowing people, nor any of the other heralds that might've shown themselves to him. It was Django's refusal to listen—to acknowledge them—to heed their call once and for all. That alone is what triggered his untimely end. Believe it or not, the visions are our allies. Their arrival signals that it's time for us to wake up, acknowledge our calling, and heed the destiny we are meant for. The signs are sporadic at first, then, sometime around the sixteenth year, they intensify. There is only a short window to act. The training must begin without too much delay. If not . . ." She pauses, struggling with just how much to divulge, before she adds, "Let's just say there are other forces at work—those whose sole purpose is to defeat the Seekers so they can rise up and rule. It's a battle as old as our time here on earth, and I'm sorry to say, but there is no end in sight."

I squint, unsure I heard right. My voice gone high-pitched and screechy when I ask, "Did you say, *the Seekers?*" I lean toward her, wait for her reply.

But she just nods, as though it's not nearly as strange as it sounds to my ears. "Make no mistake, Daire, your calling is an important one. Many people will come to depend on you—the majority of whom won't even realize it, much less think to thank you. Still, you must learn to persist, just like all of your ancestors before you. There are other forces among us, forces so dark and powerful that at first they're hard to fathom. But not to worry, I will prepare you to face them. The training consists of several well defined steps. We all endure the same initiation—I did it, my mother did it, as did countless generations before her. Though I will warn you that there is nothing easy about it. It will test every part of your being, and at times it will feel like torture, and during those times you will hate me, blame me, and consider running again. But you won't." Her gaze levels on mine. "Now that you know where that leads, you will never run again, will you, *nieta?*" Her eyes soften, but her words leave me chilled.

"There are several purposes to the initiation—to strengthen you in ways you cannot yet fathom and to prepare you for a future that will probably seem unimaginable to you at this point. But soon it will all fall into place, and before you go thinking it's all bad, be assured you can expect plenty of enchanting moments as well. You will visit mystical worlds you never dreamed of. You will experience magick in its purest form. And then, when it's time to head out into the community again, you'll be ready. I'll make sure that you're ready, if it's the last thing I do."

Her voice so grave, gaze so far away, the jokey retort I had planned dies on my lips. I have no idea what's in store, but it's clear that she's serious and that I need to get serious too. "I think I may have already met that dark, powerful force," I say, momentarily silenced by the stricken look on her face. "I've had dreams—dreams that started off nice, but then they took a turn. And that

night at the Rabbit Hole—just before the accident, I met the boys
from my dream. At first I thought I was going crazy, hallucinating again, but now I'm not sure. They had similar eyes—strange,
icy-blue eyes. And while one is . . ." *my one true love—my fated
one*—I shake my head and start again. "While one is . . . *nice*, the
other . . . well, he turned into a demon." I stop, pick at a blade of
grass I rub between my index finger and thumb. Feeling embarrassed to voice it out loud, but sensing that, unlike everyone else
who'd prefer not to hear it, this is exactly the kind of thing Paloma
wants me to share. "I guess I didn't mention it before because
I wasn't sure it was real—but now, well, I'm thinking it might've
been some kind of warning."

Paloma nods, her face fixed, serene, though her hands give her
away—there's no missing the way they tremble when she reaches
for a tissue she then brings to her nose. "I'm afraid things have
advanced far more than I realized." She crumples the tissue and
hides it from view but not quickly enough to conceal the bright
spot of blood that blooms wide across it. "I'm afraid we don't have
nearly as much time as I thought." She shoots me a troubled look.

"So when does the initiation begin?" I ask, watching as she
rises to her feet, taking a moment to steady herself before she offers a hand.

"I'm afraid it has already begun, *nieta*," she says, helping me
settle onto my crutches. "It has already started."

thirteen

"Ever ridden before?" Chay glances over his shoulder, catching my eye as I stand right behind him, watching as he secures the saddle on the horse, a beautiful paint with a perfectly striped brown and white mane.

"A few times the grooms on movie sets let me ride. Back when I was a kid. But it's been a while. I've pretty much forgotten everything I learned," I say, feeling both nervous and excited by the prospect of riding this big, gorgeous animal as soon as I'm free of my cast. According to Paloma, graduating from crutches to the Frankenstein boot just isn't enough.

"Not to worry. I think you'll find Kachina to be a gentle sort. You two will get along fine," he says, voice smooth as a smile. "In fact, giving her a treat usually works as an icebreaker. If you look in the back of the truck, you'll find a cooler." He nods in that general direction. "And if you look in the cooler, you'll find a few carrots to feed her."

I do as he says, returning with two big carrots that, in a bout of overeagerness, I'm quick to shove toward her mouth. The move sloppy, inexperienced, and when she curls her lip to accept them, the size of her teeth causes my hands to shake so badly the carrots fall to the ground, forcing Kachina to lower her head and swipe them up off the dirt.

My cheeks heat with embarrassment as I wipe my palms on the back of my jeans, forcing a laugh as I say, "Do you think she'll hold a grudge?"

"I'm sure in time she'll forgive you." Chay grins, causing his eyes to fan at the sides and his forehead to crease under the rim of his bandanna. "Horses startle easily. For such large animals, they're all a bunch of scaredy cats. You have to approach them slowly, gently, same way you'd like someone to approach you. Call her by name, coo to her softly. Then take a moment to stand quietly beside her. Keeping your breath nice and even so she can have a chance to adjust to your energy as you adjust to hers. And then, when the time is right, you may pet her like this." He demonstrates the move, his large hand smoothing her mane in a way that causes his eagle ring with the yellow stone eyes to glint in the sun, as he works his way down the swoop of her neck. Giving her a series of gentle pats, before scratching the space between her eyes, just under her forelock.

"Is she yours?" I watch as Chay presses his mouth close to the horse's ear and mumbles something in an unfamiliar language, whispering for so long, I'm not sure if he heard.

"Is she mine?" He chuckles, glances at me. "Technically, I suppose that she is. I got her from a client who'd lost his job and could no longer afford to care for her. But in the grand scheme of things—no. Kachina belongs to herself. Now that she's entered my life, I've agreed to watch over her for however long she chooses to stay. Unless you'd like the job, that is?"

I squint. Sure I misunderstood.

"I know Paloma will be keeping you busy with your training, but this also plays a part. Horses have a lot to teach us about stamina, strength, and companionship. And on a more practical level, they make for good transportation—at least until we can get you your license. Paloma has plenty of room at her place for a stall—what do you say?"

My own horse?

I've never owned a pet before, even though, according to Chay, I won't actually *own* her—still, there's no way I can turn down an offer like that.

Yet I manage to say, "Shouldn't she be the one who decides? I mean, I'm the one who made her eat her snack off the floor. She may not want me looking after her."

Chay takes a moment to consider my words. "Okay then, let's give you a leg up and see how you two get along."

I balk, unsure how to respond. "Seriously?"

He nods.

"But what about my cast? Paloma said I should wait 'til it comes off, which might be as early as tomorrow. Still, she specifically told me I could look, touch, but *not* ride."

Chay smiles in a way that makes his eyes appear hooded. "Paloma can be a bit overcautious. You'll be fine. And I doubt Kachina will mind. I tell you what—I'll take full responsibility should anything happen to either one of you, deal?"

I hesitate, though it's not long before I nod my consent, and the next thing I know he's lifted me onto her back.

We ride for a while, my paint and his Appaloosa walking the trail side by side, kicking up dirt. Though we don't run, we don't lope, we don't so much as break into a trot. Chay says there's plenty of time for that later, but for now, I need to get used to the feel of being on horseback again.

"So, do you live here on the reservation?" I ask, my voice competing with the rustle of wind moving through the trees, the leaves jostling each other like chimes. A bit embarrassed by the question, it seems like something I should already know, but I was looking for something to say, something to break up the silence, and it's the best I could do.

He squints into the distance, his gaze searching long past the nearby grove of trees, focusing hard on something I can't quite make out. His voice vague, noncommittal, when he says, "Not anymore. Though my father does. He's a tribal elder."

He yanks on the reins, and I do the same, our horses coming to a halt as I strain to follow the length of his stare. But other than a juniper tree with branches so twisted they appear almost deformed, I can't see much of anything. "He's nearly eighty," he adds, returning his attention to me and pulling on Kachina's bridle until we're both turned around and heading back the same way we came. "Nearly eighty and still strong as a bear." He grins in a way that tells me he's struggling to find his way back to my question, though his mind resides elsewhere. "He lets me keep some of the horses at his place, while the rest stay at mine."

I gaze around a wide open plain marked by the occasional adobe, thinking that other than the absence of a town (though there is a casino just off the main road, along with a gas station/ convenience store), it doesn't look all that different from the neighborhood where Paloma lives.

"Have you always lived in Enchantment?" I ask.

"Went away to college." He shrugs. "Then from there, I went on to vet school at Colorado State—but it wasn't long after I graduated when I found my way back."

"Why?" I ask, my tone betraying what I'm really thinking: *Why would an educated person—a person with choices—choose to remain in this place?*

But if Chay's offended, he doesn't show it. He just laughs, shakes his head, and says, "Oh, I suppose there's all sorts of reasons—some more compelling than others." Then, without stating what those reasons might be, he adds, "So, what did you think of your first ride?"

"I liked it." I shrug. "I think I'd like to ride her again, if it's okay with you. And, of course, okay with her." I reach down to pat Kachina's neck, but again I'm not very graceful, not yet used to her movements, and I end up teetering so precariously it takes all of my strength not to tumble right off her back. "By the way, what is it you saw back there?" I ask, once I've gotten myself straightened out. Jabbing my thumb in the direction we came from, knowing that whatever it was, it was enough to turn us around and cut our ride short.

Chay veers ahead, the words breezing over his shoulder when he says, "You're not ready to go there just yet."

I squint at his back, my curiosity more piqued than ever, but recognizing a dead end when I see one, I choose not to pursue it.

Choose to just nod in agreement when he turns to me and says, "So, what do you say we return our rides to the stall, get 'em settled in for the night, and grab ourselves a couple of sodas? Soon as your training kicks in it's going to be a while before you taste one again."

Once the horses are brushed, watered, and fed, with their stalls lined with fresh straw, we hop into the truck and head out. Stopping at the gas station/convenience store where Chay runs inside to get our drinks, while I field yet another frantic phone call from Jennika.

I slip out of the truck, head over to the edge of the lot where I park myself on the curb next to the water and air pumps. Struggling through really bad reception that strangles her words, making it sound like she's calling from somewhere deep underground.

Though it's not much of a struggle to fill in the blanks—it's pretty much a repeat of the same conversation we've been having for the past several weeks. Ever since the day she woke to a string of angry messages from me, only to call Paloma and learn I'd been hit by a car. Her questions coming so fast, it's like an assault. One blending into another until there's no way I can answer them all.

"I'm fine, seriously. There's no reason for you to come here,"

I say, which pretty much serves as my standard reply every time she mentions quitting the gig in Chile so she can come get me.

But it's not like it works. It never does. She just goes on to say, "Daire, you can tell me—has Paloma done anything *weird*?"

I roll my eyes. From Jennika's perspective everything Paloma does is weird, but I no longer see it that way. Paloma may be strange, definitely on the outside of mainstream, but there's no doubting her healing powers—no doubting that she's the only one who truly understands what's happening to me.

"Define *weird*," I say. It's what I always say.

"*Daire* . . ." She drags out my name, wanting me to know that kind of reply no longer floats. "Answer the question. You know *exactly* what I mean."

"Paloma's fine. I'm fine. Chay's fine. Enchantment is . . . *fine*." My fingers curl around the phone as I try not to choke on the lie. "I've already told you, I had a first-day freak-out. That's all. And trust me, you'd be amazed by what Paloma's been able to do. My wounds are healed and I don't have one single scar—including the cuts on my arms that I got in Morocco. Oh, and the cast is coming off soon—maybe as early as tomorrow."

"I need pictures! I need proof! You need to send me lots and lots of pictures. It's the only way I'm going to believe you're okay. The only way I'm going—"

I sigh, yank the phone away from my ear, and place it on the curb just beside me. Jennika's frantic voice screeching, threatening, pleading—a song she's sung too many times. Leaving me to bury my face in my knees and wait for the chorus to end.

Glancing up in time to see Chay waving to me as he heads back to the truck, the sight prompting me to say, "Jennika, I gotta go. Seriously though, there's no need to come here, no need to worry. I'm perfectly okay. I'll send you a photo—a whole slew of photos. I'll send you so many photos, you'll be sick of looking at me, okay? But until then, try to chill. Try to believe what I tell you."

I rise to my feet, brush my hands against the seat of my jeans, and hobble across the lot. Maneuvering around an old, primer-gray Mustang pulling up to the pump, as a boy with beautiful, long, dark hair climbs out of the driver's side, and an older female draped with the most exquisite turquoise jewelry opens the passenger door.

"Oh—excuse me!" she says, when the door nearly hits me. Her eyes meeting mine, exchanging a look that's admittedly brief, but still enough to wash me in a cocoon of all-encompassing kindness that holds for a moment before succumbing to a sadness so deep, so insistent, I'm frozen in place even though she's moved on.

Paloma told me about this. Said this sort of thing—these kinds of impressions—were to be expected. Claims it's a gift that'll serve me well in the future—that I should take time to hone it whenever I can. Every time I come across someone new, she says, I should rely less on what I see and hear and more on what I feel deep down inside.

Thing is, other than the trip to the graveyard and today's outing with Chay, I've been recovering in bed. And from what I'm told, any future trips out of the house will be as tightly monitored as those were. Paloma claims it's too dangerous for me to head out on my own, and Chay seems to agree. Though so far, neither of them has bothered to explain just exactly what that danger might be.

I switch my gaze to the boy at the pump, watching as he leans against the car and keeps a close eye on the meter—grimacing at the way the dollar amount multiplies as the gallons lag far behind. My eyes grazing over his dark glossy hair, his strong shoulders, and well-defined arms that spill out of his black short-sleeved T-shirt, seemingly immune to the weather. His torso long and lean, sexy and sinuous—narrowing into a pair of dark denim jeans that hang low on his hips. The sight of him so mesmerizing, so distracting, I'm forced to shake my head, close my eyes, and

start over. Paloma's words replaying in my head, reminding me
it's not what I see that counts but what I feel.

*"A Seeker must learn to see in the dark—relying on what she knows
in her heart."*

I close my eyes, keeping my breath steady, even, as I try once
again. Instantly overcome by yet another swarm of kindness—
much like the older woman before him; only this particular wave
is so open, so pure, my knees grow weak in response. And instead
of disappearing into sadness like hers, it leads to something else.

Something that—if I didn't know better—I'd mistake it for
love.

The true, unconditional kind of love.

The kind of love I've experienced only in dreams—and once,
for a brief fleeting moment, right before fleeing the Rabbit Hole.

I should go. Escape while I can. Leave before he catches me
staring, gawking—but I'm too stunned to move—too stunned to
make sense of all this. And the next thing I know, he's turned. His
icy-blue eyes finding mine—mirroring my image thousands of
times.

His gaze deepening, lips parting, as though preparing to speak.

The sheer sight of him causing my limbs to tremble, my body
to sway toward his—much like it did in the dream. The two of us
drawn to each other—bound by forces unseen. But before he can
get to the words, I break free of the spell and make a mad limping
dash for Chay's truck.

Taking a long, greedy swig of the soda Chay offers as he pulls
out of the lot—my gaze tracking the dry, barren landscape until it
fades into night. Unable to shake the lure of the boy—the weight of
those icy-blue eyes meeting mine.

fourteen

Chay pulls up to the gate as Paloma helps a girl my age into the passenger seat of a dust-covered SUV. Folding a long white cane with a red tip, she hands it to her, waves good-bye, and makes for the truck. Her eyes lighting on mine when she leans through the driver's side window and says, *"Nieta,* did you enjoy yourself?"

I give a quick nod and hop out. Landing on my good leg, backpack in hand, I hobble toward the house, hoping she won't ask if I had a good time riding Kachina, since I'm pretty sure I can't lie with conviction—or at least not to her. She's far too intuitive—able to sense the truth behind my words well before I can speak them.

"Bueno." She smiles, watching as I push through the gate. "Go get yourself cleaned up, and I'll meet you inside. It is almost nightfall—almost time to begin."

I give her an odd look but do as she says. Heading into the house, down the short hall, and into my room, wondering what the sun's descent could have to do with my training. Should I have taken her literally when she said all Seekers must learn to see in the dark?

I reach for the clean pair of sweats she left folded at the foot of my bed and carry my dirty sweater and jeans to the hamper, frowning when I take in the seam we had to tear from the ankle to the knee in order to make room for my cast. Despite Paloma's promise to replace them with a new pair as soon as I'm healed—I seriously doubt I'll find anything that compares. Those jeans are my favorite, dark and skinny—I practically live in them. Not to mention I got them in Paris, a place I won't be returning to any-time soon. From what I've seen of Enchantment, there's not one decent boutique. Heck, there's not even a Target or Walmart.

But Paloma doesn't view clothes the same way I do. For her, they're less an expression of individuality and more a sensible way to cover the body. Although her clothes are clean and pressed, and well kept, it's obvious that for her fashion is more of an afterthought, if she even thinks of it at all. From what I've seen, her wardrobe consists of a handful of light cotton shift dresses she wears in the house—her feet always bare—and those same dresses paired with a tattered sky-blue cardigan and navy blue espadrilles when she heads out. And yet, as strange as it is, I can't help but find it refreshing.

Paloma's indifference is a welcome change compared to the fashion meltdowns I used to witness on movie sets. When emer-gency meetings were called in order to discuss the pros and cons of some starlet's hemline, as though the fate of the world, much less the movie, depended upon it. Not to mention Jennika's pen-chant for treating my own meager wardrobe as an extension of hers.

It's like, Jennika got an overload of the girly gene, I got a smid-gen, and Paloma got none.

Or at least that's what I think until I tie my hair back into a ponytail and head for my window to close the curtain. Seeing the gate still open and Chay still parked right beside it, only now the driver's side door is flung open in a way that allows Paloma to lean in and embrace him.

I watch them together—I can't help it. It's just so unexpected.

Surprised to see it's less the brief, back-patting kind of embrace exchanged between friends, and more the slow lingering caress shared between two people who deeply care about each other.

I knew they were friends, but I always assumed. it was platonic. It never occurred to me that their relationship might extend a bit further.

Though just as I begin to talk myself out of what I'm seeing, sure I've read too much into it, they kiss and confirm it. Prompting me to snap the curtain shut and head for the kitchen where I sit at the table and wait for my first official day of training to begin.

My father never made it this far. He refused to take part, and I can't say I blame him. But, in an effort to avoid the same grisly fate, I promised myself I'd at least give it a chance and see where it leads. If I don't like it, I'll do what I can to find a way out. But it won't be rash. And I won't end up dead. Unlike Django, I plan to be smart about my exit.

Paloma steps inside and closes the door behind her. Her fingers working the buttons on her cardigan, she rubs her palms together and makes for the fireplace where she prods the wood with a long, iron poker until she's satisfied with the way the fire sparks and spits, then turns to me and says, "Chay has a sweet tooth."

I stare, the words so odd and unexpected, I have no good response.

"He is a good man but a bad influence." She laughs, claiming the seat opposite mine and folding her arms on the table. "Your training will require many lifestyle changes, the first being diet. I'm afraid you and Chay have enjoyed your last soda together, so I hope you enjoyed it." She reaches forward, places her hand over mine. Hers appearing so tiny and dark it makes mine look like a large, pale blob in comparison. "From this point on, you will eat only that which nature provides, in its purest possible form. Which means no sugar additives, no processed foods, no fast food—in short, no junk."

I gulp. Stare at her wide-eyed and dumbstruck. Wondering what could possibly be left—she nixed pretty much all of my favorites.

"The first few days will prove difficult, as you will soon see. Sugar is a powerful substance and highly addictive. But it won't be long before you start to feel better, stronger, and healthier in body, mind, and spirit. The results will be so pleasing, I've no doubt this new way of eating will become second nature. But if not, if you find the opposite to be true, I'm afraid you must find a way to live with it. There is really no choice in the matter."

"But . . . *why?*" My face scrunches in a way meant to convey that not only do I object, but I also doubt the validity of what she just said. It reminds me of the carb-free cult all the celebrities embrace before a big shoot, regarding the bread basket as their number-one enemy. "Other than my injuries, which are almost all healed, I'm healthy. So I really don't understand what difference the occasional Coke or candy bar can make."

Paloma pushes away from the table and heads up the brick ramp to her office. Motioning for me to take a seat at the square wooden table, as she fills a small copper pot with bottled water, sets it on a single burner, and busies herself with pinching off bits of dried herbs hanging from a multitude of overhead hooks.

She rolls the pieces between her forefinger and thumb, singing a soft, lilting tune I can't quite decipher. Then she drops the tiny herb balls, one by one, into the pot, adding a small dark stone she retrieves from the soft buckskin pouch she wears at her neck.

The rock landing with an audible *plop,* when she says, "We hail from an ancient line of shamans."

I stare at her back, face scrunched in disbelief. "Shamans?" I shake my head, trying to tame my annoyance, reminding myself to be patient, to give her a chance. Surely that's not what she meant. "I thought you said we were Seekers?" I frown, doubting I'll ever get used to the random things she says. From the moment I arrived

I've been in a state of perpetual confusion, and I'm beginning to doubt it will end.

Paloma shrugs off her cardigan, drops it onto the counter beside her, returning to pot stirring when she says, "Shamans, medicine men, healers, Light Workers, seers, mystics, miracle workers, those who know, those who can see in the dark—" Her shoulders rise and fall. "Different names for what is essentially the same thing at heart." She glances over her shoulder, ensuring I heard before she gets back to stirring. "Shamanic concepts date back thousands of years—its origins have been traced to Siberia when a shaman's primary role was to care for the community. To maintain the well-being of the tribe by providing healing when needed, tending to the weather to ensure the availability of crops and food, leading sacred ceremonies, serving as the primary link between this world and the spirit world, and more. It was a revered and sacred role—a calling of the highest order. Fanned out across several continents, separated by great bodies of water with no way to communicate—their ceremonies and rituals were found to be shockingly familiar. Though unfortunately, in later years, when we all became *civilized*," she forms air quotes around the word, "shamans were persecuted and forced into hiding. They were deemed witch doctors, sorcerers, accused of conjuring evil. They were said to be dangerous, when really they were just misunderstood by those too ignorant to look past their own narrow concepts of how the world works. Ignorance is one of the greatest evils known to man." She turns to me, her dark eyes flashing. "With ego and greed trailing a very close second and third."

She tends to the pot, giving it a few more stirs before placing a strainer over the top and pouring the brew into a mug. Then, grabbing a pair of small tongs, she lifts out the wet, steaming stone and places it on the table before me.

"Over the years, the role has evolved, and the name along with it. Among our kind, we are now known as Seekers. We are Seekers of the truth—Seekers of the spirit—Seekers of the light—Seekers of the soul. And it is our job, our calling, our destiny, to keep things in balance—a balance that requires us to walk in the spirit worlds just as easily as we walk in this world. There was a time when keeping the balance was much simpler, but those days are gone. And, to answer your original question of *why,* the ability to walk between the worlds depends on your commitment to purifying yourself, both inside and out. Which, my sweet *nieta,* begins with your diet."

She peers into the mug and inhales deeply. Then, deeming it ready, she places it before me and says, "And now you must drink."

I screw my mouth to the side and stare hard at the mug. Not entirely on board with her agenda but not wanting to reject it outright and end up like Django either. The horrific image of my father's battered, bloodied head hanging from a spike and screaming to get my attention providing all the motivation I need to empty the cup until there's not a single drop left. Surprised to find the liquid offers a comforting warmth as it slips down my throat, and though the aftertaste is bitter, I don't really mind it.

"There is much more to the world than it seems," Paloma says, returning to her seat. "It is actually made up of three worlds—the Upperworld, the Lowerworld, and the Middleworld. Each of those worlds consists of many dimensions—including the Middleworld, which is the one you are used to—the one we reside in during our normal, daily lives. Though most people never look past the surface—never realize it's populated by unseen forces that influence their lives in ways they could never imagine. What you see is not what you get, *nieta.* In each of those worlds you will find many lovely, compassionate beings available to help you on your various quests. They'll appear in the form of animals, humans, mythological creatures, even something as simple as a blade of grass is able to help us. Everything has its own energy—its own life force—and someday you will communicate with the earth and its elements as easily as you communicate with me—all in good time." She looks at me, her fingers steepled, fingertips pressed tightly together. "I know you might feel a little over-whelmed by it all, it's a lot to take in. That's why it's important for you to remember that you are never alone. I will serve as your guide, though I'm not so much here to teach you as to help you retrieve what you already know deep down inside."

I glance around the room, taking in shelves filled with tonics, potions, all manner of herbal remedies—while others are crammed with books, rattles, an assortment of crystals and rocks, and a red-painted drum. And though I try to keep an open mind, try to do my best to play along, I have no idea what she means. I'm the kid of a traveling makeup artist—everything I know I learned from a movie set, the Internet, or direct, hands-on experience. Though I never learned anything like this. I'd never even heard of shamans or Seekers until I came here.

I shake my head, start to protest, but she's quick to silence me. "Trust me, nieta—all the knowledge you need is already within you. It's your ancestral legacy—it's in the blood that flows through your veins, it's the pulse in your heartbeat, and it's my job to help you discover it. It won't be long before you move between the Upper and Lowerworlds as easily as you move through this Middleworld. You will learn to navigate all the various dimensions until you know them quite well. When the time is right, you will make the trip physically, but for now there are several steps that must first be completed. So this journey, your first journey, will be a soul journey. It will feel like a dream, though I assure you it's real. It will prove to be both profound and revelatory, and one you will not easily forget. Its purpose is for you to connect with your spirit animal—the one you will grow quite close to and come to rely on. He will show himself three times, that's how you'll know it is him, and so you must pay very close attention. This is the first and last time you will drink this brew, and the things you see and experience are never to be revealed to anyone but me. This is im-perative in ensuring your safety. So tell me, nieta—how are you feeling? Are you ready to make the journey?"

I struggle to answer. Struggle to slog through the words. My head's filled with fog, my mouth stuffed with cotton, allowing nothing more than a muffled groan to creep forth.

And the next thing I know, my fingers fold around the small black stone, my face meets the table, and my soul leaps from my body, traveling faster than sound.

fifteen

I stand before a tree—a very tall tree with a large, gaping hole gouged in its trunk. A tree that I recognize from the time Jennika and I went zip-lining in the Costa Rican cloud forest.

But this time, instead of climbing the inside ladder to reach the platform above, I duck into the hole and tunnel deep into the earth. Careening along a root system so far-reaching and complex, it reminds me of long, spindly, tangled-up fingers with no conceivable end.

I'm enveloped in darkness—a dank wind slapping hard at my cheeks, stuffing my nostrils with the scent of rich soil that churns out before me, providing passage for my journey. And while at first it's kind of fun, reminding me of the times I went sledding as a kid, it's not long before I grow anxious, claustrophobic, my breath becoming panicked and labored in such a cramped space.

I dig in my heels, flop onto my front, and claw at the dirt in a fight to scrape my way up. I'm not fit to be a Seeker. If this is what it entails—being buried alive with insects, and worms, and roots swirling about me—I want no part of it.

My fingers continue to shovel, digging deep into the loam, but it's no use. I can't fight it, can't get any traction.

There is no going back.

Not when the tunnel behind me closes the second I'm through.

Not when the tunnel before me continues to open and yawn—churning faster and faster to hasten my fall.

I flip onto my back, refusing the scream now lodged in my throat. Telling myself to keep calm, to preserve what little oxygen I have left—when I swoosh into a field of light so bright, I'm forced to clamp my eyes shut and reopen them slowly, allowing enough time to adjust.

My body jamming so hard into the sand I'm like a runaway truck. And after a few dazed moments, I rise to my feet and take a good look around. Finding myself in pretty much the last place I expected—a beautiful white sandy beach with clear turquoise waters, a postcard of paradise.

I head for the shore, thrilled to find myself free of my wounds, free of my cast. Allowing my toes to inch into the water, and smiling when the foamy spray rushes over my feet, soaking the hem of my sweatpants before slipping away and leaving a faint trace of bubbles that pop on my skin.

There are dolphins at play in the distance, along with a small pod of breaching whales, their sleek, broad bodies diving and lifting—and closer still, several schools of tiny shimmering fish racing circles around my ankles and feet. Though not one of these beings is my teacher—of that I am sure.

I abandon the shore in favor of the place where the coast transitions into a beautiful forest sheltered by trees with wide, sturdy trunks bearing branches so thick with leaves they block all but the faintest glimmer of light. The colors so vibrant it appears more like an oil painting than an actual place. The blooms bigger, the moss springier, the cocoon of silence broken by the rush of wind dancing among the leaves, causing them to rustle and sway and chime softly together—a whisper of song urging me to keep going, keep moving on.

I follow the wind. Taking Paloma at her word when she said

everything has a life force, a way to communicate—I follow it all the way to a clearing I know from my dreams, and I'm not at all happy to find myself here.

My gaze darts, searching for a rock, a stick, something I can defend myself with should this go wrong again—when I hear a low, deep croaking sound and turn to find the raven hovering in the space right before me.

I narrow my eyes and stare hard at the enemy—the raven with the piercing purple eyes, the one that led me to the horrible scene with the demon boy.

I stoop toward the ground, curl my fingers around a small solid stone, but before I can so much as take aim, he's gone.

I turn, casting about, until I hear his *calhing* cry once again and find him perched on the ground just a few steps behind me.

Rock still in hand, I raise my fist high—my aim careful, more deliberate this time but just like the last time, before I can release the rock, he's vanished from sight.

My heart races, my breath goes ragged and quick as I spin on my heels, stopping when he appears just before me again—his curved bill yawning wide as he emits a deep croaking sound and his eyes flash on mine.

I tighten my fist. Raise my hand high. Eyes narrowed on my target when I say, "Third time's a charm!" Seeing him blink as I let go of the stone, my aim wild, way off—as Paloma's words replay in my head:

"He will show himself three times, that's how you'll know it is him, and so you must pay very close attention."

"You!" I stare. A whispered accusation directed at him.

And the next thing I know, he lifts into flight. Pointed wings spanned wide as he flies a perfect circle over my head, before soaring ever higher and trailing the wind.

Paloma's hand on my shoulder, coaxing me back to the comfort of her warm adobe home, her voice no more than a whisper when she says, "Come back, *nieta*. It is time to return."

sixteen

I lift my head from the table, tousled and blinking as I push my hair from my eyes and secure the loose strands behind my ear. Marveling at how clear my head is—not at all soupy and thick like my meds made me feel.

"How long was I out?" I stretch my neck from side to side, muscles pulling, loosening, as though waking from a nice, long nap.

Paloma smiles. Places a glass of water before me and urges me to drink. "About thirty minutes—though I suppose it felt quicker for you. Your journey was successful, I hope?"

I take a sip of water, then push it away. Tugging my sleeves until they cover my knuckles as I try to come up with some kind of reply, not realizing at first that I still hold that small black stone in my fist.

Successful?

Not really the word I'd use. Still, I look at her and say, "I met my teacher, if that's what you mean. Though I'm not sure it's a good thing . . ."

That last bit spoken so quietly it trails off completely, but even though I'm pretty sure she heard it, she moves right past it and says, "Which direction did you travel? Up, down, or sideways?"

I pause for a moment, remembering the tree, the roots, the tunnel, the worms . . . "Down," I say. "I journeyed deep into the earth."

"The Lowerworld." She nods. "It is almost always the Lowerworld on one's first visit. The Upperworld is much harder to reach—even for the well-practiced Seeker. It took me many years to get there." She looks at me. "So, tell me, how did you find him?"

I glance down at my hands, two cloth-covered mounds, saying, "I followed the wind." I kick a leg up under me, squirm in my seat, feeling more than a little ridiculous for admitting such a thing.

"And your teacher, he showed himself three times?"

I nod. My fingers curling tighter, pressing the rock so hard it makes my hand ache. "He did indeed. But just so you know, it's not the first time we met. He came to me in a dream that didn't end well. No thanks to him."

Her eyes grow dark and serious in a way that prompts me to continue.

"Long story short, someone close to me, someone I really care about—or at least in the dream anyway—well, he died. And my teacher's the one who purposely led me to witness that death. It's the dream I told you about when we were in the graveyard—only I guess I failed to mention that part."

Her gaze grows wide as her hand flutters over her heart like a hummingbird searching for nectar. "*Nieta,* this is wonderful!" she says, her eyes beginning to glisten. "This is more than I ever could've imagined—more than I ever dared hope! And you say the wind led you there?"

I frown. Pull my shoulders in. More than a little put off by her excitement, my failure to make myself clear. "Someone *died,* Paloma." I level my gaze on hers. "*Murdered* by a *demon.* And my so-called *teacher* is the one who's *responsible* for leading me there. It may sound dumb to you, but the dream felt so real, I haven't been able to shake it no matter how hard I try." I stare at her, pleading to be heard, but despite all the emphasized words, she still doesn't get it. I can tell by the way her face softens, as her eyes grow increasingly misty.

She lowers her lids, keeping them closed when she says, "Dreams cannot always be taken literally, *nieta*. Sometimes death is really just a metaphor for rebirth. Allowing the old version of one to slip away so that a newer, better, stronger version can stand in its place." Her eyes meet mine. "If your teacher led you there, then I'm sure there was a reason. Though there is only one way to be sure that he is your teacher—do you still have the stone that I gave you?"

I uncurl my fingers and present it to her. Watching in dismay as she carries it over to the burner and motions for me to join her as she drops it back into the pot, sets the water to boil, and stares into the cloudy mixture of herbs with an infinite patience I can't even fathom.

She murmurs in Spanish, her hand fisted, pressed close to her heart. And though I stare into the pot right alongside her, I can't, for the life of me, determine what she's so excited about.

A few moments later, she reaches for the strainer and drains the hot water into the sink. Then lowering the pot onto the counter, she turns to me and says, "Is this what you saw? Is this the teacher you met on your journey?"

I lean over her shoulder, not expecting to see much of anything, and gasping in shock when I find that the small black stone morphed into the shape of a raven. Its wings clearly etched, its eyes glimmering purple.

"Is this the teacher you saw?"

I gulp. Nod. It's all I can manage. The sight of it has rendered me speechless.

I continue to stare at the stone-turned-raven, knowing there's no way it can be true, and yet there it is, sitting right smack in front of me. Reminding me of the stone animal fetishes I once saw in a tourist shop in Arizona—so shiny and intricate, hand-carved by the Zuni tribe, bearing a close resemblance to the one in this pot.

"We all have an animal guide—each and every one of us." She gazes upon the stone replica. "Though sadly, most people live long full lives without ever realizing theirs. Different animals bear different purposes, different meanings. And as it just so happens, yours, the raven, is a very fortuitous one indeed. He represents magick, a change in consciousness, and the power of stunning transformation." She looks at me, eyes shining with pride when she adds, "He soars into darkness only to return with the light. He will whisper the secrets of magick—though those secrets must never be revealed. Raven's arrival heralds the fulfillment of prophecy." She presses a hand to her mouth, overcome by a rush of emotion I can't quite grasp. "It also appears that the wind is your element. Oh, *nieta!*" she cries, her voice hoarse, thick. "I didn't expect you to determine that so quickly, which is why I didn't bother to mention it. That sort of thing usually comes much later in the training. This is very unexpected, to be sure."

"Is that . . . *good?*" I ask, still trying to make sense of the rock and her words, but feeling more confused than ever.

"It is more than good!" She smiles, hands clasped together. "It is wonderful! Though I suppose I should have guessed. You come from a very strong bloodline—a bloodline that contains powerful magick on both sides. And, in addition, you're infused with Django's untapped potential, it had to go somewhere, so it found its way to you," she says, her words triggering a question I didn't think to ask until now.

"When you say 'a very strong bloodline with powerful magick on both sides . . .'"

Paloma shoots me an apprehensive look, as though she already senses the question to come, which she probably does.

"What does that mean? Who is Django's father—my grandfather?"

She sighs, her voice as resigned as her face when she says, "His name is Alejandro."

I lean toward her. "*Is*—so he's still alive then?" Brightening at the idea of having two living grandparents.

"No, *nieta*. Sadly, he is not alive in the way that you mean. Though, like Django, his presence is everywhere, which is why I refuse to refer to him in the past tense. Alejandro and I were brought together for a purpose. His family hails from a long line of very powerful shamans—Alejandro was known as a Jaguar Shaman of the highest order. Our match was arranged by our parents in the hopes that our union would result in offspring bearing the kind of gifts I'm seeing in you. Though it wasn't long before we grew to love each other, which is why I was devastated when he was called back to Brazil on a family emergency only to have his plane crash shortly after takeoff. It wasn't long after when I learned I was pregnant—not unlike what happened with Jennika and Django. I'm afraid Seekers aren't known for their happy, long-standing unions, *nieta*. That's a part of the legacy I hope you'll escape."

It takes a moment to digest—three grandparents lost to a plane crash—Paloma discovering she was pregnant just after losing him—what a strange way history has of repeating itself.

"It's no accident, *nieta*." She addresses the thoughts I failed to speak. "The dark forces are responsible for these tragedies. It's their attempt to prevent us from producing offspring who will one day join the fight against them. But both times they were too late, a child was already well on the way—one of them you."

"So, that's why you think I'm advancing so quickly—because of all this untapped potential that's finally unleashed?"

Paloma's face lifts, her sadness easing when she says, "To heed the call of the windsong on one's first journey . . ." She shakes her head as her gaze travels a very long distance. "It is virtually unheard of. You know this makes you a Wind Dancer, *nieta*? Which means the wind is your elemental teacher. If you honor it, follow its song, it will never steer you wrong. The wind is a powerful force, one to be reckoned with, for sure. And as it turns out, soon, much sooner than I thought, you will be a force to be reckoned with too. You have surpassed all my expectations. You have accomplished in one single journey far more than any of your ancestors before you."

I pick at the ribbed hem of my sweatshirt, wishing I could drum up the same kind of excitement but unable to get there.

She's wrong about the dream. No one was reborn. Nor were they transformed. The boy was slain pure and simple—left for dead in my arms. And Raven's the one who forced me to be there.

"I've been having that dream for a while now." I pause, my eyes meeting hers. "The first night I came here, I had it again, and that was when I watched the boy die. The other times were more . . ." I struggle to find the right word, a grandmother-friendly word. "Well, the other dreams were more playful . . . more romantic. But the last one was more like an expanded version. It had an actual beginning, middle, and a very unfortunate end."

She nods, her gaze urging me on.

"I saw the boys that night at the Rabbit Hole, and then, just now, I saw one of them when I was at the gas station with Chay. It's the eyes that give them away. In the dream they're a strange icy-blue—and while one boy's eyes reflect, the other one, the evil one, his absorb like a void—and it's the same in waking life too. I don't know why I'm dreaming about them—about real people I've never actually met. I don't know what any of it means, but the thing is, the boy who died in the dream—he *didn't* transform and he *wasn't* reborn. His soul was stolen, pure and simple. So if this dream is supposed to be prophetic, I want nothing to do with it. It was horrible to watch, there was no way to save him, and I can't help thinking if I hadn't followed Raven, it never would've ended that way. So excuse me if I'm unable to be as excited about Raven as you are!" My voice breaks, I can't help it, and as much as I try to blink back the tears, one still gets away.

I mash the heel of my hand hard against it, obliterating it and all the others that follow. Paloma's voice gentle, her hand on my shoulder, she says, "You are on the verge of a very important transformation. Make no mistake, *nieta*, you will return to the Rabbit Hole. You will meet the boys again. And yes, you will even learn to trust Raven, for his wisdom is far greater than yours. But first, we must get you prepared. It is time to skip forward in your training and get you started on your vision quest."

seventeen

"Make no mistake, *nieta*, your powers will be great—greater than you can comprehend at this point." Paloma flies down the hallway in a bustle of activity it's all I can do to keep up with. Charging into my room, she grabs jeans, a white tank top, a black V-neck sweater, my olive-green army jacket, and some dusty old tennis shoes that belong to someone else. Thrusting them into my arms, she tells me to change, while she retrieves a small, black bag from a high closet shelf she needs a step stool to reach. Then she bolts from the room and heads down the hall, storming toward her office when she says, "You must never forget that great power comes with great responsibility." She glances over her shoulder, making sure that I heard. "You will gain much knowledge. You will discover the healing powers of herbs, along with a variety of songs and chants that contain powers that must never be underestimated or abused. Some of them can harm, most of them can heal—though it's absolutely imperative that you always hold your skills in the highest regard. You must never use them for trivial things. And, more important, you must learn to overcome any and all small-mindedness." She leans against the arched doorway, her eyes meeting mine in a serious stare. So caught up in her talk, she fails to notice the small trickle of blood that drips from her nose. "If someone does you wrong, you must learn to turn your cheek. Your powers must never be squandered on protecting your ego— rather they must be channeled toward the greater good of all."

She retrieves a crumpled tissue from her pocket and heads inside. And I'm just about to ask if she's all right when she faces me and says, "There is an old and very wise Native American saying: *Every time you point a finger in scorn—there are three remaining fingers pointing right back at you.*" Her gaze settles on mine. "You must always bear that in mind, *nieta*. You must never be quick to judge. Though, that said, you must also be aware that Seekers have enemies. There are those whose sole intent is to overpower us, if not destroy us. Which means I will teach you how to deal with the dark, just as I will train you to embrace the light."

She moves toward the shelf along the far wall, thumping the red-painted drum as she passes—the move causing it to reverberate in a way that prompts me to cover my ears and cower in fear. My reaction so odd and unexpected, Paloma turns, eyes narrowing when I say, "Sorry. It's just . . . that sound really bothers me. I know you didn't mean to hit it—but, still, I really prefer not to hear it."

She leans against the shelf, tissue still pressed to her nose. "The drum is a sacred instrument," she says, pausing long enough to allow the words to settle, take shape. "It's like I told you before, everything contains energy—everything maintains its own spirit— and the drum is no different. Its sound is akin to a heartbeat, a life pulse. It's often referred to as a Spirit Horse as its tempo provides a portal, allowing one to journey to the otherworlds." Then, catching my expression, she adds, "There is nothing to fear, *nieta*."

I toy with the hem of my sweatshirt, not the least bit assured by her words. "That may be so," I say. "But back in that Moroccan square, as well as in the Rabbit Hole, it was the sound of the drums that made the world stop and urged the glowing people and crows to appear."

Paloma's eyes shine as she crumples the bloodstained tissue into a ball. "And so you have already experienced its power," she says. "Tell me, *nieta*, did the air grow hazy and shimmery?"

I twist my fingers, digging my nails hard into my flesh. Watching as she makes for the sink where she disposes of the tissue and washes her hands.

"Had you followed them and done as they asked, you would've found yourself in another world—another dimension." She drops the towel, reaches into a cupboard, and pulls out a small black bag.

"So . . . you're saying I should've gone with them?" I tilt my head and shoot her a skeptical look.

"No." She flings her braid over her shoulder, allowing it to fall down her back. "I'm not saying that at all. It's better you ignored them. You weren't ready to heed their call, and there's a good chance you would've been lost. Of course, I would've found you . . . eventually. But no, you did the right thing. Much like the tea allowed your soul to journey, the drumbeat allows your body to journey. Though it's just a matter of time before you will require neither. Soon you will be able to determine the portals on your own. Enchantment has several, as you will soon see."

"And exactly why do I want to travel to these other dimensions?" I ask, tracking her moves as she whirs about the room, collecting an assortment of what appear to be random, completely unrelated things: a small box of matches, a red bandanna, a slim white candle, a few stubs of chalk, a small rattle made of rawhide, along with a few other items I can't quite make out.

"Because you have important work to do there. You're about to journey down the Spirit Road where many things will be revealed—your greatest gifts, your greatest weakness, along with your true purpose for your time here in the Middleworld. Though be aware, they may not all be revealed at once. In some cases, it takes years to decipher them—though I have a feeling that for you, the reveal will come quicker than most."

"But I thought you said I was about to start my vision quest, and now you're talking about a walk down the Spirit Road, and, well, I'm a little confused. Which is it? What's the difference?"

"It is all a part of the same, and it will all become clear soon enough." Her shoulders rise and fall, signaling the explanation is over, despite the fact that she only succeeded in confusing me more.

She motions for me to sit as she riffles through a drawer, returning with a small buckskin pouch that looks a lot like the one she wears. Draping it around my neck, she says, "A Seeker has many tools, and this is probably the most important of all. You are to wear it at all times. You may remove it to sleep and bathe if you like, but you must always keep it well within reach, well within sight. You must never leave home without it. And you must never allow anyone else to wear it or look inside it, not even briefly, or its power will be lost."

I hold it before me—a soft, yellowish piece of leather that hardly looks all that significant, and I'm just not sure I'm on board with it. Not quite sure how to incorporate it into my usual, minimalist uniform of dark skinny jeans, fitted green army jacket, and tank top. I prefer to keep it simple. I'm not all that big on accessorizing.

Paloma makes for the counter, fussing for a moment before she returns with the pot and places it before me. The two of us gazing at the purple-eyed raven resting on a bed of faded, limp herbs.

"Since Raven has revealed himself as your spirit animal—this talisman must remain with you at all times. Place it inside your pouch so that you will always be able to access his wisdom and guidance whenever you find yourself in need of it. What he wants may not always make immediate sense, but you must learn to trust him. Over time, you will add other items as well—items that will be revealed to you along the way. For now, it is just you and Raven. Do you understand, *nieta*? Do you understand the seriousness of all this?"

I nod, like I do even though I really, truly don't. But it's what she expects, and as soon as I've shoved Raven inside, she seems to relax.

Then the next thing I know, she grabs the small black bag and motions for me to follow as she makes for the courtyard and over to the old white Jeep she keeps in the detached garage.

"Where are we going?" I ask, straining against the strap of my seat belt as the Jeep bounces down the rutted dirt road. Squinting into the dark, trying to get my bearings, but it's no use—this town is a mystery to me.

"To your vision quest," she says, tightening her grip on the wheel as the road takes a turn for the worse. Looking at me when she adds, "Please use this time to rest, *nieta*. You will need all of your strength if you are to endure."

"*If?*" I swivel in my seat until I'm fully facing her. My eyes practically popped from their sockets, challenging her to explain.

"There are no guarantees," she tells me, her voice calm and sure. "Though I've no doubt you'll prevail."

I turn back toward the window, having no idea how to reply. Too wound up by her words to even think about resting.

We travel for miles. Travel over unfamiliar terrain that grows increasingly rugged the farther we go. And when we finally stop, braking just a few feet from the water, I see we're not the only ones here—Chay's luring two horses from their trailer, one that I recognize as Kachina, the other his Appaloosa.

"I'm afraid I must leave you now," Paloma says, voice laced with regret. "This part of your journey involves a long ride on horseback, and these old bones aren't fit for the saddle." She tries to smile, but there's something behind it, something I can't quite grasp. Though it's only a moment later when she's turning away, retrieving a tissue she presses over her mouth, coughing up a thick spray of blood she can't hide no matter how hard she tries.

"Paloma—are you okay?" I ask, having no idea what's going

on with her, but knowing that coughing up blood never leads to anything good.

"I am fine, *nieta*. I assure you." She waves away my concern. "Chay will accompany you and see you there safely. Though once you've arrived, he will leave you as well. A vision quest is a solo journey, and your supplies are quite meager. Though please be assured you need far less than you think to survive. Rely upon the matches and candle only when necessary, for they must last the duration. As for food, there is none. The fast is deliberate—it is how you'll begin to purify yourself. You will stay for as long as it takes—there is no time limit. And you will head back when it is right to do so. You will know when that is."

"You seriously expect me to go, *now*?" I fold my arms before me, hugging myself hard around the waist. "But it's nighttime—it's cold—and, for the record, I'm starving. I never even got a chance to eat dinner!"

Though my arguments are all good and valid, the words are lost on Paloma. She dismisses them with a wave of her hand.

"What about my cast?" It's a last-ditch effort, about as obvious as it gets, but still worth a shot.

Paloma smiles. "You are already healed, *nieta,* as I'm sure you have guessed. You are no longer in need of it, and I have no doubt you will return without it. Its materials are nonpolluting and biodegradable. The cast will take care of itself."

Chay approaches, announcing the horses are saddled and ready, but I'm not. I have so many questions I'm not sure where to start. Though I don't get the chance to say much of anything before Paloma's hugging me tight, whispering, "Good-bye and good luck."

And the next thing I know, Chay's lifting me onto Kachina's back and we're heading into the dark.

eighteen

We ride through the night. Our horses picking their way across a difficult trail, guided by the moon, the stars, and not much more.

Our conversation kept to a minimum, with mostly Chay asking: "You okay? Need anything?"

And on the two occasions when I dozed off and almost fell from my saddle: "Careful now!"

Until finally, when the dawn begins to break and the sun begins its slow ascent over the ridge, he looks at me and says, "We're here."

I gaze all around, my eyes so tired and bleary I'm unable to see what makes this particular place any different from all the other places we passed earlier. It's got dirt, weeds, rugged cliffs, and barren trees. There's nothing of note, nothing special about it—just more of the same.

"What do you say we leave the horses here and get you settled?"

I screw my mouth to the side and hold tight to my mount.

"Daire, it's time," he says, voice as gentle as the fingers that pry Kachina's reins from my hand.

"I don't want to go." I chew my bottom lip, embarrassed by

the words, by the way my voice broke, but still I continue. "I'm tired and hungry and . . . I don't like it here. I don't feel safe." My gaze pleads with his, but he stands firm and offers a hand.

"C'mon." He coaxes me to my feet, motions for me to walk alongside him. "It's better to hurry. The sooner we get you started, the sooner we can get you back home."

He keeps his tone light, almost playful, but it doesn't quite work. Chay's a good and trustworthy man—a man of good character and noble intentions. This alone makes him a terrible liar.

When the trail narrows, he veers to the front, leading me up a long, winding path that leaves us both winded. Stopping before a large dark opening that appears to be the mouth of a cave, he says, "Many of your ancestors have endured their vision quest here, including Paloma back when she was your age." He turns to me. "As you know, Django never made it this far, which means it hasn't been used for many, many years."

"How can you be sure?" I glance between him and the cave. "Paloma's vision quest must've been what—almost forty years ago? So how can you be so sure no one's used it since then?"

Chay nods toward the ground, the toe of his boot nudging at some grainy white substance that forms a thick border along the entrance, reminding me of the white line that lies inside the adobe wall and coyote fence that surrounds Paloma's house. "I said it hasn't been used in many years. I didn't say it hasn't been tended to. The salt works to protect it—keeps the energy pure and the predators at bay."

Predators.

Now there's a word I wish I hadn't heard.

I peer into the mouth, not liking what I see. Not that I can see much of anything, but still, just knowing it's deep, dark, and cavernous is enough to give me the creeps.

"I'm not going in there," I say. Even though we both know I will. But I'm not ready yet. I need a little more convincing, a little more time to gather my courage.

Chay nods, waiting patiently as I peer in again. But it's the same as before—all I can see is a solid wall of black. "What's in there?" I ask, figuring he must've checked it out once or twice.

"Beats me." He shrugs. "Only the vision quester is allowed entrance. It's a sacred space. I just swing by on occasion to maintain the border for Paloma, no more."

I frown. That hardly makes me feel better. "How long have you two been dating?" I ask, aware that I'm just stalling, though I am a little curious.

Chay laughs, rubs a hand across his brow. "Is it still dating at our age?" He laughs again, shaking his head as he hands me the small black bag Paloma packed, saying, "Daire, don't worry. You'll do fine. Really."

I swallow hard, not believing a word of it but taking a long deep breath and stepping across that thick line of white anyway.

"What am I supposed to do in here?" I ask, testing my surroundings by running a finger down a wall that's surprisingly smooth to the touch.

Seeing Chay squint when he says, "Well, it's been a long time since my own vision quest, but—"

"Wait—you did this too?" I step toward him, staring incredulously. "Are you a Seeker too?"

He shakes his head. "Can't say that I am. Though the idea of the vision quest is no stranger to my people—my people being the Native Americans." His eyes twinkle when he says it. "When I was a young man, about the age you are now, I felt conflicted about my future, wasn't sure which direction to take. My quest helped me realize my affinity for animals was more than a hobby—it was an actual calling. So, I enrolled in vet school and never looked back."

"And how long did you have to starve in a cave to come to that conclusion?" I ask, sorry about the way my voice sounded much snottier than intended. It's not his fault I find myself here. Still, when Paloma said I'd have to change my diet in order to purify myself, I didn't realize that meant fasting in a dark, abandoned cave until I pass out.

"I spent three full days on the mountain." His gaze grows distant, carried away by a long-ago memory. "It was an intense experience—one that revealed many things—many prophetic things. Some that have already happened, others that might still happen—the kind of things I will never forget. I expect you'll have a similar experience. So it's best you get started."

I glance behind me, finding it so dark I can't even see how deep it is, can't see much of anything.

"Remain calm," Chay tells me. "Find a place to sit quietly, and it won't be long before your eyes adjust to the dark so the light can find you."

I turn to face him. That's exactly what Jennika used to say back when I was a child to wean me from the night-light she found so annoying. Same thing I told myself when I followed Vane into that deserted Moroccan alleyway. In both cases, it worked to quell my fears—so hopefully, it'll work here as well.

"The white line will keep you protected, ensure that no intruders find their way in. But make no mistake, Daire, you're only safe as long as you remain inside. If you head out, if you're lured from the cave before the time is right—all bets are off."

I nod, watching as he retraces the border with a fresh pour of salt. Clinging to his parting words, "You can do this," as he disappears down the trail, leaving me to face the dark on my own.

nineteen

I hover by the entrance—toes on the right side, the safe side, of that thick white border. My heart leaping into my throat when a rattlesnake slithers past, paying me absolutely no notice, and I watch in fascination a few minutes later when a scorpion follows suit.

Well, it works on reptiles and insects. Let's hope it works on bigger animals too—like those of the warm-blooded, carnivorous, mammal variety.

It's not until the sun rises high enough to hang in the middle of the sky that I venture farther in. Noting how the cave's smooth walls narrow—how its ceiling shrinks until it ultimately ends at a point in the dirt.

It's not nearly as big as I thought.

It's not nearly as scary either.

I consider that a good thing. I'll take what I can get.

At first glance, it seems there's nothing special about it. Seems like any other cave I've ever seen on TV or in movies, despite the lack of stick-figure battle scenes and other kinds of hieroglyphs.

Though a closer look reveals that I'm wrong. There's a series of scrawls on the far part of the wall that I somehow missed at first glance. A long list of names left there by my ancestors.

Each of them leaving their first and last name, along with a sketch of an animal just alongside it that served as their guide.

Valentina Santos is the first—her name appearing at the highest possible point—scrawled in the space where the wall curves into the ceiling. Her writing faded, angular, with a dark-eyed raccoon drawn in intricate detail placed just beside it.

Esperanto Santos is next, and just beside him is a large black bat.

Piann Santos was guided by a fox—a red fox according to the color of the chalk that she used. While Mayra Santos was guided by either a leopard or a cheetah—she wasn't much of an artist, so I can't say for sure.

There are several more names that follow—Maria, Diego, and Gabriella, who were guided by a horse, a monkey, and a squirrel, respectively. And there, down toward the bottom, I spy Paloma's strong, loopy scrawl, seeing how she went to great lengths to etch a very detailed white wolf with piercing blue eyes.

I lean back on my heels, struck by the enormity of what truly lies before me: family.

My family.

A long tradition of Santoses—both male and female—who survived the same ordeal I've only just started. (Well, I'm assuming they survived.)

I guess I'm so used to being a loner, so used to Jennika and my solitary existence, I never realized there was a whole other side beyond my quirky single mom, a black-and-white photo of my long-dead dad, and a few random stories about grandparents who perished well before I was old enough to form any lasting memories of them.

This is so much bigger than I thought.

So much bigger than enduring my tests and succeeding in my training as a Seeker.

I'm a Santos.

Part of a rich, deep, long-standing ancestral legacy.

A calling that stretches back through the centuries.

And now it's time for me to add my name to the list, to claim my rightful space alongside them.

I reach for my bag, retrieving the chalk stubs Paloma tossed in, and taking great care to allow enough space between my name and Paloma's, in order to acknowledge that Django's is missing. Having decided that's what the other blank spaces were for and feeling relieved to count only two.

I bite down on my lip, noting how my freshly scrawled name, standing on its own, without the addition of *Santos*, looks oddly alone. And yet it feels a little too weird to add it just yet. I've never gone by that name. Jennika and Django never married, never had a chance to, which means I've always been known as Daire Lyons—the surname stemming from Jennika's side.

I grip the chalk tighter, start to add an *S* but don't make it past the uppermost curve before I stop. I can't write Lyons—can't write Santos. For the moment, I'm just Daire—a girl straddling two bloodlines. One I was given—one I must earn.

If I live through this, I'll add it. If not, then my first name and Raven will be my only legacy.

Not that anyone will venture in after me. If I don't survive this vision quest, there will be no one to follow. According to Paloma, it all ends with me.

I take my time drawing Raven, adding pointed wings, a curved beak, a squared tail, long sharp talons, and glimmering purple eyes. Then I sit back to admire it, figuring if nothing else, this wall will keep me company.

My Irish side finally meeting my Hispanic side—I'm curious to see how the two get along.

I consider adding a few more doodles to pass the time, but it's a fleeting thought I'm quick to discard. It doesn't feel right, seems

almost disrespectful. It's like Chay said, this is a sacred space—
any extraneous scribbles will only amount to graffiti.

I get up. Take another lap. In search of anything I might've
missed the first time. But in the end, I'm just walking in circles.
Other than the long list of names, there's not much to it. So after
going through a series of stretches, followed by a handful of yoga
poses an on-set hair stylist once taught me, I take a quick peek
outside, fail to see anything of note, then plop myself down in the
middle of the cave deciding to do what Chay suggested: Go quiet
and still and wait for something to happen—for a life-defining
revelation.

Though I'm only a few minutes in when I grow hungry and
restless and bored. I'm no good at meditating, no good at sitting
still unless I have a good book. So I reach for the small bag, hold it
upside down, and dump the contents before me. Counting the
small book of matches, the slim white candle, the red bandanna,
the three pieces of chalk, a small jar of white grainy salt like the
kind that forms the border, the small rawhide rattle, and a folded-
up note among the offerings. I check the bag again, turn it inside
out, shake it as hard as I can, but that seems to be it.

No water.

No food.

Apparently Paloma wasn't joking about the purification fast.

Hoping for a few words of wisdom, I unfold the note, and read:

Dear Nieta,

The directions are simple and few:

Do not leave the cave until it is time.

Do not venture past the white line for any reason
whatsoever, until you are absolutely certain it is the
right thing to do.

Use your supplies sparingly—they must last
throughout the entirety of your vision quest.

Seek the truth.

Seek the light.

Release your attachment to old attitudes, as well as
old beliefs and ideas, in order to make room for much-
needed insight.

Go quiet, keep your activity to a minimum, and do
what you can to connect to the mountain.

When the mountain has accepted you—approved of
you—you will know.

Though please be aware that the mountain is tricky—it
requires you to distinguish between the real and the
false and see past the mirage.

Call upon Raven when you need him—he is always
there to guide you.

Call upon your ancestors as well—a shake of the rattle
will alert them.

But do not, under any circumstances, venture outside
until you are absolutely certain it is time.

Godspeed.

Safe return.

Paloma

I glance between the note and the border beyond. According to what I just read, along with the warnings Chay gave me, they're not exactly joking about my staying put until it's time to move on.

And though I try to meditate again, it's no use. I can't silence my mind. Can't silence my stomach from groaning in hunger. So I lean against the wall of my ancestors' names, hoping it'll make me feel less alone, remind me that I'm hardly the first to endure this ordeal. Making my way down the list, I call upon them for guidance—shaking the rattle as I do, which feels a bit weird, but then weird is all relative here—and when I reach the end, I call upon Raven as well.

Then I wait.

Stomach clenching so tightly, I reach for my soft buckskin pouch, squeeze it gently, and say, "Raven, please get me through this. Show me whatever I need to know. Put me to the test. And help me do whatever it takes to survive." Barely reaching the end before my lids start to droop, becoming so heavy I can no longer lift them, and just a few seconds later, I'm swallowed by sleep.

twenty

I'm tired.

Hungry and thirsty.

Cold and lonely too.

Terrorized by a long stream of shadow dancers that swarm all around me—their lurid forms mocking—taunting—teasing—cajoling—tempting me to leave—to find my way out of the darkness—out of this cave—and it's not long before I agree.

I never asked to be a Seeker.

Never asked for greatness or victory.

I'm more Lyons than Santos—not cut out to be a hero.

All I ever wanted was to be a normal girl with a normal life—living in a place of blissful ignorance where gruesome monstrosities—things born of darkness—no longer exist.

I scrunch against the wall, one arm wrapped tightly around me in a vain attempt to slow the train of ache storming my belly—while the other hand clutches high at my throat—so itchy and dry my tongue feels too big—as though it no longer fits. Determined to ignore the gang of monsters—demonic, foul beasts—dancing circles around me—until I flounder to my feet, eager to flee.

My movements so clumsy and quick, I reach for the wall to steady myself, as a constellation of bright, twinkling stars swirl before me. My fingers pressing into Mayra's wildcat, slipping past Diego's monkey—the vibration of their long-lingering energy proving I'm not fit to join them—unworthy of their legacy—of claiming their name.

It's better to cut my losses, apologize to Paloma, and be on my way.

I slip my bag over my shoulder and bid good-bye to the demons. Just about to step over the line when my exit is blocked by a beautiful dark-haired boy standing before me, his icy-blue eyes meeting mine in a way that reflects my sad, sorry image thousands of times.

"You know you can't do that, right? You know you can't leave before it's time?" His tone is sharp, but his eyes flash in kindness, belying the words. "You have to see this thing through. You have to endure. They're depending on you."

I roll my eyes. Huff under my breath, telling myself he's not real—he's a boy made solely of ether—the product of delusional reveries and outlandish imaginings.

He has no sway over me.

"You and I aren't like the others," he says, working hard to persuade. "We don't get to choose. Our path has been chosen. It's our job to follow it—to live up to the task."

I roll my gaze up the length of him—starting at his black shoes and skimming past the slink of long legs, the elegant V of his torso, up to his broad rectangle of chest. Greedily tracking every square inch—until I return to his eyes and realize I'm content to remain there for as long as I can. His words repeating in my head until I finally say, "Us? Are you a Seeker too?"

He wipes a hand over his chin and quickly looks away. Dodging my question when he replies, "You and I are the last of our lines."

My mouth grows grim as I force myself to look elsewhere, settling on the fiends jeering behind me. The boy doesn't know me, doesn't know the challenge I face. Doesn't know it'll be much better for me—much better for everyone—if I admit my defeat and go home.

Home.

Wherever that is.

Besides, if this is just a dream like I think, what difference could it make? So what if I go in search of a little relief?

I take a deep breath. Push to move past him. The toe of my shoe edged up to the grainy white line marking the entrance, when his eyes fix on mine and he blocks me again.

"It's a dream!" I cry, voice filled with frustration. "You're a phantom—a fantasy—no different from them!" I motion toward the demons. "So do us both a favor and let me out of this place."

He shakes his head slowly as his eyes tug down at the sides, the sudden transformation making me want to take it all back, renege on my words if only to see him smile again. "I can't let you do that," he says. "Everything that happens here—whether in the dream state or the waking state—it's all part of the test. The actions you choose bear significant consequence. You must determine the mirage from the truth. It's the only path to success."

"You're the mirage!" I shout, eager to move past him, be free of this place. "It's all a mirage! I just want to be free—why won't you let me?"

My tirade cut short by the press of his finger just under my chin as he tilts my face toward his and urges me near. Our lips swelling—meeting—the first taste tentative and unsure—though it soon melds into something much deeper—something surging with untold promise—cresting with hope.

Something I've no doubt is real.

His hand slips to my shoulder—dips into the valley of my chest—circling the soft buckskin pouch lying close to my heart as he says, "They want this—they want to see you defeated more than anything else." His gaze intense, voice a soft, whispered warning. "Don't let them win."

I press hard against him, his touch so enticing, magnetic, I can't bear even the slightest divide to stand between us. My progress halted by his hands gripping my shoulders—the forced backward shuffle of my feet—moving me well behind the white line—only satisfied when an expanse of blank space yawns wide between us.

"You must stay until it's over. You must see this thing through. It's all a mirage, everything but this anyway—" He leans past the barrier and kisses me again, his touch light, fleeting, but leaving me breathless all the same.

Leaving me staring into the dark, his words lingering in the space he once filled: "We're all counting on you . . ."

twenty-one

I wake again.

For the second time. Or is it the third? I can no longer tell.

Time's so intangible, so fleeting—the day turns to night, and the night becomes day. Indecipherable flashes of dark and light meshing together, blurring into a series of smoldering images that spark and flare—lure and seduce—until I can no longer determine what's real and what's fake.

Can no longer distinguish between dreams and reality—between evil and good.

All I know for sure is that the cave is now as dark as it is cold, but I'm too weak from hunger and thirst to light that candle or do much of anything to comfort myself.

I push hard against the wall, the tips of my fingers seeking my ancestors, reading their names like braille. Reminded of the words Paloma wrote in her note, about learning to see through the mirage—to see in the dark, see with my heart—and knowing I can't go it alone. I need them to help.

I hold tight to my pouch, seeking comfort in the hard, curved edge of Raven's beak, but my resolve is wearing so thin, stepping over the line before it's time seems like a small price to pay for a reward that's so great.

I stumble to my feet, my gait so stiff and uncertain, I kick the rattle, causing the small beads to spin and loop crazily, as I move toward the exit, eager to be free. Free of the darkness and cold—free of the vision quest—my training as a Seeker—eager to say good-bye to it all—when someone tugs hard on my arm, pulling me backward, and I turn to find Valentina standing behind me.

I recognize her from the spirit animal she's brought along with her—a dark-eyed raccoon with its head lowered, back raised. Its sharp teeth bared as it paces back and forth, careful to never veer too close to the line marking the cave.

Valentina is young. Pretty. Reminding me of what Paloma must've looked like at that age, with her long dark hair, flashing brown eyes, and bare feet. She grips my arm hard, pulling me to her. Murmuring a long string of words I can't comprehend, though the message is clear—I'm not to go any farther. I'm to stay right where I am, next to her.

If she'd brought some food and drink, heck, even a small blanket, something to warm me—I might reconsider. But as she came empty-handed, she's soon overpowered by more immediate needs.

I yank free of her grip and make for the exit, focusing on the thick, white border, the freedom that looms just beyond. Telling myself there's no shame in failing—nothing wrong with rejecting this world. Their practices are barbaric, too primitive to work in this new, modern time.

Just one step away from all that I crave, when another voice drifts from behind me and says, "Daire—my sweet baby girl, won't you do this for me?"

It's Django.

The Django from the black-and-white picture I keep in my wallet.

And just like Valentina, he's brought his spirit animal with him—a huge, menacing black bear that growls loudly, angrily, as it paces behind me.

One step . . . just one more step and I can move past all of this. I don't have to end up like him—don't have to face a premature death. Now that I know what I'm up against, I'll find a way to outsmart them—but for now, I just need some relief . . .

Sorry, Django.

Sorry, Valentina.

I really did try. But I'm refusing this life.

One more step, a rather large one at that, and freedom is mine.

My toe aiming for the line's other side, when the boy appears before me—head shaking sadly, arm raised in warning—as Valentina lets out a bloodcurdling cry—and Django remains right behind me, his voice low and serious, urging me to reconsider, to *look,* to *think,* to stop seeing with my eyes, my stomach, my immediate needs, and start seeing with my heart—to distinguish the mirage from the truth.

I stare into the boy's eyes—his brilliant blue eyes—seeing my bedraggled reflection transform to something brilliant—incandescent.

The promise of the me I can be.

Will be.

But only if I see this thing through.

I press my foot downward, sick of being ruled by hallucinations and dreams. Ready to cross the line, wipe that hopeful look from his eyes, when my pouch begins to thump so hard against my chest I can't help but flinch.

Can't help but stumble backward, away from the boy, away from Valentina who lets out a terrible cry, as Django rushes forward and I land in his arms. His dark gaze burning on mine—filling me with all the fatherly love and devotion I'd missed all these years. The moment holding, growing, filling me with the most beautiful, expansive burst of hope—only to be broken by a wicked rush of hot air and a horrible howling wind bearing a hail of black feathers that rain all around—the herald for a giant, purple-eyed raven that swoops down from above.

I fight.

Scream.

Try like hell to free myself.

But it's no use. Django's too strong. And when Valentina joins in and grabs hold of my feet, the fight becomes hopeless.

The two of them working together, working against me—allowing Raven's beak to pierce through my skin and snap all my bones. Plucking out my entrails, my organs, my heart—before systematically ripping me apart.

And it's not long before the other spirit animals join in as well. Valentina's raccoon, Esperanto's bat, Maria's horse, Diego's monkey, Mayra's wildcat, Gabriella's squirrel, Piann's red fox, along with a huge, raging jaguar I suspect belongs to my grandfather, Alejandro. Even Paloma's blue-eyed white wolf is here—and they've brought the rest of my ancestors with them. Several generations of Santoses forming a circle around me, watching in dull fascination as I'm torn into pieces.

No matter how much I plead—no matter how much I beg, cry, and demand for it to stop—my cries fall on deaf ears. The boy's disappeared, and those who remain, willfully choose to ignore me.

And it's not long before I'm gone. My body reduced to small shredded crumbs that litter the floor. My life force fading, dissipating—as a river of blood seeps into the ground, blending with the dirt—becoming one with the mountain.

My energy mixing with the earth's until whatever's left of me—my soul, my spirit, my essence—is rewarded with the mountain's sacred song:

> I am constant and strong
> Eternal—everlasting
> A provider of shelter and solace

Strength and perspective

Look to me when you're lost—and I'll give you direction

The words continuing to swirl all about me, though it's too late to do any good.

I am nothing more than a small wisp of energy.

To the eyes of the world, I am already dead.

twenty-two

A soft, insistent tickle brushes my nose—tapping lightly against the tip, forcing me to chase it down over my lips, well past my chin, until I grasp it at the base of my neck, pop an eye open, and peer into a hard slant of light at the single black feather—a raven's feather—I hold in my hand.

Knowing instinctively it came from my Raven—the one who ripped me to shreds—I spring to my feet, my gaze darting, heart racing, as memories of my horrible dismemberment blaze in my head.

I went through a war.

Fought a battle I was sure I had lost.

Yet the only thing out of place, the only thing that wasn't here from the start, is this single black feather—carried by the wind that raged in this cave.

My leg's fully healed—my cast nowhere to be seen.

While the grainy white border is left untouched, intact, and my small black bag is propped neatly in the corner just as I left it. And the place near the center, where the spirit animals plucked out my heart and tore off my limbs, remains undisturbed.

No blood.

No shredded bits of tissue and flesh.

Not even so much as a bone scrap.

No sign of anything out of the ordinary, and yet there's no doubt in my mind that it happened. All of it. I'm absolutely certain of it.

I'm reborn.

Renewed.

Having fused my energy with the energy of the earth, I've been resurrected with a surge of power the likes of which I've never known—never could've imagined.

My fellow Seekers—my fellow Santoses—my family—allowed me to be ripped apart so I could be rebuilt. And because of it, I am now bigger, better, and stronger than I ever thought possible.

I have earned their approval, their trust.

I have earned the right to carry their name.

And with the mountain's song still fresh in my mind, I know it has accepted me as well. My time in this cave has come to an end. It is time to move on.

I riffle through my bag, find a stub of chalk, and add the name *Santos* right beside *Daire*. And then, in the space above that, I add *Django Santos*, taking a moment to include a sketch of Bear—the spirit animal he never had a chance to acknowledge as his.

My father may have failed to heed his calling, but his spirit lives on, and he helped me heed mine. I couldn't have survived it without him.

I run a hand over my hair, surprised to find that my braid is more or less intact, but since I've been here for days, I'm pretty sure my scalp's a greasy mess. And with no immediate way to remedy that, I cover my hair with the red bandanna Paloma packed. Knotting it tightly at the back of my head, wondering if that was its intended purpose when she saw fit to add it.

Then, after tossing my bag over my shoulder and stuffing the raven feather into my pouch, knowing it's another talisman, a gift from the wind I should never be without—I head for the grainy white border. Having no way of knowing if the boy really did stand just outside of it or if the scene only played in my head—but dropping the thought just as quickly. All that really matters is that I got what I came for—I survived my vision quest. The rest is just details.

I pause for a moment, long enough to take one last look at the cave, knowing I'll never come here again—then I step out of the dark and into the light, ready to face whatever comes next.

twenty-three

I head down the same way I came, and when I reach the bottom, I'm not the least bit surprised to find Kachina saddled and waiting for me.

Though I am surprised to find I don't rush to get back like I thought I would.

Instead, I take it slow. Take my time. Wanting to linger, to hold onto the experience, the magick of the mountain, for as long as I can. Stopping every now and then to let Kachina graze for a bit and drink from a cool, rushing stream—while I wander through a grove of cottonwood, juniper, and piñon trees, communing with a variety of birds who introduce themselves as purple martins and red-tailed hawks. Eagerly testing the new powers I've gained—increasingly amazed at the magick I hold.

When I come across a mesquite tree swarming with bees, instead of avoiding it like I usually would, I stand directly beneath it. Humming the mountain's song under my breath as I shake the two lowest branches, causing an army of agitated bees to swarm all about me, though not a single one of them so much as stings.

Then later, when I come across a nest of scorpions, I kick off my shoes and step in the middle. Humming the tune the mountain revealed, and not the least bit surprised when the scorpions choose to ignore me.

And though I have no idea how to get back to Paloma's, Kachina and I now share a bond like never before. We have an innate understanding of each other. We've discovered a new way to communicate—and because of it, I've no doubt she'll lead me wherever it is I most need to be.

We continue the journey—Kachina carefully picking her way through the woods, as I remain in deep communion with all that surrounds me. The plants, the streams, the mountains, the wind—all of it brimming with energy—eagerly revealing their secrets.

Paloma was right. Everything really is thrumming, illuminated, alive. And now that I've discovered the truth, now that I'm merged with its power and energy, I can't imagine how I ever existed without it.

I cluck my tongue against the roof of my mouth and press my heel to Kachina's side. Urging her to go faster, and then faster still, until she's galloping down the trail with her mane lifting, ears pinned, tail swooshing behind her, as her hooves beat hard against the ground. I close my eyes, let go of the reins, and fold my hands around my buckskin pouch, allowing my body to rise and fall as I part my lips wide and sing the mountainsong at the top of my lungs.

And, as it turns out, even the wind has a song to reveal:

> *I am cloudy and clear*
> *Stormy and bright*
> *I am the chaos and silence that lives in your mind*
> *I watch over all with unfailing vision*
> *Look to me when you face indecision*

With my horse charging beneath me, my vision quest behind me, the elements singing in harmony—I've never felt so free, so empowered, so alive. One song fading into the next as my voice continues to rise—until Kachina veers a sharp right, causing her to tilt in a way I didn't expect.

I lose my balance. Land on the saddle all wrong. Blinking, fumbling, and flailing for the horn, the reins, her mane—searching for something that'll help me right myself again.

She skids to a stop, rises on her hind legs, and snorts in protest, as her front legs kick before her. And I'm so preoccupied with fighting to stay on her back, it's a moment before I see what caused her to spook in the first place:

A shiny, black, fully loaded, four-wheel-drive pickup truck crowded with teens.

The girls laugh—a horrible, howling, snickering sound. While the boys all stare—wide-eyed and uncertain, having no idea what to make of me.

I yank hard on the reins—try to maneuver around. Having just cleared the bed of the truck, when the driver jumps out, moves right before me, and lifts his dark glasses onto his forehead.

"You okay?" His icy-blue gaze lands on mine, though just like the dreams, it fails to reflect.

I swallow. Try to steer around him. But it's no use. He just mimics my moves. Everywhere I go, he appears right before me, frustrating me to the point where I shout, "Go away!" Practically spitting the words, seeing no need for fake courtesies.

"I'll get out of your way when I'm sure you're okay," he says, going for Kachina's bridle, but she's on my side, which means she rears her head back and slips from his grasp. "Your horse had quite a scare, and I'm afraid it's my fault. I probably shouldn't have parked on the trail like I did. You okay?" He arranges his face into a mask of concern.

I huff under my breath and avert my gaze. Refusing to answer, to engage any more than I have.

"Hey, come on, now. Throw me a bone, will ya? A simple *yes* or *no* will do. I can't help being concerned about you." He grins, not at all daunted by my unwillingness to play. "Every time I see you, you're in some kind of trouble, and I have to confess—I find the whole damsel-in-distress thing completely irresistible. I blame it on Disney movies and fairy tales, what's your take?"

I frown, eyes leveled on his when I say, "I'm not looking to be rescued. I do just fine on my own."

His gaze grows deeper, the flat expanse of his irises becoming a fathomless void that lures everything in—everything but me. "Wow, you really know how to hurt a guy, don't you?" He shoots me a wounded look I don't buy for a second. "Isn't there some way we can move past this? Convince you to give me a chance?"

I roll my eyes, tug on the reins, ready to leave this behind, when he reaches for Kachina's bridle again, and I jab my heel so hard into her side she ends up charging right at him.

It's only after he's lunged out of her way that I realize how close I came to killing him, if not seriously maiming him. And the realization fills me with doubt.

Doubting my ability to distinguish between reality and dreams.

Doubting my ability to seek the truth behind the mirage.

Every time I've seen him he's been smarmy but kind. The only time he's ever proved himself to be evil is in my darkest moments—and during my sleep.

Our gaze meets—mine horrified—his flat and unreadable.

And that's how I leave him.

Kachina and I storming the trail as fast as we can, unable to rid myself of the overwhelming burden of doubt that chases me all the way home.

the
raven's
song

twenty-four

Chay pulls up to the curb, stopping outside a large two-story building that, despite its efforts to mimic the ever-popular adobe style, is really no more than a concrete slab with a sandstone façade, surrounded by a big iron gate, with a scowling man standing guard at the entrance and a large painted sign on the side stating: MILAGRO HIGH—HOME OF THE MAGUS—with a cartoon wizard just underneath it.

Milagro High.

Miracle High.

From the looks of it, it's as poorly named as the town it resides in.

My face goes grim as I try to take a fortifying breath, which comes out shaky. Reminding myself how I came away completely unscathed and empowered from full-body dismemberment in the cave—so surely I can survive this: my first day of eleventh grade at this prison-like school.

Though try as I might, the pep talk's a fail. Today marks a major letdown in more ways than one.

After leaving the cave in triumph, I was eager to face whatever came next, excited about this whole new world that was open to me—sure that being a Seeker would be way more Superhero than

Student. But despite my praising the wonders of Internet school—explaining how it improved my vocabulary and made me a math whiz—Paloma still wouldn't budge. According to her, now that I've completed my vision quest, it's imperative I get out into the community, and, unfortunately for me, that involves going to school.

"They need you, *nieta*," she'd said, her gaze fixed on mine. "They don't yet know it, but they do. You alone will keep the community in balance. No one else can do what you do."

"What about you?" I'd asked, seeing her turn away, her fingers curled around a bloodied tissue in an attempt to hide it from view.

"My powers are diminishing." Her gaze grew distant, far away. "It was never meant to be this way, it's supposed to be parent and child working in tandem. But I've been on my own for so long, trying to compensate for Django's loss, I'm afraid it's taken its toll. And now I must hang on to whatever's left, so I can pass it to you. Soon you will be stronger than any other Seeker that's come before. There is nothing to worry about, *nieta*—you are more than ready for this." She turned to me then, her expression telling me the discussion was over.

The decision was made despite all my protests, and now I'm clinging to the door of Chay's truck, staring down my new school on a gloomy Wednesday morning, which still seems ridiculous. Who the heck starts school on a Wednesday?

"It is better this way," Paloma says, in her uncanny way of tapping into my thoughts. Her hand patting my knee when she adds, "You will take a few days to get adjusted, meet a few people and find your way around, and by Monday, you'll be ready to face the whole week, and all those that follow."

Despite her words of encouragement, I can't help but feel disappointed. I had high hopes for this school. It's the first one I've ever attended, and I was hoping it would be prettier, more inviting. I was hoping it would look more like the fancy schools you see on TV, and less like the bleak house of doom that sits right before me.

"Remember what I told you, *nieta*."

I lick my lips. Flick my gaze toward hers.

"Cade will be here, so you must be on guard. Do not let him intimidate you. Do not let him manipulate you. And never allow yourself to doubt his true nature again. Your impressions of him were right all along. He is a powerful sorcerer—his entire clan, the Richters, also known as El Coyote, are masters at manipulating perception. Controlling the consciousness of others is the very thing that's allowed them to hang on for so long. It's a skill the Seekers have yet to accomplish and have fought hard to over-come. Though even if we do find the key, we would never use it in the way they do. They've chosen to play in the dark—while you, my *nieta*, are a Santos, a Seeker, and we always remain firmly en-trenched in the light, no matter what. You are ready to face him, I assure you of that. Otherwise, you would not be here, so there is no reason to worry."

I swallow hard. Press my palm against the window. Despite what she says, I don't feel ready, not in the least. My stomach's a jumbled mess of nerves, and yet I'm all too aware that there's no use fighting it. Paloma is right. It's time I head inside and face up to my destiny.

I push the truck door open and slide from my seat. Doing my best to quash my fears, but I'm pretty sure no one's fooled.

"I'll be back to get you at three," Chay tells me. "I'll meet you right here." But as nice as the offer is, I can't accept it. He has a life, an important career. He doesn't need to waste his time playing chauffeur to me.

"No worries. I can get myself back," I say, my words met with a skeptical look that prompts me to add, "What kind of Seeker would I be if I couldn't find my way home?"

Before he can reply, before Paloma can say another word, I step away from the truck and head through the gate. Making my way across large squares of gravel and dirt standing in for a lawn, before pushing through the big double doors and stealing a moment to orient myself. But, as it turns out, I pause for too long, and a second later I nearly fall victim to a trio of girls storming the hall.

They're the kind of girls I instantly recognize as being in charge.

The kind of girls determined to snag the lead role.

Marquee girls.

Pretty much the opposite of me—the lowly kid of a crew member, used to keeping quiet, out of sight, doing whatever it takes to avoid the spotlight.

This may be my first day at school, any school, but I've spent enough time on various movie sets to recognize a social caste system when I see one.

Their gazes are piercing and gleaming—darting like crazy—calculating the number of students checking them out, which is just about everyone within a ten-foot radius. The majority of students content to stand on the sidelines—smiling, waving, and striving to be noticed—knowing never to approach unless summoned. Never to breach the invisible red-velvet rope that separates the popular crowd from everyone else.

I duck my head low and maneuver around them, about to make my way down the hall in search of the office, when the girls stop. Their jaws dropping, eyes popping, as the one in the middle, the one with the long dark hair and brassy blond highlights, approaches and says, "Hey."

I nod, force a half-smile, and meet her *Hey* with one of my own.

"You're the girl I saw on the horse." Her eyes are dark, kohl rimmed, and narrowed on mine.

I stand before them, refusing to confirm or deny—having dreaded a moment like this ever since Paloma broke the news about my enrolling in school. With only one high school to choose from, it was only a matter of time before I ran into the kids I saw that day on the trail. Though I was hoping I'd at least make it a little farther into the building before I was outted.

"You are her, aren't you?" She checks with her friends, her gaze turning first to the girl on her right wearing the gloppy pink lip gloss, and then to the one on her left with the overplucked eyebrows and iridescent purple eyeshadow, turning back to me when she says, "Even without the bandanna and the horse, I know it's you. You were singing too—weren't you? How'd that song go again—something about *strength, perception, and giving direction*? Maybe you should sing it for us?" Her dark eyes flash on mine as her friends fall all over themselves, laughing hysterically into their hands.

I start to walk away, only to have her slip right before me, and say, "Seriously." She nods, smiling like she means it. "We'd really like to hear it. So go ahead—sing your psycho song."

My hands curl to fists. She's mocking the mountainsong. Has no idea how much power it holds—how much power *I* hold. I could crush her in ways she couldn't begin to imagine. Or, at the very least, humiliate her in a way she'd never live down.

But I can't.

Won't.

Paloma warned me about that. Said I had to use my skill for the greater good—to not squander my powers on protecting my ego.

I try to move around them, but they move right along with me. Their arms linked together in an impenetrable wall of designer knockoff jeans, padded bras, and pop-star perfume. Still, as much as I make fun of them in my head, the actual effect is far more intimidating than the big iron gate that surrounds the school grounds. Without the use of my magick, I'm no match for them. I have no idea how to deal with this. No idea how to get out of this.

"How'd you get to school?" one of them says, the one on the right with the glossy pink lips. "Is your horse parked out front?"

She laughs well before the joke is out, which kind of ruins the timing. Still, her eyes flick toward the girl in the middle, seeking her approval, as I stand there and stare, telling myself that they're silly and stupid and not worth my wrath. But even though I know it to be true, the crowd of students growing around us pretty much deletes all that.

They press closer, everyone wanting to get a better view of the kind of new-girl hazing they don't get to see every day—every last one of them relieved that it's me and not them. The sheer size of the audience encouraging the girl in the middle to speak up again, voice rising when she says, "Clearly nobody told you we don't allow psycho girls at this school. So maybe you should go back to your mental ward."

I swallow hard. Tell myself to let it go, to not make it any worse than it already is—but discard that thought just as quickly. It's better to nip it right now. Let them know I'm not one to be messed with. My silence will only encourage them to stalk me until graduation.

Despite a lifetime of being told to remain unobtrusive, in this case I've already failed. I've been spotted, picked out of the crowd, so there's really no point in acting submissive.

"No psychos?" My eyes dart among them, until I settle on the ringleader and take a step toward her. "Then how do you explain yourself? Did they bend the rules for *you*?"

Her eyes bulge. Her face burns with rage. As her sidekicks stand mutely beside her, too shocked to react, or at least not right away.

She steps toward me, face scrunched and feral, but I remain in my place, staring her down and keeping my cool.

She has no idea who I am. Has no idea what I'm capable of, the kind of magick I've been practicing since I completed my vision quest. A verbal insult is nothing. She's getting off easy.

With her face just inches from mine, so close I can just make out the circle of pink, unhealed skin surrounding her Marilyn piercing, she reaches for my shoulder, presumably to give me a nice good shove—start a fight she cannot, will not, win—when *he* appears, masquerading in his favorite role as the noble white knight on a mission to save me.

"These girls messing with you?" He stops the girl from going any further by sliding his arm tightly around her and pulling her close to his side, the move instantly subduing her to silence. His gaze fixed on mine when he adds, "Or, maybe it's the other way around—you bothering them?" He throws his head back and laughs, the sound so alluring, so magnetic, it causes the girls to forget about me and train their focus on him. "Sorry you got off to a rough start." He smiles. Extends his right hand. "Maybe I can make up for it. We've met a few times already, I know, but never formally, so now's my big chance—I'm Cade. Cade Richter."

His hand hovers before me, but I make no move to take it, no move to acknowledge it. "I know exactly who you are," I tell him, noting the way his lip twitches with delight, as his gaze connects with mine. The two of us knowing what no one else does, I'm no longer hiding.

It's me against him.

Santos vs. Richter.

Seeker vs. El Coyote.

The game is now on.

I turn, determined to leave it at that, or at least for now anyway. There's no need to rush into anything, especially when Paloma still has so much more to teach me.

Doing my best to ignore him when he calls out from behind, "Allow me to be the first to welcome you to Milagro High! If you should need anything, I am at your service." His words met by a chorus of laughter that bursts out all around him.

I pick up the pace, moving so fast I'm practically sprinting. Slowing only when I've rounded a corner where I stop, sag against the wall, and fight to catch my breath. Relieved to know it's not Cade who set my heart beating triple time, I can and will deal with him. It's the mean girl stuff that got me off kilter. Having avoided school all these years, I've never had to deal with that sort of thing.

On the set, the snootier stars always kept to themselves, figuring they were far too important to mingle with the likes of the lesser cast and crew. This is my first time being bullied. And while I'm sure I could've done better—I definitely could've done worse.

Much worse.

She'll think twice before she messes with me again.

Or not.

There's just as good a chance she's roaming the halls, sharpening her talons, gathering the troops, and gearing up for a grisly round two.

Great. First day of school and I'm doomed. The enemy turns out to be someone Paloma never even warned me about.

"Coulda been worse."

I lift my head to find a small slim girl with light brown hair, delicate features, a beautiful heart-shaped face, and soft gray eyes that look just to the right of me.

"Being a brunette's safer. If you were blond, they would've eaten you alive, for sure."

I peer at her closer, noting the way her gaze fails to meet mine, how she grips a red-tipped white cane in her hand—all of which leads me to believe there's no way she could know what hair color I have.

"Last new girl didn't fare so well," she continues. "Mostly on account of her being a natural blue-eyed blonde, she didn't stand a chance around here. Lasted just shy of two months before she called it quits and enrolled in Internet school." She shrugs. "It's too bad. I really did like her. But I have a feeling you'll do a lot better. Try to hang in there. Though I'm not gonna lie—chances are they'll never come around. Yet, with your dark hair and green eyes, at least you'll blend in, which makes you way less of a threat. If you stay out of their way, eventually they'll grow bored and stay

out of yours. That said, Cade could pose a problem. He seems to be
pretty intrigued by you—and Lita, the ringleader, is not going to
like that. They've had an off-and-on thing for years now. Even
when they're officially off, she doesn't quite see it that way, and any
girl who goes after him ends up regretting it." She cocks her head
to the side, as though working a serious mental equation—
calculating the statistical probability of my surviving this school.

Then focusing on me again, well, not really *focusing*, more like
acknowledging, she says, "I'm Sochee. That's how it's pronounced:
So—chee. I tell you that because if you saw the way it was spelled,
you'd never guess. Anyway, It's X-O-T-I-C-H-L, and just so you
know, it means flower. Some people pronounce it with a soft *T* at
the end, or even a *shee* or *sheel* sound instead of *chee*—but Sochee
is the way I was taught to say it, so that's how I say it." She nods,
signaling that's the end of it and I can't help but feel relieved; my
head is spinning from just about everything she just said.

"And it's my guess that right about now your eyes are darting
like crazy, frantically searching for an exit, figuring you've gone
from the scary mean girls to a downright crazy girl with a weird
name, and you can't decide which is worse." She laughs, and the
sound is as light and bright and beautiful as she is.

"How do you know all that . . . when you're . . . well, it seems
like you might be . . ." Several choices flit through my head, but
I'm not sure which is politically correct, so I just let the sentence
dangle unfinished.

"Blind? Vision impaired? Lacking in visual perception?" She
leans toward me, flashing a generous smile that displays a row of
straight white teeth. "Well, just so you know, the answer is yes
to all three. So tell me, was this your first clue?"

She taps her cane against the gray-tiled floor, the move causing my cheeks to heat so much I'm glad she can't see me. Still, I'm
not about to let her off the hook. "So with that in mind, how
could you possibly know I'm a green-eyed brunette?" I ask, looking her over again, wondering if she's faking it, wondering if there

was some kind of school bulletin warning all the students about the incoming new girl.

But Xotichl just smiles and says, "Some might say I'm perceptive."

"And what would *you* say?" I ask, my voice a little edgy, tired of being toyed with.

"I'd say I agree." She lowers her head, tries in vain to hide the grin that sneaks onto her face.

I fidget. Heave my bag high onto my shoulder as I try to drum up some kind of reply. But before I can gather the words, the bell rings, and a swarm of students burst into the hall, while Xotichl stands in the middle, with an army of students careening around her.

"Do you need help?" I ask, not wanting to offend, but they all veer so close, it's like they don't even see her.

"Don't we all?" She laughs, tapping the tip of her cane against the toe of my boot. "But in this case, I'm pretty sure you need way more help than I do. So, if you're looking for the office, it's straight ahead. Fifty-two steps from where we now stand. Though for you, it may be as few as forty-five—forty-seven tops— considering how much taller you are. And your legs are much longer too—lucky you." She laughs again.

I squint, wondering how she could possibly know all that. Is she mocking me? Having fun at my expense? Is she not really blind? Is anyone in this town who they present themselves to be?

But before I can reply, she's gone. Cane sweeping before her, heading down the hall as a path clears all around her.

twenty-five

I wish I'd prepared.

Wish I'd taken the time to do a little research by watching a weekend's worth of high school–themed movies.

Because this—this school—this insane social scene—feels as foreign and chaotic as the day I got lost in the Moroccan medina.

It's all about the bells. Bells are in charge around here—they rule everything. They usher us to class, scold us when we're late, then prod us again when it's time to move on. The sequence repeating over and over—until I'm just like everyone else, numbly reacting to that abruptly shrill sound.

Except, I'm not like everyone else. I'm not like anyone I've seen so far. And despite my attempts to blend in, thanks to the events in the hall between the mean girls and Cade, I now stand out in the very worst way.

Nothing in my life has prepared me for this. Not one single thing. I feel like a lab rat stuck in some horrible experiment meant to measure how I adapt to brutal forms of social segregation and weirdness. And the sad news is, I'm producing way below average results.

I stand to the side of the lunchroom, or cafeteria, or whatever they call it. The vegetarian lunch Paloma packed with great love and care tightly clutched in my fist, though I've no clue as to where I'm supposed to go eat it.

Having already committed the most heinous crime of all by sitting at the *wrong* table, I'm not sure I'm up for trying again. I'm still shaken by the way those girls acted—so self-righteous and territorial, so *burdened* by my presence at the end of their bench.

It's the seniors' table, I was told. I have *no right* to sit there. *Ever*. And that includes holidays and weekends.

"Duly noted," I replied, grabbing my lunch and standing before them. "I'll do my best to steer clear of it on Christmas. Easter as well. Though Valentine's Day is a wild card I just can't commit to." And though it felt good at the time, I've no doubt it was a reckless act that only made things worse.

I heave a deep sigh and survey the room, wondering how Jennika might've handled such a thing back when she was my age. Barring the fact that she was already in her first trimester of carrying me, she'd probably head straight for the table where the bad boys sit, making them fall madly in love with her during the first five minutes.

And while the bad boys' table isn't all that hard to spot—just aim your dart for the guys dressed in leather jackets, trying too hard to look dangerous and jaded—and you've got yourself a bull's-eye—I'm not the least bit like Jennika. I could never pull it off.

Besides, there's only one true bad boy here, and as it just so happens, he's the one no one suspects. He's too pretty, too popular, too charismatic, too athletic, and smart, and alluring. Praised by both teachers and peers, he's pretty much the king of everything. Class president, the star quarterback, a sure thing for prom king, no doubt. As far as I can tell, I'm the only one who remains unimpressed.

I take another glance—noting how the tables are systematically segregated. There's the cowboy table, filled with kids wearing jeans, Western-style shirts and cowboy boots; the hippie table, where they all sport tie-dyed T-shirts, bandannas, and ripped jeans; the Native American table, where the majority wear flannel shirts and faded denim—all of them talking and laughing but clearly keeping to themselves. And after seeing all that, well, I finally understand the true meaning behind the sayings: *Like seeks like.*

And: *Water seeks its own level.*

They were talking about high school.

Or maybe just life in general.

The point is, people will always cling and conform in order to belong to something they want to be part of.

Even the fringe group, the ones who think they're so arty and different, so outside the mainstream—no matter how outrageously indie they strive to be, it only takes one informed glance to see that they're all conforming to each other. Without even realizing it, they're keeping within their own defined boundaries.

That's just the way it is. It's never gonna be any different. And even though the day's half over, I've yet to see anyone who'd consider sitting with me.

Well, Cade might, judging by the way he's smiling and waving and gesturing for me to join him, but I know he's not serious. It's all a big show, designed to make him look funny and make me feel awkward and bad about myself.

As far as Xotichl goes—I can't quite get a handle on her. Besides, I have no idea where she is. Haven't seen her since that weirdness in the hallway this morning.

I turn my back on it all, push through the door, and slink down the hall. In search of a nice, quiet place where I can eat my lunch in silence and wait for yet another bell to tell me where to go.

Spotting a place at the end of a long row of lockers, I drop to the floor, reach into my bag, and smile when I discover Paloma packed one of my favorites: a small plastic container filled with goat cheese enchiladas covered with her amazing, homemade tomatillo sauce.

With my plastic fork at the ready, I'm about to dig in when I'm stopped by a soft rustling sound that could only come from a lunch sack. Wondering who could possibly be as big an outcast as me, I scooch forward just enough to peer around the bend where I spy a pair of long legs, dark jeans, and heavy, thick-soled black shoes so large I hope they belong to a guy. Then I retreat to my corner, happy to know I'm not nearly as alone as I'd thought—that I'm not the only friendless loser who doesn't belong in this school.

twenty-six

The bell rings—again. That awful, shrill sound blaring through the hall, bouncing off the ugly beige walls and red metal lockers, sparking a stream of students into a flurry of movement, as I try my best to find my next classroom.

I pause by the door, schedule in hand, taking a moment to confirm I'm in the right place, since I really don't need to make that particular mistake yet again.

Independent study. Right. Last class of the day—praise be, hallelujah, and more.

I make my way inside and introduce myself to the man at the podium bearing a squinty mean gaze, a cruel slash of a mouth, a size-too-small T-shirt forced to stretch over a belly that will always arrive well before the rest of him, and a crew cut so tight it's mostly just scalp. Pausing when he places a red checkmark next to my name and tells me to grab any seat.

If I've learned anything today, it's that it can't be that easy. It may not be obvious at first sight, but somewhere in this deceptively innocuous classroom, territory has been staked, boundaries drawn, and an invisible wall erected, bearing an equally invisible sign that states clueless new girls like me are not welcome here.

"Any seat," he barks, shooting me a look that's already pegged me as just another moron in a succession of many.

I give the room a thorough once-over, noting how instead of the usual desks, it's divided into a series of tall, square, black tables and old metal stools. All too aware of the way my fellow classmates track my movements, sighing with overblown relief when I pass them in favor of the back where I toss my bag onto a table, grab an empty stool, and ask, "This seat taken?" My eyes grazing over the only other occupant, a guy with long glossy dark hair with his head bent over a book.

"It's all yours," he says. And when he lifts his head and smiles, my heart just about leaps from my chest.

It's the boy from my dreams.

The boy from the Rabbit Hole, the gas station, and the cave—sitting before me with those same amazing, icy-blue eyes, those same alluring lips I've kissed multiple times—but only in slumber, never in waking life.

I scold my heart to settle, but it doesn't obey.

I admonish myself to sit, to act normal, casual—and I just barely succeed.

Stealing a series of surreptitous looks as I search through my backpack, taking in his square chin, wide generous lips, strong brow, defined cheekbones, and smooth brown skin—the exact same features as Cade.

"You're the new girl, right?" He abandons his book, tilting his head in a way that causes his hair to stream over his shoulder, so glossy and inviting it takes all of my will not to lean across the table and touch it.

I nod in reply, or at least I think I do. I can't be too sure. I'm too stricken by his gaze—the way it mirrors mine—trying to determine if he knows me, recognizes me, if he's surprised to find me here. Wishing Paloma had better prepared me—focused more on him and less on his brother.

I force my gaze from his. Bang my knee hard against the table as

I swivel in my seat. Feeling so odd and unsettled, I wish I'd picked another place to sit, though it's pretty clear no other table would have me.

He buries his smile and returns to the book. Allowing a few minutes to pass, not nearly enough time for me to get a grip on myself, when he looks up and says, "Are you staring at me because you've seen my doppelganger roaming the halls, playing king of the cafeteria? Or because you need to borrow a pencil and you're too shy to ask?"

I clear the lump from my throat, push the words past my lips when I say, "No one's ever accused me of being shy." A statement that, while steeped in truth, stands at direct odds with the way I feel now, sitting so close to him. "So I guess it's your twin—or *doppelganger,* as you say." I keep my voice light, as though I'm not at all affected by his presence, but the trill note at the end gives me away. Every part of me now vibrating with the most intense surge of energy—like I've been plugged into the wall and switched on—and it's all I can do to keep from grabbing hold of his shirt, demanding to know if he dreamed the dreams too.

He nods, allowing an easy, cool smile to widen his lips. "We're identical," he says. "As I'm sure you've guessed. Though it's easy enough to tell us apart. For one thing, he keeps his hair short. For another—"

"The eyes—" I blurt, regretting the words the instant they're out. From the look on his face, he has no idea what I'm talking about. "Yours are . . . kinder." My cheeks burn so hot I force myself to look away, as words of reproach stampede my brain.

Why am I acting like such an inept loser? Why do I insist on embarrassing myself—in front of him—of all people?

I have to pull it together. I have to remember who I am—what I am—and what I was born to do. Which is basically to crush him and his kind—or, at the very least, to temper the damage they do.

He shoots me an odd look, moving right past my words when he says, "What I was going to say is we're only identical on the outside, inside is a whole other story. He's far more social, always surrounded by large crowds of fawning admirers who follow him around like some kind of starstruck entourage."

"And you don't have one of those—an entourage?" I ask, wondering how that could possibly be. With his good looks and easy demeanor, he's way more attractive than his brother.

I shake my head. Clear the thought from my mind. No matter how cute he may be, no matter how kind his energy seems, he's still a Richter—a bona fide member of the El Coyote clan. He's someone to keep a close eye on, but no more.

He leans toward me, his eyes so piercing, so blue, I have to force myself to meet them. "Me? An entourage?" He laughs, pushing a hand through his hair. "It really is your first day, isn't it?" He lowers his arm, allowing the strands to fall to his shoulders when he adds, "At any rate, welcome to Milagro. This school's not really known for being hospitable, so I doubt anyone got around to saying that."

"Your twin did." I meet his gaze, striving to get a deeper, more reliable impression than the first time around, but all I get is that same cloud of kindness and love, so I turn away, force it from my mind.

"Guess good manners run in the family. Who would've thought?" He laughs, quick to chase it with "Oh, and sorry if I didn't mention it before, but I'm Dace."

He shoots me an expectant look, but I offer no response. If he really is a Richter, and there's no doubt he is, he's been made all too aware of my arrival. According to Paloma, they've been waiting for some sign of me ever since Django's demise.

"Just in case you're wondering how this class works." He moves past the snub. "You can work on whatever you want, and if you choose not to work, at least try to make it look like you're busy. Coach Sanchez will be out of here soon, but see that camera at the front?"

My eyes follow the length of his thumb as it jabs toward a

point just beyond. The two of us peering into the eye of a camera perched dead center over the chalkboard—an all-seeing, unblinking eye recording all of our actions.

"Get out of line and they got you on video." He lifts a brow and rolls his eyes. "This was supposed to be an art class. That's what I signed up for, anyway. But when the budget got slashed, art and the teacher who taught it were the very first casualties. No one cares about the arts in this town—it's all about sports and the people who play them. So now, instead of drawing and painting, we have independent study hall, a surly coach who takes roll, and a camera to record all our actions. Though I'm sure it was probably the same thing at your last school?"

I shrug, refusing to either confirm or deny, refusing to engage any more than I have. I'm too freaked by his presence—too angry with Paloma for her failure to prepare me for him. My fingers seeking the pouch I wear at my neck, reassured by the faint outline of the feather and Raven, before reaching for the waterlogged paperback I've been trying to finish since that mess in Morocco. Immersing myself in the magickal world the author created, scribbling notes in the corner, underlining favored passages, and doodling in the margins, until the bell rings again and I'm free.

It's over.

I made it.

It was never a given. There were definitely moments I wasn't so sure.

I shove my book in my bag and shoot for the exit. Surprised to find Dace just beside me, holding the door, and motioning for me to go first.

It's such a kind and decent thing to do in a day that's been anything but—I can't help but soften toward him. And when I accidentally brush up against him as I make my way out, I can't help the way my breath hitches, the way my heart skips a few beats, the way all of my nerve endings seem to ignite—all because of his touch.

"You never told me your name," he says, his voice so hauntingly familiar it causes a rush of heat to blanket my skin.

I sigh, staring blankly down the hall when I say, "Psycho Girl—Psycho Horseback Singing Girl . . ." I shrug. "I've heard it both ways."

He squints. His hand reaching for my shoulder, then falling away the instant he catches the look of reproach on my face.

"Look," I say, knowing I need to stop him before he can go any further. His kindness will only distract me at a time when I need to stay focused. "I've had a really bad day. And if my calculations are right, I have three hundred and eight more, give or take, before I get to graduate and get the heck out of this place. So, why don't you just call me whatever you want. Everyone else does. It's not like it matters . . ." My cheeks go hot, my eyes start to sting, and I know I'm rambling like a lunatic, but I can't seem to stop, can't seem to care. The world's most socially inept Seeker—that's me in a nutshell.

"Don't let them reduce you to that," he says, his gaze intense, his voice surprising me with its sincerity, its urgency. "Don't let them define how you see yourself, or your place here. And if you ever need someone to talk to, I'm not hard to find. I'm either in class, reading in the library, or eating lunch in the North hallway."

The second he says it, my gaze flies down the length of him. Slipping past a gray V-neck tee and dark denim jeans, not the least bit surprised when I land on the same heavy, black, thick-soled shoes I spied earlier.

Then before he can say anything more, I'm gone. Trying to ignore the comforting stream of kindness and love that swarms all around me.

These *impressions* as Paloma calls them, may come in handy in my life as a Seeker, but if I don't get a handle on them in my life as a student, if I don't learn to control them, they'll have me labeled as a much bigger freak than I already am.

Not that I should care what any of my classmates think—it's not like they made such a stellar impression on me.

I push through the double doors and into the light. Taking in the rush of activity—people hugging and saying good-bye, carrying on like they'll never see each other again, before hurrying to catch buses, or meet up with the long line of cars that trail along the curb. A few of them unlocking bikes, fewer still choosing to walk, and I can't help but regret my decision to tell Chay not to come get me. I don't have it figured out nearly as much as I'd thought.

Despite my newly honed skills and burgeoning magick, when it comes to navigating the rules of high school, I've never felt so lost and inadequate.

I can skip down the Spirit Road, survive a brutal vision quest—but can I handle high school? Not even close. The thought makes me laugh.

Though, unfortunately, the laugh wasn't just confined to my head, and before I know it, I'm met with a chorus of: "Psycho!"

The girls are back. Back in formation with Lita standing tall in the center, flanked by her sidekicks. She shakes her head in disdain, while the other two snicker. But as much as they're committed to hating me, the boys remain undecided, their eyes narrowed as they take a full inventory. Willing to risk whatever wrath their interest evokes, simply because I'm a new girl in a school where everyone knows everyone.

I take a deep breath, prepping myself for another round with Lita and company, when Cade saunters up from behind, addressing me when he says, "Sorry you had such a tough day. Milagro's not used to newcomers." Winking when he adds, "Go home. Get some rest. Tomorrow offers a fresh new start, as they say. I look forward to seeing you then, Daire Santos." He starts to turn away, then stops just as quickly as though a new thought occurred to him. "It *is* Santos now, right?" His mouth tugs at the side. "You no longer go by Lyons?"

He pauses, waiting for me to confirm it, but I don't. Can't. His words leave me stunned.

Meeting my silence with a flash of his most practiced, most devastating smile, he leads the group away, as I stay rooted in place, left to grapple with his words—the fact that he knows more about me than he rightfully should.

Knows more about me than I know about him, and it's time Paloma caught me up—nothing but full disclosure will do.

I watch him fade into the distance, disappearing into the student lot, where I assume he's parked his truck. Just about to get moving again, when I'm stopped by a girl's voice calling out, "Hey, Daire—you need a ride?" And I turn to find Xotichl, wondering how she could possibly know my name when I never told her, never told anybody. Not that anyone cares, they've already christened me Psycho, and I'm pretty sure it'll stick.

"So, do you?" She stops before me, as I hesitate, unsure what to say.

While I could certainly use a lift, I'm not so sure I'm willing to accept the offer. She seems to know an awful lot about me, even about Cade's interest in me—all without being able to see—and it kind of gives me the creeps.

"I know where you live," she says, which is not reassuring. "It's not all that out of the way either. Well, maybe a little. But not to worry, I'm a really good driver." She smiles. "I may be vision impaired, but all of my other senses are more than enough to compensate. In fact, if it makes you feel any better, you should know that I've only had one accident that I was charged with being legally responsible for. One out of five." She shakes her head. "Not bad odds if I say so myself."

When she gets to that last part, the jig is up. I know exactly what she's doing. She's trying to remove the sting of discomfort her disability brings out in others, by making light of it, treating it as though it's something to joke about. And it breaks my heart so much I just smile and say, "Sure, thanks for offering." Noting the grin that brightens her face as I walk alongside her. "In fact, you're way ahead of me. I've yet to get my license, much less my permit."

"I know." She turns in my general direction when she adds, "I know because Paloma told me."

"So that's it." I laugh. "You know Paloma." I shake my head, remembering the time I saw Paloma ushering a girl with a red-tipped cane into a dusty sedan after my first horseback ride with Chay and instantly realizing it was Xotichl. "That explains everything."

"Well, I know you're her granddaughter. I know she was so excited about your coming to stay, she told me all about you, described you in great detail. You've had one glamorous life." She shakes her head and whistles through her teeth. "What was it like growing up on all of those movie sets? Was it as cool as it sounds?"

I hesitate, wavering between answering honestly and giving her the answer she most wants to hear. People always get so excited by the Hollywood thing, assuming it's way more glamorous than it actually is. Eventually settling on some semblance of truth when I say, "It was just life as I knew it. I had nothing else to compare it to." Though still not willing to let her off the hook when I add, "So, how did you know it was me? You know, this morning in the hall?"

She presses her lips together, takes a moment to decide on her answer. "I read energy, which means I don't need to see someone's face to sense what mood they're in. Some call it intuitive vision—some call it blindsight. And I hate to break it to you, Daire, but you definitely exhibited a classic case of new-girl nerves. Your vibes were all over the place." She laughs in a way that urges me to laugh along with her.

"Well, I guess I can't deny that," I say. "But that still doesn't explain how you knew Cade was into me." I study her carefully, figuring the more info I can gather on him, the better. There's so much Paloma hasn't told me.

Noting the way Xotichl's face darkens, the way she turns away, making for the big, iron gate, her cane sweeping before her with newfound urgency. "It's like I said, I can read energy," she tells me, moving three steps ahead before she nods over her shoulder and adds, "Hurry now, our ride's here."

twenty-seven

As it turns out, Xotichl's *ride* is a really cute guy with sandy blond hair and soft brown eyes, driving an old, beater, wood-paneled station wagon that, despite its dilapidated state, turns out to be a welcome change from all the trucks, Jeeps, and SUVs everyone else seems to drive around here.

"This is Daire, the one I told you about," Xotichl tells him as he helps her into the passenger side, while I slide onto the seat just behind them.

"Aw, Paloma's *nieta*," he says, pronouncing the word perfectly, even though he doesn't look the least bit Hispanic. Then again, neither do I, despite the fact that it constitutes a good bit of my bloodline. "I'm Auden, like the poet, named after the poet. So, how was day one? Did Xotichl show you the sights?"

"There are sights?" I joke, aware of the pang in my gut when he leans toward her, brushes her bangs from her eyes, and gazes upon her with such open admiration, I can't help but look away.

It's a shame she can't see it. It's the kind of look most girls can only dream about. But the way she meets it with a smile, the way she leans into his touch, it's clear she wasn't kidding about the blindsight, she doesn't miss a thing. If anything, she's reading the energy of it—of him. The energy so palpable, I can feel it back here.

"How long have you guys known each other?" I ask, trying to get the conversational ball rolling as Auden steers the big boat of a wagon away from the curb and onto the street.

"Forever," he says. "I can't remember a single day without her."

Xotichl laughs, gives his shoulder a playful slap. Head tilted in my direction when she says, "We met last year. It was love at first sight. But unfortunately, my mom doesn't quite see it that way. She doesn't approve."

I look at Auden, taking a quick mental inventory. He's cute, sweet, and obviously lives to breathe the same air as Xotichl—what could possibly be the problem?

"I'm in a band . . . left high school early only to drop out of college . . ." Auden shrugs, his gaze meeting mine in the rearview mirror.

"How old are you?" I ask, having assumed Xotichl was a junior like me, but maybe she's older. Maybe he is too. This town has no shortage of illusions, that's for sure.

"Seventeen—" He starts to continue, but Xotichl butts in.

"For the record, he's a prodigy. Left Milagro at fifteen to go to the university. He's being ridiculously humble," she says, ruffling her hand through his hair.

"I was a full semester into it when I decided it wasn't for me. I love music." He shifts in his seat, looks at me. "I didn't want to *study* music, I wanted to *create* music. Music and Xotichl—that's my life—it's all that I need." He lifts his hand from the wheel, pulls her closer until their shoulders bump together.

"It's all true, except the last part. He loves music more than me," Xotichl says, squealing with delight when he leans in to kiss her, the sudden move causing the car to swerve slightly out of the lane before Auden rights it again.

"Never! You know it's not true, take it back!" he says.

The two of them going at it with banter so cute, it's all I can do to stay quiet and stare out the window. There's just too much love in the room. Or car. Or station wagon. Or whatever. All I know is I've had a rough day, and while I'm happy to know that not everyone is as miserable as I am, I'm more than ready to be free of them.

"Daire's had a bad day," Xotichl tells him, pushing him back toward his side. "We need to tone it down, show a little sensitivity for her mood. She had an unfortunate run-in with the Cruel Crew."

"Aw, the Three Faces of Evil," Auden says, voice sympathetic when he adds, "That bites. Hope you kicked some Cruel Crew ass? You look like you could take 'em." He peers at me again. "Well, the minions for sure, but maybe not Lita. You're on the skinny side; Paloma got you on the same vegetarian diet she's got my flower on?"

I squint, wondering why Paloma is telling Xotichl what to eat. I thought that sort of thing was reserved just for me.

"I've been seeing Paloma for a while, now," Xotichl says, answering the question I didn't yet voice. "She's nothing short of a miracle worker. You're so lucky to have her."

I nod, neither confirming nor denying. I love Paloma. She's helped me, cured me of the hallucinations, given me the keys to a world I never imagined existed. Though I'm not always sure that's a good thing. Truth is, I was happier before the visions took over, before I got involved in any of this. My life was way less complicated back then.

A moment later, Auden pulls before the big blue gate, and Xotichl is turning in her seat, saying, "Auden's band, Epitaph, is playing tonight at the Rabbit Hole and I—or rather, *we*—want you to come."

The Rabbit Hole.

Paloma did say I'd have to return at some point, though I'm not sure I'm ready just yet. If the way I handled day one at Milagro is any indication, I have a long way to go 'til I'm ready to take on something like that.

They're waiting for an answer. And knowing I need to say something, that Xotichl will not move on until I reply, I mumble, "I don't know . . . I'll have to check with Paloma . . ."

"Of course," Xotichl says, already turning away. "First set's at eight—see you then."

twenty-eight

I head into the house. Doing my best to keep quiet in case Paloma's with a client, I drop my bag onto my desk and flop onto my bed, reviewing the day's events, but only for a moment, before I push them away.

All things considered, it was a bigger failure than even I thought it would be.

Paloma was confident.

Chay reassuring.

While I tried to keep my hopes somewhere within the realm of realistic, if not reasonable.

Still, as skeptical as I was, I truly thought I'd glide under the radar. I never imagined I'd be labeled a freak right from the start—only to go on to prove it to the one boy who was nice to me, even offered to lunch with me (in an indirect way).

Though it's not like it matters. The link to his brother, the fact that they're twins—identical at that—instantly places him in the no-fly zone, no matter how cute he may be.

I kick off my shoes—a pair of soft black ankle boots I picked up in Spain—knowing I should make a stab at doing my homework but ruling it out just as quickly. Fact is, I've already read the assigned book for English, and I solved the math equations well before I left class. As far as history and science are concerned, I'm pretty sure I can wing it. Turns out I learned more in Internet school than I realized. Either that or my new school is completely pathetic.

I haul myself up, lean back against my headboard, and decide to work on something more useful, like magick. Merging my energy with the dream catcher that hangs over the window, focusing hard as I *feel* the lilt of its feathers, the light *sway* of its fringe—watching as it lifts itself from the hook, hovers for a moment, and then makes its way toward me . . .

"*Nieta?*" Paloma knocks once before opening the door and peering inside, her sudden arrival prompting me to slam the dream catcher between my palms and shove it deep under my pillow where she can't see it.

My breath coming too fast, my cheeks flushing red, having no good reason to hide it from her, and yet doing so anyway.

Though I should've known better. Paloma's gaze is all-seeing. Glancing between the empty hook over the sill and me, she says "So, tell me, how was your first day at school?"

I sigh. Shake my head. My eyes meeting hers when I say, "Terrible." Figuring there's no use lying, no point in pouring a thick coating of sugar over it. But just after I've said it, I realize the word may have been a bit overstated. It wasn't *all* bad. While Xotichl and Auden were definitely a little heavy on the lovefest— meeting them was still one of the brighter spots.

The other bright spot was Dace, though I'm not quite ready to admit that—or at least not in that way.

Paloma sits beside me, the mattress dipping ever so slightly under the weight of her tiny frame. "So, your first day was so horrible you chose to fortify your ego with magick?" She thrusts her hand before me, demanding the return of the dream catcher we both know I hid. And though her words seem judgmental on the surface, her eyes tell a whole other story—they're brimming with compassion, letting me know she understands all too well.

I slip my fingers under the pillow and hand over the goods, watching as she moves toward the window and puts the dream catcher back in its place, as I say, "I met Cade. Again."

She nods. Flicks a finger against the dream catcher's fringe, watching it sway back and forth. "And?" She turns to face me.

"*And,* if I didn't know better, I'd think he was devastatingly handsome and utterly charming. I'd think I was the luckiest girl in the world to have a boy like that notice me. But since I do know better, he just gives me the creeps."

"Good." She nods. "No matter what happens, you must never forget that."

I gaze down at my hands. Pick at a loose string on my blanket. "I met Dace too, and he's just like he is in the dreams. And every time I try to get an impression of him . . ."

Paloma returns to the bed, where she sits at the foot.

"Well, the impression is always . . . *good.* It's the opposite of Cade, and I need to know more about him. We have a class together, so there's no way to avoid him, though I'm not sure how to handle him."

She nods, folds her hands in her lap, eyes flashing when she says, "Dace is *not* your enemy." She pauses, allowing the words to sink in. "The reason I warned you about Cade and not Dace is because Cade is the one you must watch. Don't ever forget that, *nieta.* And never confuse the two, no matter what." She rubs her hands over her dress, fidgets with the hem, then after rising from the bed, she heads for the dresser, where she stands before Django's picture and says, "I didn't tell you earlier because . . ."

I clutch my pillow and wait—wait for something to happen, for some big revelation. But for a while anyway, all I get is a view of her back.

"They're only identical on the surface." She sighs, the sound heavy and deep, belying some hidden meaning she's not sure she'll reveal. "They were raised separately, didn't meet until their first year of high school. Cade grew up with his father, Leandro—while Dace was raised by his mother, Chepi. They've had very different upbringings, which makes for very different views of the world."

"Why were they raised separately? Why didn't they at least know about each other? This town is so tiny—how's that even possible?" I ask, knowing she's hiding something, though I can't imagine why, much less what.

She clasps and unclasps her hands, debating whether or not to tell me, then she takes a deep breath and says, "Dace grew up on the reservation—he and Chepi rarely left—while Cade lived in town. His father's family, the Richters, are quite wealthy, they own most of the businesses here and run all the public services, not to mention his father's been mayor for many, many years. Chepi had nothing to do with their world. When she found herself pregnant with the twins, she was the beautiful young daughter of a well-respected medicine man named Jolon—a truly revered, much-sought-after healer, who was said to work miracles and have a direct link to the divine."

"So, let me get this straight." I look at her. "Chepi, the good girl, decides to hook up with Leandro, the bad boy—trouble ensues—she gets knocked up—the news devastates her father who held such high hopes for her . . ." I frown, trying not to judge, but it sounds like the Django and Jennika story. Except Jennika was never what you'd call *good*, and Django wasn't all that *bad*; still, the stories aren't without their similarities.

But before I can finish, Paloma's already shaking her head, saying, "No, *nieta*, it's not nearly as simple as that. You see, Chepi was very young, very innocent, and very devoted to Jolon. She never would've gone off with Leandro on her own. She was studying as Jolon's apprentice, and many say she showed great promise. Everyone assumed she'd succeed him someday—but Leandro interfered, making sure to derail all their plans." She looks at me, gaze clouded with memory. "Leandro is very much the opposite of Jolon. He's a dangerous sorcerer who hails from a long line of them. The Santoses have been battling the Richters for years . . . centuries really, and not always here. While we made very good progress for a very long time, while we were able to subdue them and keep them in line, in more recent years, with the arrival of Leandro, things have changed for the worse. They're no longer happy with just amassing their fortune—their ambitions extend far beyond that. They're changing this town. It wasn't always so *depressed*, like it is now. It used to be a good match for its name—if you can imagine such a thing. But over the past few decades it's becoming increasingly difficult to keep them contained. They've messed with so many minds—the townspeople feel alternately awed by them and indebted to them. And without Django's help, I'm afraid I'm no match for them on my own, their ranks are too strong." She takes a deep breath—runs both hands over the lap of her dress. "Anyway, Leandro was determined to use Chepi for his own sordid purposes, and so, on the night of *Día de los Muertos,* he set out to find her, and from that moment on, life as she knew it was over."

Reading my look of confusion, she says, "The Day of the Dead, *nieta.* It's a ritual that's been celebrated for thousands of years, traced all the way back to the Aztecs. It's a time when the veil between the living and dead is lifted, as well as a time to honor all those who've passed. Here in Enchantment, we celebrate it in place of Halloween, and the whole town takes part. People don masks resembling skulls—they head to cemeteries where they decorate the graves with marigolds, beads, and old photos. And they remain by those graves throughout the night—dancing, drinking, turning the dirt, and communing with their deceased loved ones. Though lately, over the last several years, many have abandoned the graveyards in favor of the Rabbit Hole, which, as you know, the Richters own."

I stare at her wide-eyed, urging her to continue. It's the first I've ever heard of it, and I'm fascinated by the idea.

"There was a time when death wasn't viewed so much as the end of life but rather a continuation of life. It was life that was regarded as a brief fleeting dream, while death allowed one to truly wake up. The Bone Keeper presides over the festival. She rules the lowest level of the Lowerworld where she keeps watch over the bones. They say she has a skull for a face, wears a skirt made of serpents, and her mouth is extra wide in order to feed off the stars during the day. And yet, despite my numerous journeys to the Lowerworld, I have yet to run into her. But maybe you will, *nieta,* who knows?"

"A skull face, a snake skirt, and a steady diet of stars?" I shake my head and balk. "No thanks, I'd prefer to avoid her if it's okay with you."

"You don't always get the journey you want, *nieta.* Though you always get the journey you need," she says—yet another sage statement in a collection of many.

"You paraphrasing Mick Jagger now?" I laugh. It feels good to laugh, lessens the creepiness of her story.

Paloma grins, but it's not long before she tucks a leg underneath her and says, "Now, back to Chepi—while she had no interest in Leandro, no interest in *hooking up with bad boys* as you put it," she winks at me, "she was no match for Leandro, whose proficiency in the black arts is unrivaled. The Richters have misused the power of the Day of the Dead for centuries. They don't so much honor and commune with their relatives as *resurrect* them."

I lean toward her, chin tucked to my knees, eyes practically popped from their sockets.

"Oh, not for long, *nieta,* and not physically. They're not necromancers, or at least not yet, anyway. It's more like they call upon the energy of the dead and infuse themselves with the dark power of their lineage—an effect that lasts a few days at best. But, as it turns out, on that day, it proved enough. And that, coupled with Leandro's ability to alter perception, is what made it so easy for him to seduce Chepi. He knew about the powerful magick that flowed through her bloodline, and he was desperate to harness it and merge it with his. The Richters' power was beginning to falter. While they've never had access to the Upperworld, on the occasions they've managed to breach the Lowerworld, they were quick to corrupt it along with the spirit animals, which caused chaos to reign here in the Middleworld, leaving people unprotected, easily misled—becoming both victims and supporters of insane, corrupt leaders. The rise of Atilla the Hun, Vlad the Impaler, Stalin, Robespierre, Idi Amin, Pol Pot, Hitler . . ." She looks in my direction, but her gaze remains far away. "It can all be traced to the Richters' dark influence in the Lowerworld, and it took great sacrifice on behalf of Seekers and shamans everywhere to evict them. The Lowerworld, just like the Upperworld, is populated by loving, compassionate beings that guide us and aid us without our even realizing. We are dependent on their well-being and wisdom in more ways than we know. It's only the Middleworld that contains beings that both help us and harm us."

It's not until she pauses that I realize I've been holding my breath, doing my best to take it all in and try to make sense of it.

"And so, desperate to beef up their ranks, Leandro purposely set out to father a son whose blood would run thick with the magick of both sides, hoping that would enable him to infiltrate the other worlds so long denied him. Chepi didn't stand a chance— he kept her captive for the entire ceremony—and when she awoke, she was nude, battered, and her body was covered in black-magick symbols."

I'm speechless, haunted by the images that flare in my head. Remembering the night I met Leandro in the office at the Rabbit Hole, the creepy impression I got when he caught my hand in his.

"Leandro wasn't looking for just any son, he wanted a son

with a soul even darker than his own. Knowing the soul contains equal parts light and dark—that a person's life story and the sort of nurturing they receive often determines which side emerges as the dominant one—he set out to dissect the child's soul right from the start. He called upon his long-deceased ancestors to aid him, worked terrible magick and ritual to split the soul and nurture the dark part at the expense of the good. Though, in the end, things didn't go quite as planned. Instead of giving birth to one black-hearted son, Chepi gave birth to twins, one with a light soul and one with a dark one."

My mind spins with the news—unable to think of one good response.

Twins.

One evil. One good.

The stuff of myth—only in this case it's real.

"Okay," I say, struggling to understand. "But if Chepi's dad, Jolon, was so powerful, why didn't he stop it?"

Paloma nods as though she was expecting the question. Wasting no time in replying, she says, "When Chepi arrived home disheveled and disoriented, Jolon was distraught to find his beloved daughter violated and used in that way. Little did he know, but Leandro was waiting nearby, and he used that moment of weakness to penetrate and alter Jolon's perception—something he was never able to accomplish before. Some claim Leandro terrorized Jolon with images of the future, the havoc his grandson would wreak. All I know for sure is that Jolon didn't survive. He dropped dead of a heart attack, leaving poor Chepi an orphan. When Leandro learned he'd produced twins, there was no doubt which one he favored. He immediately took custody of Cade, warning Chepi that if she tried to fight him, tried to get the boy back, he'd take Dace as well. And so Chepi turned her attentions to Dace, while turning her back on the healing, and magick, and all that Jolon had taught her. Claiming she'd lost her gift along with her faith—that she was good to no one, but she'd try to be good to her son. To support herself, she began making beautiful turquoise jewelry she sells in the square. Hers is a very sad story, *nieta*. She refuses to forgive herself for something that was never her fault."

"So, how is it the boys never met?" I ask, my head spinning with the story she weaves.

"Dace didn't leave the reservation until his teens when he decided he wanted to attend Milagro, and Chepi, tired of fighting him, knowing she couldn't shelter him forever, finally consented. The day before he left, she confided the truth, told him about the brother he never knew. Though I doubt she told him the full truth. She can barely admit it to herself. And I can't see how it would do Dace any good to know his true origins."

I grow silent, not quite knowing what to make of it. Remembering the day at the gas station, the older woman with the beautiful turquoise jewelry, cloaked in deep sadness, and I've no doubt it was Dace's mom, Chepi.

"Now that I've revealed this to you, you must never repeat it. Not to anyone, and certainly never to Dace. Someday he may learn on his own, but it's not our place to intervene. The boy is truly a pure and beautiful soul. He is no threat to you. I wish nothing but the best for him."

Beautiful—no argument there.

"And you must never confuse the two. You must never allow Cade to trick you into thinking he's his brother, or vice versa. You must find a way to set them apart—you mentioned the eyes?"

I nod, picturing them in my head. "They're almost exactly the same, except Cade's absorb light, while Dace's reflect it."

Paloma clasps her hands to her chest, her face glowing with excitement. "You're the only one who's ever been able to see that, *nieta*. And now that you know it, you must never forget it. When in doubt, seek the eyes—no matter what guise they wear, their true nature remains. They will never lead you astray."

I exhale slowly and deeply, my head spinning with everything I just learned, when Paloma places her hand on my knee and says, "And now, sweet *nieta*, seeing as how you've managed to teach yourself telekinesis without my instruction, I suspect it is time for you to learn something far more exciting, and I see no further need to delay. So tell me, are you ready to fly?"

twenty-nine

Paloma leads me to the yard tucked away in the back, which, no matter how much time I've spent here, I've visited only once, and even then it was brief. But now, as we make our way down the stone path, I can't help but gawk at its sheer size and scope—not to mention how fragrant and lush the plants are, considering we're well into fall.

The yard seems to sprawl forever, consisting of carefully designated areas for the healing herbs she uses in her clients' therapies and the organic vegetables we eat for dinner. There's even a space brimming with beautiful, fat, blooming flowers sitting adjacent to another area reserved especially for her hybrid experiments, where all sorts of odd, misshapen plants sprout from the earth.

She murmurs in Spanish, her voice soft and lilting, her fingertips grazing over everything she passes. It's a song I've heard her sing on other occasions, only now I recognize it as her garden song—the one that encourages the plants to stay strong and thrive, to reach toward the light, even when there appears to be none.

But the lyrics belong only to her. They've yet to reveal themselves to me. Probably because my thumb has always been more brown than green. And though Paloma promises to remedy that, it's usually followed by, *"First things first! There is still so much to teach you, nieta, and so little time."*

It's that last part that bothers me: *So little time.*

It's not like she's old. Statistically speaking, she should have several more decades ahead of her, at least. But between the nose-bleeds and blood-spewing cough, I can't help but worry about the state of her health. Yet every time I ask her about it, she just waves the subject away, tells me she's fine, and moves on to something else.

I watch her lead the way, her step light, her long dark braid swaying behind her, as I say, "I met Xotichl."

Paloma turns, a smile lighting her face. "Aw, Xotichl. A girl who is sweet, and mischievous, and wise beyond her years. Which of those faces did she share with you, *nieta*?"

I think for a moment, then I look at her and say, "Pretty much all of them. She says she's a client of yours—she's not sick, is she?"

Paloma shakes her head, and I'm surprised by the flood of relief that washes over me.

"While the content of our meetings are confidential, I can say that Xotichl has the rare ability to see what most sighted people miss. What she lacks in outer vision, she makes up for in inner vision—her insight is unsurpassed." Paloma nods, leans down to admire a particularly fragrant bloom that I can smell from where I stand. "She's unmoved by the usual superficial things most people get too caught up in to look any deeper. And without that sort of distraction, she's able to get right to the heart of the matter—to read the true energy behind a person's actions and words. Which is one of the reasons she's always remained unswayed by the Richters. They're unable to reach her, unable to alter her perception. She is a rare child indeed and has a great sense of humor. I'm sure she had quite a bit of fun at your expense. Though I have to admit, I supplied her with all the information she needed. I know you had a rough day, I hope you won't hold it against her?"

I think about our strange first encounter in the hallway and quickly dismiss Paloma's concern. "Her boyfriend, Auden, drove me home. They invited me to meet them at the Rabbit Hole tonight to see his band, but . . . I don't know. I'm not sure I'm up for it, much less ready to go back to that place—or at least not just yet anyway."

Paloma gestures for me to take a seat on the mosaic tiled bench that sits adjacent to the birdbath, saying, "You're right, *nieta*. You are not quite ready yet. But by the end of our lesson, you will be."

I squint, wondering what she could possibly teach me in the next few hours that'll prepare me to return to the place where I nearly lost my mind, not to mention my life. Surely she was speaking in metaphors when she asked if I was ready to fly?

"I'm going to teach you to hop with the rabbits, to slither with the snakes, to run with the horses, to crawl with the scorpions, and to fly with the ravens. And you'll be surprised to find that it's so much easier than you think."

My eyes light on hers, not knowing which part to believe, if any. It seems like such an impossible feat, and I highly doubt I'll succeed.

"Much like you merged your energy with the energy of the dream catcher to lift it off its hook and bring it to you—you will now practice merging your energy with true living spirit—with flesh-and-blood creatures—in order to share their experience."

"You mean, like . . . *shape-shifting*?" I ask, already dead set against it. What if I get stuck? What if I get lost and can't find my way back? I like being a girl. I have no desire to live out the rest of my life as a lizard, a scorpion, or anything else.

Paloma laughs, her voice soft and reassuring, as she says, "No, *nieta*. You will not become them, but rather you will experience what it's like to be them. You will learn to see what they see, experience what they experience. It's a skill steeped in much magick and mysticism—one that normally comes much later in the training, but you're ready right now. I can feel it. It is time for you to begin."

I don't say a word. I have so many questions, I don't know which to ask first.

Paloma turns, her gaze surveying the yard, moving past the empty stall waiting for Kachina's arrival, and landing on the first animal she sees, which happens to be a mangy white cat carefully picking its way across the thick adobe wall.

She gestures toward it, her voice a mere whisper when she says, "Concentrate. Focus. Picture him for what he *truly* is—not just an underfed feline with matted white fur but rather a mass of vibrating energy that's assembled itself into that form. He is energy just as you are energy, just as your thoughts and words are energy too." She sneaks a peek and continues. "Now, focus harder. Block out everything around you, until it's just you, and the cat, with nothing standing between you, no barriers of any kind. Merge into his energy stream, delve into his experience. Go ahead, *nieta*, you are perfectly safe. Let your energy blend, and mix, and merge. Allow your soul to ride tandem with his."

I do as she says. Staring at the cat for so long everything around me goes dark. Watching as he stops, sits, lifts a delicate paw to his mouth in order to clean it with his sandpaper tongue. And the next thing I know, I'm *in*. It's like I've *become* him. My energy merging with his until I'm deep inside his experience.

I'm light.

Fluid.

Graceful and agile in a way I've never known—never could've imagined.

Crossing the wall with my tail pitched high, I stop in midstep, alerted to some kind of change, aware that something's intruded, though it's only a moment before I realize the intruder is *me*.

I rise up on my paws and arch my back high, enjoying the stretch and holding the pose for a few seconds more before I set

off again. Moving with such delicacy and finesse, I'm absolutely
giddy with the feel of it.

Then, without any warning, his body springs forward as he
leaps away from the wall and lands out of sight. Our connection
so suddenly severed, I collapse on the bench in a heap.

Paloma stands before me, hands clasped over her heart, ex-
claiming, "Wonderful, *nieta*! You blended your essence with his,
I could see it on your face. You became one with him! Tell me,
what did you experience?"

I take a moment to settle myself, find the right words. "I felt
peaceful . . . and light. I felt a deep profound joy at being alive . . .
I felt all of his deep-seated instincts that guided him to do what he
does . . . and I was painfully aware of the deep stirrings of hunger." I look at her, push my hair from my eyes. "I think we should
leave him some food so he doesn't always have to hunt the fields
and fend for himself."

Paloma sits beside me, slips an arm around my shoulders, and
says, "You are very kindhearted, *nieta*. Consider it done. Though I
warn you, you will never get rid of him once you start feeding him."

I shrug. Sounds good to me. For someone who was never allowed a pet, I'm building up quite the menagerie now with my
horse and my cat.

After merging my energy with a spider, a lizard, and another
cat—this one gray and quite fat, which pretty much covers the
variety of wildlife found in Paloma's yard—it's time to fly with
the birds.

"It's basically the same thing," she tells me. "But as you'll soon
see, it is very exhilarating, which is why it's always saved for last.
One needs to work their way up to such an experience. Though
seeing as you are a daughter of the wind, a Wind Dancer as it
were, guided by Raven, you are likely to soar ever higher. Which
is why I wanted to ensure you were fully prepared before we pro-
gressed to this step. So, what do you say—are you ready?"

I nod. I'm more than ready. I can't wait to get off the ground and soar through the clouds—or at the very least, flit from tree to tree.

Paloma's eyes narrow, performing a quick survey of the land. Her arm lifting, gesturing toward a large, shiny black raven perched on a nearby branch.

"This is no accident." She nods, turning toward me. "He is here for a reason. He senses who you are—knows he shares the bloodline of your spirit animal, and he is ready for you to make the bond. While he should not be mistaken for your actual spirit animal—the raven you met in the Lowerworld as well as the cave—he is still considered a brother, as are all ravens that inhabit the Middleworld. Crows are also part of the family—your arrival was heralded by them. Along with the other things I've already told you, Raven is a messenger of the spirit realm—the things he will show you can shift your life dramatically. He will teach you to venture into the dark in order to bring forth the light. And in some legends it is said he stole the sunlight from Coyote who was determined to keep the world shrouded in darkness—a legend that happens to be true, as it was during Valentina's time, and she made sure to document it in some writings I will one day share with you. Though, as you well know, everything is cyclical, *nieta,* and it was just a matter of time before El Coyote regrouped and came back stronger than ever . . ." She picks at the hem of her dress, as her gaze joins her thoughts on a long-distance journey. Then shaking her head, she returns to me and says, "Anyway, enough of that—now it is time for you to join him, to soar with the raven."

Just like I did with the cats, the lizard, and the rest, I narrow my gaze until I see only him, and a moment later it clicks. With a minimum of effort we've merged, and when the raven springs from his perch and soars overhead, I'm soaring right along with him. The experience so freeing, so exhilarating, it's like every cell in my body is vibrating with the pure life force of his energy.

I gaze down upon treetops. Get a bird's-eye view (literally!) of my neighbors' roofs. I am the surveyor of everything. My eyes see all. Tracking the white cat I will soon claim as a pet, I watch as he stalks his prey, a small gray field mouse, then move on well before he can leap.

I soar above rutted dirt roads, over small adobe homes with rusted-out cars in the yards. Wishing we could soar all the way to the mountains, the Sangre de Cristo range that looms in the distance, but the raven has other plans. And while I'm pretty sure I could steer him, if not convince him, there's something specific he wants me to see.

We arc left, dipping lower, gliding just shy of the telephone wires, before stopping on the shelter of the bus stop just opposite the Rabbit Hole. And it's then that I realize what's really happening here—while my body remains with Paloma, by merging my energy with the raven's, I can watch the goings-on in various locations—see what he sees, no matter the distance.

We flit closer, the raven and me landing on a light post overlooking the alleyway. Seeing Auden's station wagon parked near the back door as he and his bandmates haul equipment into the club.

My interest further piqued when Dace exits through that same door, lugging two heavy trash bags, one in each hand, stopping to allow passage for Auden's bandmates, before making his way down the alleyway. Arms flexing from the weight of the bags, gait confident and long, moving in a way that makes the diminishing sunlight seem to shimmer around him.

I note every detail. Track every move. Torn between feelings of exhilaration and shame for spying this way. Repeating Paloma's words in my head:

He's not your enemy—not like the other Richters—his soul is good and pure.

He stands before the Dumpster, taking a moment to survey the alley, ensure no one's watching, before he closes his eyes, lets go of the bags, and I stare in astonishment as they leap from his hands and dunk straight into the large metal bin.

Guess I'm not the only one around here who enjoys a little tele-kinesis.

He wipes his palms down the sides of his apron and makes for a redbrick building, where he pulls his phone from his pocket, inserts his earbuds, and shutters his eyes as he leans against the wall and listens to a melody that leaves him looking so peaceful and dreamy, I'm tempted to land on his shoulder and listen in too.

I flit from my perch, desperate for a better view. Using the raven's eyes to soak in the casual slant of Dace's shoulders, the gleam of his hair falling down the front of his tee, the long, lean line of his body, the way his apron dips low at his waist and skims over his thighs. Content with watching him for as long as it lasts, regretting the moment he sighs, pushes away from the wall, and heads back.

I follow his lead, careful to keep close to the buildings, remain unobtrusive, unseen. Tracking him all the way to the back door of the club, where Auden and his bandmates have been replaced by the waitress who served me the last time I was here.

She stands in the doorway, posture stooped, arms folded across her chest, while Cade looms before her, berating her in a way that leaves her wincing in shame.

I creep closer, wondering if I should do something to stop him, jab my beak into those creepy blue eyes—when Dace moves in and handles it for me in a less violent way.

He slips an arm around her, murmuring soft words of comfort, as he fixes a hard stare on his brother, and says, "That's enough."

Cade glares. Dismisses his brother with a wave of his hand. "Stay out of it, Whitefeather. This is none of your business," he snaps, returning to the waitress, picking up where he left off, when Dace interferes once again.

"You've made it my business," Dace says, turning to the waitress and ushering her into the club.

Her sudden departure causing Cade to erupt in fury when he shouts, "You've no right to interfere!"

Dace lifts his shoulders, shoves his hands into his pockets, and says, "She works hard, you need to cut her some slack."

"Who the hell are you to tell me what to do?" Cade's voice bearing the same outrage he wears on his face. "Unless you've decided to change your last name to Richter, I don't see how you have any say in it. You're nothing more than hired help around here. Never forget that."

Dace stands before him, not the least bit intimidated. "You'd get a lot more out of your employees if you treated them with a little respect," he says, not so much as flinching when Cade steps forward, face fully inflamed.

"What gives you the right to tell me how to run *my* business—huh?" His hands curl to fists as he reaches for his brother, only to have Leandro appear in the doorway, his large form crowding the space.

"*Your* business?" He stares hard at his favored son, the one he engineered to his exact specifications. "Don't you think you're getting a bit ahead of yourself?" He grips Cade's shoulder and yanks him away from Dace. "Stop making trouble. Leave your brother alone. I mean it, Cade, do not make me warn you again." He nods at Dace, motions him through the door, returning to Cade, voice lowered when he says, "I don't like him any more than you do, but your actions only prove that you're nowhere near ready to take over this business or any other business. It's time you learn a little diplomacy."

He heads inside, leaving Cade to grapple with his words—grapple with an anger so intense, so palpable, it transforms him into the blazing-eyed, snake-tongued, demon boy I know him to be.

The effect lasting only a moment, yet long enough to shock me in a way that causes the delicate balance of energy to shift. So when the raven springs from the roof and soars toward the heavens—he goes without me. Leaving me an inert, glassy-eyed mess, slumped over a bench in Paloma's backyard.

thirty

"Isn't this kind of weird?" I glance at Paloma through the bathroom mirror. "You know, the grandmother urging the granddaughter to go clubbing, and even offering to drive her?"

Paloma forces a smile, as though she's in on the joke, but the way it fails to reach her eyes tells me her mind is preoccupied with a new set of worries.

"What is it?" I take a moment to face her, mascara wand hovering before me.

"I'm afraid this isn't just about going clubbing with your friends, *nieta*." She meets my gaze with a look of regret. "While I want you to have fun with Xotichl and Auden, you should know that there's much more at stake than listening to music and enjoying yourself."

I nod, waiting for her to reveal the agenda. But Paloma being Paloma—a person who likes to dole it out slowly—she turns her focus to fussing with her sky-blue cardigan instead. Taking way too long to get it draped over her shoulders *just so*, despite the fact that she rarely wears it inside. It's a delay tactic, no getting around it, but I decide not to push it and return to coating my lashes the way Jennika taught me—swiping the brush horizontally at the base, then nudging it vertically all the way to the tips.

"As I mentioned before, Enchantment is a place of many vortexes that provide portals that lead to the various worlds," Paloma says in a voice that's dry and tight. "But what I didn't tell you, is that there's one at the Rabbit Hole as well. The Rabbit Hole holds many secrets, though their portal is not only difficult to find but also well guarded. Only the most gifted Seekers have been able to locate it—though no Seeker has ever been able to enter."

I shoot her an uneasy look, wondering if that's what she's expecting me to do—not only find it but enter it too. If that's the plan, then I'm sorry to say that kind of espionage is way out of my league.

"Make no mistake, *nieta,* I don't ask you to access it tonight. In fact, I strictly forbid it," she says, her hands clasping as her gaze locks on mine. "Even if you are able to find it, under no circumstances are you to enter. You're not yet ready, and there will be plenty of time for that later. For now, all I ask is that you try to locate it, then report back once you've succeeded."

I take a deep breath, turning to face myself again. My hair is lank and straight, and that's the way it'll stay; I'm not one for fluff and curls. And after enhancing my eyes with dark liner and a third coat of mascara, I add a hint of peach blush at my cheeks, and complete the look with my usual dab of lip salve. No need to overdo it. No need to look like I'm trying too hard to impress.

I return to Paloma, leaning against the counter when I say, "Okay, so, how do you suggest I do that? How will I recognize it? What does a portal even look like? And didn't you say that it's guarded? So how am I supposed to get anywhere near it?" The second the words are out, my eyes bulge in horror when I realize I sound exactly like Jennika—shooting a full stream of questions, without once pausing for breath. Which isn't exactly one of the traits I'd hoped to inherit.

"I guess it's safest to say that you'll know it when you see it. I'm afraid there is no set standard for what a vortex looks like.

Sometimes you know it by the way the air grows suddenly hazy and shimmery—like you saw in Morocco. Other times, it's more dense, greasy, and bleary looking. Sometimes, it's more of a feeling—a perceptible rise in energy—as though the area is vibrating higher and faster than anywhere else. In that case, you will often notice the entire area affected as well. Twisted Juniper tree branches are always a good indication," she says, her words reminding me of the time I rode on the reservation with Chay, when I saw a twisted juniper tree, and he wouldn't let me get anywhere near it, said I wasn't ready just yet. But I don't mention it to Paloma, I just nod for her to continue.

"What you need to understand is that you can't hear anything, feel anything, or see anything unless you focus on it with intent." She pauses, the blank look on my face prompting her to explain. "Right now you're focused on me. You're looking at me, listening to me, struggling to understand me—" She flashes a grin. "And you're successful in this endeavor because I am already a solid part of your consciousness. I already exist within the field of all the things that you know and have come to expect of the world. But now that you realize there is more to this world than you thought—now that you know that this particular Middleworld dimension is just one of many and that there are vortexes and portals that lead to other worlds, and other dimensions within those worlds—it won't be long before you'll become proficient enough to locate them easily. But for now, for tonight, all I ask is that you take a good look around, stay alert, and if you do notice something that appears out of the norm, take careful note, observe the area well, then get yourself out as quickly as possible."

I fumble with the strap on my watch, remembering the first and last times I visited the Rabbit Hole. How the whole place seemed odd, off, and definitely out of the norm. From the bleary-eyed patrons at the bar, to the bartenders, bouncers, and waitstaff who worked there, and now I understand that they're all under the spell of the Richters.

"The place is rigged with surveillance cameras," I say, my eyes meeting Paloma's. "Right before I left, I went into an office where I saw Cade monitoring the entire building, inside and out, from a large set of screens. It won't be easy to poke around in there. No matter where I go, they'll be able to watch me. And believe me, once they realize I've entered the premises, they'll be watching for sure. There's no way I can sneak under their radar."

But despite all I've said, Paloma meets my words with a smile. "But you *will* sneak under their radar, *nieta*. And you'll do so quite easily, with very little effort, as you will soon see. They won't even notice you, I promise you that."

I peer at her, having no idea what she's getting at, and not sure I want to. "So . . . you've got an invisibility cloak for me to wear?" I say, hoping the joke will calm my nerves, and it does. But only until she reaches into the side pocket of her dress and retrieves a small glass jar with tiny holes poked in the lid and an unhappy cockroach inside.

"Much like you merged your energy with the cat, and the lizard, and the spider, and the raven—when you get to the club, you will go into the bathroom, find an empty stall, and you will merge your energy with this cockroach, which will allow you to get a good look around without getting noticed."

"A *cockroach*?" I glance between the jar and her. There's no way. The mere thought makes my skin crawl. "Seriously. *La cucaracha*?" I say, using up all the Spanish I know.

"Yes, *nieta*." She grins. "And while I'm sure there is no shortage of them at the Rabbit Hole, in this case, we just can't take the chance that they run a much cleaner establishment than I suspect. So, I'm afraid you'll have to bring your own."

She hands me the jar, and even though I can hardly wrap my head around what's being asked of me, I find myself taking it with less hesitation than I ever would've thought. After checking the lid and making sure it's screwed on good and tight, I tuck the jar deep into my bag, heave it onto my shoulder, and say, "So, out of all the vortexes and portals in Enchantment, what makes this one so important?"

Paloma faces the mirror, assessing her reflection as she pulls her cardigan tightly around her, then turning away well before she can spot the small pool of blood gathering at the corner of her nose. She looks at me and says, "Because that's where the secret of their strength lies. If you can locate it and, eventually, breach it, you can stop them forever."

thirty-one

After slipping on the same dark skinny jeans I wore to school—the only ones spared the fate of Paloma's scissors, intent on making room for my cast, I add a clingy, hip-grazing, black tank top, my favorite black ankle boots, a large pair of silver hoop earrings, and, of course, my olive-green army jacket. Arranging my soft buckskin pouch inside my clothes, where it rests against my skin, I'm just exiting my room and careening down the hall, when Paloma steps before me.

"Here, *nieta,* you will need this." She offers two worn and crumpled twenties, but I'm quick to wave them away. I can't take her money. From what I can tell there's not a lot of it, and it doesn't feel right.

She sighs, tucks it into her pocket, and leads me outside to her Jeep. And for all the talk and excitement we engaged in from the moment I got home from school, I'm surprised to find how quiet we are for most of the ride into town. It's only when she brakes at a stoplight just a half block away from the Rabbit Hole, and reaches for a fresh tissue to dab away the bright spots of blood accumulating at her nose, that I say, "Paloma, about the nosebleeds—"

But just like every other time I've mentioned it, she's quick to silence me. Her foot moving from the brake to the gas when she says, "When you're ready to leave, Chay and I will be happy to come get you, all you have to do is call. And if you fail to find the portal and want to stay late and have fun, that's okay too. I'm sure Auden or Xotichl will find you a ride, they're good kids."

She stops before the club, but I make no move to leave. Not until she tells me, once and for all, just what the heck is going on with her.

But, as usual, she senses my mood and turns in her seat, placing her hand over mine, giving it a nice, reassuring squeeze as she says, "Now go, *nieta.*" Her tone along with her gaze signaling she has no intention of answering my questions, so I might as well get on with it. Softening a bit when she adds, "And try to have some fun—you've certainly earned it."

I sigh, wishing she'd confide in me. But knowing there's no point in pushing it, I hop out of the Jeep and make my way down the alleyway to the side door, thinking how different the place looks from the other two times I was here. First as a terrified, hallucinating, confused train wreck of a girl, which only served in making everything appear dark, foreboding, scary, and sinister. Then, just a few hours earlier, when I saw it through the eyes of the raven—when it seemed almost ordinary, mundane, boring even. Though that's what the Richters want you to see. It's like Paloma said, now that I'm trained as a Seeker, now that I know the truth about the world, I definitely get the the sense of something much darker lurking beneath.

I head for the door, edging my way toward the front of the line, unable to keep a grin from slipping onto my face when the bouncer stamps my hand with the same stamp they used the first time I visited: a cartoon coyote with gleaming red eyes.

El Coyoté, it's time to meet a new generation of Seeker.

My bravado lasting all of ten seconds, until I step inside and the first thing I see is Lita and the rest of the Cruel Crew, as Xotichl called them, hovering just steps from the door.

But instead of the usual sneers I expect, I'm met by three pairs of narrowed, interested eyes that carefully track my progress as I make my way past the bar, through a maze of crowded tables and chairs, all the way to the front of the stage where Xotichl stands with her eyes squeezed shut, palms pressed flat against one of the speakers, as Auden runs through a series of sound checks.

"You made it." She smiles, eyes still closed, head turning toward me.

"I did indeed," I say, wondering what it is that she's doing, but she tells me well before I can ask.

"I can see the music's energy." She opens her eyes, though her gaze remains unfocused, far away.

"You can . . . *see* it?" I study her closely, taking in her cute denim miniskirt and black tee, the word EPITAPH scrawled in silver across the front. "But . . . *how?*" I ask. I've never heard of such a thing.

"Amazing—isn't it?" She grins in a way that makes her whole face illuminate. "It's probably not what you think. It's not like actual images or anything. It's more like bright, intense flashes of color. Music is energy—you know that, right? Well, actually, everything is energy, it's been scientifically proven. But anyway, back to music—you see, each note contains its own energy, its own vibration, which in turn contains its own corresponding color. I'm not sure if Paloma told you, but this is how Auden and I met. I mean, not here at the Rabbit Hole, but because of the whole energy/music/color/connection thing. Actually, when you come right down to it, it's all Paloma's fault." She laughs. "We've been working on this for about two years now—she's the one who helped me discover it. Then when Auden agreed to help me fine-tune it, she put us together and it was love from the start! His music is amazing," she gushes, her face soft and dreamy. "You should see how much color it radiates. It's as vibrant as he is."

I stand beside her, having no idea what to say. Having never imagined I'd find myself jealous of a blind girl—or any girl, for that matter. I've always been more or less content with just being me, for better or worse. But Xotichl's joy is so contagious I can't help but wonder what it might be like to be her. To live in her skin. To be so filled with happiness and love it can't be contained.

To never face the burden of merging your energy with that of a cockroach in order to go vortex hunting.

I wonder if she has any idea just how good she's got it? But when I look at her again, I'm pretty certain she does.

"Oh, and just so you know." She lowers her voice to a conspiratorial whisper. "Word's out about your Hollywood past."

I gape, overcome with the feeling of air rushing out of me.

"Apparently you're quite the cover girl." She nods. And I can't decide if her voice contained a hint of glee, or if I'm just crazy and paranoid, which is such a real possibility I decide to give her the benefit of the doubt and move past it.

"They *saw* it?" I close my eyes, wondering how this could've happened. It's a *weekly* tabloid. It's been off the shelves for a while now.

"Apparently the hair salon has a copy," she says, answering the question I hadn't yet voiced. "And there was one laying around the Laundromat too. Oh, and just in case you haven't heard, there's this new thing called Google—apparently you can find it there too."

"Great. That's just . . . *great*." I study my feet. "Nothing like going from really bad to way worse all in the course of a day."

"Maybe . . ." Xotichl bends toward me. "Then again, maybe not. For the first time in a long time—quite possibly ever—they're hit with the kind of dilemma they're not used to facing. Now they're torn between hating you and admiring you, when before they just hated you. You should consider it progress."

I survey the room, and yep, sure enough, there they are—three sets of eyes keeping track of everything I do. Then I turn back to Xotichl and say, "Well, for the record, the cover wasn't exactly flattering, and the story wasn't true. But it's not like anyone ever cares about that. The more salacious the better. Why wreck a potentially blockbuster issue with the cold, hard facts?" I shake my head, determined to not just locate that secret portal but also to find my way inside no matter what Paloma says. The sooner I can locate the source of El Coyote's power, the sooner I can destroy it, complete my job as a Seeker, and get back to my life as I knew it.

"But see, that's what you don't get," Xotichl says. "Lita and the Cruel Crew—otherwise known as Crickett and Jacy—well, they don't care if it's flattering. They only care that you were in the *same general vicinity as Vane Wick.* And, while we're on the subject, what was *that* like?"

I shake my head, thinking: *Et tu, Xotichl?* Only to glance over my shoulder to see just about every girl in the room, every guy too, staring at me, presumably wondering the same thing, so I might as well get used to explaining. "It wasn't nearly as good as most people want to believe," I tell her, knowing that's about as false as the story on the cover of that tabloid. From what I remember, Vane was a damn good kisser. So good I came very close to doing something I would've regretted. But the fact that he so easily betrayed me, means that from this point on, that's the story I'll stick with.

Xotichl laughs, facing the stage when she says, "Yeah, I had a feeling about that."

A moment later, the lights dim and Auden stands before us with a guitar strapped to his front. "This one's for Xotichl," he says. "Actually, they're all for Xotichl."

His fingertips meet the chords, causing a crescendo of music to swell through the room, as I lean toward Xotichl and say, "I'm gonna take a walk, have a look around. I'll find you later, okay?"

Already moving away, when she catches my wrist, her face grim, voice competing with Auden's strumming guitar and plaintive wail when she says, "Careful out there. Cade's here."

thirty-two

A crush of teens surge toward the stage. So many it forces me to shove my way through, mumbling, "Excuse me," over and over again until I finally burst free and smack straight into Dace.

My body slamming so hard into his, it sets him off balance. His fingers going for my arm in an attempt to steady me, steady himself, when he says, "You okay there?"

I nod. Look away. Unable to reply—unable to meet his gaze. My immediate field of awareness narrowed to the space where his hand clutches my arm—reducing the world outside to blurred shapes, white noise.

"That's the second time you've smacked into me here—must be a sign." He grins, eyes shining, as his skin fans at the sides. The two of us suspended—staring hard at each other—until I release myself from his grip, break free of the spell, immersed in a whirl of music and people swarming all around us. "The last time you seemed a little out of it—in a bit of a hurry," he says, looking chagrined when I fail to respond. "So you probably don't remember."

"I remember." I nod. Wanting to say: *I remember everything—all of it—the question is: Do you?* But instead, I stare down at my feet, smiling stupidly. Everything I do around him is stupid. Some

Seeker I've turned out to be. Attempting to redeem myself, say
something normal, not let on that I already know he's employed
here—thanks to the raven who allowed me to spy on him earlier,
I say, "So, I guess you hang out here a lot then?"

He pushes a hand through his hair, as his eyes—the color of
aquamarines—glide down the length of me. And damn if I can't
feel their trajectory. It's like showering in a stream of warm, mol-
ten honey—dripping from the top of my forehead all the way
down to my feet. "I guess you could say that," he says, voice low
and deep. "More than most, anyway." He waves a damp towel,
tugs on the string of his apron, and I blush in reply. The sight of it
reminding me of what I saw in the alleyway—watching him lean
against the wall, his face so soft and dreamy I longed to touch
him—kiss him—like I did in the dream.

I study him closely, seeking traces of recognition,
remembrance—some small token of evidence to assure me that,
as odd as it seems, that kiss in the cave was as real as it felt—but
coming up empty.

"So, how long have you worked here?" I ask, returning to the
topic at hand. My gaze drifting over the black V-necked T-shirt
skimming the sinuous line of his body—telling myself it's all
part of my reconnaissance, my need to gather as much information as I can about him and his kin. But knowing that's not really
it. The truth is, I like looking at him, being near him.

"I guess you could say somewhere between too long and not
long enough—depending on the state of my wallet." His laugh is
good-natured and easy—the kind that starts at the belly and trips
all the way up. "It's pretty much the only decent game in town." He
shrugs. "One way or another, you end up working for the Richters, and believe me, this is one of the better gigs."

I peer at him closely, remembering what Cade said when I was
here via the raven. How he referred to him by another name.
"You're not a Richter?" I ask, holding my breath in my cheeks.

Despite what Paloma told me, I need to hear it from him, confirm that he doesn't identify with their clan.

"I go by Whitefeather," he says, gaze steady and serious. "I was raised by my mom, didn't even know the Richters when I was a kid."

Despite getting the answer I wanted, I frown in return. His being a Richter was a good reason to avoid him—without it, I'm out of excuses.

"Is that okay?" He dips his head toward mine, his mouth tugging at the side. "You seem a little upset by the news."

I shake my head, break free of my reverie, and say, "No—not at all. Believe me, it's more like a relief." I meet his gaze, seeing the way it narrows in question. "Guess I'm not a big fan of your brother," I add, watching as he throws his head back and laughs, the sight of that long, glorious column of neck forcing me to look away, it's too much to take.

"If it makes you feel any better, most of the time I'd have to agree." He returns to me, the warmth of his gaze solely responsible for the wave of comfort that flows through me.

The feeling lasting only a moment, before everything changes. His demeanor grows cautious, guarded, as he focuses on a distant point just beyond and says, "Speaking of . . ." He frowns, barely looking at me when he adds, "I should get back to work . . . see you around?"

I watch as he weaves through the crowd, only to be replaced a few seconds later by Cade.

"Hey, Santos." His voice rises above the noise and chaos, as his eyes move over me, devouring me, but unlike his brother, his gaze leaves me cold.

"Hey, Coyote." I smirk, seeing no use in pretending. We both know which team we play for.

He laughs in response—a real and genuine laugh I didn't expect. "Of course I have no idea what you're talking about," he says, eyes twinkling, as though we're just two friendly conspirators sharing a joke. "Though I have to admit, I could definitely learn to like you."

He moves closer, too close for my comfort. But as much as I'd like to take one giant step back, I force myself to stay put. He will not intimidate me, no matter how hard he tries.

"You may not believe this, but I'm really glad to see you. You're exactly what we need to shake things up around here."

I quirk a brow, taking in smooth, poreless skin—a flash of white teeth—having no idea where he's going with this.

"This is a great town, don't get me wrong, and Leandro, my dad, is pretty much responsible for everything in it—you do know we run this town, right? My dad's the mayor. My uncle's the police chief, my cousin's the judge . . ."

I roll my eyes, wanting him to know I'm not the least bit impressed by the Richters' long list of bogus accomplishments.

"Anyway." He dismisses my reaction with a wave of his hand. "As much as I love it here, lately things were starting to get a bit stale. I mean, you're a world traveler . . ." He pauses, waiting for me to confirm that I have indeed seen a lot of the world, and when I don't, he goes on to say, "All that globe-trotting and location hopping—with that kind of experience, your views are probably much broader than most. Something that, I'm sorry to say, my family places little value on. They've grown comfortable, complacent, and for a while there, I was feeling so stifled I threatened to leave. I wanted to expand my horizons, see more of the world. You probably don't know this since you're new here, but people don't often leave Enchantment, and when they do . . . it rarely ends well."

I narrow my gaze, knowing that was a reference to my dad but also sensing something far more sinister behind the words.

"Anyway," he continues, "ever since you arrived, it's like I've been given a new lease on life—got my second wind—and all that." He tilts his head toward me, causing his hair to sweep into his eyes. It's his signature move, meant to be alluring, but it's totally wasted on me. "So, here's the thing—I have a proposition to make, one that I think will surprise you . . ." He licks his lips, inching so close he pelts my left cheek with his breath. "I know we're supposed to be sworn enemies. I know we were born to fight each other to the death. But honestly, I don't see the point. You may find it strange, it may go against everything you've heard about me, but I see no reason why we can't work together. I see no reason to fight when we could both benefit from waging peace instead of war."

"You're joking," I blurt out, unable to keep the shock from my voice.

"I'm dead serious," he says, eyes ablaze with his vision. "My goals far exceed those of my family, and you're just what I need to help me achieve them. Of course, you'll be well compensated—*very* well compensated, in fact." He leers in a way that leaves me cringing. "We have far more in common than you think, Daire. And I've no doubt I could learn as much from you as you can from me. Just think—the two of us together—pooling our talents to bring all the otherworlds and their various dimensions under our rule. How's that for broad thinking?"

I stand before him, having no idea what to say—other than: *No!* And: *You're crazy!* But mostly I'm too stunned to speak.

"Anyway, it's nothing you have to commit to just yet. I know it'll take some getting used to, but I do hope you'll give it serious consideration."

I nod, unsure what to say, what to do. Paloma did not prepare me for this.

"So, tell me, was my brother bothering you?" He leans toward me again, his proximity setting me on edge. "He's not really one of us, you know. He's sort of the black sheep. Every family has one. Kind of like your dad, Django, I suppose."

I swallow hard. Fight like hell not to react. He's baiting me. Purposely pushing all of my buttons in search of the sweet spot—the one that'll transform me from a totally in-control Seeker to an overemotional teenaged girl who loses her cool. But he can say what he will, I won't fold.

"Anyway—" He shrugs, back to his fake-smiling-self once again. "It's nice that Paloma let you out of the house long enough to have a little fun." His gaze sweeps over me, and while he may look just like his brother, the resemblance stops exactly where it starts. To those who never manage to look deeper, he's a god—to me, he just gives me the creeps. "So, can I show you around—get you anything? Something to drink, maybe? After all, I do own the place."

I shoot him a dubious look, remembering the scene in the alleyway when his dad called him out in front of Dace for suggesting the same thing.

My expression prompting him to laugh when he says, "Okay, maybe it's technically in my dad's name, but I'm the first on the list to inherit. I'm considered quite a catch in this town—in case you hadn't already guessed."

"That sort of thing probably works better on Lita than me," I say, watching in fascination as his face transforms from what I've come to know as his glib, self-satisfied look to something much harder and darker—though it's a far cry from the demon I know him to be.

"Lita," he scoffs. Dismissing the thought when he says, "Lita's too easy. I'm in the mood for a challenge. Though, from what I hear, you have a thing for smooth Hollywood types."

"You shouldn't believe everything you hear," I say, the words flung from over my shoulder. I've had enough of him for one night.

Not getting very far before I'm stopped by the feel of his fingers circling my wrist, as he pulls me close to his chest, saying, "Whatcha looking for, Daire?" His voice a mere whisper, as his hand squeezes tighter.

"I'm looking for *the ladies' room*," I tell him. "But I'm pretty sure I can find it on my own." I try to yank free, but he's incredibly strong and it's not quite that easy. And while I'm sure I could do it if I really put some effort behind it, I'm not sure how much of a scene I'm willing to make.

His voice dropping all pretense at flirtation when he says, "And I'm sure you plan to take several detours first, don't you?" He trails a finger down the length of my cheek, the feel of it causing me to suck in my breath and try to wrench free. "In order to spare ourselves that kind of embarrassment and preserve our budding new friendship, allow me to direct you to the other side of the room—just opposite the dance floor—you can't miss it."

I swallow hard, make another attempt to yank free, only to have him pull me even closer, his lips pushing into my hair when he says, "I meant everything I said—I want us to join forces. So don't disappoint me by poking your pretty head where it doesn't belong. The future is ours for the taking—so try not to blow it."

I reach around, grab hold of his fingers, and peel them off my wrist, aware of his knuckles creaking in protest and not feeling the slightest bit bad about it.

"Don't touch me," I say, my gaze fixed on his. "Ever. Again. Do you hear me?"

"Oh, I hear you," he says, voice steady and even. "And just so you know, I see you too. There are cameras everywhere, Santos. No place is safe. Except for maybe the bathroom. After all, we do have our standards." He grins, a sickly sight of flashing teeth and cold, vacant eyes. "Try not to do anything stupid. Try not to do something you'll live to regret."

His words trailing behind me as I make my way across the dance floor, heading in the direction he sent me.

thirty-three

I slam my palm against the door and shove in. Shooting for the row of white sinks jutting out from the blue tiled wall, I thrust my hands under a surge of cold water in an attempt to cool myself, calm myself—the encounter with Cade left me more shaken than I first realized.

I meet my gaze in the mirror, seeing a flushed, harried face staring back. And just behind me, just to my right, I watch as the waitress from the first time I came here, the one Dace consoled in the alleyway, bursts out of a stall, straightens her apron, cuts a wide arc around me, and heads for the very next sink, where she washes her hands, dries them on a handful of crunchy brown paper towels, and leans toward the mirror, erasing a mascara smudge with the tip of her finger.

"Miss your bus?" She continues to peer at herself, assessing her appearance, though the question's for me.

I turn. Surprised she remembers. But then again, Enchantment's not exactly a destination town. It doesn't get many tourists.

"Something like that." I focus on the name tag teetering high on her chest: MARLIZ! That's right. Only, the view from the mirror makes it read backward.

"They leave every few hours, maybe you should try again?" She pushes away from the sink, looks right at me.

"Why are you so anxious to be rid of me?" I ask, digging through my bag for my lip salve and swiping a thin coat across my mouth.

"Maybe I'm just trying to help you." She shrugs.

"And why would you want to do that?" I counter, seeing her sigh, turn back toward the mirror, where she surveys her face once again. Combing a hand through her bangs, getting them settled across her forehead, her left ring finger bearing a large diamond solitaire on a slim gold band I'm pretty sure she wasn't wearing the last time I saw her.

"I'm kindhearted, what can I say?" She smiles in a way that reminds me of Cade—unfeeling, unreal. "I commit one selfless act a day, and today it seems to be you. So, take my advice and get out while you can."

I lean against the edge of the sink, careful to keep my face clean of emotion. "Ever consider following your own advice?"

She tugs on her black bra strap, secures it under her tank top. "Sure." She fusses with the other strap too. "All the time."

"And . . . so . . . how come *you* never left?"

"Who's saying I didn't?" She looks at me, her gaze hinting at something I can't quite grasp.

"So why'd you come back then?"

She shoves a hand into her apron pocket, sighing as she fiddles with a pile of change, the coins' jostling causing a dull clinking sound. "I was born and raised here. I guess the longer you stay, the easier it is to lose your perspective. Thought I was the only girl headed to L.A. with bleached roots and big dreams—turns out I was wrong. So I enrolled in beauty school—but it was too hard to make a go of it, and, after a while, it just seemed easier to return." She heads for the door, presses her palm flat against it—her new diamond ring catching the light, winking at me. "I've seen the way they look at you," she says.

"Who?" My eyes travel the length of her.

"All of them—but mostly Cade and Dace. The brothers hate each other—or at least Cade hates Dace. I don't think Dace is capable of hating anyone." Her gaze grows soft, far away, probably remembering when Dace stopped Cade from berating her just a few hours earlier. "Anyway—" She shakes her head. "Watch yourself."

That last part spoken no louder than a whisper, prompting me to call, "Hey—what's that supposed to mean?" My voice competing with the swoosh of the door closing behind her, leaving my question unanswered.

thirty-four

I claim an empty stall, check the lock twice, flip the toilet lid down, settle myself on the seat, and dig through my purse in search of the jar with the tiny holes in the lid and the inch-long cockroach inside. Equally repulsed and excited by what I'm about to do, I loosen the lid, set the jar on the floor, and stare at the roach as hard as I can.

Stare at him until everything dims but his three sets of legs, brownish-red shell of a back, extra long antennae, and the wings that enable him to flit, more than fly.

His antennae twitching before him, discovering the lid is now gone, he moves forward—too fast. Scurrying out of the jar well before we've had a chance to properly blend.

I watch, horrified, as he picks up speed, veers out of my stall and into the next, just as someone walks in and takes up residence.

I slide my foot over, attempting to coax him back to my space, only to have the person beside me see my foot invading, and cry, "Excuse me, but *do you mind?*"

She kicks her foot against mine, using way more force than necessary, causing my boot to slam smack into the cockroach so

hard I let out an audible gasp. Ignoring the tirade of hateful comments drifting from the next stall, I lift my foot carefully—terrified
I've inadvertently crunched him, killed him, before I even had a
chance to put him to work.

But cockroaches are much tougher than that. There's a reason
they're one of the oldest surviving groups of insects on earth.
Other than having rolled onto its back, it appears in good shape.
So I take a deep breath, focus on its frantically writhing body, the
three sets of legs spinning in circles in a fight to right itself again—
all too aware that the second I merge, I'll be joining that struggle.
But also knowing there's no way I can risk turning him right side
up until I've had a chance to join him.

The girl in the next stall flushes and vacates, banging the door
so hard, it makes the blue metal walls rumble and shake. Forcing
me to bide my time while she visits the sink, the sound of the
door closing behind her allowing me to focus on the cockroach,
and it's not long before I'm *in*.

I'm alive.

Surging with adrenaline.

A primal fight for survival firing up all of my nerve endings.
All I have to do—all *we* have to do—is right ourselves again.

The longer we remain belly-up, the more this overwhelming
feeling of panic kicks in. Knowing that's only going to waste
much needed energy, I drive into him harder—mixing my will
to live with his primal fight to survive. Pushing his legs even
faster—like a cockroach on steroids—until I manage to flip him
over and land smack on the belly. The antennae twitching, scoping, until it locates the side of the jar, equates it with danger, and
sprints for the opposite wall. Instinctively seeking the place where
it's darkest—and that's when I remember that cockroaches are
true creatures of the dark—they live in it, hunt in it, doing whatever it takes to shun the light and remain undetected.

Paloma knew exactly what she was doing when she chose him
for me to merge into.

For something so reviled—so hated, abhorred, even feared—
I'm amazed by how very powerful I feel now that I've joined him.
I'm like a tiny, commanding tank, trekking my way across a vast
expanse of gray-tiled bathroom floor that, from this perspective,
seems to go on forever.

I pick my way around a crumpled paper towel that fell short of
the bin and pause in the corner, body still, antennae twitching,
trying to determine if I can sneak under the door or if I have to
wait for someone to open it. Determining it's too close to the
ground to chance, I'm left with no choice but to wait. So I squeeze
into the corner, hoping that soon, someone will push their way
in, so I can seize the moment to sneak out.

The door opens, banging so hard against the wall I cram into
the corner and give silent thanks for the little rubber stopper that
keeps it from doing any real damage. Watching as a pair of knee-
high black boots, pointy-toed red flats, and sky-high silver stilettos
walk in—trying to determine just the right moment to make my
move when I realize the shoes belong to Lita and the Cruel Crew.
And from what I can tell, they're discussing me.

"What's up with that jacket she wears?" the girl with the bright
pink lips says, who, according to Xotichl, is either Jacy or Crickett,
though I'm not sure which is which.

"Seriously," the other one echoes, the one with the best blond
highlights of the bunch. "What's up with *all* of it?" she adds, looking to Lita for approval—they both do.

I glance between the door and them—it's closing but is still
open enough to provide an easy escape. If I make a run for it *right
now,* there's no way they'll notice me and I'll be well on my way.

I'm just about to do exactly that when Lita heads for the mirror, stands right before it, and says, "I don't know . . ."

The door's closing—one second more and I'll have to wait 'til
they leave.

I start to move, start to make a run for it, my legs short, spindly, but powerful nonetheless, propelling me forward faster than

I ever would've imagined. But just as I've reached it, pink lips
heads for my stall—the one the real me is currently occupying—as
opposed to the obviously empty one right beside it with the door
hanging wide open.

I freeze. Unable to risk it. If she somehow manages to push her
way in, if the lock I double-checked somehow fails, she will catch
me slumped over the toilet seat—my body present, my consciousness in limbo—and I will never live it down.

I slip back to my corner, it's the only thing I can do. Antennae
twitching with frustration when she finally gives up and claims a
vacant stall, just as the bathroom door closes—my perfect chance
for escape now lost.

Except it's not.

Not entirely.

Not for something as small as a cockroach.

That same paper towel I avoided before must've been inadvertently kicked by one of their heels, as it's now firmly lodged between the door frame and the door. Leaving a crack just wide
enough for me to slip through and get on with the job Paloma
sent me to do.

I creep toward it. Keeping a close eye on Lita still standing before the mirror, cupping a hand around each breast, heaving them
higher into her bra, as she smiles seductively at her own reflection, and says, "Take *that*, Cade Richter."

She rubs her lips together, fluffs her hair around her shoulders,
and when she twists her head from side to side so she can verify
just how pretty she is, I can't help but agree. I mean, she could
certainly learn a thing or two from Jennika on the proper appli-
cation of eyeliner—and the highlights could definitely be a lot
better—but she's still pretty. And no matter how awful she's been
to me, it breaks my heart that she's so willing to waste that beauty
on Cade.

I'm so engrossed in my thoughts, it takes a minute to register when she says, "Anyway . . . I think her boots are kind of cool." Returning to a conversation I was sure had already ended.

Her statement causing pink lips to cough in her stall—as the other one gapes at the sink beside Lita's, striving to adjust to this new way of seeing me. Quickly recovering when she says, "Yeah, and her jeans are cool too." Shooting Lita a sidelong glance, eager to get a jump-start on agreeing with her before pink lips has a chance to bang out of the stall.

Lita rolls her eyes as though she's sick of being surrounded by suck-ups, even though it's obvious she wouldn't have it any other way. Sighing deeply as she says, "I'm talking about *the boots*. The jeans are *common*. But the *boots* . . ."

Common if you buy all your clothes in Europe! I start to say. Until I realize I can't.

I'm a cockroach.

A cockroach with a mission.

I have no business caring about this kind of nonsense.

"I'm so glad you said that," pink lips says, taking her place on the other side of Lita. "Because all this time I've been secretly thinking they were awesome."

Oh, brother. I creep forward, eager to get out of here before it gets any worse.

Glancing toward the mirror to see Lita roll her eyes, shake her head, and say, "Jacy . . . *really* . . ."

"What? It's true. I totally did!" pink lips/Jacy says.

"Whatever." Lita sighs. "It's just—do you have to agree with *everything* I say?" She snaps her bag shut, hikes it high onto her shoulder, and makes to leave.

But I need to leave first. I've seen more than enough of the inner workings of their clique, and now I need to get out while I can.

I crawl toward the door. Unwilling to use my wings, knowing it'll attract too much notice, I begin scaling the crumpled paper towel that holds the door open, which, from my new, low-to-the-ground perspective, may as well be Everest.

Having just made it to the summit, when Jacy falls in place behind Lita, causing Lita to heave a great sigh, boost the door open, and say, "Please—after *you*," in the most sarcastic voice she can manage. And all it takes is the reshuffling of feet just behind me, along with the careless kick of Jacy's red pointy shoes spiking my back end, to force me off the paper towel mountain and send me flying out of the bathroom and into the club.

My body grazing the pant legs of more unsuspecting club-goers than I can count. Veering wildly out of control but trying not to panic, since panic will only result in a lost connection—until I land with the kind of heavy, unexpected thud that rever-berates throughout me.

I'm stunned. Watching as an army of shoes stomp all around, and knowing I can't just sit here like the universally hated target I am, I start moving. Making slow, cautious progress until the band takes a break and the journey becomes increasingly perilous when the same crowd that swarmed the stage, now suddenly leaves the stage in search of the bathrooms, a drink, and each other.

Heels slam down all around me until I can't decide which is scarier—the spiky tip of a stiletto or the heavy, rubber tread of a boot?

In a desperate fit to survive, I wind up the wings on my back and propel myself from shoe to shoe, pant leg to skirt hem, until I'm in the clear. Then I make for the wall, clinging to the shad-ows, until I'm free of the busier part of the club and into that weird hall of corridors, where I make for the office I visited last time I was here.

I pause by the door, watching as Cade perches on the edge of a desk, flipping a baseball bat against the palm of his hand. The sound of wood slapping, dull and continuous, as another man, a man who's clearly older and most likely related, talks to him about something that, though I can't quite make it out, has clearly captured Cade's interest.

I sneak closer, straining to hear, but before I can glean much of anything, Marliz appears. The sight of her causing Cade to abandon the bat and slip out, as Marliz approaches the desk. Her face slack, eyes resigned, loosening her apron strings as the man tilts his chair away from his desk, and growls, "Close the door."

I steel myself against the force of the slamming door, watching as Cade makes his way down the hall, pausing briefly to light a cigarette despite the fact that he fails to smoke it past the initial drag. He just waves it around—the tip sparking, flaring, as a blizzard of ashes drift to the ground. Unknowingly leading me down a series of halls so confusing I take note of all manner of landmarks so I can find my way back.

There's a gum wrapper on the ground, just before the door with the chipped paint near the bottom, that looks like the shape of a heart. A real heart—the kind with aortas, and ventricles, and arteries—as opposed to the Hallmark kind.

There's a squashed cigarette butt in the corner where the wall is warped and bubbled in a way that could be the result of water damage.

But while I'm off to a good start, it's not long before there are so many doors, so many hallways, so many little bits of debris to keep track of, I completely lose count. So I tell myself it's not my concern what becomes of this cockroach when I'm finished with him. From the looks of things, I've done him a huge favor by leading him to an area where the carpet is crusted with a wide assortment of his most favored treats. Bits of hair, flakes of dried skin, an unlimited supply of unidentifiable small greasy things that just the mere thought of prompts his instincts to kick in. Making him hungry enough to try to turn around so he can go hunt some of that down. And it's all I can do to convince him to work past it, to get back to what I need him to do.

I pick up the pace, sneaking dangerously close to Cade's heels but feeling pretty good about the move until he stops without warning and I slam so hard into the back of his big brown boot, it takes a moment to reorient myself.

I'm just about to scramble backward in a bid to keep a safer distance between us, when I realize we're here.

Watching as Cade waves the smoldering tip of his cigarette before what at first appears to be a large blank wall—but that's before I remember Paloma's advice and train my focus on the invisible, the unknown—coaxing it into my immediate field of consciousness—and it's not long before that brick wall has morphed into something entirely different.

And all I can think as I gaze at it wide-eyed is that Paloma was right.

The portal looks nothing like I would've imagined.

thirty-five

Cade stops. Stiffens. His spine straightening, head tilting as though he senses something out of place—something out of the ordinary.

Could it be me?

He turns a slow circle, head swiveling from side to side, gaze running the length of the hall. And when he lowers his gaze to the ground where I wait, I take my chances, spread my wings, and flit toward his pant leg. Assuring myself I can easily extricate my way out of the situation if necessary—all I have to do is sever the bond and I'll find myself right back in the bathroom, no worse for the wear.

Though I'm not sure I believe it.

I'm in deep.

Maybe too deep.

It's as though the cockroach and I are now one.

I cling to the hem of Cade's jeans, keeping silent and still while he shakes his head, mutters under his breath, and moves forward again. Then I scurry up the back of his leg where I stop at his waistband and sneak halfway into his belt loop, hoping for a more secure ride and a much better view.

My eyes dart like crazy, taking note of all the details—ugly, greenish/gray industrial carpet, hideous white walls that have seen so much tobacco smoke waved before them they're streaked a dull yellow/brown. Desperate to find something that sets it apart from all the other hallways I've seen but coming up empty. No wonder most Seekers couldn't find it—it's something extraordinary hidden well within the confines of the painfully ordinary.

He stands before the wall—or at least the place where the wall was before it became a soft, yielding, grayish-tinged swirl of energy that's neither welcoming nor unwelcoming but definitely intriguing.

Paloma's warning repeating in my head: *Under no circumstance should you enter. You're not yet ready—there will be plenty of time for that later . . .*

Though it's too late to heed—we're already in.

The first thing I notice is the darkness.

The second thing I notice is the demons.

Two huge, scary, malevolent beings with the requisite tails, hooves, and horns you'd expect, along with obscenely grotesque faces that appear to be a mixture of animal, human, and some other unidentifiable beast that originated in a place I prefer not to visit.

Cade stands before them, greeting them in an ancient tongue I can't understand. Presenting the cigarette like some kind of offering, he tosses it to the larger one who wastes no time shoving it into his mouth and devouring it whole—smoldering tip and all—as the other beast looks on with unconcealed envy. His blatant hunger causing me to burrow even deeper into Cade's belt loop, assuming that if they'll eat burning cigarettes, they'll have no qualms eating a cockroach.

Cade speaks, but again the words make no sense. Though whatever it was, it got the demons laughing—if you can call hideous, gaping, fanged mouths flapping wide open before snapping shut again *laughing*. Then after a few more words are exchanged, he nods and moves past them. His step echoing so loudly, it's as though we're moving through a hollow tin drum, and it's only a moment later when I venture out a little farther, take a good look around, and confirm that we are.

It's a long, hollow tube—the kind they use to build sewers. The soles of Cade's shoes banging hard against the bottom, making for a sound that's so unsettling, so unpleasant, I'm overcome with relief when he steps out of the tunnel and onto a dirt-covered area that marks the mouth of a cave.

But unlike the small, spartan cave of my vision quest, this one is large, seeming to ramble and sprawl without end. Consisting of a series of rooms—very well-appointed rooms from what I can see. The one we currently occupy posing as some kind of grand entry.

Cade slips two fingers into his mouth and whistles long and low. Then he waits. Waits for . . . something. I can't imagine who or what he expects to find here, though I'm braced for more demons.

But when I see a long-nosed, red-eyed coyote racing toward him—I'm not one bit surprised. Of course El Coyote isn't just a name—it's his spirit animal, just as Raven is mine.

Coyote leaps toward him, plops his long, gangly legs up high on his chest as he nuzzles his snout into Cade's neck. His nose pushing, prodding, sniffing—then, catching a whiff of something unexpected, he darts his face toward me, bares his sharp teeth, and growls.

With no way to defend myself, I burrow into Cade's belt loop, all too aware that this hard shell of a body will do nothing more than provide a nice, satisfying *crunch* once Coyote's had his way with me.

"Hey, boy—how's my boy? Huh? How's my boy?" Cade pushes Coyote's paws back to the ground, scratching his head and ruffling his fur like a favored family pet. Then he straightens, pats the side of his leg in a way that urges Coyote to follow. The two of them bounding deeper into the cave until they come to a well-furnished den, where Cade uses his silver-and-turquoise lighter to set the wall torches blazing.

"She's here," Cade says, settling onto a red velvet sofa that sits low to the ground. Pulling Coyote closer as he smooths the fur at his crown. "The one we've been waiting for, Daire Santos, has finally arrived."

Coyote growls, snarls, as though he understands—or maybe I'm reading too much into it—maybe it's just a coincidence. Though probably not—as Cade's spirit animal, they're deeply connected.

All I know for sure is that when he shoves that long snout toward me again—when his nose starts twitching and his growl deepens—I'm overcome with relief when Cade misreads the whole thing.

"Not to worry, you know I can handle her." He lowers his face to Coyote's, nuzzling him with affection. "It's just a matter of time until I convince her we're so much better together. So much better to wage peace and not war. Though she's tougher than I figured. Prettier too. It won't be easy to convince her—but then easy is overrated. The reward is so much sweeter when it requires a little conniving—and man is she sweet. Exactly what I was hoping for."

Coyote throws his head back and howls, spinning in a quick series of circles before he rests at Cade's feet, tail thumping with anticipation. The move practiced, a much-rehearsed ritual, prompting Cade to make for a large icebox I hadn't noticed 'til now.

He flips the lid and retrieves a large crystal bowl filled with bloodied, dark, squishy things. The sight and smell of which triggers the coyote into an absolute frenzy.

I peek past the belt loop, determined to get a better look. Overcome by the scent of something so putrid, it kicks the cockroach's most primal instincts into high gear when he senses what lies just before him: random, chopped-up bits—either animal or human—something that repulses me just as much as it drives the roach insane with desire.

Cade returns to the couch, where he sets the bowl on the glass table before him and scoops his fingers into the sludge. His hand held in offering, tempting the coyote with a heap of putrid, bloodied chunks. Face shining with pride when Coyote slurps it right off his palm with a finesse that's surprising.

Coyote licks his chops, gives a quick yelp that comes off as a cross between a growl and a bark, then he goes through the whole spinning ritual again—his version of begging for seconds.

The performance causing Cade to laugh when he says, "You know the drill—gather the troops and there's more in it for you."

Coyote obeys, streaking from room to room until I can no longer track him. Leaving me alone with Cade who settles back on the couch and readies a snack for himself. Slipping his hand into the bowl, he retrieves a long, stringy bit of *ick* he's quick to plop into his mouth. Taking a moment to close his eyes and savor the flavor, before leisurely licking his slick, bloodied fingers, and dipping his hand in for more.

thirty-six

I creep under Cade's T-shirt. Using extreme caution to cling to the fabric and not him. The last thing I need is to tip him off—from what I've seen, he might consider me less a nuisance and more a nice little morsel to eat.

It's a risky move, being this close. Yet it's one I'm willing to take. I can't risk the cockroach's instincts overpowering me—making a dive for the bowl of bloodied bits in search of a little late-night nourishment.

If that happened on my watch, I just couldn't bear it. There's just not enough toothpaste and mouthwash for something like that.

The wait feels much longer in here. Probably because there's not much to see other than the flicker of torchlight that penetrates the thin weave of Cade's T-shirt, highlighting the Calvin Klein waistband of his black boxer briefs like a Times Square billboard. I also detect the all-pervasive scent of a musky body spray for men—and while at first I found it repellent, after a while, I have to admit, it goes a long way in masking the horrible scent the bowl of crud emits.

I wait. Growing so bored I'm tempted to nap, but instead I

spend the time eavesdropping as he hums a few songs I don't
recognize—songs that sound tribal and ancient. And when I do
decide to take a quick peek, due to sheer boredom if nothing else,
I watch as he gives himself an impromptu manicure by gnawing
a hangnail right off his thumb.

I'm just about to duck back inside when he jumps to his feet
and says, "There you are. Well done, boy. Well done."

I make for the belt loop, in search of a better view. Thankful to
be here in cockroach form and not human form, if for no other reason than it keeps me from shrieking in horror when my gaze darts
from Coyote to the group gathered before us, which can only be
described as an army of . . . undead beasts.

A small army of truly monstrous beings with partially decayed faces and protruding bones, some with crucial body parts
missing. The sight of them gathered like that reminding me of
some of the more intense, special-effects makeup jobs Jennika
used to do for the scarier horror movies.

Only this is much worse.

This is real.

They gather before him with their tongues—well, those who
have tongues—lolling with anticipation, eyes bulging expectantly—
as Cade makes for the icebox, returning with a large, metal container he places on the glass table before him.

"Back off," he says, glaring at one in particular that's creeping
too close. Waiting until it returns to the group, rejoining the rest
of the freak show, before he plunges his hand into his pocket,
fishes around, and retrieves a small silver key he uses to open the
lock.

The group presses forward, their gruesome faces naked with
craving, as I brace for a big, messy pile of squishy gray matter.
Figuring the brains will most likely be human, since, according to
legend, that's the preferred undead/demon/monster treat.

But instead of the sludge I expect, when Cade pops the top,
the most beautiful, incandescent glow fills the room. The sight of

it causing a hushed chorus of *Ahhhhh*s soon chased by excited yips, snarls, and growls, as Cade cups his hands, scoops them both in, and comes away with a heap of beautiful, gleaming, white orbs he admires briefly, before tossing them to the beasts, as though tossing bread crumbs to pigeons.

The freaks dive-bomb each other—going absolutely mad in their attempt to score more than their share of orb. A spectacle Cade seems to enjoy, judging by the way he takes his sweet time doling it out. Preferring to make them fight for it, no matter that there seems to be more than enough to go around.

"That's it," he says, wiping his hands on the sides of his jeans, the lined expanse of his palms hovering dangerously close to me. "Show's over. Feel better now?" He glances among them and laughs. "You certainly *look* better," he adds.

And that's when I see it.

That's when I see the way they've transformed into something not nearly as gruesome as they were just a few moments earlier.

Some of that decayed flesh is intact.

Some of those broken bones are repaired.

Some of those missing parts have regenerated.

Regenerated.

What the heck is he feeding them?

I study them again, taking in dark hair, dark features, light eyes . . . and I know—I immediately know it's more than a coincidence.

When Paloma spoke of them communing with their long-dead relatives on *Día de los Muertos* or Day of the Dead—claiming that they don't so much *honor* their relatives as *resurrect* them—she was also quick to assure me that it wasn't what I assumed. That it wasn't the physical bodies they resurrected but more their spiritual essence.

They call upon the energy of the dead and infuse themselves with the

dark power of their lineage—an effect that lasts a few days at best . . .
they're not necromancers, or at least not yet, anyway, she'd said.

But as I gaze upon them again, I realize Paloma is wrong.
Cade *has* brought them back. There's an entire army of long-dead
Richters lined up before me.

"Leandro's gonna freak when he sees you," Cade says, his voice
nudging me back to the present. "And once Daire's on board . . .
the whole world is ours . . ."

I swivel around until I'm peering at him—staring into the eyes
of a narcissistic roadkill-snacking psychopath who seriously thinks
he can convince me to join him.

This is far worse than I was warned it would be.

I squinch my eyes tight, striving to break my bond with the
cockroach, when Cade slams the lid of the metal container so hard
it severs the thought. Turning away from his family of freaks, he
yells at them to scram, and they do. Not necessarily leaving in the
most orderly manner, though they are obedient, leaving no doubt
who's in charge around here.

"Now what?" Cade glances between his watch and Coyote.
"Time for a run?" Coyote howls, excited by the idea, but Cade
hesitates, scrunching his face when he says, "I don't know. I should
probably get back, keep an eye on things in the club."

Coyote ducks his head low, looks up at him with sad, red-
glowing eyes. The sight causing Cade to laugh softly, chucking
him under the chin as he says, "Okay, but just a quick one. I can't
let that Santos out of my sight for too long."

They move through the place, heading toward a wall at the far
end. But just like the wall that led us here, this one is also a mirage
that allows us to push through to its other side—staring upon a
wide, seemingly endless expanse of desert, with hard-packed, well-
traveled sand.

Cade kicks off his left boot as the coyote races excited circles
around him, and I hang on for dear life, convinced there's no way

I can survive a run without falling off and getting lost here forever. Even though it's not technically *me* who'll be lost but rather the *cockroach,* it's still not something I'd wish upon him. He's served me well. He deserves better.

I steel myself. Committed to making the journey, doing whatever it takes to hang on so I can eventually find my way back to the club, where I can deposit the cockroach in a nice, dark, damp spot where he can live out the rest of his days with hopefully no memory of all the wretched things I forced him to witness—when Cade unbuckles his pants.

It's a move I didn't expect.

His jeans dropping to the ground as I spring toward the hem of this T-shirt, where I cling with all of my might. Overcome with relief to have nailed my target, when he begins to remove that as well, and I'm swept across his torso, up over his armpit (*ick*)—and then—

"What the—?"

He shrieks.

Or maybe that was me shrieking in my own head, I can't say for sure.

All I know is right after he yells, "Filthy . . . disgusting . . ." time seems to stop as we glare at each other.

The moment suspended, on pause, and I'm just about to break it, just about to make a run for it, when his eyes turn to slits of rage and he snaps the T-shirt toward the ground so hard I lose my grip. Sent sailing, soaring, flying through the air—so startled and flustered and helpless, I'm unable to use my wings to propel myself anywhere.

Then the next thing I know, I'm belly-up on the ground. Staring into a pair of cruel, nonreflective, icy-blue eyes, as Cade lifts his shoe high and slams it so hard I become one with the heel.

thirty-seven

"Hey—hey there. You okay?"

The voice sounds male. Concerned. A male who's concerned about me?

It's gotta be either the ghost of Django or Chay's come to get me—those are the only two males who would care.

"Do you need a doctor? Come on, open your eyes and look at me, *please?*"

I do as he says. I see no reason not to. And I find myself staring straight into a pair of icy-blue irises.

I flinch at the sight, squirm backward, try to get away. But then when I see my own reflection gleaming back, my entire body goes soft once again.

"Whoa, there." He eases me back onto the seat.

Onto the . . . *toilet seat?*

I sit up straighter, gaze around wildly, wondering what I'm doing here, in this stall, and why Dace is here with me.

I start to stand, but my head's too dizzy, refuses to allow it, and it's only a second later when I'm down again. Landing so awkwardly my foot kicks at something that rolls across the ground.

A jar.

An empty jar.

And then I remember. I remember it all.

"I have to go—" I push against him as hard as I can, which, in my weakened state, isn't hard at all. Visions of Coyote, demons, and long-dead Richters flooding my mind. And when I get to the part where his twin licked slimy globs of gore from his fingers, I say it again and push harder this time. But for the moment anyway, he's stronger than me.

"Relax," he coos, voice hushed, soothing—a melody hummed solely for me. "There's no rush. Take all the time you need to gather your strength, get your bearings again."

"No. Really—I have to . . ." I look at him, having no idea how to explain. "I have to find Xotichl," I say. It's the first reasonable thing that springs to mind.

"Xotichl's gone." He squints in study. "The club closed a while ago. I was just making final rounds when I found you. What happened?" he asks, voice laced with concern.

"I . . ."

I merged with a cockroach—caught a ride next to your twin's Calvin Klein underwear label—and after I watched him play with a demon coyote and snack on bloodied bits that could've been either animal or human, he fed glowing, white orbs to the walking dead—then crushed me under the heel of his boot . . .

"I'm not sure," I say, willing my head to feel better, to stop spinning, and a moment later it does. "I guess I passed out, or something . . ." I cringe, hating the lie but knowing there's no way I could ever present him the truth.

I start to stand, pretending not to notice when he offers a hand. "I need to call my ride." I fumble for my phone, reluctant to bother Paloma and Chay at this hour, but they're pretty much my only real option.

"Don't be silly. I'll drive you." Dace follows me out of the stall, watching as I call Paloma's number, then Chay's—face scrunching in confusion when they both fail to answer. It doesn't make any sense.

"Daire—why won't you let me help you?" he says. My name on his lips sounding just like it did in the dream. Our eyes meeting in the mirror, mine astonished, his chagrined, when he adds, "Yeah. I asked around. Uncovered your real name. So shoot me."

And when he smiles, when he smiles *and* runs a nervous hand through his glossy, dark hair—well, I'm tempted to shake my head and refuse him again.

Maybe he goes by the name of Whitefeather, but technically, he's still a Richter. A good Richter—a kind Richter—still, I need to do what I can to avoid him. To ignore that irresistible stream of kindness and warmth that swarms all around him.

Need to cleanse myself of those dreams once and for all. We are not bound. Nor are we fated. I'm a Seeker—he's the spawn of a Richter—and my only destiny is to stop his brother from . . . whatever it is that he's doing.

But, more immediately, I need to get home. And there's no denying I could do a lot worse than catching a ride with gorgeous Dace Whitefeather.

Dropping the phone in my bag, I reluctantly nod my consent. Heading out the door as I ask, "Are we the last to leave?" I survey the club, noting how different it looks now that it's empty. Wondering if Cade's holed up in his office, watching us from his wall of screens.

"Naw, my cousin Gabe is still here. Probably Marliz too, since they're engaged. But Raul, my uncle, is always the last one out. Especially on the nights when Leandro leaves early."

I wait for him to mention Cade, but the name never comes, and it's not like I'm about to bring it up. "Sounds like you come from a really big family," I say, wanting to learn more about that family—greedy for whatever he's willing to divulge.

He holds the door open, exiting behind me when he says,

"Feels like I meet a new member every day." He laughs—the sound magnetic and deep, the kind of laugh you want to hear again and again. "I grew up on the reservation—my mom and I lived in our own little world, which didn't leave room for much else. But when I hit my teens, I wanted more. And after some initial reluctance, my mom agreed to let me go to Milagro. That's when I learned I had this whole other family."

"That must've been . . . strange." I peer at him sideways, the question more baited than it seems.

"It was." He shrugs. "*Strange* is definitely the best word to describe it." He falls quiet, stares into the distance.

"So you still live on the reservation?" I ask, desperate to keep the conversation going, remembering how Paloma failed to say either way.

"Only when I visit my mom. The rest of the time I rent a small room in town, paid for with what I earn working here."

My stare hardens; I have no idea how to reply. Shocked that he'd go to all that trouble, work so hard for his creep of a brother, just so he could attend a school that hasn't been all that accepting of him.

He meets my gaze, reads the unspoken question written on my face, but instead of elaborating, he stops beside a primer-gray Mustang—same car he drove at the gas station that day—saying, "You're staying with Paloma, right?"

I nod in reply, duck my head low, and settle inside. Noting the interior is a little worn, a little worse for the wear, yet surprisingly neat and clean. And it definitely smells really nice—sort of earthy and fresh—like him.

"So, now that you know about me—what about you?" He starts the engine, backing out of the space and onto the street. "Or should I ask around to uncover that too?"

I stare out the window, tempted to say something glib, noncommittal, but he's so kind and sincere, I go with the truth. "For as long as I remember, it's been me and my mom. She's a Hollywood makeup artist—though the job title's a little misleading, since we spend most of our time traveling the world, only stopping in Hollywood between gigs."

He swerves onto a rutted dirt road, the first of many, eyes slewed toward me when he says, "Sounds rough."

I sharpen my gaze, searching for signs of sarcasm, insincerity, something—but coming away empty, which really surprises me. Usually when people respond like that it's with an undertone of envy.

"I mean, I'm sure it had its good parts." He recovers quickly, worried he might've upset me. "Still . . . never having a real place to settle, to call home . . . I'm not sure I could do it."

"Sometimes it was tough," I say. "Sometimes it got really lonely." I settle deeper into my seat, wondering why I saw fit to confess that when I've never admitted it to anyone, much less myself. Quick to add, "Then again, when it's the only life you know, then you don't really know what you're missing." Not wanting him to feel sorry for me.

My fingers twist in my lap, watching as he considers my words. Gripping the wheel tighter as he slows to a crawl in order to navigate a particularly rough patch of road.

"So I'm guessing this is the reason everyone drives four-wheelers around here?" I grip the edge of my seat, cringing when the bottom of his car scrapes hard against the ground.

"I have an old truck I usually save for these roads. I'm a bit of a grease monkey. I like fixing up cars and other broken-down things. But since I didn't plan on coming this way . . ." His shoulders lift, ending that topic as he segues to the next. "So tell me, for someone who's traveled the world, what do you make of Enchantment?" He removes a hand from the wheel to tuck some loose strands of hair back behind his ear, and it's all I can do to keep from reaching toward him—entwining my fingers with his.

I bite down on my lip, having no idea what to say. So instead

I just stare at his profile—noting how it's so perfectly chiseled it should be minted on coins.

"That bad, huh?" He shakes his head and laughs.

"Aside from school and Paloma's, I really haven't seen all that much." I shrug, deciding to leave out my visit to the graveyard, the cave, and the time I went riding on the reservation with Chay.

"Well, I know it pretty well, and I'm more than happy to volunteer as your guide—just say the word. It's not nearly as bad as you think. There are some truly enchanting places, if you know where to look."

I nod as though I'm already considering it, but as tempting as it is, I know I can't do it. After tonight, I have to do whatever I can to avoid him. Getting to know him is not a viable option. I have a job to do—one that'll require all of my focus. I can't allow myself to get distracted by a boyfriend—or even a boy that's a friend.

The rest of the drive passes in silence, but, strangely, I have no need to fill it and neither does he. It's only when he pulls up to the big blue gate that he turns to me and says, "This is it, right?"

I reach for my bag, intending to give a quick thanks for the ride and be on my way. But when our eyes meet again, the words melt on my lips.

He holds the look. Holds it with such intensity, no matter how hard I try, I can't break away.

Everything my head is telling me: *Open the door—say your good-byes—and get the heck out of this car!*—is in direct conflict with what my heart is saying: *Stay—talk—hang out for a while—give it a chance—see where it leads* . . .

His blue eyes gleaming, lips parting and curving, as a slant of moonlight creeps through the window and finds its way to the top of his head where it glows like a crown.

The sight of it forcing me to shut my eyes, shut out the whole glorious sight of him. Needing to see if I'm merely drawn to his beauty, since it wouldn't be the first time. But when I turn the

focus from my eyes to my heart, when I tune in to what it tells
me—well, the impression I get is the same as the first time I saw
him that day at the Rabbit Hole and again at the gas station, then
today at school, and earlier tonight when I ran smack into him in
the club . . .

A swarm of kindness, followed by the deepest, most unconditional love—all of it directed at me.

"Daire . . ." he says, voice husky and thick.

The lilt of my name on his lips causing me to sway toward
him. Ignoring the warning in my head, in favor of the yearning in
my heart. Lured by the invisible magnet throbbing between us.

"Daire," he repeats, the words barely a whisper. "Someone's
here."

My eyes open wide and I turn to find Jennika glaring into the
window.

thirty-eight

"Why'd you have to embarrass me like that?" I follow Jennika down the walkway and into the house as the rumble of Dace's engine fades into the distance. Admiring the way he held his own, kept so steady and calm, but those icy-blue eyes told a whole other story—he couldn't wait to be gone.

I've seen it before. An angry Jennika is a scary Jennika, and she was—correction, *is*—undeniably angry.

But I'm angry too. And unlike Dace, I'm not the least bit intimidated by her.

"Seriously—why'd you have to be so incredibly rude?" I throw my bag on the kitchen table and head for the sink, where I retrieve a blue handblown glass from the cupboard, fill it with water, and down it in three easy gulps in an attempt to calm myself.

"Oh, well—excuse me for *embarrassing* you and acting so *rude*. Please accept my most heartfelt apologies." She shakes her head, clearly not meaning a word of it. "Maybe you can tell me just exactly what is going on around here? Maybe you can explain how you'd like me to react upon finding you parked in a beat-up wreck of a car with a boy who's up to no good—at one thirty in the morning—on a *school* night, no less?"

I lean against the counter and stare hard at my boots. Struggling to get a rein on my emotions—arguing with her won't solve a thing. But I'm far too annoyed to take my own advice, so I lift my chin and say, "Well, for starters, you really didn't have to yell. That was completely uncalled for. And for another thing, you really didn't have to jump to conclusions. *Nothing* was going on. It wasn't at all what you think—you misread the whole thing. I only just met him today! He gave me a lift, nothing more. But instead of trusting me, you just go off on a rant and assume the worst. Way to go, Jennika. Seriously."

"Oh, so now I'm supposed to *trust* you?" She fumes under her breath, surveying Paloma's home as though she's suspicious of everything in it, most of all me. "How can I *trust* you when you go for days on end without returning my calls? How can I *trust* you when you renege on our deal?"

I sigh. Roll my eyes. Hardly able to believe we're back to this—the same argument we've already had over the phone. Twice. But apparently she's gearing up for round three, and once she gets started, she's hard to contain.

"That was *one* time, and it was only for *three* days, as you well know—"

But I barely get to finish before she's shaking her head, practically shouting, "It was *four* days, Daire. *Four.*"

"That's only because of the time difference and you know it," I mumble, thinking how sad it is that after weeks of not seeing each other, this is the way she chooses to greet me. But now that she's started, I'm not in much of a hugging mood either. "The point is, it was just once, and there were special circumstances involved since I was"—*enduring a vision quest/full-body dismemberment in a remote cave*—"not feeling well . . . due to my injuries from the accident and all."

"Yes, so you say." She looks me over, brow quirked, eyes appraising. "And ever since then, you've been very good at keeping our conversations to a minimum and evading all of my questions.

And the ones you do choose to acknowledge are answered in a way that's intentionally cryptic. While you may not believe it, I was once a teenager too. You're not pulling anything with me that I didn't pull on my own parents. So if you think your coming out here is a free pass to party, well, I hope you enjoyed it because the party just ended."

"*A free pass to party?*" I scowl. "Surely you don't mean that?" I eyeball her carefully, seeing she does indeed. "Have you even seen this place?" My voice rises in outrage. "Out of all the places I've been—Paris, London, Rome, Mykonos—heck, even Miami—why on earth would I chose to rebel *here*—in barren, boring Enchantment, New Mexico?"

I chase it with some additional phrases I mutter under my breath not meant for her ears, which is why I'm caught by surprise when she says, "Good. I'm glad to know you see it that way. That means you won't miss it when you go."

I narrow my gaze, my skin prickled with cold.

"You're out of here. So take a good look around and say good-bye to this place because after tonight, you'll never see it again."

"You can't be serious?" I stare. There's no way I can leave. I'm a Seeker—the town needs me—and tonight I saw all the proof that I need to convince me it's true. While I have no idea what Cade's up to, he's definitely up to something, and it's up to me to stop it. I'm the only one who can.

Jennika nods, a self-satisfied smile hijacking her face. "I've taken a TV gig, which means no more traipsing the globe—"

My eyes go wide, my mouth hangs open and dumb, while my mind replays her words again and again until they begin to make sense. "But you hate those," I say. "You always say that—"

She flashes a palm, letting me know that's just the beginning. "*And*, along with the new gig, we have ourselves some new digs. I've rented a two-bedroom apartment in West L.A. But it's just a temporary arrangement until we can find the right place to buy.

I'm considering Venice or maybe even Silver Lake. We'll look around—see what feels right."

I stare at her without really seeing—my mind's too busy trying to catch up with my ears. I have no idea what to say—no idea what to think. Everything she just said stands in direct opposition to everything I thought I knew about her.

"Yep." She nods, one hand tracing the seam that runs down the side of her black, leather leggings, the other pushing through a chunk of hair that used to be pink but is now bleached platinum to match the surrounding strands. "It's all taken care of. So go pack up your things so we can get a move on. I've got a rental car waiting with a full tank of gas. And for once in my life, jet lag seems to be working for me—I plan to drive through the night."

She flicks her fingers, gesturing for me to get crackin', but I just stand before her, rooted in place. "No," I say, hating how small the word sounded. I chase it with a much stronger chorus of, "Forget it, Jennika. Uh-uh. There's no way."

She tilts her head, eyelids squinching as she appraises me. "Is this about the boy?" The tone of her voice implying she's convinced that it is.

"What? No!" I shake my head, assuring myself it's not *at all* about the boy—has nothing to do with Dace. It's about my duties as a Seeker—something I'm not about to confide to her. For one thing, she'd reject it outright, refuse to believe—wouldn't even try to understand. For another, she'd fear for my safety, end all negotiations, and insist that I leave. As long as she doesn't know, there's still hope—and when she's acting like this, hope is all I can cling to.

She moves toward me, her face softening along with her tone. "Daire, you can tell me. I get it. Believe me, I do. It's not like I didn't see him. It's not like I'm blind. He's gorgeous. Exactly what teenage dreams are made of. Falling for a boy like that is easy to do. But make no mistake, a boy like that has *heartbreaker* written all over him, and the last thing I want is for you to get hurt—or worse."

I glare, my face a mask of defiance, hating her words. Partly because I don't want to believe them and partly because I fear that they're true. "By *worse*, you mean *pregnant*? Like when you got knocked up with me at sixteen?"

"Yeah," she says. "Is that such a bad thing?" She fiddles with the long line of small silver hoops that hang from her multipierced ear—a sure sign she's searching for just the right words. "Look, Daire, as much as I don't regret having you—not for one single second—I don't want you to end up sixteen and pregnant like I did. Is that such a crime?"

I roll my eyes and look away. We've had this talk countless times, starting way back when I was too young to hear it and it bordered on wildly inappropriate. "It's not like that," I say. "He's not like that. You've got it all wrong."

But no sooner are the words out when I realize I waltzed straight into her trap. Her eyes widening, lips curling in triumph when she says, "How would you know? I thought you just met him *today*?"

I turn away. So annoyed I have to fight to keep quiet—keep the storm of angry retorts confined to my head.

"Come on, Daire." Her voice rings much sterner than the words imply. "Get your stuff, so we can get the heck out of here. Oh, and when you're done packing, be sure to leave a note for Paloma, thanking her for doing such a stellar job at screwing up as badly with you as she did with your dad."

"What?" My eyes widen, casting frantically around the room.

But Jennika just shakes her head, brows slanted, lips flattened in fury.

I push away from the counter and race down the hall—the sight of Paloma's empty bed confirming the worst. "How'd you get in?" I whirl on Jennika, voice filled with panic.

Reading her look of confusion when she glances between the bed and me, saying, "What do you mean? The door was wide open."

thirty-nine

"I stopped by with Kachina—had just gotten her secured in her stall when I found Paloma collapsed at the table in her office." Chay meets us at the door of the tiny adobe. His eyes are bloodshot and red-rimmed, tainted with worry. "Looks like she hit her head pretty hard when she went down, which only complicates matters."

"And so you brought her *here*?" Jennika plants herself in the entry—hands clutching her hips as she eyeballs the room and everyone in it with a disapproving glare.

But Chay knows how to handle her, which means he ignores her by directing his focus to me. "She's slipping in and out of consciousness, but every time she wakes up, she asks to see you."

"Hey, I've got a question." Jennika pipes up, her voice as condescending as the look on her face, insisting on being heard even though no one wants to listen. "Why isn't she in a hospital? Don't you think they can help her more than these people can?" She arcs her arm in a wide sweeping motion, indicating the older Native American, who I assume is the medicine man, and his much younger apprentice who sits at a small hand-carved table beside him. "No offense," she adds, looking at them, but their faces remain stoic, immobile, completely unmoved by her words.

"Just because you don't understand something doesn't mean it lacks validity," Chay says, his voice calm and even, his gaze prompting Jennika to clamp her lips shut and find a wall to go sag against.

"Can I see her?" I direct my words at Chay, the medicine man, and his apprentice, unsure who's in charge.

The medicine man nods his consent, as Chay reaches for my elbow and steers me toward her room. The sight of it prompting Jennika to push away from the wall, eager to follow, but I nix it just as quickly. Shaking my head in warning, I chase it with my very best *don't even think about it* look. Knowing I'm just buying time—that I'll pay for it later—but I'll face that hurdle when it comes, for now I just need to deal with the present.

Chay ushers me into a small, spare room, stopping beside a dark-haired woman leaning over Paloma, her hands moving in the space just a few inches above Paloma, as though working the energy.

"Chepi," he says. "Her granddaughter is here."

Chepi?

I watch as Dace's mom—Cade's mom too—finishes her ritual and turns away from the bed. Her eyes meeting mine with a look I can't read, before Chay escorts her from the room and closes the door behind me. Leaving me to stand in the entryway as I study the space, taking in a scattering of handwoven Navajo rugs hugging a dark wood floor, a short, sloping ceiling, and three identical niches along the far wall crammed with fetishes, carved wooden santos, large silver crosses, and other assorted objects of worship. My breath catching when I face the small, slim figure on the narrow bed, with a fan of silver-streaked hair spread wide across her pillow, and realize it's Paloma. Her pallid complexion providing sharp contrast to the trickle of blood that seeps from her nose and onto the sheets.

I claim the seat beside her, reach for a tissue, and gently bring it to her face. But the moment the blood's cleared away, it starts flowing again—a constant stream that refuses to cease.

"*Nieta,*" she murmurs, the word requiring obvious effort, demanding the kind of strength she no longer has.

I stroke her cheek softly, lean closer, and say, "It's me, *abuela.*" My voice catching on the word—Spanish for grandmother. And though I took the time to learn it, I could never bring myself to use it. I guess it felt too risky—hinted at the kind of bond I wasn't sure I could handle. But now, seeing her like this, there's no denying how much she's come to mean to me—how much I've come to trust her, rely on her, love her. I have no idea what I'd do without her. I can't stand to see her this way—so vulnerable and frail.

I rub my lips together, steady my voice, and say, "Don't worry, I'm fine, perfectly fine." I swallow hard, blinking back the tears as soon as they come. "Please don't waste your energies worrying about me. You need your rest. We'll talk later. For now, get some sleep."

She lifts her hand from the bed, ignoring my words. Her fingers cold and thin as she makes a grab for my wrist, asking, "Did you find it, *nieta?*"

I glance behind me, ensuring we're alone, that Jennika didn't find a way to sneak in. "Cockroach worked like a charm." I smile, wanting her to be proud of me. "I not only found it—I got *in.* And I know you warned me against it, but I didn't have much of a choice. It just sort of happened, though I made it out fine, with no one the wiser, so all's well that ends well, right?"

"And which way did you travel? Up, down, or sideways?" she asks, voice disturbingly frail.

"Sideways," I say, remembering the sewer-like tunnel that led to the well-appointed cave, noting the way her face floods with relief.

"The Middleworld." She sighs, her lids drooping halfway, fluttering for a moment, struggling to rise, until they lift once again. "Still just the Middleworld. I am grateful for that."

Not wanting to upset her, but knowing she needs to hear it, I take a deep breath and say, "Well, even if it was just the Middleworld, what I saw wasn't good. He's planning something . . ."

I lean back in my chair, gaze flitting toward the niche and its collection of carvings. The memory of everything I saw blazing in my mind so brightly I wish there was a way to transmit it to her. I'm not sure I can relay it with the kind of accuracy it deserves. Though knowing I have to try, I lean toward her and say, "He has big plans to break away from the family tradition—wants to extend his reach—rule all the worlds—and the bizarre thing is, he's asked me to join him. He sees no reason why the two of us can't work together. He thinks of it as a peace treaty, but that's because he's totally crazy. No peace could ever come of such a thing." I study her carefully, see the way her lips tighten, pulling under her teeth. "While I have no idea how he plans to pull it off, I'm sure it has something to do with a bunch of dead Richters. They're no longer just communing with their spirits—Cade's communing with the ancestors *themselves*—apparently without Leandro's approval. You should've seen it—there was an entire army of undead Richters, and I watched as Cade fed them these strange, glowing white objects, which made them transform right before me. Making them a lot less gruesome and zombie-like, and a lot more . . . human-like."

Paloma gasps. Her face stricken, blanching so badly I'm about to call Chay. Only to have her fingers find mine, her voice a forced whisper when she mumbles something in Spanish I can't understand. Figuring she's too exhausted to say it in English, but sensing it's important, I start to rise so I can get someone to translate—only to have her shake her head in frustration and blurt, "What day is it?"

I consult my watch. "After midnight, so that makes it November first. Why?" Wondering what sort of significance the day might hold.

Only to watch her face pale even further when she says, "He's prepping them . . ."

Her lids droop as her gaze grows so cloudy and vacant. I know I should let her rest, but I also know it's important, so I shake her shoulder and plead, "Paloma—please, hang in there—what's he prepping them for?"

Her lips move, but her voice is so faint I'm forced to press my ear to her lips and beg her to repeat it.

"*Día de los Muertos*," she says, the words a croaked whisper.

"Day of the Dead, yeah—what about it?" I urge, my tone frantic, eager. She's slipping away, drifting into that painless place of sleep, and while I can't say I blame her, I also can't let her go there—not yet anyway.

I cup my hand to her cheek, press my ear directly to her lips. Struggling to piece together the words when she says, "He's prepping them . . . the glowing objects . . . the white orbs . . ."

"Yes? Paloma, please, what is it?" I beg, holding my breath.

She fumbles for the soft, buckskin pouch she wears at her neck—her fingers curling around it in a bid for one last burst of strength—receiving it when she says, "They're souls, *nieta*. He's feeding them souls. Human souls. He's prepping them to invade the Lowerworld, and he will use the magick of that day to do so. What happens in one dimension ultimately affects all the others. It's a sacred balance the Richters will start to corrupt the moment they gain access—allowing havoc to rule in the Lowerworld, the Upperworld, and the Middleworld too. If he succeeds, it's just a matter of time before they expand their influence, and once that occurs, it's the end of the world as we know it."

forty

When I exit Paloma's room, Jennika takes one look at my face, and says, "Listen, Daire, I know you're worried about her, but I'm sure she'll be fine, and we really need to get out of here, so . . ."

"I'm not leaving." I push past her, barely pausing long enough to look at her when I add, "I'm staying in Enchantment and there's nothing you can do about it."

"Excuse me?" She grabs my arm, swings me around until I'm facing her again. Her brow shooting halfway up her forehead, mis-reading my words as a challenge even though I meant what I said.

I'm staying. I have no plans to leave. It's as simple as that.

And yet there's really no use in arguing. It'll just make her more stubborn, cause her to dig her spiked heels in even further. So I soften my tone when I add, "At least not until she gets better. When I'm sure she's okay, then fine, whatever. But *not* before then." My gaze meets hers, and I hope she can't see the lie behind the words. The things Paloma told me have left me shaken to the core, but there's no way to explain it to Jennika.

When Paloma gets better—and she *will* get better—she has to, I can't do this without her—when that day comes, Jennika and I will negotiate again.

I plop down on the chair the medicine man vacated when he went to check on Paloma with his assistant and Chepi in tow. Fully determined to wait it out here, to not budge from this seat until I'm sure she's turned the corner. But it's not long before Chay places a hand on my shoulder and insists I go home.

"Get some sleep," he says. "It meant a lot for her to see you, but now that she has, there's nothing more you can do. Leftfoot, the medicine man, is doing all that he can. It's far more important for you to rest up before *school*."

The way he says *school*—well, I know he's thinking the same thing I am: School equals Cade, and I need to keep a close eye on him.

School also equals Dace—though that's really not something I can think about now.

And it's not long before he's bundling Jennika and me back into the rental car, promising to call at the first sign of change, as Jennika sighs long and loud and pulls away from the curb. Continuing her chorus of sighs all the way back to Paloma's, though I do my best to ignore her.

I just wait until she pulls into the drive, then I bid a quick *good night* and make for my room. Only to find a beautiful, carved wooden chest placed next to my bed that Paloma must've put there before she fell ill.

I run my hands over the top, my throat closing in on itself when I look inside and find it filled with the same kinds of things she keeps in her office. There's a small black-and-white hand-painted rawhide rattle on a long wooden stick; a large drum bearing the face of a purple-eyed raven stretched over a round wooden frame; three beautiful feathers bearing tags that identify them as a swan feather to be used for transformative powers, a raven feather bearing magickal powers, and an eagle feather used for sending prayers; along with what looks to be a pendulum with a chunk of amethyst attached to the end—all of it lying on a soft, handwoven blanket, including a small, white card from Paloma that reads:

Nieta—

These are but some of the tools you will use on your journey as a Seeker. Soon I will teach you how to use them all—their power will amaze you!
I am so very proud of you.

Paloma

    I gaze upon it, my eyes burning with unspent tears, wondering if Paloma will last long enough to teach me. Other than the rattle, I have no idea what to do with any of it. For someone who's supposed to be brimming with untapped potential—I feel just the opposite. Powerless. Useless. With no idea how to access the gifts of my ancestral legacy. Unable to do anything more than collapse on my bed.
    Jennika was right.
    She was right all along.
    If this is what loss feels like, then I'd prefer to have never known it.
    I'd prefer to have never come to this place—never been foolish enough to allow myself to care as much as I do.
    This horrible feeling goes way beyond pain—miles past debilitating.
    It's reduced me to a numb, frozen shell, huddled on my bed—forced to remind myself to breathe in and out.
    I curl into a ball, trying to silence my mind and shut down my heart. Yanking the blanket high over my head, desperate to block out the room since everything in it reminds me of Paloma. Though it's no use. Turns out, the scent of lilac laundry soap that clings to the sheets is just as big a culprit as the dream catcher that hangs over the windowsill. Enough to prompt the image of her that blooms large in my mind—kind, loving, trusting me to live up to my birthright. But I've no idea where to start.

According to Paloma, every time the El Coyote clan has managed to break through to the Lowerworld, chaos reigned in the Middleworld. And now that they're planning to draw upon the power and chaos of *Día de los Muertos* to use all those regenerated ancestors to penetrate the Lowerworld—with more power than ever before—I have no idea how I can possibly stop it.

I have to do something, but I've no idea what. No idea how I'm supposed to face off against Cade and his army of undead ancestors.

There's no way I can beat them. Heck, I haven't even completed my full Seeker initiation. And yet I have to find a way to fight them. I can't let them win.

I gaze at my father's photo, remembering what Paloma said about him being everywhere—that I can call upon him anytime. But without Paloma's guidance, without her beside me, I can't seem to summon his presence.

Without her, this house feels too lonely, too empty. A cold, blank space that only magnifies my inability to deal with all this.

Too wound up to sleep, too wound up to do much of anything, I dress for the day and head out. Finding my way to Kachina's stall and feeling a tiny bit better when she lifts her head high, paws hard at the dirt, and lets out a soft snort of greeting when she sees my approach. Her reception far more enthusiastic than my newly adopted cat's, who was perfectly content spending time with Kachina until he caught sight of me and decided to scram.

I duck into the stall, busying myself with filling her feeding trough and replenishing her water, then I stand just beside her while she eats, telling her all the things I'm too worried to voice to myself.

My long list of worries multiplying until I've lost track of time. And the next thing I know the sky is draped with thick ribbons of orange and pink, the sun is hanging much higher than it was when I arrived, and Jennika has managed to find me. Her eyes darting between Kachina and me when she says, "Don't get too attached to her."

I pretend not to hear. I don't want to start this again. But despite the gaunt cheeks and deep purple half-moons that swoop under her eyes—the result of too many nights of missed sleep—Jennika's clearly lost none of her steam.

She hands me a mug of freshly brewed coffee, and I'm quick to receive it. Enjoying its rich piñon scent, when she says, "I'm serious, Daire. I know you think you can talk me out of it. I know exactly what you're up to. But as soon as Paloma's better, and I mean the very second we get word, you and I are out of here. Which means you'll have to say good-bye to your horse, this house, the boy, and everything else. This was always meant to be temporary—I thought you knew that."

I sip my coffee, stare at the sky, and refuse to engage.

"I mean, I don't get it. Just what is it you see in this place? What's the attraction? Is there something I'm missing? Because from what I've seen, it's a socially backward trash heap."

I turn to face her, taking in her pale face, the bulky sweater too big for her frame. Hanging on her shoulders in such a haphazard way, it leaves her looking as tiny and vulnerable as I currently feel. "It may be a dump," I say, holding tight to my mug as I turn away from her and survey the yard. Unable to see anything but the love, care, and devotion Paloma supplied to make it this way—a private oasis tucked away in the desert—though it's all lost on Jennika. All she sees is a horse, an abundance of plants, a strange border of salt inside a strange coyote fence inside a thick, adobe wall. The magick is lost on her. But that doesn't mean I can't try to make her see why it might be important to me. "It's not like I can deny it. But it's also the first place I've ever felt like I just might belong. It's the first time I've ever felt like I had a real and stable home."

She starts to speak, probably wanting to defend herself and all the choices she's made over the last sixteen years, but there's time for that later. I need her to hear me while the words are still with me.

"And I know you've spent a lifetime trying to protect me from the staggering pain of grief that comes from losing the things and the people and the places you allowed yourself to care about—but guess what, Jennika—that's no way to live. As much as it hurts to lose something you love, there's a much greater joy in getting to experience it for as long as it lasts." I suck in my breath, my eyes meeting hers. It's the opposite of what I thought I believed, but now I realize it's true. "And I know you meant well. I know you were only trying to spare me from the feelings that overwhelmed you. And who knows, maybe you did spare me a load of regrets and hurt feelings? What I do know is that I *like* being part of something. I like being a member of a family, a community, heck, even a school. I don't care if it's small time—I don't care if it lacks excitement and glamour—this is the place where my *abuela* lives. A woman who's given me a home—a purpose. And for the first time in my life, I—"

"A *purpose*?" Jennika squints, as she cocks her head and steps closer. "And just what exactly might that be? You planning to take over her garden? Apprentice as an herbal healer? I had much higher hopes for you, Daire."

The way her gaze meets mine—outraged and incredulous— well, I know I've gone too far. I never should've said it, should've stopped while I was barely ahead.

"Forget it," I say. "Just forget the whole thing." I give Kachina one final pat and make my way back toward the house. Carefully avoiding Jennika's gaze when I add, "You should probably just take me to school. The first bell's at eight."

forty-one

The second I walk past that big iron gate, I start searching for Cade. Though it's not until lunch when I run into Xotichl in the hallway that I learn why I've been unable to find him.

"So, you taking part in *Día de los Muertos*?" she asks, employing her uncanny ability to know it's me before I've even had a chance to announce myself.

"Don't tell me I'm still giving off that new-girl energy?" I say, watching as she slams her locker shut and taps her cane on the ground, nailing the space between my boots and hers.

"Now it's more like nervous, paranoid energy—what gives?"

My eyes scan the hall, knowing I should mention what happened to Paloma but not wanting to upset her, I say, "Guess I'm on the lookout for Cade, Lita, and the Cruel Crew. I'd rather spot them before they can spot me."

"Not to worry." She smiles. "Cade's absent, and as for the rest, I'm pretty sure they're too starstruck to approach you. But that still doesn't answer my question. Day of the Dead—you in?"

"In for what?" I check out her cute blue sweater and jeans, struck once again by how pretty she is. Knowing I'm most certainly in for observing *Día de los Muertos*, though probably not in the way that she means.

"You probably noticed we pretty much skip Halloween and go straight to Day of the Dead. It takes over the whole town, so the only way to avoid it is to leave. Some places celebrate it all week, but here in Enchantment, we wait until the last day, November second, when everyone dresses in costume, and eats, drinks, and makes merry all night. And while plenty of people sleep in the graveyards, hanging with the spirits of their dead ancestors, most people go to the Rabbit Hole since the Richters throw a huge, crazy party where the whole town gets to eat, drink, and listen to music for free. Which, as you probably already guessed, makes it a pretty big draw."

"Sounds fun," I say, knowing *fun* is definitely not the right word, though it's the one that's most appropriate, considering the circumstances. "Wouldn't miss it," I add, suspecting this year's celebration will provide a party experience like no other—especially if El Coyote has his way.

"Good." She nods. "Epitaph is on the lineup, so you'll get another chance to hear them since you totally vanished last night. What happened? We looked everywhere—how'd you get home?"

I fumble for an excuse, knowing it's virtually impossible to lie to her, but that doesn't stop me from trying. "I wasn't feeling well, so . . ."

She makes for the North hallway, the place where Dace eats lunch on his own. But after last night and the whole thing with Jennika, I'm too embarrassed to face him.

I pull back, searching for a detour, when I realize there's no sign of his shoes—no sign of him anywhere. The hallway is empty. And despite my initial reluctance to face him, his absence makes me feel even worse.

Xotichl stops, head tilted toward me, lips tugging at the sides, as I stare at the empty space where Dace would normally be.

"What's going on with you?" she says. "There's no use lying, I can sense it, you know?"

She stands before me—a tiny force of nature who will not be fooled by my fictional stories. Leaving me no choice but to laugh when I say, "I know. You're too intuitive for your own good, but I'm not quite ready to spill, so you'll just have to bear with me."

Her lips flatten as she considers my words—her cane sweeping the space before her again as she says, "Fair enough." She leads me into the cafeteria with far more confidence and authority than I could ever manage. Heading for a table in back, where she slips onto the bench, nods toward the boy on her left, and says, "Daire, Dace—Dace, Daire." Shooting me a knowing smile when she adds, "Or perhaps you've already met?"

She cocks her head to the side and digs into her lunch sack, and all I can think is that there's more to this blindsight thing than I ever would've guessed.

I mumble a quick *Hey* and claim the opposite space. Feeling awkward and embarrassed, unable to rid myself of the image of Jennika's glaring face peering into the window—the horrifying things that she said. Not to mention how dumb I must've looked with my eyes squeezed tight—lips all puckered and ready—leaning in for a kiss he probably never intended to give.

"You okay?" His gaze moves over me, voice marked with concern. "Your mom seemed pretty upset."

"She was." I peer into my lunch bag, avoiding his eyes—unwilling to catch sight of my burning red cheeks reflecting thousands of times. "She gets like that sometimes, though deep down, she means well." I lift my shoulders, deciding to leave it at that. Unwilling to explain how Jennika's history has a habit of bleeding into my present. How her somewhat irrational yet well-intended desire to save me from things like heartbreak and unplanned pregnancy, along with all the other detours life offers, sometimes gets in the way of my journey.

"I'm not sure I handled it well," he says, his face so open, gaze filled with such raw regret, my heart aches on his behalf.

"Considering the circumstances, I think you did fine. Besides, it's not like you stood a chance, her mind was made up the moment she saw you."

Dace jerks back, his expression slighted, voice unsure when he says, "I don't understand . . ."

I fumble with my lunch sack, wondering why I can never say the right thing around him. Having no way to explain in a way that won't sound completely embarrassing, when Xotichl steps in.

"What's not to get? You're hot—Daire's gorgeous—it's a recipe for parental distress if there ever was one. Guess that means she got a ride home from you, since Auden and I couldn't find her?"

Dace and I exchange a look, mine flushed and panicked, his amused and reassuring when he says, "She wasn't feeling well, and I was on my way out . . ."

His voice drifts away with his gaze, as Xotichl's foot finds mine, giving a swift kick when she says, "Incoming." And it's only a few seconds later when Lita appears at the end of our table.

She looks at me, her gaze surprisingly shy when she says, "Hey."

I glance to either side of her, amazed to find she made the trip on her own. Leaving me to wonder if she truly is tired of hanging with suck-ups, like she implied in the bathroom.

"Listen," she says. "I just wanted to apologize for the other day." She swallows hard, forces her gaze to hold mine.

"By *the other day*, do you mean yesterday—or the first day I saw you on the trail?" I ask, figuring there's no use denying the fact that she's had two occasions to be nice to me, and both times she chose not to.

"Um, both, I guess. I just . . ." She tries to find the right word, quickly abandons the search, and starts again. "I know it wasn't cool of me, and I just want to—"

But before she can go any further I flash my palm and say, "It's fine. Whatever. Apology accepted." Noting the way her shoulders soften, her jaw loosens, the effect short-lived when I add, "But just so you know, before you start spending all your energy being nice to me, my Hollywood connections aren't all that you think."

Xotichl sucks in her breath, while I brace for an onslaught of denials and anger that fail to appear.

"Wow," she says, her heavily made-up eyes surveying me with a hint of approval. "You really don't take any crap, do you?"

I glance at Dace who's watching me intently and knowing it's true, and that I have Jennika's influence to thank, I say, "Nope, I really don't." I meet her gaze again.

"So, we're good, then?" she asks in a voice that's ridiculously hopeful. So hopeful I'm pretty sure she didn't believe me—still thinks I have unlimited access to Vane Wick, or whoever else she might have in mind.

But not wanting to start up again, I say, "Yeah. Sure. We're good."

She nods. Smiles. Starts to move away, then turns back as though a thought just occurred to her. "I'll look for you at the Rabbit Hole. You know, tomorrow night, for Day of the Dead? You'll be there, right?" Her eyes drift from me, to Xotichl and Dace, acknowledging them as though she hadn't realized they'd been sitting there all along. "I thought we could maybe hang out?"

I gape, rendered dumbstruck by the offer. Eventually gathering my wits enough to say, "Sure. Whatever." Watching as she retreats and thinking how my prospects for tomorrow night keep getting weirder.

Xotichl whistles under her breath, saying, "I'm not one to shock easily, but that was just . . ." She screws her lips to the side, drums her nails against the side of her water bottle, searching for just the right word.

"Oddly sincere," Dace supplies, his gaze finding mine.

I lift my shoulders, having no idea if he's right, but then nothing in this town is ever what it appears.

The moment broken by the shrill sound of the bell, telling us it's time to pack up and move on.

forty-two

When I reach my last class, independent study, the one I share with Dace, there's no denying the excitement I feel at the prospect of seeing him again. But my excitement soon turns to disappointment when I find his chair empty. For whatever reason, independent study is not on his agenda today.

I claim the table near the back and retrieve my book from my bag. Determined to settle in for a nice long read, but not getting very far before my mind wanders back to Paloma.

I have to help her.

As her granddaughter—as a Seeker—there must be something I can do.

Something more than sitting idly in this room, being babysat by a video monitor.

I sling my bag over my shoulder and bolt for the door. My classmates staring in shock, as the strict surveillance of the all-seeing camera tracks my escape. Making my way down the series of halls, I burst through the double doors and blaze past the guard, trying to come up with some kind of plan.

While I may not know how to stop the Richters from invading the Lowerworld, I'm still a day away from their being able to do so. And since that's the place where Raven lives, and since it's his job to guide me, I figure it's as good a place to start as any.

Only I have no idea how to get there.

My only other visit was the soul journey when I drank Paloma's tea.

Knowing of only one other way I might be able to find it, I head for her house, sneak through the gate without Jennika knowing, and go straight for Kachina's stall where I toss on a bridle and hop on her back. Smoothing my hand over her brown and white mane, I press my mouth to her ear, and say, "Take me there. Take me to the cave of my vision quest so I can consult with my ancestors."

The second I get to the cave, I leap past the grainy, white border and head straight for the wall featuring my long list of ancestors with their spirit animals lined up beside them. My eyes grazing over Valentina, Esperanto, Piann, Mayra, Maria, Diego, Gabriella, all the way down to Paloma, Django, and me. Holding the pouch at my neck with one hand and shaking the rattle with the other, I call them to me—letting them know that I need their assistance— need them to show me how to make my way to the Lowerworld.

I sit beside them, back propped against the wall, legs sprawled before me. Forcing my mind to go quiet and still—shut down the restlessness that often plagues me and remain open to some kind of sign. Instantly alerted to a gentle nudge of wind that twists into the cave. Swirling and lingering before me, making sure I take notice, before breezing right past, wafting all the way to the place in back where the ceiling meets the dirt.

The wind is my element. According to Paloma that makes me a daughter of the wind—something she was very excited about. But one look at that solid wall of rock—so dense and forbidding— is enough to make my head fill with doubt.

No way will that budge.

No way will it lead to a mystical land hidden deep underneath.

It's not like I didn't touch it before. Last time I was here, I made the full rounds, ran my hands over every square inch in an attempt to see how big the cave was. Yet that was before I knew the full truth of how the world works. Before I learned how to focus on the unseeable, the unknown—how to coax it into my immediate field of consciousness, until it presents itself.

And it's not long before that seemingly impenetrable stone wall wavers before me, as my buckskin pouch begins to throb like a heartbeat. A solid reminder that I need to stop seeing with my eyes. Stop running everything through my logical mind and start trusting what I know in my heart—no matter how improbable it may seem.

I duck my head low, stretch my arms before me, and sprint toward it. My palms slamming into the stone, impacting for a moment—only to break through the rock as the surface softens and fades. The wall crumbling to a finely milled dust that swirls at my feet, as the ground just beneath me gives way. Sending me falling, spiraling, tumbling down a long, steep tunnel that plunges straight into the core of the earth. My arms flailing, body somersaulting head over feet—unable to stop or slow down, unable to gain control of myself.

But unlike the last time, I don't try to stop it. I just trust that I'll somehow end up in the mouth of the Lowerworld.

The tunnel ends without warning—spitting me straight into a bright shaft of light where I land in a heap. Only to find Raven sitting on a nearby rock, purple eyes flashing, waiting for me.

I rise to my feet. Wipe my hands across the seat of my jeans. Keeping a careful eye on Raven as I approach him and say, "I need help. Paloma's sick and I don't know what to do. Will you guide me?"

My words halted by the sight of him preparing for flight. His wings lifting, spreading wide, as he thrusts himself forward, lifts from his perch, and executes a perfect wide circle over my head, before he soars with the wind, and I set off behind him. Grateful for the way he stops on occasion, allowing me a chance to catch up, before he takes flight again—leading me all the way to the beautiful clearing I know from my dreams, as well as the time I drank Paloma's tea.

I glance all around, taking in the tall swaying trees, the way each blade of grass seems to dance at my feet. Not quite sure how to feel about his leading me here—but definitely leaning toward uneasy at best, when Raven swoops toward me, lands on my shoulder, and thrusts his beak forward, urging me to keep going, to move all the way through to the other side of the forest where I come across the same hot spring I saw in my dreams.

And just like in my dream, Dace is here too.

forty-three

I stand before him, keeping quiet and still. Hoping to observe without notice, prolong the moment before he senses my presence.

His hair is wet, slicked away from his forehead—the light filtering through the trees in a way that slings a series of shadows over his face. And when Raven lifts from my shoulder, glides to a nearby branch where he looks down upon us, the beat of his wings causes Dace to look up, not the least bit surprised to find me wandering through a mystical dimension that remains hidden to everyone else.

"From the moment I saw you, I knew you were different." His head tilts in a way that darkens his face, as my hands curl to fists, my body braces for just about anything. The last time we were here, it didn't end well. And there's no way to prove this isn't a setup—that I won't be forced to relive the nightmare again.

"Yeah?" My voice is curt, edgier than planned. "And why's that—what gave me away?" I focus hard on his eyes, seeing thousands of images of me glimmering back—a long, rigid line of a girl with dark flowing hair.

He shrugs, shoulders rising and falling as though he's truly perplexed. "Guess my instincts are good. Some things you just know without question," he says.

"Was it instincts that brought you here?" I move toward him, the toes of my boots edging up to the spring. "Or did you see it in a dream?" My pulse thrumming triple time the second the words leave my lips. But I have to know, and there's no way to ask coyly, no other way to phrase such a thing.

Was he really there too—or was it all just a product of my wildest imaginings?

"Waking life—dreaming life—who's to say where reality lies?" He grins, a glorious flash of sparkling eyes and white teeth, before he goes on to add, "This place is like a dream, but I'm pretty sure we're awake." He fingers his arm, gives himself a quick pinch. "Yep, I'm awake—you?"

My eyes roam the length of him—drinking in strong shoulders, a smooth bare chest, stopping where the water dips low at his hips. So distracted by the sight, I nearly miss it when he says, "But to answer your question, it was my mom who introduced me to this place when I was a kid, and it's been a favorite of mine ever since."

I swallow hard, noticing how gracefully he avoided my question, but I decide to let it pass, there's no reason to push it.

"So, you coming in?" He motions toward the bubbling space just beside him, as I look to Raven for guidance. Only to watch him flit from the tree to the back of a beautiful, black horse I hadn't noticed 'til now. He's brought me where he wants me—it's up to me to see it through.

"I'm not really dressed for it." I sweep a hand over my jeans, point toward my boots. Not exactly the clothes I wore in the dream, and I'm hoping that's a good omen.

Dace lifts his shoulders, causing tiny droplets of water to sluice down his sides. "You're gonna let that stop you?" He looks at me, slicks a hand through his hair, as I gnaw the inside of my cheek, unsure what to do. His voice warm and coaxing when he says, "C'mon, water's great. Besides, I promise not to peek."

He makes a show of turning away and placing his hands over his face, as I stand before him—weighing my options.

Should I do what Raven wants and join Dace in the hot spring, which could turn out as badly as the dream?

Or should I ignore them both and be on my way—even though I'm not really sure where that is?

Remembering what Paloma told me about Raven having more wisdom than me, that it may not always make sense but I have to learn to trust him—I slip off my jacket and shoes, shimmy out of my jeans, then yank my tank top well past my thighs and wade in. Unaware I'd been holding my breath until I reach the far side where Dace waits—taking my place beside him like I did in the dream.

He lowers his hands, revealing a face so kind and disarming, I'm tempted to believe this couldn't end badly. But knowing better than to believe what I see, I take a moment to grab a large, sharp rock from behind me. Folding my fingers tightly around it as I settle it onto my lap. If his brother shows, he won't stand a chance. I'm more than ready to bash in his ugly demon head at first glance.

"The first time my mom brought me here, she said a lack of money was no excuse not to travel to enchanted places." His gaze wanders to a long-ago past. "But she didn't take me very often, she liked to save it for special occasions. Didn't want me to grow bored of it—though I can't imagine such a thing."

"Do you come here a lot now?" I ask, observing the exact moment he returns to the present.

"Whenever I can." His voice going soft and wistful when he adds, "But between work and school, it's hard to find time."

"And yet you found time today." I glance all around as I pat the rock in my lap, reassured by its sharp edges and heft.

He settles against the stone ledge at his back and spreads his arms wide. Fingers drumming just shy of my shoulder, he says, "I had an irresistible pull to come here, so I followed my instincts, and now I know why."

He grins in a way so hopeful, I can't help but meet his smile with one of my own. Though the look is deceptive, just underneath my heart beats in a frenzy, worried that *pull* he felt was less about running into me and more about reliving the dream.

He holds the look for a moment, then takes a deep breath and disappears under a blanket of bubbles, only to emerge a few seconds later so glistening and gorgeous, it takes my breath away. The two of us sitting in silence—he with his eyes closed, his face soft and dreamy—as I sit right beside him, tense and alert, fingers clenching a rock I have every intention of using if his brother shows up.

The quiet broken when he pops one eye open and says, "So tell me, how'd you find it?" Then opening the other, he adds, "How'd you get to the Enchanted Spring?"

I rub my lips together, unsure how to answer.

"You're the first person I've ever run into." His face is thoughtful, gaze appraising.

"So that means you've never come here with Cade? Never even told him about it?" The words rush from my lips before I can stop them.

Dace frowns, face dropping as though my words have left a bad taste. "Why would I do that?" he says. "In case you haven't noticed, we're not exactly close."

I turn the rock in my hands, sidestepping his original question when I say, "Is that your horse?" I gesture toward the beautiful black stallion grazing nearby.

Dace nods. "Is that your raven?"

I clamp my lips shut. Try to focus on the bubbles, the warmth of the water, the flowering vines that drift down from the trees and sprawl among the rocks, but it's impossible. I'm too wound up. Prepared for an epic battle or an epic embarrassment—it could go either way.

"So, you're not going to claim that raven, and you're not going to tell me how you found the Enchanted Spring?" He tilts his head, studies me closely, but I just look away, refusing his gaze. His eyes are a vortex leading to a place of no escape. And yet I don't have to look at him to be irresistibly drawn to him. His presence alone is enough.

He pushes forward, moving away from the rock until he's looming before me. His hair shiny and slick, revealing a collection of features so lovely and sharp, they appear to be sculpted by a talented hand. Eyes gleaming darker than normal, less like aquamarine and more like the deep shade of turquoise found in his mother's jewelry, he says, "However you managed, I'm glad you found it. From the first day you ran into me at the club, I knew you weren't like the other girls around here. I knew in that instant you were different."

"How can you be so sure?" I ask, my voice hoarse, thick, affected by his nearness—the way he hovers so close he's just a razor's width away. Remembering what I saw when I spied on him via the raven, the way he used telekinesis to deposit the trash bags into the Dumpster—knowing I'm not the only one who's different around here.

He throws his head back and laughs, the sight so beautiful I wish it could last. Leveling his gaze on me when he says, "I guess we're right back to instincts again—so far, they've yet to steer me wrong."

"And what are your instincts telling you now?" I whisper, knowing I can no longer trust mine. He's thrown me so off kilter, I don't know what to expect, what to do next, other than tighten my grip on the rock in my lap, and wait for his twin to show up.

He swallows hard. Takes a deep breath as though he's about to dip under the water again, but instead he says, "They're telling me to kiss you."

He leans forward, gaze steeped with intent. And when his hands find my cheeks—when his thumbs smooth my skin—when

his gaze wanders over me, devouring all that he sees—well, I
can't help but notice that it's happening now just like it did in the
dream.

I squeeze the rock hard, shift it high on my lap—determined
to go with it, see this thing through. Raven brought me here for a
reason, and clearly that reason is now.

His face looming before me, lips swelling toward mine, I close
my eyes and meet them—telling myself it's just part of the progression, it's how the dream goes. The kiss so sweet, warm, and
familiar—yet far more soulful than I remembered it being.

"Daire . . ." he whispers, his voice husky and deep, as his hands
explore the length of me. Slipping under my tank top, discovering
every hollow and curve. And I'm so lost in the kiss, the heady
nearness of him, I hardly notice when he entwines my fingers with
his, causing me to lose my grip, as the rock falls from my lap and
rushes down past my feet.

I slide my palms over his taut, smooth chest, and anchor my
arms around his neck. Hooking my legs around his, I pull him
closer, yearning to taste even deeper—when he curls a finger
under my strap, pushes it down past my shoulder, clearing a path
for his lips as he bends his head toward my breasts—and it's then
I remember—this is how it went down.

This is the moment he'll be replaced by his demon twin with
a snake shooting out of his mouth.

And now that he's rid me of the rock—I'm left with no way to
defend us.

I pull away—the move so abrupt, so unexpected—the strap on
my buckskin pouch snaps and sends it flying into the water.

My eyes blaze on his, gasping in panic, when he goes under to
retrieve the pouch well before I can move.

I take a quick breath and submerge myself too. Grappling for
the pouch, seeing it just below us, resting on a rock, I push him
aside, try to fetch it for myself, but he's quicker, his arms longer,
and he's claimed it well before I can get there.

Heading for the surface, I break free of the water, only to find his face shining with triumph, as he takes a moment to tie the ends back together. Paloma's voice filling my head, warning me to never allow anyone else to wear it, look inside it, not even briefly, or its power will be lost. And though he's made no move toward either of those things, I can't take the chance that his curiosity might get the better of him.

"I'll take that," I say, snatching the pouch from his hands, and securing it back around my neck, where it clings to my chest.

His brow slants, his mouth goes grim, hands fumbling help-lessly in his lap, as he says, "I'd never look inside, if that's what you're worried about. Believe me, I know better."

I clutch the pouch to my chest, fingers seeking the shape of Raven, the feather, relieved to find all is okay, but even more re-lieved when it suddenly dawns on me:

This is not how the dream goes.

The realization coming too late, and the next thing I know, Dace is out of the water, reaching for the towel he left folded on a rock. Running it over his hair, his body, before draping it over his shoulders and saying, "Listen, I'm really sorry. I wasn't going to keep it, and I'd never look inside. I just hope I didn't scare you from this place. You're free to visit for as long as you like, when-ever you like. If it makes you feel better, I'll steer clear of it."

He turns his back, starts to head for Horse. The sight of it prompting me to rush from the water, my breath coming shallow and quick, tank top molding and clinging in the most embarrass-ing way, as I stop just behind him and say, "So, you're giving me custody of the Enchanted Spring?"

He turns, his expression shifting from troubled to confused.

"Or are you just granting me visitation rights? You know, like an every other weekend kind of thing?"

I stand before him—a wet, soggy mess with a wide, hopeful grin, which, thankfully, he's quick to return. His gaze moving over me, so heated and intense, I can't help but squirm under the weight of it. Then remembering the towel draped over his neck, he flushes in embarrassment, and hands it to me.

We dress quickly, and with my tank top so wet, I decide to abandon it, and just wear the jacket buttoned up the front instead.

"I should go." I shoot Raven a pointed look, but he just remains rooted in place, refusing to move from Horse, no matter how hard I glare.

"Spirit animals have their own agenda," Dace says, glancing between Raven and me. Replying to the shock on my face when he adds, "I grew up on the reservation, and, as it happens, I descend from a long line of healers and medicine men. You tend to pick up on these things. Horse has been with me since birth, got me through some rough times."

I study him carefully, sensing there's more.

"Other than the occasional trip to this place, my mom did her best to shelter me from the more mystical side of life, despite the long line of Light Workers in our family. But I was always drawn to it. I was never a normal kid. I preferred spending time with the elders to kids my own age, and because of it, the other kids shunned me, made fun of me. My mom's attempts to get me to fit in made for some rough, awkward times. But the times I spent with the elders, hearing their stories and learning their magick . . . that's when I was happiest. They're the ones who introduced me to Horse. They also convinced me I had a natural gift that shouldn't be wasted. That it was my legacy, and that there's no shame in nurturing it. That's another reason I left the reservation. I wanted a shot at growing my gifts, without my mom's constant interference. I know it sounds crazy—but this world is full of untapped possibilities—the potential is limitless. You wouldn't believe some of the magick I've seen." He shakes his head, his focus returning to me. Cheeks heating with embarrassment when he says, "And now you probably think I'm a lunatic." His body tenses, bracing for the emotional blow I have no intention of giving.

I shake my head and move toward him, cupping his face with

my hand, as I whisper, "Not even close." My lips meeting his—
softly, warmly—pulling away only when Raven emits a low croaking sound, telling me it's time to move on.

"Do you ride?" Dace grabs my hand, leads me toward Horse.

"Chay gave me a horse to look after, but I'm not very good, I'm
still learning. Though Kachina, the horse, is really patient."

"We should ride sometime." He smiles, then, coaxing Raven
onto his finger, he says, "In fact, why don't you hop on now—
there's something I think you should see."

I glance at Raven, noting how quickly he hops from Dace's
finger to a space high on Horse's neck, his glimmering eyes urging me to take Dace's hand and get settled behind him, as we head
back through the forest, back through the clearing, and into a
heavily wooded area, where Horse stops beside a thick clump of
shrubs and Dace says, "This is it."

He eases me to my feet, entwines my fingers with his, and
leads me to an area sheltered by trees and low-growing bushes.
Pushing the brush aside, he stands behind me as I stoop down to
see better. My eyes growing wide, throat closing tight—dropping
Dace's hand as quickly as I took it, when I gaze upon a dying white
wolf with blue eyes.

forty-four

I drop to my knees, place my hands on the wolf's head with no hesitation, no fear of any kind. From what I've seen, the animals of the Lowerworld have no need to fear us, which means they're not at all vicious. Besides, this is Paloma's Wolf—her spirit animal—I know it in my heart—and he's far too ill to pose any threat.

"What happened?" I glance over my shoulder, Dace's expression transforming from confusion to hurt when he misreads the whole thing and assumes that I blame him.

"I found him this way," he says, quick to explain. "I've tried everything to nurse him back to health, but it's no use. He's dying—which means his human attachment is dying as well."

"You don't know that!" I scowl, my voice snappy, edgy, though he barely reacts.

He moves closer, places a tentative hand on my shoulder. His gaze as sad as his voice when he says, "I agree that it's strange—spirit animals aren't supposed to die. From everything I've learned, this shouldn't be happening. And yet there's no doubt he's fading. If he does die, I'm pretty sure his human attachment will die too—and if that happens, I fear for what will become of that human's soul."

I swallow hard, rising to my feet as I gaze all around, saying,

"We can't leave him here. If you'll help me lift him, then we can . . ."

I bend forward, inch my fingers under the poor dying wolf that's too weak to move, ignoring Dace's warning when he says, "Daire, you can't do that. It'll only cause him to suffer even more than he is."

I mutter under my breath, doing my best to heave the wolf into my arms. Struggling to keep my movements gentle and slow—I don't want to hurt him or make him feel worse—still, the wolf is so much heavier than I expected.

"I have to get him back to Enchantment," I say, my voice frantic, betraying the full depth of my anxiety. "Chay's a vet—he can fix him. I'm sure of it. So please, either help me or move out of my way."

Dace stands behind me torn between doing what he thinks is right and upsetting me further, he slips his arms under Wolf until they're pressed close to mine. His face inches away, his breath warming my cheek, he glances between the poor dying animal and me, saying, "Daire, do you know whose spirit animal this is?"

Remembering how Paloma once stressed the importance of keeping one's spirit animal a secret, I look to Raven for guidance. Shocked to find him lingering nearby, along with Dace's Horse, Django's Bear, my grandfather's Jaguar, and a golden-eyed Eagle that reminds me so much of Chay's ring, I figure it must belong to him—the sight of them gathered together making my eyes brim with tears.

It looks like the end, like a memorial of some kind—but it can't be—not while Wolf is still alive.

"Do you know them?" Dace follows my gaze to the strange menagerie of animals. Watching the way they circle and pace, Jaguar and Bear growling and anxious.

"Yes." I turn to him, trying not to give too much away. "They care about Wolf and his human attachment as much as I do."

Dace looks at me, his eyes reflecting my sadness too many

times."Well that person is very lucky to have so many caring beings on their side," he says, voice edged with regret when he adds,
"but you still can't move him." He glances at Wolf, frowning
when he sees his eyes are now shut as his head hangs limp on my
chest. "If you try to bring him back, he'll die. He's too weak to
survive the journey. Daire, I'm sorry, but if you insist on doing
that, you'll only succeed at putting them both at greater risk."

"So, what am I supposed to do?" I ask, the words laced with
anger, though it's more at the situation than the messenger.

"Accept the natural progression," he says, his voice soft and
low.

"Not happening." I shake my head. "There's no way. Besides,
you're the one who said it was strange—that there's nothing *natural*
about this."

He sighs, more out of sadness than frustration, saying,
"Daire—is this about Paloma? Is she in some kind of trouble?"

I swallow hard, bury my face in the wolf's coarse white fur,
my tears turning it clumpy and damp.

Taking my silence as a yes, he says, "Okay, here's what you do:
You head back and find Leftfoot so you can tell him you found
Paloma's Wolf. You describe the location, Wolf's condition, and tell
him that I, along with Bear, Jaguar, Eagle, and Raven, are watching
over him—and he *might* be able to help. But, Daire, you need to
know, there's no guarantee."

"How do you know about Leftfoot?" I ask, wondering what
else he might know about this strange new world I'm only just
learning to navigate for myself.

"He's my great-uncle. My grandpa Jolon's brother. He's the
only one Chay would trust to look after Paloma, besides my mom.
But Chepi doesn't do healings anymore. Not since she got pregnant
with Cade and me."

I'm about to tell him that from what I saw earlier, Chepi's come
out of retirement, or at least temporarily. But before I can get to it, he
says, "Paloma's been good to my family. She's been a huge support

to my mom. We'll get through this, okay? I promise to help in every way that I can."

My throat is too tight to reply, so I nod my consent. Allowing him to lift me onto Horse, his hands strong and sure, as he says, "There are quicker ways to get where you need to go, but it's best if you exit this place the same way you came. Horse will know where to take you, so no worries there."

I reach for Horse's mane, my gaze meeting Dace's when he says, "Daire . . ."

I blink back the tears, swallow past the lump in my throat, seeing the full range of sentiment displayed in his gaze, all the things he longs to tell me—but instead he just says, "Good luck."

Then he slaps Horse on the rear, and I ride like the wind.

forty-five

When I reach the reservation, I burst through the door of the small adobe, confronting Chay with a torrent of words so jumbled, he's forced to put a hand on my shoulder and coax me into the nearest chair until I can calm down enough to start again.

"I found Paloma's Wolf," I tell him, my breath slowing as his eyes grow wide. "He's in bad shape, but he's being looked after by Dace, along with a couple other spirit animals, including your Eagle."

At the sound of her son's name, Chepi peeks around the corner, her gaze meeting mine, holding the look, until Chay summons Leftfoot into the room and tells me to repeat the same thing to him. After describing the location as well as I can, Leftfoot takes off, leaving specific instructions for his apprentice, Chay, and Chepi to look after Paloma, as I stand in her doorway, my heart plummeting when I see her looking so much smaller than before. Even in the dim, flickering glow of the candles placed all around her, she looks paler, weaker. Her breath coming too shallow, too slow, reduced to a horrible rattling sound that emanates from deep in her chest.

I drop beside her, enclose her hand in mine. My throat gone so lumpy and tight I can't get to the words. My vision so frantic and blurry, the room swims before me.

"She was doing better. We were sure she'd made the turn, but then . . ." Chay looks at me, his eyes filled with sorrow. "I'm afraid she's not long for this world."

I shake my head. Refuse to believe it. Glaring at him when I say, "No. No! I won't let her go. She can't—not now—not when I'm just getting to know her! Leftfoot will fix her Wolf, and Paloma will be healed—you'll see!"

He squeezes my shoulder, his voice saddened but even. "I'm sorry, Daire. But from what you said about Wolf's condition, I'm afraid it won't be much longer."

His eyes meet mine, revealing the full depth of his loss, the truth behind his words, but I cannot—will not—accept it. "Why can't they heal her? Why can't she heal herself? Why can't some-one make some mystical medicine or something?" My eyes search the room, accusing everyone in it. The medicine man's apprentice running a wildly spinning pendulum up and down Paloma's body, pausing on each of her chakras, his brow creased as he turns on occasion and makes odd, little spitting sounds. Even Chepi, who sits in a corner, her eyes clamped shut, hands waving before her, as her lips move in silent communion. Each of them employ-ing the same ritual I've seen Paloma work to help others—so why is it not helping her? Returning to Chay when I add, "She's a healer. A Seeker. How could this happen? How'd she get sick in the first place?"

He takes a deep breath, nodding in a way that encourages me to slow down, calm down, and take a breath too. When my energy settles, he says, "Healers do all that they can to keep themselves strong, grounded, and well. Good health allows them to do what they do. But, once they fall ill, they're forced to seek help just like anyone else. Leftfoot will tend to Wolf as best he can, but some things are not for us to decide. The toll of losing Django—of hav-ing to keep her powers going for much longer than normal—have

come at a price. She's suffered significant soul loss. I'm afraid
there's nothing more to do but let her transition into the next
world as comfortably and easily as possible."

I turn, my face scrunched in confusion.

"In the end, that's what all illness amounts to," he says. "A loss
of power. A loss of the soul."

Soul loss.

A loss of the soul.

The words ringing in my ears so loudly they're almost
deafening—as visions of long-dead Richters devouring glowing,
white orbs blaze in my head.

"So—get her soul back!" I say, aware that I'm not making the
slightest bit of sense. *Could one even do such a thing?*

"I'm afraid it's too late for a soul retrieval." Chay looks at me,
having already accepted what I'm dead set on refusing. "It is time.
The signs are all present. So please say your good-byes so she'll be
free to move on."

"No." I glance between Chay and Paloma. Repeating, "No.
Not yet. No way. This is no accident—the Richters have done
this—Cade in particular."

Chay looks at me, his narrowed gaze implying his surprise
comes not from the sentiment so much as from hearing me
voice it.

"How does one lose a soul?" I set my jaw and focus on him,
needing to learn all that I can if I've any hope of saving my *abuela.*
"And once it's lost, how does one get it back?"

Chay fingers his ring, the eagle's golden eyes glimmering as it
twists back and forth. "A soul loss can occur in a number of ways.
Some trade their power to malevolent beings in exchange for
fame, fortune, even love. Sometimes it's the result of trauma—
death of a loved one, a violent event—something that leaves a
person in a state so weakened they've lost their will to live, which
inadvertently allows the soul to become vulnerable to those same
malevolent beings who are eager to claim it. And in other cases . . ."

He looks at me, unsure if he should say it, but I nod for him to continue—sparing me from the truth won't make it any less real.

"In other cases, the entire soul, or even bits of the soul, are taken outright—the result of being targeted by a very powerful sorcerer with ill intent. And I'm afraid once one is targeted, it's nearly impossible to undo without the aid of an equally powerful Seeker or shaman—a Worker of Light."

"Well, I'm a Seeker—so where do I start?"

My tone is frantic, my gaze all over the place. Nothing about me inspiring the least bit of confidence, so Chay can hardly be blamed when he says, "Soul Retrieval is very dangerous work. It requires one to journey to the place where the soul is being kept, then confronting the malevolent being that stole it, which often involves lengthy, extremely costly negotiations to get it back. Only the most gifted shamans and Seekers are able to do this— those with many years of experience." He looks hard at me. "You're nowhere near ready. I can't let you risk it. Paloma would never allow it."

At the sound of her name, my grandmother stirs. "Daire . . ." she whispers, prompting Leftfoot's apprentice to move aside, as my grandmother, my *abuela,* strains to open her eyes.

"Sweet *nieta* . . ." She struggles to focus. Her voice so labored, so forced, the sound makes me shiver. "Do not worry for me. I've lived a good life. Focus on them. You must stop El Coyote, no matter the cost. I haven't taught you everything, but I've taught you well. And now you must let me go, *nieta*—"

"No, Paloma—no, don't say that! I can't do it—not without you! I don't even know where to start!"

My voice breaks, my eyes fill with tears, as I gaze upon my grandmother, her essence fading when she says, "You cannot, must not, save me. Do you understand? Today is the day, *nieta*. Please go—you must hurry . . ."

Her eyes already closing, shutting me out, as I turn to Chay and say, "What day is it?" Wondering just how long I spent in the Lowerworld with Dace.

"November second, *Día de los Muertos*," he says, his hand reaching for my shoulder in an effort to comfort, but I've already slipped out of his reach, am already racing toward the door.

dark
harvest

forty-six

I hop on Kachina and make for the Rabbit Hole. My horse racing down the road at full speed—her mane lifting, ears pinned, as the wind lashes hard at my cheeks.

I may not know what I'm doing—I may not be properly trained—I may have no idea how to stop the Richters from invading the Lowerworld—but Paloma's counting on me to stop them, and I won't let her down.

She always said I showed great promise, that someday I'll surpass all of my ancestors . . . well, maybe that someday starts now.

I lean forward. Bury my face in Kachina's neck. Focusing on the reassuring beat of her hooves meeting the dirt—a reminder that every stride brings us closer—when the sky cracks loudly overhead, releasing a blast of thunder so piercing the earth vibrates beneath us, causing me to cringe and squeeze the reins tighter, eager to get there before the rain starts to fall, not wanting to be caught out in the open in a New Mexico rainstorm.

The thunder rolls again, louder than before—the sound spooking Kachina enough for her to throw her head back and snort in distress—as I clench my legs tighter, fight to stay on her back, keep her on track. Murmuring softly into her neck, telling her there's no need to worry, to hang in there, it will all be okay—when a massive bolt of lightning bursts from the sky, slams into the earth, and scorches a wide swath of dirt not far from her hooves.

The sky darkening, becoming increasingly ominous, as the wind blows surprisingly hot—and when I lift my head from Kachina's neck and take a good look around, I'm horrified to see a flood of large black ravens plummeting down.

They plunge from the sky.

They drop all around.

Emitting horrible, high-pitched screeching sounds seconds before they smash to the ground. Their numbers so great, the sky appears to be vomiting massive chunks of black hail.

I duck my head low—whispering soft, soothing words to my horse—but it's no use, she's as spooked as I am. Her eyes rolling crazily, she snorts, whinnies, careening wildly in a vain attempt to avoid the torrent of ravens.

They slam hard onto my shoulders. Pummel my back. Only to roll down Kachina's side and become a gruesome mess of feathers, blood, and gore under the crush of her hooves.

My horse so terrified, so terrorized, I start singing the mountainsong in an effort to calm her. Remembering the power each song holds, I sing the windsong as well. The two of them blending together until my voice grows tired and hoarse, forcing me to pause for a moment before continuing with a renewed burst of strength.

While it doesn't keep the ravens from falling, they no longer fall near us. A path has been cleared, allowing Kachina safe passage to race down the road.

The sky finally brightening as we make our way into town. The raven storm halted at last—though its memory lingers.

Like a postcard from the Richters—letting me know the hourglass has been flipped.

Time is slipping through my fingers like sand.

forty-seven

I slide off Kachina, slap her on the rump, and tell her to head back to Paloma's where it's safe. Then I stand before the Rabbit Hole, observing a scene of organized chaos, as I fight to get my bearings and try to drum up some kind of plan.

They've tripled the number of bouncers working the door, making a big show of stamping all those under twenty-one with the red ink coyotes, yet the moment I make my way in, I see that it's pretty much a free-for-all—everyone's drinking, no one is checking.

I glance all around, not the least bit surprised to find most of the crowd already inebriated. Encouraging everyone to drink themselves into a stupor is a well-planned move on the Richters' part. The more compromised the consciousness, the easier it is to alter the perception—allowing them free rein to do as they please.

A band is on stage, a really loud opening act that has the dance floor crammed with writhing bodies—everyone wearing wildly painted skull masks, along with a wide array of costumes. The entire club decorated in the way Paloma described—with colorful beads and skull masks hanging from the walls, and tables sagging under heaps of beeswax candles, marigolds, and large heaping platters with decorated sugar skulls and homemade bread with bone-shaped pieces arranged across the top, which I think she called *pan de muerto*.

Though no matter how hard I look, I can't seem to find Cade, which fills me with worry that I might be too late—that he might already be at the vortex, starting the festivities without me.

"I brought this for you."

I turn to see Xotichl thrusting a colorful skull mask into my hands that bears large grinning teeth, marigold petals surrounding the eye sockets, and a lavender background—an almost exact replica of the one she wears, only hers has a backdrop of blue. "I figured you might not have one, and it'll help you blend in," she says. "Though I'm afraid it won't save you from Lita and the Cruel Crew. From what I can tell—" She lifts her chin, twitches her nose, returning to me when she adds, "You've been spotted, they're headed here now."

"I'm amazed at how you can do that," I say, pretty sure she just grinned, judging by the way her mask twitched in response.

"While I can sense her presence, what I can't sense is whether or not she's wearing her Marilyn Monroe skull mask again," she says, shaking her head when I glance toward Lita and confirm that she is, along with a trashy white wedding dress that's short, low-cut, and at least one size too small. "It's her way of honoring Marilyn, while trying to commune with her spirit, and I can never decide if it's morbid, creepy, pathetic, or all three."

I watch as Lita makes her way toward us. Her Marilyn mask offset by a blond wig that's spent a lot of time with a curling iron.

"I think she's pretty serious about hanging out," Xotichl says. "Question is—what are you going to do about it?"

"I'm going to get serious about hanging out with her too," I reply, not bothering to explain that I'm less interested in making meaningless chitchat and more interested in locating Cade. If anyone knows where he is, it's Lita. She never lets him out of her sight for too long.

Lita stands before us with her friends just behind her. All of them giving me a thorough once-over, struggling to say something nice when it's pretty clear I'm not looking my best. "Cool mask—and nice boots," she finally says. "Not really a costume, but still cool."

And though I'm tempted to laugh, remembering the scene my boots inspired in the bathroom when I was a lowly cockroach cowering in the corner, eavesdropping on them—I decide to thank her instead.

"I don't think you've met everyone," Lita says, going into full-on hostess mode. "This is Jacy . . ." She points to a girl wearing a skull mask bearing the same flaming pink lips she favors in real life, and a sexy bunny suit. "And this is Crickett . . ." She gestures toward the girl with the best blond highlights of the bunch, whose mask pretty much mirrors Jacy's except the lips are more red than pink, and her costume is that of a naughty French maid. Then turning to Xotichl, she says, "When's Epitaph playing?" Making me wonder if she might be sincere after all.

"They're up next," Xotichl says, the news prompting so much excitement and chatter between Lita and company, you'd think the news was way more fascinating than it is.

But even though I nod and laugh when I'm supposed to, I'm not really present—not really paying attention. I'm too busy searching for Cade, knowing I need to make a quick exit, find a way to lose them, so I can seek him.

"Who are you looking for?" Lita's eyes flash from behind her mask.

I shrug in response, but the way she tilts her head and folds her arms across her bridal dress, it's clear she's not fooled for a second.

"I see the way he looks at you," she says, her tone even, the words unmistakably accusatory.

I swallow hard, shake my head, and say, "Who?" Hoping it sounded more convincing to her than it did to me.

"Please." She scoffs. "I may not be all hip and Hollywood like you—I may come from a tiny, little dump of a town—but I'm not stupid. I know when a girl's after my guy. And I know when my guy's intrigued by a girl."

I stand before her, realizing she's done such a good job of convincing herself, I'm not sure I can make her think otherwise.

"I get it, okay? I really do. He's hot. He's the hottest guy here—the hottest guy anywhere. He's even hotter than Vane Wick—and don't even pretend you haven't noticed. But as it just so happens, he's taken. And while I'm sincere about us being friends, I gotta warn you, Daire, if you decide to go after him, despite what I've told you—well, you should know right now that it won't end well for you."

I picture him snacking on slimy, bloodied bits, enjoying it so much he licked the remains right off his fingertips, and I can't help but feel sorry for her. As far as creeps go, Cade's reached the pinnacle. But knowing she wouldn't believe me if I told her, I say, "Duly noted."

She nods, the move curt, dismissive, lifting her mask onto her wig so I can see that she's serious when she adds, "I know you don't really trust me. I know you're suspicious of why I'm suddenly acting so friendly. But the thing is, we don't get many newcomers in Enchantment, much less Milagro. I've known most of these people my whole life, and, because of it, I guess I'm not so great at adapting to change." She lifts her shoulders, causing her dress to strain at the seams. "So when you showed up with your cool boots and don't-give-a-crap attitude—well, you seemed like the kind of girl who could easily shift the balance of everything I've worked so hard for, and I couldn't allow that to happen. Then, when I saw the way Cade looked at you, and the other boys too . . ."

"So what changed? You spot me on the cover of a glossy tabloid and decide to give me a chance?" I ask, having no idea where she's going with this, but hoping she'll get to it soon. I've got a job to do.

"Yeah." She nods. "Only not for the reason you think. I mean, even though the cover wasn't all that flattering, it made me realize just how small my world is. So small I perceive everything new as a threat." She shakes her head. "I don't want to be like that. I'd much rather we try to be friends."

"Me too," I say, surprised by how much I mean it. I've never had a friend before—not one that lasted for more than a few months anyway. And now between Dace, Xotichl, Auden, and possibly Lita and company—well, that's pretty much a record. Though I'm guessing it'll require tolerance, understanding, and, especially in Lita's case, a whole lot of patience—but I'm willing to try if she is. "But if we're going to be friends, then you have to believe me when I tell you that I'm not into Cade," I say. Going one step further when I add, "In fact, I can't freaking stand him."

She shakes her head and laughs, blond polyester curls bouncing on her shoulders, assuming it's a joke—I couldn't possibly be serious.

Her laughter halting when I say, "But you were right about one thing—I am looking for him. Just not for the reason you think."

Her face grows dark, her voice suspicious when she says, "Yeah? And what reason might that be?"

"It's about his brother."

"Dace?" Her eyes widen, the name spoken so loudly Xotichl turns, Crickett and Jacy stare, while Lita slaps a hand over her mouth, shakes her head, and says, "I mean, I guess he's hot too—but I've always thought of him as like a fake Cade. Like a knockoff, poor man's version of the real thing, you know? But seriously—you're serious?" She stares hard at me, waiting for the punch line that never comes. Still in a state of disbelief when she says, "Okay, whatever. I'll give you the benefit of the doubt on this one. Cade's in his office. As for his twin—it never occurred to me to keep track."

I turn, reminding myself to not be annoyed. Like everyone else in this town—well, everyone but Dace, Xotichl, Auden, and a few others—she's totally brainwashed where the Richters are concerned.

"Oh, and Daire . . ." She grabs hold of my arm, her eyes meeting mine, fingers circling my elbow when she says, "If you play me for an idiot, I'm going after you."

"I wouldn't do that." I yank free of her grip. My tone softening when I add, "Trust me, you have nothing to worry about."

"I don't trust anyone," she says, her gaze changing until it becomes empty and vacant, leaving me to wonder if Cade's been harvesting bits of her too.

I turn to Xotichl, about to tell her I'm taking a walk, when she says, "Wherever you're going, I'm going with you. But we better hurry; in case you didn't notice, your mom's here, and I get the feeling you'd rather avoid her."

forty-eight

I follow Xotichl, her glow-in-the-dark skeleton suit making her movements seem odd, almost eerie. And sure enough, it's not a second later when I spy Jennika across the crowded room. As the only one not wearing a skull mask and costume, she's easy to spot.

"This is the only show in town," Xotichl says, trailing alongside me as I duck around a corner and pause. "It was just a matter of time 'til she showed." She makes a show of sniffing the air, as she tucks her hand into my jacket's front pocket, fishing around until she finds the pack of cigarettes I swiped from Leftfoot on my way out the door, and dangles them before me.

I swipe at the pack, telling her it's not at all what she thinks, when she tilts her mask high on her head, her gray/blue eyes seeming to find me when she says, "Oh, so you're *not* going to use them as an offering for the demons that guard the Rabbit Hole's vortex?"

I gape, having no idea what to say.

"I read energy, Daire. I know all about the vortex." She shakes her head and frowns. "I know about *all* the vortexes in this town. I also know that there are some extremely unnatural beings that

lurk inside this place, and I'm not just referring to the Richters."
She grins. "Their magick doesn't work on everyone, you know.
They prey on the weak—those with weak wills, weak personali-
ties, weak sense of self—the usual targets. But they can never touch
me. They need your sight in order to change your perception.
They're powerless when it comes to blindsight. Besides, everyone
knows demons crave tobacco."

I exhale long and deep, relieved to share the burden of truth
with someone other than Paloma and Chay. "I had no idea you
knew," I tell her, seeing her nod in reply.

"I can also locate Cade if you'll let me. The vortex too. It's
tricky; most people can't find it. And no matter how many times
I offered to help, Paloma always refused me."

I start to speak, wanting to tell her about Paloma, but she
raises a hand, alerted to something sensed only by her. She tugs
hard on my arm and says, "Quick—in here!"

She ducks inside the office, and I slink in behind her. The two
of us holding our breath, pressed hard against the wall, as someone makes their way down the hall.

When Xotichl's sure that they're gone, she reaches beside her,
grabs hold of Cade's baseball bat, and thrusts it into my hands,
saying, "You might need it to defend yourself in case the cigarettes don't work."

I run my palm down the length of the bat, testing its weight
and heft, as we exit the office and she leads me down the series of
halls, searching for signs of the vortex or Cade, whichever comes
first, while I track all the same landmarks from the last time I was
here: the stray gum wrapper, the heart-shaped piece of missing
paint, the bubble of water damage, Cade's squashed cigarette
butts. Training my focus on the things that go unseen, hoping to
coax them to spring into view.

Though unlike last time, there's a strange chemical scent per-
vading the air that seems to intensify the farther we go. And it's

not long before Xotichl stops, tilts her head toward me, and whispers, "This is it."

I stare at the wall, noting how it's still soft, malleable, recently breached, with no sign of the demons, but that doesn't mean they're not waiting inside.

"You know you can't join me," I say, overcome by guilt for allowing her to take me this far and hoping she can find her way back unharmed.

"Don't worry about me, I'm stronger than I look. I'll deal with your mom, while you deal with Cade. And, Daire . . ." I look at her—see the way her lip trembles, surprising me when she says, "Go kick some Richter ass!"

I lunge toward the wall that's already closing. Shoving right into it, bat first, pushing so hard it's like merging into a solid wall of taffy—sticky, gooey, molding around me—until it finally gives way and I burst through, slamming headfirst into one of the demons—the big one who guards the vortex.

We stare at each other, the two of us momentarily stunned, until he growls so loudly it alerts the others to join him.

They surround me, their massive paws and razor-sharp nails swiping at me from all sides, leaving me no choice but to shake the cigarettes loose from the pack, toss them behind me, and bolt.

Glancing over my shoulder to see the demons dive after them, snarling and hissing in an effort to get to them first, I race for the tunnel that leads to the cave. The crash of my boots against the metal trilling too loudly, leaving me with no choice but to ditch them and tiptoe the rest of the way. Careful to keep my breath light, shallow—allowing only the briefest sigh of relief when I reach the end undetected and creep past the entry into a room lit by bright blazing torches. The frenetic lick of flames sparking and flaring in a way that illuminates the ribbons of strung marigolds and beads draped across the walls—the skeletons propped among the furniture with hand-painted skull masks secured to their heads—the usual Day of the Dead décor, but in here the effect is especially chilling.

That strong chemical scent growing in intensity, as I move through the rooms, forcing me to clasp one hand over my face to block out the smell, as the other clutches hard at the bat, and it's then that I see him.

See them.

The whole lot of them wearing identical black-and-white skull masks with red dripping mouths—waiting for the party to begin.

Coyote sees me first. Ducking his head, he snarls in protest, as Cade stands before an elaborate altar draped with a starched white tablecloth, covered with flaming beeswax candles, decapitated marigold heads, a plate piled high with ornately decorated sugar skull candies, a crystal carafe filled with something resembling red wine but that could just as easily be blood, and at least a hundred black-and-white photos of blank smiling faces strewn along the top. His back turned, arms embracing a glowing metal container that floods the room with a brilliant spectrum of light.

"So you made it," he says, not bothering to face me. Taking a moment to shush Coyote when he adds, "And just in time too. I knew you'd see the beauty of my plan. And now, because of it, the victory is ours to share."

The undead Richters make horrible yipping sounds, as Cade turns, his eyes red and glowing behind his own gruesome skull mask that looks a lot like the demon face I know from the dream.

"Smell that?" He tosses his head back, makes a show of inhaling deeply. "It's the sweet scent of insecticide. Had to spray the whole place. Seems a cockroach managed to sneak his way in just the other day." His gaze levels on mine, flaring in amusement when he adds, "Wasn't you, was it?"

I don't reply. Don't so much as flinch. I just secure the bat from his view and tighten my grip. Determined to at least give the appearance of holding my own, even though deep down inside, I'm quaking all the way to my toes.

"I can't tell you how happy I am that you've come. That you've decided to join me in a moment so great." He hugs the container close to his chest. "The second it's over, we'll go straight to my father—though don't be surprised if Leandro doesn't accept you at first. He may even move in to kill you—but I'll be right by your side and I won't let that happen. Besides, once we've had a chance to explain it, once he sees for himself just how much we can accomplish by working together, I know he'll see the brilliance of my plan." He lifts his shoulders in a way that causes the orb to lift, surging so precariously toward the lip, it's all I can do to remain rooted in place, to not rush forward and snatch it away. "This is the perfect ending to a ridiculous, primitive feud. It's also a wonderful beginning to a partnership that's long overdue. You see, Leandro had it all wrong. Not only did he fail by accidentally conjuring my aberration of a brother—but he failed to understand that the reason we've been unable to penetrate the Lowerworld for so long is because our souls have become too dark for admittance. And mine, as I'm sure you know, is the darkest of all." His eyes flare with pride. "Then again, it's the pure blackness of my soul that led me to them—the solution."

He nods toward the gathering of undead Richters—the entire lot of them yipping and yelping with excitement over the meal to come. Their enthusiasm causing Cade to shout, "Silence! Can't you see that I'm talking? Sheesh!" Shaking his head and returning to me as he says, "So anyway, where were we?"

"Your dark and desolate soul." I tap the bat against the back of my calf, prepared to use it at the first sign of trouble.

He nods again. "Little does Leandro know, but during last year's *Día de los Muertos*, I brought them all back. And not just their essence. I actually *raised* them. They're all Richters—resurrected Richters! I started by feeding them bits of animal souls. I'm telling you, there's no shortage of worthless pets in this town." He shakes his head, as though he can hardly believe the nuisance, the folly. "But then, over the last year, I've started feeding them human souls. Sometimes taking entire souls—sometimes just prying off little bits. It's amazing how easy they are to obtain. Some people just hand 'em right over, they have no regard for their lives. Though most have no clue they've been taken, and even when they do suspect, they're usually quick to convince themselves it was merely a nightmare." His eyes fix on mine, and I can't help but wonder if he's referring to my own dream-turned-nightmare. "Anyway, for the record, I learned how to do it all on my own. Leandro refused to teach me the fine art of soul stealing—claimed I wasn't ready, but I think I've proved otherwise." He pauses as though awaiting my praise, and when it fails to appear, he says, "Oh, don't look so sorry. It's not like any of those people were using their souls for anything truly worthy or good. Our cause is much greater. And now, with you on board, it won't be long before we rule the Middleworld, the Lowerworld, and ultimately the Upperworld too. My dad's really gonna be proud of me then." His eyes blaze at the idea, proving once again, he's a psychopath. "Take off your mask and join me," he says. "It's time."

I shake my head. I don't take orders from him.

"Take off your ridiculous mask and put down that bat you think I can't see. We're a team now. We have to learn to trust each other if we're going to work together, no?"

I tighten my grip, braced for just about anything. Watching as he shrugs and says, "Fine. Have it your way." Then, nodding at the metal container, he adds, "Have you ever seen anything more beautiful?"

I gaze at the orb, seeing the way it illuminates the room in a kaleidoscope of color—like a beautiful prism refracting the light.

"Do you see how much power it holds?" His eyes flare as though mesmerized by the sight of it, the thought of it. "Notice the way it shines brighter than all of those other souls you saw last time you were here?"

My fingers start to itch, my body fills with dread.

"You know why that is?" he taunts, willing me to say it.

But I won't.

Can't.

There's no way.

"C'mon, Daire, you're a smart girl—*think!* Who do you know personally whose soul would shine far brighter than anyone else's? Who do you know who's so full of magick, and goodness, and purity, and light—their soul would radiate in precisely this way?"

I move toward him, fingers shaking so badly the bat trembles against them.

"I'm afraid your dear Paloma is not long for this world. Django's death came with a price, and by the time you came around, it was already too late. I've been harvesting little bits all year, and now I have the whole thing. But then, you already knew that, didn't you? You've been watching her fade since the moment you arrived. It's too late to save her—so you may as well make your peace and take this moment to join me. Because I promise you, Daire, if you choose to fight me, I'll have no choice but to steal your soul too."

He dips his fingers into the container, then turns toward his undead family, presenting Paloma's bright and shining soul on a single splayed hand he raises before them. The sight of it causing them to lurch forward, teeth gnashing, bodies lunging, unable to contain their hunger—themselves. Worked into an absolute slobbering frenzy, when Cade glances over his shoulder, wanting to make sure that I see it.

My feet spread wide, I grip the bat tighter. Knowing I have one second to act. One second to stop him.

There are no do-overs here.

"Still time to join me," he says, sparks shooting from eyeholes surrounded by bright yellow marigolds.

I rush toward him, bat held high, Paloma's words swirling through my mind:

Do not worry for me. Focus on them—you must stop El Coyote, no matter the cost. I haven't taught you everything—but I've taught you well—and now you must let me go, nieta. *You cannot, must not, save me—do you understand?*

She wants me to crush it.

She knew it would come to this and she wants me to do whatever it takes to stop him. Willing to sacrifice her own eternity in order to spare mankind the horror of the Richters invading the Lowerworld again.

It's what a Seeker does.

He smiles when he sees me—eyes flaming, teeth gleaming—as I take a deep breath and swing with all of my strength. My gaze never once leaving the orb as I bring the bat down as hard as I can—begging Paloma to forgive me—good-byes were so much easier before I allowed myself to care.

The bat crashes down hard, causing shards of glass to scatter, fly about the room, as it bounces off the altar, sending the table, the candles, the candy, the photos, the carafe with the strange red substance crashing to the ground—as I stare at Cade, breathless and horrified, both of us knowing I just couldn't do it.

His eyes meeting mine when he hurls the gleaming white orb—my *abuela's* soul—to the crowd of undead Richters. Shouting in triumph as the largest of the group snatches it from the air and swallows it whole.

forty-nine

Cade's face is exultant, victorious—having misread the whole thing, he thinks I've gone crazy, decided to join him.

The moment holding, growing, until I rid myself of the mask, gaze down at my feet, and see the rug blazing beneath me. The corners of those nameless pictures scorching and curling—recognizing first one face, then another, and suddenly realizing they're not what I thought.

They're not pictures of long-dead Richters—they're pictures of those whose souls have been stolen for Cade's horrible cause.

He stands before me, hand reaching toward mine as white hot flames lick at his shoes and dance up his sides. The enormity of what I've just done looming before me, as I bolt toward the army of undead Richters, chasing the beast that ate my grandmother's soul. Noting the way it allows him to grow and transform as a wondrous halo of light seeps out all around him—having no idea if it's too late to save her, but knowing I have to try, have to stop them from invading the Lowerworld, or the whole world will suffer.

My legs spin beneath me, carrying me faster than I ever

thought possible. My flight spurred by Cade's haunting trail of laughter, along with his horrible coyote nipping close at my heels.

I sprint through a long series of rooms—heart pumping too hard, lungs about to burst from my chest. Only a handful of steps yawning between me and them, when they burst through the wall that leads to the desert, and Coyote leaps forward and sinks his fangs into my jeans.

I whirl on him, stare into his glowing red eyes, and give him a swift, hard kick in the snout before he can pounce again. The move stunning him just long enough to allow me to dive through the wall before it snaps shut.

Sand.

I forgot about the sand.

It meanders for miles. And though it's packed hard, which makes it easier for running, with so many undead Richters ahead of me, it's not long before I'm sandblasted in their wake.

I trudge forward, eyes squinched against the spray, trying to stay focused on the big one, when they sprint up a hill, only to scale it and drop out of sight—disappearing so quickly my heart leaps into my throat, sure I've lost them for good. Only to find myself falling as well—swallowed by a tunnel of sand that ingests me deeper and deeper into the earth.

The Lowerworld.

That's where I'm going. That's where they're going too. Intent on wreaking unspeakable damage—fueled by the power of my grandmother's soul.

But they're so far ahead, there's no way to catch up—no way to stop them from entering.

All I can do is go with the fall—my body tumbling, rolling, getting sucked in so deep I can no longer see. My eyes squeezed tight, lips clamped shut, and yet I'm still inundated with great gobs of sand that slip into my ears, grind between my lips, and spread across my teeth.

It's horrible.

Unbearable.

I can't breathe, can't survive it much longer.

The sound of them flailing before me the only thing that keeps me hanging on—reminding me of my purpose, giving me the incentive to keep going.

My ears filled with the sound of their howling and yelping, so tantalizingly close yet so far away. And the next thing I know, I'm out. Slamming hard against the ground, surrounded by undead Richters sprawled all around me.

I blink. Spit. Jump to my feet and dive for the big one, determined to catch him, to stop him at last. But Paloma's soul has empowered him and he moves far too fast.

They circle and scatter—zigzagging around him in an effort to confuse. And just as I start to gain ground, they split into several small groups that go several different ways. Leaving me with no choice but to forfeit the majority to get to the one.

Trying not to think about all those Richters now loose in the Lowerworld.

Trying not to think about how I've failed Paloma, failed as a Seeker in every conceivable way.

All I can do is keep my eye on the prize—racing after him as he heads for a thick grove of trees, causing the spirit animals to dart from our path. So unused to any unrest, much less the invasion of evil, they go into hiding, unsure what to make of it as he continues to move through the brush so quickly, I know I can't do this alone. I either do something serious, something to stop him, or I'm seconds away from defeat.

I call upon the elements.

Call upon Raven.

My ancestors too.

If what Paloma says is true—that they're everywhere, part of everything—then they'll find me here too.

The wind shows up first, wafting and whirling, kicking up great clouds of dust that cut all visibility. And when the earth begins to quake, causing the freak to lose his footing, well, it's just the boost that I need to push him to the ground, clamp my legs on either side of him, and slam his face into the dirt.

Shouting in victory as I tighten my grip—my triumph short-lived when I realize I have no idea what comes next.

fifty

He struggles against me, fights to break free, but I use all my strength to cling fast to his back and tighten my hold. One hand fisting around a greasy clump of black hair, I yank his head back, and shove my free hand into his mouth. Having no idea if I'm on the right track, but knowing that one way or another, I have to get this thing out.

The soul no longer lost, it's time to retrieve it—time to wrench it from him so I can return it to Paloma. But with no idea how to do that, I shout, "Give it to me!" Fingers pushing past his tongue, going straight for his throat, when he bites down so hard it threatens to break through my skin.

I yank my hand free, shrieking in frustration and pain, as I grasp his hair tighter and slam his face into the dirt so hard bits of mask break free and embed in his flesh—repeating the move so many times I lose track.

Stopping only when a voice drifts from behind me and says, "I can't say I blame you, but we really need to keep him alive."

Dace!

He kneels beside me, answering the question in my gaze when

he says, "I heard your call. Horse brought me here as quickly as he could—Raven led the way."

He heard the call?

Along with the wind, the earth, and my spirit animal?

Maybe there really was more to the dream than I think—a reason we found each other before we'd even met?

Maybe we really are bound in some way?

I look to his right, seeing Raven perched high in a tree, while Horse stands off to the side. The two of them keeping a protective eye on us and a wary eye on the undead Richter, unsure what to make of him.

"Is this the freak that stole Paloma's soul?" Dace asks.

I swallow hard and nod in reply. Unwilling to tell him that the freak merely ate it—that it's his brother who stole it and served it to him.

He turns. Casts all about. Focusing on a vine hanging from a nearby tree, his breath slows, his lids narrow, and the next thing I know it's found its way to his hand, and he's using it to bind the freak's arms and feet.

Then he looks at me. I smile at him, and without a single mention of it, he says, "Wolf is stabilized for now." His brow slants with worry. "Still, we don't have much time."

"What do we do?" I loosen my grip on the freak now that Dace has subdued him.

"I don't know," he admits. "Soul extraction requires years of training. Though I do know you can't just reach in and grab it, you have to know how to handle it. One false move and you can lose it for good. Back when I was a kid, the elders used to talk about a particular . . ." He pauses, searching for the best word. "A particular *denizen* of the Lowerworld who they sometimes turned to for help. She's considered quite dangerous, and in our case, she has no reason to cooperate. Though if the barter is right, she might consider it . . ." His voice fades, unwilling to say any more, fearing he's gone too far.

"Do you know where to find her?" I ask, determined to speak to her one way or another.

He shakes his head. "All I know is that she resides in the nethermost level. And while our spirit animals may not want to join us, they can probably at least get us started."

I rise to my feet, facing Raven and Horse as I say, "Show us the way."

We head for a shallow trickle of river, Raven and Horse leading, as Dace and I drag the undead Richter behind us. Stopping at the place where the water meets the sand, Raven and Horse refuse to go any farther, as the three of us continue to trudge along the path.

The water soaking my jeans, the rocks ripping the hems to shreds, and when Dace looks down, asks what happened to my shoes, I just shake my head, tighten my hold on the freak, and keep going. The three of us making good progress until the river grows deeper and the current changes so swiftly, we're swept downstream and abandoned to a series of falls that send us hurtling deeper and deeper into the earth. Reminding me of what Paloma said about the Lowerworld consisting of many dimensions, and sensing we're getting pulled into yet another one, and then another, the lower we go. Finding our way to the nethermost.

The torrent growing in intensity, becoming so fierce, we lose our grip on the undead Richter, who breaks free of his restraints and tumbles ahead of us. Until the falls suddenly end in a swiftly moving stream that washes us onto a narrow bed of sharp rocks, where Dace and I pick ourselves up and race toward him.

Dace charging forward, gaining in speed, fingers falling just shy of the target when a figure looms large before us, catches the freak in one hand, and says, "I'll take it from here."

My eyes widen. Dace stops in midstride. The two of us panting and drenched, standing before a beautiful woman with eyes as black as onyx—a lush and generous mouth—hair that undulates down her back, in waves of amber so glimmering it perfectly mimics the tinge of flaming New Mexico sunsets—and skin so pale and translucent, its hue is unearthly.

"This one is mine. They're all mine." Her arm sweeps wide, revealing what we'd failed to notice before—a full roundup of undead Richters strung up by their feet, left to dangle from a grove of tall trees. Their hideous black-and-white skull masks seeming to mock the predicament they find themselves in. Her gaze flicking between Dace and me when she adds, "And now, it seems you are mine too."

I take in her swishy black skirt, her black lace-up boots, her snakeskin corset of a top, then I look past her—look all around her. Suddenly understanding what I missed at first glance.

The stream didn't feed into a bed of rocks like I'd thought.

It fed into a bed of bone chips.

There are bones everywhere I look. We're completely surrounded by them.

There's even a house made of bones—a large, rambling, dull white palace with knobs and joints on the corners, teeth decorating the windows and doors. And the fence that surrounds it is made of bones too, mostly femurs and spines, with the occasional elbow thrown in.

And that's when I see that what I first took for trees aren't trees at all—or at least not living trees. No longer sprouting leaves, no longer providing oxygen or shade, no longer functioning in the usual way. They died long ago, their scorched and bony carcasses are all that remain.

The woman spreads her arms wide and gazes up at the sky. The move causing the sky to darken into a glittering canopy of black velvet, as her face transforms into a skull, her skirt becomes a whirl of snapping, writhing snakes that circle her legs and waist, and her eyes turn into horrible empty sockets that level on me.

Her jaw yawning wide, emitting a horrible bone-on-bone scraping sound, as she throws her head back and feeds on a long line of stars that funnel into her mouth.

The sight leaving no doubt in my mind that Dace has brought me to the Bone Keeper's house.

fifty-one

"You can't have him." I glare, as Dace finds my hand. The press of his fingers warning that this is not the best way to proceed, though it's not like that stops me. "You can have all the others. I don't care what you do with them—but this one is mine."

"None of them are yours!" She shrieks, eye sockets glowering, skirt thrashing and slithering. "How dare you even consider it! Don't you know who I am?"

I nod. Not only do I know, but the Richter we're fighting over finally guessed too, judging by the way he snarls and yelps and fights like hell to free himself. But it's no use. With a single flick of her wrist, a knot of snakes swarm him, binding his throat, his arms, his legs—holding him captive like the vines once did.

"Then you know those bones belong to me. *All* the bones belong to me. And these particular bones have been denied me for too many years." She glowers at the undead Richter beside her. "Today is *Día de los Muertos*—the day when the dead bring me their bones. It is *not* a courtesy. It is *not* an offering to appease me. It is the price one pays for their final admittance into the afterlife. This family of Coyotes has eluded me for centuries, but no more. Their bones will be mine, and since you found your way here, yours are mine too."

Dace tightens his hold, but I'm too stunned by her words to edit myself. "You can't take my bones!" I cry. "I'm not even dead!" Dace moves to hush me, subdue me, but it's no use. I came here to get Paloma's soul, and there's no way I'll let myself fail.

The Bone Keeper stares, weighing my words as her fingers pick at her hissing, slithering, twist of a snake skirt. "That's easy enough to remedy," she decides, her shiny black boots gliding across the dirt until she stands just before me. Her skin so translucent it looks like a sheen of wax paper has been pulled over her thin, bony frame—her skull of a face glistening as a result of all the stars she just ate.

Her fingers reaching for me, ready to join me with the undead Richter beside her, when Dace steps between us and says, "We're not interested in bones. The only ones we want to keep are our own. We're here for another reason entirely—it's my understanding you've been known to work with the Light Workers from time to time—helping them retrieve stolen souls. This one here—" He motions toward the freak held hostage by the snakes. "He's stolen a soul we desperately need. If you'll help us retrieve it, we'll leave the bones to you."

Her skirt of squirming snakes shoots around Dace to lash at my legs, their flickering tongues finding all the spots where my jeans have ripped, stinging and lashing my skin as she says, "I don't make deals."

Her eye sockets darken in dismissal, as though that's the end of it. But we didn't come all this way to give up so easily. I swipe hard at the snakes, watching as they dart back to the protective bed of her hips, as I stand beside Dace and say, "I need that soul, and I need it now. A good woman is dying, and I can't let that happen. And while you may not care about that, you might care to know that these undead soul stealers and the sorcerer who made them, have terrible plans for this place. They're going to destroy the Lowerworld as you know it, and all the other worlds too. But you can help stop it. If you'll just return this soul to me, then—"

"I don't care about their plans!" she cries, her voice as outraged as her skull face. "It's *bones* I'm interested in. Every time Coyote invades the Lowerworld, it results in millions of deaths in the Middleworld—a bounty for me!"

"But you'll get those bones eventually!" I practically spit in frustration. "Don't you get it? By not even trying to fight this, you're letting them win at their game. You claim to hate them for eluding you all these years—and yet you're helping them go through with their plans! It just doesn't make any sense."

While she doesn't instantly cave like I'd hoped, it's clear my words have had an impact. She grows quiet, pensive, making no further move either toward me or away from me. Her face transforming, returning to the beauty she was when we first came upon her, though the snake skirt remains. She turns to me and says, "Paloma is on my list."

I swallow hard. Wondering what it means but too afraid to ask, so Dace does it for me.

"The list of the dead," she says. "Or soon to be dead. She's on today's list. It is done. There is no going back."

"But she's not gone yet." Dace strives for calm, though the way he grips my fingers tells me he's as worried as I am. "It doesn't have to be this way. You have plenty of bones to keep you busy. You have theirs"—he points toward the freaks hanging from the tree—"and you have his"—he motions toward the Richter bound by snakes. "That's a lot of fresh skeletons in exchange for one soul. Seems like a pretty good trade, no?"

She flips her hair over her shoulder, a glimmering rainbow of reds that momentarily steals my attention. Nodding toward the undead Richter, she says, "You're willing to sacrifice Coyotes for Seekers?"

Dace shrugs, face confused when he says, "Why wouldn't I?"

Having no idea what that means. But I do, and the words leave me chilled.

"I find that very intriguing." She steps toward him, her onyx eyes moving over him, drinking in his wet form, the way his T-shirt and jeans mold and cling. Licking her lips slowly, lasciviously, she says, "Actually, I find *you* very intriguing."

Dace freezes, eyes locked on hers, hand clasped in mine, as she runs a slender finger down the length of his cheek, around the curve of his ear. Holding his gaze for so long I suddenly understand what I didn't before: She doesn't just keep the bones, she *knows* the bones.

Knows where they came from.

Knows their full history—how they found their way to her.

She removes her hand from his flesh, returns to her place. Continuing to gaze at him with an expression I can't quite decipher when she says, "Why wouldn't you sacrifice a Coyote for a Seeker?" She shakes her head, eyes sparkling, teeth glittering when she adds, "Because you're the Echo, that's why." She throws her head back, allowing great peals of laughter to boom in the sky—a cacophony of mockery that swoops down around us. Leveling her gaze once again when she adds, "Then again, as the Echo, your destiny is not only a strange one but a shared one." Her eyes switch to mine.

"I don't know what that means." Dace searches her face, his voice steeped with worry. "What the heck is an Echo? What're you getting at?"

She grins, her face so beautiful, so seductive it's impossible to look away. Moving forward again, she cups his face in her hands, pressing her forehead to his when she says, "Oh, but that is for both of you to discover. Just know, that when you do—I'll be watching. I've been waiting for something like this—this is going to be good fun, indeed!" She moves away from Dace and turns to the Richters still hanging from their feet. "And whose souls have they stolen?" she asks.

"I don't know." My gaze moves among them. "All I know is they don't belong here. And if the souls are not reunited with their beings, then how will their bones find their way to you when there will be no afterlife for them to aspire to?"

Our eyes meet, and it feels like something clicked, like I finally convinced her of what I know to be true. But maybe that's just wishful thinking. Her face is so vague and unreadable, her mood so volatile, I'm braced for just about anything when she turns away from me, focuses hard on her snakes, and shouts, "Extract them— set the souls free and leave the bones for me!"

They dart from her legs, slithering across the ground at astonishing speed. Winding their way to the line of undead Richters, they spring into their mouths and dive straight down their throats, before emerging with numerous glowing, white spheres they're quick to spit out. The souls bouncing, soaring, winking out of sight as they go in search of their owners—all those poor people I saw in the photos. The sudden loss of energy causing the bodies to give way, dissolving to a mound of old bones and dust.

With just one Richter left, she looks at me and says, "Perhaps you'd like the honor?"

I nod, watching as she plucks a snake from her skirt and thrusts it toward me. Its eyes flaring, tongue striking—reminding me of the snake from my dream, the one that stole Dace's soul— only this soul extraction won't fail. I won't let that happen.

She grabs the freak, her bony fingers working into his hair, yanking back, as Dace pries his jaws wide apart, and I feed the snake in. My chest squeezing tight, my breath held fast in my cheeks, praying Paloma's soul will emerge unharmed, delivered safely to me.

Gasping when the snake returns with a glowing white orb delicately clasped in its jaws, amazed by how light and airy it is when it lands flat on my palms.

The Bone Keeper's voice hissing in my ear when she says, "You got what you wanted—now go! Leave them to me!" Her face transforming back into a skull when she takes in the bounty of bones at her feet.

I do as she says, eager to get as far from her as I possibly can. Glancing over my shoulder to say, "There's more. I have no idea where they are by now. But they're out there, somewhere, of that I'm sure."

She kneels before her bones, getting them organized, sorted, appearing to ignore me, until we're walking away and she says, "No matter. I will watch for them, just as I will watch the two of you. It'll be a good show, of that *I* am sure. The Echo and the Seeker." She laughs among her treasures. "Who would've thought?"

fifty-two

With Raven's guidance, we find our way back to Wolf. My excitement vanishing when I see him just barely hanging in there.

"Leftfoot did what he could," Dace says. "But without the soul, he couldn't do much. Whatever happens next, depends on you. Have you done this before?"

I shake my head. Gnaw the inside of my cheek. All too aware of how big the risk is. Failing at this means losing Paloma—an option I cannot accept.

"Have you?" I turn to him, my voice sounding too small for the stakes I now face.

"No," he admits. "This is way out of my league."

"What should I do?" I switch my focus between the orb and Wolf.

"I think you're supposed to go with your instincts," Dace says, his voice quiet but sure, and the moment our eyes meet, I've no doubt he's right.

It's like Paloma said—this is part of my ancestral legacy, my bloodline. The knowledge lives inside me—all I have to do is find a way to discover it.

"Open his mouth," I say, the words sudden but sure. Remembering how the Richters swallowed the souls—how the souls seemed to survive it without being harmed, including this one. Besides, Wolf would never do anything to intentionally damage it. And who knows, maybe the infusion of energy will help save him too? A quick look at Raven's purple glimmering eyes confirming I'm on the right track.

"Hurry!" I say, watching as Dace opens Wolf's jaws, careful to move out of the way as I bring my hands to Wolf's mouth and ease the soul in. Dace's arm sliding around me, as we search for some sign of change, some sign of life that wasn't there earlier. Overcome with relief when Wolf's ears perk, his eyes open, his tail thumps hard on the ground, and he lets out a long, plaintive howl as he struggles to his feet.

"Can I?" Dace sweeps toward him, ready to lift him, the question so much bigger than it seems on the surface.

He's asking if I'll trust him enough to carry this out.

Trust him enough to let him deeper into my life.

Trust him enough to give him my heart.

I close my eyes for a moment, blocking out all that I see with my eyes, in order to see in the dark—see with my heart—it's what a Seeker does.

Overcome once again with the same impression I had from the start: one of kindness, compassion, and unconditional love—and it's all directed at me.

I nod my consent. There's no need to question or push him away.

He's a pure and beautiful soul—a Whitefeather. That Richter bit is a mere technicality.

With Wolf in his arms, he leads me through the bushes and out to the clearing. Glancing at me when he says, "Since you're trusting me with this, I'm going to trust you as well. We're going to return the way I came in. It's a sacred vortex that leads straight to the reservation. It'll allow us to reach Paloma much quicker, though you can never tell anyone about its existence."

I'm quick to agree, watching in fascination as he leads me to an area where the energy feels palpably lighter—where the light shines just a little bit brighter. And the next thing I know, we're swept away in a whirl of uplifting energy, spinning and swirling until it deposits us in a field of deeply twisted juniper trees.

The same juniper trees I saw on the horseback ride with Chay that caused him to cut the ride short and turn away. I may not have been ready for it then like he claimed, but it seems I am now.

We rush to the small adobe home where Paloma lies dying. The sight of us bursting through the foyer, Wolf in tow, causing Chepi to gasp—clutch her hand to her heart—as Chay sags with relief, and Leftfoot and his apprentice rush us into the room where Paloma lies prone on the bed.

Taking Wolf from Dace, Leftfoot settles the animal next to Paloma, watching as he licks her cheek in a gesture so tender and caring, it stirs Paloma from whatever deep state of unconsciousness she found herself in. Her fingers seeking his muzzle, stroking softly, using the minuscule strength that remains to mutter a long stream of words I can't comprehend, as Wolf throws his head back and lets out a terrific howl that prickles my skin.

And that's when I see it.

That's when I watch as the soul leaves Wolf's body—hovering for a moment, shiny and bright, before it finds its way back to Paloma where it belongs.

Her cheeks instantly coloring, her lids lifting, gaze seeking mine when she says, "*Nieta. Nieta*, you did it!" Our shared elation lasting only a second before I realize it's not at all like she thinks.

"No, *abuela*," I whisper, my lips close to her ear, not wanting Dace or Chepi to hear. "I didn't. I only managed to save you and a few other souls—lots of souls actually—and believe it or not, it was the Bone Keeper who helped me. Still, despite my efforts, there are many who were lost. I'm so sorry—I just couldn't do it. I couldn't bear to lose you. Couldn't do what you asked. And though I tried to stop them, I failed."

Paloma's eyes meet mine, brimming with compassion, though her lips tell another story, turned pale with worry. "And how did you find her, *nieta*—the Bone Keeper?"

"Raven led me." I smile. "With a little help from Horse and Dace."

At the mention of his name, her gaze switches to the place where Dace stands at the far wall with Chepi. Studying him closely, her attention claimed for so long, I'm just about to speak, when she returns to me and says, "Now that you have found each other, it is time for you to realize your destinies. It's all in motion, there is no going back. The raven heralds the prophecy, and the prophecy is here. You two are fated, *nieta*."

"I—I don't understand," I say, wondering why her gaze is so consoling when her news is so good.

"A Seeker's life requires great sacrifice," Paloma says. "And I am sorry for that. But you must stop Coyote no matter the cost. You have no idea how much havoc just a few of them can wreak."

"I will." I nod, desperate for her to believe me. "I'll do what it takes, just point the way."

"I've lost most of my magick." Her lids droop, voice fades with fatigue. "I've relinquished it to you. So while I can guide you, sweet *nieta*, in the end, the task belongs to the two of you. You must work together—you must do all that you can . . ."

Her voice lulls, as her breathing sputters and slows, but I'm not yet finished. I've still got one more question to ask, and she's the only one who might know the answer.

I lean closer, lips at her ear as I whisper, "Paloma, what is the Echo? What does it mean?" I hold tight to her hand, hoping for a response that will ease these deep-seated fears gnawing inside me.

But my words are met with silence—she's already claimed by sleep.

fifty-three

Leftfoot ushers us out of the room, insists Paloma needs her rest. And while I don't disagree, I'm not entirely ready to leave. Not until she wakes and I'm sure she's on the mend.

"She's experienced quite a bit of trauma," he says. "It is rare for one to survive a complete soul loss—it is usually only a partial. But as you know, Paloma is not like most people. She is stronger, more resilient, and because of your efforts, she will make it just fine. But for now, you must allow her to sleep. And you must allow me to return Wolf to the Lowerworld. It's no good for him here. You two have done enough for one day."

"Yes, you certainly have," Chepi says, her eyes grazing over my snarled hair, torn jeans, and bare feet, telling me I look even worse than I think.

Her anger dissolving the instant Dace slips an arm around her, murmuring in their native tongue. Then he leads us outside, where the three of us pause on the road, silent and awkward, until Chepi says, "I remember your father."

Her eyes meet mine as I stand rooted before her, unsure how to react.

"You are just like him," she adds, confusing me further.

Does she mean I'm impulsive and reckless?

Does she mean I'm destined to break her son's heart just like Django broke Jennika's—even though it wasn't his fault?

Does she mean I'm part of a world she's vowed to turn her back on, in an effort to protect herself—protect her son—and she resents my dragging him into it?

Does she mean all of those things, along with plenty more I've yet to think of?

I lower my lids, shutting her out in an effort to see with my heart, but all I get in return is a woman who's deeply concerned for her son.

Dace moves to intervene, desperate to smooth things over, but he's soon stopped by his mother who says, "Paloma was there for me when I needed her, and so I spent the last couple days doing what I could to return the favor. Though I never imagined my son, along with you, would come through when it really mattered."

I duck my head and stare hard at my feet, unable to come up with a suitable reply. The sentiment was simple, hinting at kind, but the tone it was spoken in seemed accusatory at best. Then again, maybe I'm just tired, and maybe my fatigue is making me paranoid.

"It's been many years since I observed *Día de los Muertos*—but perhaps today I should." Her gaze lingers on mine in a way that reminds me of all the horrific, unthinkable things that happened to her on that day, when she was just a young girl my age.

She turns to her son, invites him to join her back at her house, but when he shakes his head in reply, she's quick to turn and be on her way. "You be careful out there," she says, the words drifting over her shoulder, more loaded than they appear.

She heads down the road, seeming to diminish the farther she goes, and when I'm sure she's out of earshot, I turn to Dace and say, "Your mom hates me."

He laughs, wraps an arm around me, and hugs me close to his

side—the warmth of his body instantly emanating to mine. "She doesn't hate you," he says. "She just has to get used to the idea, that's all."

I peer at him, taking in a face so beautiful it's almost hard to fathom. "Get used to what?" I ask, having no idea where he's going with that.

Noting the way he flushes, looks away, stopping beside a beat-up white pickup truck when he says, "Of me having a girlfriend."

I lean against the passenger door, trying to adjust to the thought. I've never been anyone's girlfriend. The word alone implies permanence, stability, longevity—all things I've long been denied.

Misreading my silence, along with the contemplative look on my face, he says, "Great, now I've scared you." He rakes a hand through his hair, stares down at the dirt, but I reach for his sleeve and pull him back to me.

"After all we just went through, you think you can scare me so easily?"

He lifts his eyes to meet mine, face flooding with relief when he says, "Maybe we can just start with breakfast? There's this great little tucked-away place that serves the best blue-corn pancakes in the state—though it might seem a little too normal compared to a soul retrieval."

I look past his shoulder, spying the first rays of sun sneaking up the mountain range just behind him. And if I tilt my head just right, it turns him into a dark silhouette surrounded by a nimbus of brilliant gold light that matches the ones in his eyes. "Trust me." I grin. "*Normal* is looking particularly good about now."

"So it's a yes, then?"

"To blue-corn pancakes or being your girlfriend?" I tease, enjoying the way his cheeks redden.

"Both would be great, but I'll leave that to you."

I bite down on my lip, realizing I've never been in this position before. It's always been: Hey, *meet you at the Pont Neuf at eight.* Or, in Vane's case: *Meet you by the snake charmer at dusk.* By the time the movie wrapped and the premiere rolled around, I always found myself sitting with Jennika. I've never had a real date, much less a boyfriend. Never even had the prospect of one until now.

Realizing he's still waiting for an answer, I look at him and say, "Okay."

"Okay to breakfast . . ." He tilts his head, studies me closely.

I take a deep breath, my heart beating triple time at what I'm about to do. "Okay to both." I exhale softly. "Oh, and if I didn't already say it—*thanks.*"

"For what?" His brows merge, as he studies me closely.

"For helping. For understanding. For not pushing me to explain things I'm not quite ready to answer. And for being so kind."

He leans his head back in a way that leaves him gazing down at me. "Haven't you heard?" He smiles. "I'm the good twin."

I freeze, wondering how much he knows.

"You know—good twin, evil twin? Lame joke, I know. And according to the Bone Keeper, I'm also the Echo—what do you think she meant by that anyway?"

I shrug, watching as he shakes his head and moves to unlock my door, but just as he leans past me, I stop him. My fingers curling around his bicep, I pull him closer, and say, "I have no idea what an Echo is, but I've no doubt you're the good twin." And I kiss him under the rising sun.

fifty-four

We drive by the Rabbit Hole, and at first sight I can't help but think it looks like the sight of a self-contained apocalypse. The doors are wide open, the bouncers are gone, and when Dace parks in the alleyway and peers inside, it's clear that the place is abandoned—there's not one person left.

"I don't think the party's ever ended this early," he says. "It usually goes on until noon, if not later."

I lean past him to get a better look, wondering if we might've had anything to do with that. If we might've had more effect on Cade's plans than I thought. There may be Richters in the Lowerworld—it may not be a complete victory—but we retrieved Paloma's soul, along with a whole host of the others that were restored to the citizens of Enchantment. No wonder they no longer want to be here—they finally got their mojo back.

"Think anyone will notice I never made it to work?" Dace glances my way, and I shrug in response. "Guess the only thing left is to make peace with Jennika."

He checks both mirrors and merges onto the road, as I stare out the window, gazing upon streets littered with skull masks and marigolds—jagged bits of grinning teeth and flowering eye sock-

345

ets gazing up from the asphalt, staring vacantly into space, as though mocking the very people who lost them.

"Good luck with that." I turn to face him. "She's predisposed to hate you. Convinced you'll be my downfall. Says you've got *heartbreaker* written all over you."

Dace grips the wheel tighter, eyebrows quirked, gaze stricken in a way that makes me feel bad for saying it, but it's only a moment later when he laughs and says, "Funny, that's the same thing Chepi said about you." Addressing my confusion when he adds, "That day at the gas station, when I saw you sitting on the curb, talking on the phone—Chepi caught me looking and warned me right then and there to keep my distance, to not get involved."

"Why do you think she said that?" I ask. "It's such a strange thing to say about someone you've never met."

Did she get an impression of me like I did of her? Is that why she hates me?

Dace reaches toward me and places his hand over mine, giving it a reassuring squeeze when he says, "That's what mothers do."

I lean back in my seat, determined to push it out of my mind. Staring blankly out my window as the truck bounces down the dirt road before pulling onto Paloma's street that's crowded with cars, one in particular I can't help but notice.

Barely allowing Dace enough time to park before I'm leaping from the truck and racing through the courtyard. Heart firmly wedged in my throat, as I bolt through the door, terrified by the thought of what I might find, only to see Jennika sitting at the kitchen table with Marliz right beside her. The two of them surrounded by a group of girls I recognize from school—all of them waiting their turn at a professional Hollywood makeover.

"Daire." Jennika's gaze slews toward me as she applies mascara to Lita's top lashes. "I've been looking for you." Then seeing Dace right beside me, she adds, "And why am I not surprised to find you together? You guys look terrible by the way. Where the hell have you been?"

I dismiss the question with a wave of my hand, my eyes frantically scanning the room, searching for Xotichl and relieved to find her curled up on the couch next to Auden—flashing me two thumbs up the second she senses me. Jacy and Crickett are there too, laughing and talking with some of Cade's guy friends—all of them lounging on the woven rugs and chairs, no one seeming to notice that Cade Richter is missing.

My attention returning to Jennika, taking note of her disapproving glare, and knowing it's time for us to hash through this mess and find a way to compromise.

"We need to talk." She pushes away from the table, her expression turned grim.

Her flight interrupted by Lita, face only half-finished, who cries, "But you're gonna finish me first though, right?"

Jennika shakes her head and motions for Marliz to take over. "I think she can take it from here," she says, nodding for me to follow her into Paloma's office.

Dace looks uncertain, but I drag him along. The two of us united before an angry Jennika, when he says, "You can blame me. I take full responsibility." Which is probably one of the worst things he could've said. It's an honorable attempt, but definitely not the best way to get on her good side, and when I see her sarcastic expression, I can't help but cringe. "She was worried about Paloma," he continues, desperate to make things right. "So I took her to the reservation to see her, and it must've worked because Paloma is better."

Jennika smirks, her focus on me when she says, "So, I guess that settles it then." She pushes away from the sink, as though it's been decided that easily. Motioning for me to follow, and when I don't, when I remain right beside Dace, she says, "We had a deal, Daire. Now that Paloma is better, it's time to say good-bye to your friends and go back to L.A."

I stand rooted in place. My eyes grazing over the herbs, the drum, the piles of books on the shelves—this is my home, I'm not going anywhere. Not when Paloma still has more to teach me. Not

before I find a way to evict those Richters from the Lowerworld—
not before I stop Cade in his insane quest for power—and maybe
not even then.

Jennika places her hands on her hips, her voice rising in anger
when she says, "Daire!" She glances between me and Dace, as
though silently asking if I really want to do this in front of him.
And while I'd really prefer not to, now that it's started, I don't feel
like I have much of a choice.

"I'm not leaving," I say, noting the look of outrage clearly displayed on her face. "I know you think it's crazy, but I like it here,
and I don't want to leave. It's as simple as that."

Dace squeezes my hand, his palm warm and sure. But when
my gaze meets his, it's clear he's way out of his comfort zone, so I
tell him to wait in the den.

Barely making it halfway down the ramp before Jennika says,
"He's gonna have an awfully long wait, 'cause you're coming
with me."

I sigh long and deep. Stare down at my feet. Arguing won't get
me anywhere. If I want to be heard, I'll have to tread softly. Careful to keep my voice tempered, I say, "Jennika, what do you have
against this place?"

She scowls, sweeps her arm wide, saying, "Isn't it obvious? I
want better for you than some dump of a town and a cute boy with
no future." She places her hand on her hip, clenches her jaw, and I
struggle to remind myself that she truly means well, only wants
the best for me, even though she's not always sure what that is.

"But what if I like it here?" I lift my shoulders, fiddle with
the torn hem of my jacket. "What if this dump of a town feels like
home? What if I'm not even looking to that cute boy to provide
my future—what if I'm perfectly capable of providing my own?
What if I just want to see what it's like to have a real home, a real
family, real friends, and yeah, even a boyfriend? And what if this
place can provide a sincere shot at all of those things—would you
really deny me? Would you really insist on taking me to L.A. just

because it feels better to you?" I suck in my breath, confident I lodged a good case, though Jennika's not easily swayed.

"You can have all those things in L.A.! And trust me, it's a much better, much nicer environment than this place could ever be. You just need to give it a chance, that's all."

"Or maybe *you* need to give *me* a chance," I say, my words silencing her. "Why can't you just give me this? One year of high school. If I blow it, fail, start getting in trouble, you'll have every right to yank me, and there'll be nothing I can do about it. But first, why can't you just give me a chance to see how I do?"

"Because you're not Paloma's responsibility, you're *my* responsibility!" she cries.

"But you can visit anytime—it's not like it's far. One year, Jennika. Please. Give it a chance. Give *me* a chance to see how I fare."

She sighs, casts a glance all around. Focusing on the general vicinity of the den when she says, "You be careful with him. And don't say I didn't warn you, 'cause I did—more than once."

I nod. Shoulders sinking with relief, knowing that's Jennika's way of giving in.

"Thank you," I say, taking her by surprise when I rush toward her and hug her tightly to me. Pulling away and blinking back tears, finally realizing just how much I'll miss her, no matter how much she annoys me sometimes.

The thought causing me to realize something else—how much Jennika probably misses me. I'm all she's got. For sixteen years we've been a team. She's purposely avoided getting close to anyone else. Even with Harlan, she's careful to keep a safe distance. And while I know it frustrates him, he chooses to accept her on her limited terms. But as much as she tries to avoid it, there's no doubt Jennika needs a home just as much as I do. She needs friends—a life outside of work. She needs all the things I now have for myself—only in L.A., not here.

"So what now?" I ask, a new idea forming in my head.

She sighs, folds her arms across her chest, looking tired when she says, "Well, now that you're here, I guess I'll grab a short nap, check in with Paloma, and be on my way."

"What about your makeovers?" I motion toward the kitchen. "Looks like you've built quite a fan club."

Jennika laughs, the sound light and weary, making her way down the ramp when I decide to just say it, just toss it out there and see where it lands.

"You know, if you're looking for a roommate in L.A. . . . ."

She stops, unsure where I'm going.

"Well, you might consider Marliz. I mean, I know she's engaged and all—but he's kind of a jerk, and—"

My words cut short when she says, "They broke up."

I stare at her, speechless.

"It's been a crazy night." She lifts her shoulders, her gaze growing distant as she mentally reviews it. "The stuff I saw . . ." She shakes her head, causing her hair to flop in her eyes. "Well, I'm clearly running a serious sleep deficit."

"So you'll consider it, then? Asking her, I mean?" Jennika shrugs, pushing past me when I add, "Listen, I need to step outside—will you tell Dace I'll be back in a minute?" Allowing her no time to reply before I'm slipping out the back door and making my way past the detached garage, through the gate, and halfway down the dirt road where a black, four-wheel-drive pickup truck is parked on the shoulder.

Barely making it to the driver's side window when Cade says, "You hurt my feelings." He shoots me a wounded look.

"I wasn't aware that you had any." I stand before him, gazing into those cold, vacant eyes.

"The way you just ran off like that—you didn't even stick around to celebrate." He shakes his head sadly. "Wasn't the same without you. You know I had those sugar skull candies made especially for you, ended up feeding 'em to Coyote instead."

"Sorry," I say, my expression anything but. "I had a soul to retrieve."

He nods, face thoughtful when he says, "I hear Paloma recovered."

I lift my shoulders, my gaze locked on his. "Funny, I heard the same thing."

"You must feel pretty good about yourself." He squints, pushes his fingers through his hair, checking his reflection in the rearview mirror, and despite having left him engulfed in flames, he looks no worse for the wear.

"Actually, I think you're underestimating it. I feel pretty damn awesome."

His icy-blue eyes meet mine, striving to absorb my energy, my essence—trying to change my perception, make me see things his way—but it won't work. I'm totally onto him.

"You know Lita's inside? In fact, *all* of your friends are inside. And not one of them seems to miss you."

He studies his hands, inspecting his cuticles, not saying a word.

"What's the matter?" I taunt. "El Coyote can't make it past Paloma's coyote fence? Is that why you're waiting out here, hoping they'll come to you? 'Cause I gotta tell you, Richter, from what I saw, they're not even thinking about you. Out of sight, out of mind, as they say."

"So, why don't you invite me in, and we can remind them?" He grins, face lit with possibility.

"Never," I say, but he laughs at the word.

"Saw you with my brother." His gaze moves over me. "Guess that explains your attraction to me—he looks just like me."

His cocky grin fading when I roll my eyes in response.

"Well, you sure spend a lot of time thinking about me—searching for me—don't you, Santos?" he says, determined to make me admit the ridiculous.

"Don't flatter yourself, Coyote. It's an occupational hazard. Purely job related," I say, seeing the way he drums his fingers against the steering wheel, wearing a smirk so smug and arrogant, I long to wipe it right off his face.

"You're truly gifted, Santos. I saw that tonight. A little too soft in the heart, but there's no reason we can't remedy that. Shame to see you waste your gifts on my brother."

"You'd rather I waste them on you?"

"Yes," he says, not a hint of irony in his voice. "I've been nothing but nice to you and yet, look how you treat me. I don't know what you've been told, but you've got me all wrong."

"You stole my grandmother's soul!" I say, my voice outraged. "You call that playing nice?"

He shrugs, rubs a thumb over the face of his watch. "Maybe not nice, but it had to be done. And yet, look how you managed to save it—while allowing several of my people to remain in the Lowerworld. It's pretty much a win-win, wouldn't you say? See how well we work together?"

I shake my head in frustration, about to walk away, when he turns the key, sparking the engine to life as he says, "I don't know how much you think you know about coyotes, but I'll tell you this—they go to great lengths to look after their family. It's *family* that matters most, Santos, don't ever forget that. The bonds of family can never be broken. And whether you realize it or not, you've been working for me since the day you started having those dreams."

I swallow hard. My breath quickening, palms moistening, his words reverberating through me.

"You know, the ones where you get all hot and steamy with my brother?" He laughs, flicks his tongue across his front teeth, grinning in a way that's both lurid and obscene.

"Is that it?" I cross my arms before me, trying to appear calm, cool, not the least bit disturbed, though I'm pretty sure he's not fooled. His words have shaken me to the core. "Is that all you got?"

"Hardly." He smiles. "You and I are just getting started, you'll see. But in the meantime, enjoy your time with my brother—you know, the Echo." He laughs, pulling away from the curb just as

I turn to see Dace peering around Paloma's blue gate, looking for me.

"We're all heading for breakfast," he calls the second he spots me. "Everyone's coming, it won't be just us. I hope that's okay?"

I rush toward him, eager to erase the energy of his brother and replace it with his. Barreling into his arms, I inhale his warm, earthy scent and say, "Sounds good to me. I'm starving."

He holds me tightly to his chest and looks past my shoulder, catching a glimpse of his brother's truck. He pulls away and says, "Is that Cade?" He squints into the distance.

I nod, hoping he doesn't think something weird, because there's no good way to explain the conversation we had.

"What'd he want?" he asks, his voice as confused as his gaze.

I sigh, picking my way over a bed of rocks as we head for the gate. "He wanted to warn me," I say.

"About me?" His brow slants with worry.

"No. About him. He wanted me to know he's the bad twin." I take a deep breath, knowing it's as close to the truth as I'm willing to get.

Exhaling softly when he wraps an arm around me, and says, "He's probably just upset about Lita. She broke up with him. He's not exactly used to rejection. It's a whole new experience for him."

"Sounds like Lita got her soul back," I say, taking one last glance down the street, ensuring Cade's gone—or at least for now anyway. Then I slip through the gate with Dace right beside me, the two of us heading into Paloma's adobe where all our friends wait.